MORTAL GODS

TOR BOOKS BY KENDARE BLAKE

Anna Dressed in Blood
Girl of Nightmares
Antigoddess

MORTAL GODS

THE GODDESS WAR: BOOK TWO

KENDARE BLAKE

TOR·
TEEN

A TOM DOHERTY ASSOCIATES BOOK
NEW YORK

MORTAL GODS

Copyright © 2014 by Kendare Blake

A Tor Teen Book
Published by Tom Doherty Associates, LLC
175 Fifth Avenue
New York, NY 10010

www.tor-forge.com

Tor® is a registered trademark of Tom Doherty Associates, LLC.

The Library of Congress Cataloging-in-Publication Data
is available upon request.

ISBN 978-0-7653-3444-2 (hardcover)
ISBN 978-1-4668-1222-2 (e-book)

Tor Teen books may be purchased for educational, business, or promotional use. For information on bulk purchases, please contact Macmillan Corporate and Premium Sales Department at 1-800-221-7945, extension 5442, or write specialmarkets@macmillan.com.

First Edition: October 2014

Printed in the United States of America

0 9 8 7 6 5 4 3 2 1

For the students of Lyons Township High School in Illinois.
Because that kid in the back row asked.

ARISTEIA: From the Greek word for excellence. A moment in epic poetry when a hero is untouchable, in which they display their utmost skill and valor; when they are almost a god.

Before the walls of Troy two armies met
In bronze and blood
The Trojans and the Greeks fought
For gods on both sides.
Gray-eyed Athena and Hera, white-armed queen,
Filled the Greeks with rage and righteous song
Against Aphrodite and Apollo
Who strengthened the Trojans.
At their urging the great heroes faced each other,
sword to shield
Noble Hector and wrathful Achilles
And Achilles threw Troy's hero down, killing him
and dragging his body
Around the city.
Troy, which would fall as Cassandra foretold
And leave all to waste and ruin in its wake.

MORTAL GODS

PROLOGUE

BLOOD AND IVORY

The god of war stood still as a statue, waiting for Aphrodite as he waited for prey, for foes, for anything with veins to cut. The stillness lasted only an hour or so. Then he paced and huffed and gnashed his teeth. Ares had no more patience than he had rationality or restraint. He made a fist, and the skin of his knuckles cracked and ran red. Damned Aphrodite. She kept him waiting even when the meeting was her idea.

He glanced to his wrist, like someone checking the time, but in place of a watch was a blood-soaked bandage with fraying edges. He could have been anywhere else, enjoying the end of his days. Maybe lounging on an island, eating figs and honey. Maybe killing someone.

Ares should've known better than to come early, or even on time. Aphrodite was unmindful of anyone's needs but her own. He bit down hard when a smile started at the corner of his mouth. Even her bad habits made him sentimental. The god of war had gone soft.

He flexed his arms and the muscles of his chest. Blood oozed from a broad cut on his bicep and soaked the black cloth of his shirt.

Soft, but not weak. Strong, but still dying.

His death had started to show over a year ago. All his old war wounds, long since healed, reopened on their own. Ares loved blood more than all things, so the cuts blooming on his chest and shoulders delighted him at first. He waited for the next one to open, and remembered with nostalgia the fight when he'd taken the wound. The cuts lingered and bled, but eventually closed. Then the whispers started, of other gods falling ill. Impossible stories of gods dying. By the time the half-eaten Nereid washed up at his feet on a beach in Tanzania, he wasn't feeling quite so nostalgic anymore.

Across the stream, in the trees that lined the opposite bank, something moved. Rustled. He peered into the shade. Maybe just the wind through leaves, or a careless squirrel. Only squirrels didn't usually smell like vanilla and cinnamon.

"Aphrodite."

She picked her way along the black stone that bordered the streambed, and he took her in, inch by inch. Her bare soles scraped over cold rocks and wet grass. She hopped and hummed like a little girl playing a game.

For Aphrodite it was always a game. She ran, and Ares chased. She laughed, and he fought to catch his breath.

Images flashed behind his eyes, a thousand images from a thousand years. Rose-colored lips. Gold hair. Bared breasts that brought men to their knees.

But shadows like coal smudges marked Aphrodite's calves now, long lines of darkness that disappeared beneath the uneven hem of her blue-green dress. Only they weren't shadows. They were bruises.

Suddenly Ares didn't want to see her face. To see her

changed from breathtaking to hideous, with sores on her forehead and blackened eyes.

It would be an unfair fate for the goddess of love and beauty. As unfair as for the god of war to die from battles he'd already won. Ares took a breath and looked up.

Golden blond hair twisted down to her waist, and she smiled with lips red as blood. Her curious eyes shone blue and bright. The most beautiful of goddesses was still the most beautiful, even with the hint of bruising on her jaw. Even if she was mad as a rabid dog.

"I've come, as you asked," she said. "To this river. Will you come to me now? Or must I cross?" She dipped a toe into the current and kicked, splashing Ares' shoes. The flirt.

"I've come, as *you* requested. But not to the place you dictated. I'm not your pet, Aphrodite. I never have been."

She pursed her lips. He was her pet, and they both knew it. She stood ungainly, unbalanced, the cock of her head at odds with the jut of her hip. Mud streaked her skirt. He couldn't tell whether her eyes were truly bright, or only fevered. And then there was the dog to consider: a small, golden puppy, asleep in her arms.

"Very well," she said. "I'll come to you." She walked into the river up to the waist, hugging the puppy close, careful to keep it dry.

"What do you want, Aphrodite?"

"I want you to come home," she purred. "I want you to fight, like you used to. Like the god you are."

Ares snorted. Appeal to the strength of a dying god. Tell him he was strong. She was clever still, even through the crazy.

"Things have changed," he said. "War has changed. Men don't need me to take up their cause." He lifted his arm to show her the blood. "The world sloughs us like dead skin."

"It isn't men who are asking." She pouted. "And it isn't like you to submit."

He clenched his jaw.

"I heard about Hera and Athena. About you and Apollo. Is it true about Poseidon? Is he really dead?"

Aphrodite clutched the puppy tighter, and it squirmed. Any tighter and she'd break its little neck. But then she took a breath and stroked its soft, shiny fur, soothing it to sleep. It was a beautiful little dog. Perfect. Its fur matched her hair. In another life, she might've carried it around in a designer handbag.

"Poseidon is gone," she said, swaying. "Drifted back into the sea. His blood flows, red and black streaming clouds, moving through the currents. It makes the sharks weep. His bones have dug into the sand, taken over by coral. A million fish carry his eternal flesh in their bellies." She smiled. "But we kept his head."

"You're mad."

"Don't say that."

"You killed Apollo. You killed our brother."

"He killed Poseidon! He and wicked Hermes. Weak, vile boys tore him apart in the lake. Nasty girls put their hands on Mother." Her thin fingers walked over the head of the puppy to tap its nose. "Turned her to stone."

A glaze had taken over Aphrodite's eyes, and she looked over Ares' shoulder into the trees. With the dress clinging to her narrow hips and her long waves of blond hair, she looked fragile. But that was only a costume she wore. When she wanted to be, she was as warlike as he was. *Aphrodite Areia*, they called her. Her loveliness hid rage and bared teeth. How he'd always loved that.

"You killed Apollo," he said. "But Athena and Hermes sent

you scuttling for cover. And what about the prophetess? They say she can kill gods."

"Ares." Aphrodite frowned. "We mean so much to each other. You always fight with me. For me."

"I haven't seen you in centuries," he said. "Not a word in a hundred-odd years. Not until you need me." He swallowed. Her dress clung in just the right places. "I should turn around and find Athena. Tell her you're still up to your old tricks." Aphrodite parted her lips. Old tricks, indeed. "Maybe I should help her swat you like a fly."

Aphrodite drew a long, silver knife from the fastenings of her dress.

"Don't be hasty. You haven't heard everything. You don't know." She held the tip of the knife out toward him, playful. Light from the moving current fluttered along the sharpened edge. "An offering."

She fitted the blade beneath the puppy's throat, and Ares held his breath. She would do it well. One long cut. The puppy wouldn't yelp. The knife would be hidden back in the folds of her skirts before it even woke.

Ares imagined the blood racing down her dress to dye the river red. He saw the dog's empty body carried away by the current.

"Does it please you?" she asked.

"From you? The gesture of sacrifice has no meaning." But despite his words, it touched him. The beautiful little dog. The ceremonial knife. Just like old times. Ares leaped into the stream, blindingly fast, and twisted Aphrodite's wrist. The knife fell to the water, silver sides shimmering like a fish, and the puppy slept on.

"It isn't dog's blood I want."

"Mmm." Aphrodite led him out of the shallows like a

legend: the goddess, rising from the sea, borne on the waves. "And you would draw the blood yourself. Like always. Ares. Curse of men. Sacker of cities."

"Names I haven't been called for a long time," he whispered. She was so close. The scent of her cloaked him in floral and vanilla, cinnamon and fruit. And underneath that, the sweeter, darker perfume of sickness and decay.

"Men will scream those names before we're through," she said into his ear, and pressed something into his hand. He looked down. A chunk of marbled granite, one edge smooth as a statue, the other ragged and cracked.

"Mother isn't dead. They brought her back. Healed her. And they'll do it for us, too, my love. We'll be whole again. We'll live forever."

I

SAND THROUGH HER FINGERS

The desert never changed. The same sun-dried sand, hard packed beneath Athena's feet, and the same herds of saguaros strung out across the horizon, were programmed on repeat. And maybe that's really how it was. Maybe it was the same five tumbleweeds, rolling through on the wind to fall off the edge and show up again back at the start.

Athena swallowed. Nothing in her throat today besides smooth working muscles. No quills, no itchy edges of feathers cutting into her windpipe to make her cough blood. Not today. Maybe tomorrow.

She wiped sweat from her brow. It was high noon in the desert. She'd timed the trip badly; she should've left when she could meet Demeter in the fading light of evening. But there was nothing to be done about it now. Her boots already tread lightly on Demeter's skin, stretched out for miles, half-sunk into the sand. At any minute, Demeter's wrinkled, blinking eye could show up between her feet. If she wasn't careful, she might step on it.

It was the first time Athena had gone back to her aunt since finding her in the desert and learning about Cassandra. The girl was the key to everything, Demeter had said. And she had been. Three months had passed since they'd fought Hera, since Cassandra had laid hands on her and killed her. Since she'd turned Hera to stone. Three months since Hermes and Apollo had torn Poseidon apart in Seneca Lake. Since they'd laid Apollo to rest beneath the dirt.

Athena's dark hair hung hot on her shoulders. Walking the desert the night before had practically turned her into an icicle, but under the sun she felt like a stick of softening butter. The plan had been to cover up the swirling tattoos on her wrists, to dress decently and avoid any of Demeter's harlot jibes. But that wasn't going to happen. She'd dropped her jacket shortly after hitting her aunt's skin and hadn't bothered to drag it along behind her.

"Back so soon?"

Athena spun at the sound of Demeter's oddly disembodied voice, carried on the wind from all directions at once.

"What do you want this time?"

Athena didn't answer. She scanned the wrinkled skin for the eye, broad and bleary. When she found it, she stood over the top and peered down. It swiveled over her body, blinking lashes longer than a camel's.

"The goddess of battle returns," Demeter said. "In torn jeans and barely a shirt." The eye squinted. "The jewel in your nose is gone."

"I took it out. You're welcome." Under her feet, the skin pulled and plumped: a set of pursed lips.

"If you've come to tell me your news, I've heard it. You found the girl."

"The girl who kills gods," said Athena.

The eye narrowed. "Does she? Does she really?"

"Don't get excited," Athena muttered. "I'm not going to drag her out to the middle of nowhere so she can take care of you. She's a god killer, not a god euthanizer."

"Careful, Gray Eyes. Don't insult me. You at least die with some semblance of self. I'm a bare-skin rug. Vultures loose their bowels on my face, and I'm forced to snack on passing lizards." Demeter took a breath. "Why'd you come all this way? Perhaps to gloat? To recount your victory? Tell me how my seaward brother died."

Athena crossed her arms. Victory, Demeter called it. When they'd lost Apollo. He died a mortal, and they buried him under a mortal's name in a Kincade cemetery when he should've had a temple. But yes. It felt like a victory.

"I was sent to ask whether you know what became of Aphrodite," Athena said.

"Sent? Who could send you?"

"Cassandra sent me."

Demeter sighed, and the skin dropped Athena four inches. She wondered how the lungs were laid out over the acres. It would make for an interesting dissection, if any ballsy scientists ever happened across the corpse.

"The girl wants revenge," Demeter said.

"Wouldn't you?" Athena asked. Cassandra swallowed rage and tears like candy. Her guts would soon burst with it. "The pain burns her like fire. Aphrodite's blood will put it out."

"Will it? I think you know better."

Maybe she did. But it was what Cassandra wanted, and Athena owed her that.

"What about your fight?" Demeter asked. "Your battle?"

"What of it? We found the weapon. We won the day. But we're no closer to answers. We're still dying."

"What did you think would happen, Gray Eyes? That you'd destroy Hera and the feathers would dissolve in your blood? That Hermes would plump like a fattened cow? That I would spring up out of this dirt, soft and supple and woman-shaped?" Demeter's eye closed, wearily or sadly or both. "Everyone wishes for answers, Athena. But sometimes the answer is that things just end."

"Is that the answer here?"

"I don't know. But I know you don't think so. If you did, you would wander off and let yourself be torn apart by wolves. You'd dye more harlot colors into your hair."

Athena snorted. She could be killed. They'd proven the impossible possible. But it wasn't as easy as Demeter made it sound. Her bones would break those poor wolves' teeth. A death like that would take months.

And she wasn't ready. Who would have thought, after so much time, that she wouldn't be ready.

"The point is," said Demeter, "that you stay. Why?"

Odysseus flashed behind Athena's eyes. His voice whispered in her ears. And Hermes, too. Her beautiful brother. Thinner and thinner.

"There are things, I guess, that I still need to take care of."

Demeter drew in a rippling breath. "You are tired. Sit, child. Rest."

Athena cleared her throat. "No, thank you."

"Why not?"

"Hermes says . . ." She hesitated and rolled her eyes. "Hermes said that when he sat on you he could feel your pulse through his butt."

Demeter laughed, hard enough to knock Athena off-balance. Her feet skidded apart, and she put her arms out to steady herself. Startled birds flew from wherever they'd been hiding moments before, squawking their worry at the shifting dirt.

"I wish you'd brought him," Demeter said, quieting. "I miss his impudence."

Athena smiled. Having finally reached her aunt she was no longer all that tired. Wind cooled the sweat on her shoulders and neck. The quest neared its end. Soon she could go home.

"Aphrodite," she said. "What do you know?"

"Nothing." Demeter recoiled innocently, stretching herself so thin that Athena could feel desert pebbles beneath her toes. "Without Hera to direct her path, Aphrodite will hide. So fast and so well that you'll never find her."

"We will find her."

"Why do you ask if you aren't going to listen?" Demeter snapped. "Why are you talking about a mortal girl's revenge? Why are you fighting her fight, instead of yours?"

Athena looked away, across the sand. At first it was grief. The loss of a loved brother. And then it was guilt, too many days spent staring at Cassandra, at the shell of a girl Apollo left behind. She'd made a promise to look after them all. Cassandra, Andie, and Henry. Apollo had made her promise.

"I don't know what it is," she said softly. "I never . . . understood time before. It didn't mean anything. I could never make a mistake. I don't know how mortals do this. How they only live once."

"You doubt your instincts."

"Why shouldn't I? Things just end. Isn't that what you said?"

Demeter wriggled in the dirt. "I might be wrong. You beat Hera, but it wasn't Hera who caused this. Whatever really did, you may be able to fight." The eye bulged, scrutinizing. "Tell me. What you're thinking."

Images flickered in Athena's mind: she saw Demeter rise up from the earth and shake herself off, no longer a flat expanse of skin but a woman, with brown hair waving to her waist and deep dark eyes. She saw Hermes with muscle returned to his arms, a beautiful curve in his cheek when he smiled. She saw Apollo, Aidan, bright and perfect as ever, with Cassandra by his side.

She thought and she dreamed. Of wrongs put right. Things restored that would never be. Impossibility hovered like a light in her chest and made her *want*. To be a hero. To feel alive. As alive as she'd felt that day on the road above Seneca Lake, when she'd charged Hera with iron in her fist.

"We won," she said quietly. "Hera and I both sought the oracle, but I found her first. The other side was stronger, and everything went wrong. Our side was scattered and made terrible choices, but we won anyway. We left Hera and Poseidon dead, and Aphrodite running for cover. And now I have the girl who kills gods. And I have Odysseus, who can lead me to the other weapon."

She had Hermes, and capable soldiers in Henry and Andie. And she had herself. Goddess of battle.

"You have much," Demeter agreed.

"I don't want to put them through any more," Athena said, and that was true. Hermes, Odysseus, and Cassandra had been through enough. But she couldn't deny the urge that grew daily in her gut. She couldn't deny the exhilaration she'd felt when Hera had fallen on the road.

"Going through is the only way to the other side," Demeter said.

"The people I've endangered . . . I would see them safe. I

dragged them with me before," she said, and paused thoughtfully. "But always in the right direction."

"Stop trying to make me say it for you," Demeter said. "Spit it out."

"I'm going to wage one more war."

"Why?"

"Because we're supposed to fight, and we're supposed to win."

"Ah," said Demeter. "There it is."

"Yes. There it is. I'm going to hunt down every rogue god and monster. I'll tear their heads from their shoulders. Cassandra will turn them to dust. One last rush of heroes on the battlefield. It'll be glorious. Something for the books."

"And if you win, you'll regain your immortality?"

"Even if we don't, at least we'll be the last to die."

"You're so sure," said Demeter.

"I am, Aunt," said Athena. She looked up at Aidan's sun, blazing high and hot in the sky. "I well and truly believe the Fates favor *us.*"

"The Fates favor you," Demeter said quietly. "And so. What is your first step?"

"The first step," Athena said. She'd begun pacing back and forth across her aunt without realizing it. "Try to find Artemis. Save her from the beasts in the jungle and gain another soldier."

"That's not the true first step," said Demeter. "When Hera came after you, she sought two things. Two weapons. You only control one."

"The other can't be controlled."

"Then he must be eliminated."

"Yes," Athena said. "I need Achilles kept out of the other side's hands permanently. The trick will be convincing

Odysseus to give him up. And once Achilles is gone . . . there'll be nothing they can do against me."

The eye blinked slowly. For something so sickly and close to death, it was clear as a mirror.

"Go, then, and try your tricks," Demeter said. "None of this will really be over, anyway. Not until you are dead."

2

SUN AND STONE

Snow never gathered on Aidan's headstone. Other grave markers stood half-buried, with ridges of ice packed across the tops even after family members brushed them off. But Aidan's sat bare. Snow and ice shrank from it. Out of respect? Or out of horror, maybe, at something buried beneath the ground that had no business there.

A god. A god lay dead at the feet of that granite slab. Apollo. Aidan Baxter. God of the sun.

Cassandra Weaver stood off to the side, as she had on every Tuesday and Friday afternoon since they'd buried him. Sundays were too crowded, and she hated the sound of other mourners, the ones who knew how to mourn and what to say. How to cry softly into a handkerchief instead of screaming until their noses bled.

Her fingers reached out and traced the air in front of his name. *Aidan Baxter, Beloved Son and Friend.* Every day in the cemetery she thought she'd say something that needed to be said, but she never spoke.

High on Aidan's grave marker, above his name, was a carving of an enflamed sun. No one had told his parents to put it there. They just had. One more strange thing, working its will on the world, placing symbols for dead gods and keeping the snow at bay.

Odysseus stepped up beside Cassandra and laced his fingers through her hair, drawing it over her shoulder like a brown curtain.

"It's been an hour. Should we go?" His neck was tucked into his shoulders. Londoner. Unused to the cold.

She'd asked him to be her alarm clock. Time in the cemetery tended to stretch out, and she didn't have hours to lose. Normally, the job fell to Athena. The goddess accompanied Cassandra practically everywhere she went. A faithful, and hated, hound dog. Looking past Odysseus, Cassandra could almost see her, standing quietly near the edge of the cemetery in the copse of bare winter trees. She'd used to lean against a monument of a weeping angel, looking bored, until Cassandra snapped at her and said she was being disrespectful. But Athena was hundreds of miles away, somewhere between New York and Utah, seeking another dying goddess, stretched out across the desert. Seeking word of Aphrodite.

Cassandra's hands tingled and burned even at the thought of Aphrodite's name. They'd spent two months looking, Athena and Hermes both. They threw lines out in all directions, and still Aphrodite was nowhere to be found.

Andie said it didn't matter. That Aphrodite would die eventually anyway. But it wouldn't be the same. It wouldn't be enough, if it wasn't at Cassandra's own hands.

Odysseus sank deeper into his coat. His shaggy brown hair made for poor earmuffs. Cassandra flexed her fingers to drive the burn away, and to drive Aphrodite from her thoughts.

"Cold?" she asked.

"Of course I am. It's beastly cold." He stuffed his hands under his armpits. "But take your time. We've got a while before we need to nab Andie from practice."

"We can go. Thanks for coming with me."

"Anytime. But if we don't go soon, I'm going to warm my feet on his gravestone. Think he'd mind?"

Cassandra looked at the marker. Aidan Baxter. She'd loved him from the minute she saw him, without ever knowing what he really was. Who was she to say what he'd do, or what he'd feel?

I knew him in two lives, and not at all.

She remembered what he'd done to her in Troy—driving her insane, cursing her to never be believed—and she hated him. But she also remembered the sound of his voice and the last look in his eyes. He was there, underneath the dirt, and she'd give anything to reach down and pull him out of it. Even if it was only to scream into his face.

Damn you, Aidan. You were never this infuriating when you were alive. Come back, so I can tell you so.

"'Beloved son and friend,'" she read. "If they only knew. That it isn't the half of it. That they'd have needed a gravestone a mile long to tell the whole story." She shook her head. "Four words. It's not enough."

Odysseus put his arm around her and tugged her close. He took a deep breath, and kissed her head.

"I think he'd say it's everything."

Cassandra and Odysseus walked into the ice arena and found Andie waiting on the steps leading up from the locker room. Her hair stuck to her head, steaming with sweat from practice. It wasn't that much warmer inside the arena than out, but Andie stretched her t-shirt-clad arms happily.

"First one done?" Cassandra asked, descending the stairs.

"As usual." Andie cocked her head toward the locker room. Inside, the shouts and laughter of her teammates mingled with the noises of packing skates and pulling Velcro. She snorted. "I don't know what they're laughing about. They suck. We suck."

"Still time to turn it around."

But there wasn't. February was upon them, and the hockey season neared its end. Andie waved at Odysseus as he talked to the girls running the concession stand. "Hey, heartbreaker! Get me a hot dog!"

The sheer booming volume of Andie's shout made Cassandra squint. "You're in a decent mood, considering how bad you suck."

"Yeah. It's funny, but I don't really care that much. Did you know?" she asked Cassandra. "That the season was going to blow?"

Cassandra shrugged. Of course she had. The usual, run-of-the-mill visions were still around.

"Well, anyway. What's going on in the world of weird?" Andie asked. "Does Athena still want to look for Artemis?"

"So Odysseus says."

"But you saw Artemis running to her death months ago." Andie craned her neck and gestured for Odysseus to hurry up.

Had it really been so long? Standing in the hockey arena, it felt like minutes, not months. Cassandra's eyes clouded with memories of overgrown jungle leaves streaked with blood. The slim girl with brown and silver hair, chased down by a pack of ravenous who knew what. She could almost smell the blood and the rich black dirt. "Yeah," Cassandra said, taking a breath. "But it's the only vision we have to go on. And you know Athena. Any chance for another soldier is a chance too good to pass up."

"Don't be unfair," Odysseus said, sneaking up behind them. "It's about saving her sister as much as it is finding a soldier. And Artemis was Aidan's sister, too, you know. His twin." He handed Andie a hot dog in a cardboard shell.

"Finally. What took so long?"

"Sorry. Got caught chatting up Mary and Allie." He nodded to the girls in concession, who leaned so far over the counter they were about to fall out of it.

Andie batted her eyes. "Odysseus is so witty. Odysseus is so charming! Don't you just *love* Odysseus' accent!" She took a huge bite of hot dog and talked through it. "Barf."

Odysseus had enrolled at school a month earlier. An ancient Greek hero, matriculating at Kincade High so he could dog Cassandra's footsteps. Athena's idea, though she probably regretted it now, seeing how popular Odysseus had become with every girl in their grade. But no. Having him there served a purpose, and to a goddess that was the important thing.

"You headed to Athena's place?" Andie asked, referring to Athena's new house, a few streets over from Cassandra's own, where she lived with Hermes and Odysseus. "I'll come with you if you guys can stop off and let me shower."

"When's your car supposed to be fixed?" Cassandra asked.

"Dear god, soon," Andie groaned.

Athena's house was a pretty brown cottage with four bedrooms and two stories. A walk-out porch on the second level attached to the master bedroom, Athena's. It probably made her feel like she could see things coming, but it seemed imperious. If she were home she'd be there now, looking down on them as they pulled into the driveway.

Behind them, tires crunched in the snow, and Andie turned in the backseat. A beaten-up hatchback idled behind Odysseus' Dodge Spirit.

"Chinese delivery," Andie said as the delivery guy jogged past their door holding two white bags the size of backpacks. "Did Hermes know we were coming?"

"He didn't know *you* were coming," Odysseus replied. "And I wouldn't expect to get much of that Chinese, either. Athena's got him on a ten-thousand-calorie-a-day diet. If I were you, I'd order a pizza."

Ten thousand calories or not, it wasn't doing any good. The boy who opened the door was painfully thin, the skin of his cheeks drawn, and the bones visible in his wrists and shoulders. Hermes' light brown hair shone, and his skin was smooth. Everything about him looked healthy, even as his body ate his flesh away. He waved them inside.

"I can't believe you're going to eat all that," Andie said as Hermes set white box after white box out on the kitchen countertop.

"Big sister's orders." Hermes dumped an enormous pile of sesame chicken onto his plate and placed six steamed pork dumplings around the edge. When he ate, he used a fork instead of chopsticks, to better shovel everything in.

"Is it helping?"

Hermes paused a fraction of a second before taking another bite.

"I feel better. And Stanley's Wok has incredible pork dumplings."

"It smells good," Andie said. She eyed the boxes, and Hermes' brow arched possessively.

"I told you," said Odysseus. "Order a pizza."

"Don't be ridiculous." Hermes pushed a box of dumplings in Andie's direction. "Besides, if you ordered a pizza, I'd eat that, too."

Cassandra snorted in spite of herself. Without Athena standing stone-faced beside him, Hermes was impossible to dislike. He was so much more fragile than Athena, and much more concerned about not being an asshole.

"That wasn't there when I was here last." Andie nodded toward the living room wall. A silver sword with a black handle was mounted above the fireplace. The blade glinted, long and thin, in a subtle curve.

"Beautiful, isn't it?" Hermes said with his mouth full. "It's brand new. Just a replica, though I imagine it could cut someone in half if I wanted it to. It reminds me of one I used to have during the Ming Dynasty."

"Athena will like it," Odysseus said. "It suits her, to have weapons all over the house."

"It does," Cassandra agreed.

"I don't think she'd care if I put up baskets of posies. She doesn't give one whit about decorating or style. If you really want to make her happy, we should sell this place and hobo it down by the river."

Andie stood, chewing dumpling, and walked closer to the sword. "So, you know how to use this? You studied it?"

"I did," Hermes replied. "Though fighting and killing comes fairly naturally to gods. Except maybe for Aphrodite." He glanced sheepishly at Cassandra, who shrugged, even as her hands burned. Any mention of Aphrodite's name made her think of the glee on the monster's face when she drove the broken limb through Aidan's chest.

Cassandra rubbed her palms against her jeans and the burning disappeared.

After Aidan's funeral, she had asked Athena what her

power meant. Athena had blinked and replied that it was her purpose. That she killed gods.

She killed gods. Both intentionally and by accident. Hera. And Aidan.

But Cassandra couldn't believe that. She was no loaded gun, to be pointed and fired. Yet her hands still burned, and her heart raged with a surprising ferocity. Feeling so angry was new, and she didn't know what to do with it, besides murder Aphrodite.

And maybe Athena for good measure.

She felt Odysseus' eyes on her as if he could read her mind. But her silent threat wasn't real. Much as she hated it, Athena was needed.

"Did you get the maps?" Cassandra asked. Maps of every continent known to house a rain forest or jungle that might be the one Artemis ran through. Athena wanted her to use her sight on the maps to figure out which one it was. Probably a stupid idea. She'd never tried it before, and the only thing she knew about her "gift" was that it was generally disobedient.

"I did," Hermes said. "Do you want to do it now? Or is my eating going to distract you?"

"Well, it looks like you might be eating for the next few hours, so I guess we should go ahead." Cassandra smiled and took off her coat.

"The maps are in Athena's room." Hermes jerked his head toward the stairs. "On her desk."

"Sure, I'll go get them." Odysseus crinkled his eyebrows. "Bossy."

Andie plunked down on the sofa beside Cassandra.

"Do you want me to light some candles or something? Set the mood for the voodoo . . . that you do . . ." Andie trailed off. She sounded like Aidan. Always wanting Cassandra to play the part. Trances and smoke and mirrors. Magic words.

"It'll either work or it won't."

Odysseus returned with the maps and spread them out on the coffee table. A few were rolled and needed to be weighted down with coasters. Cassandra breathed deep. Odysseus, Hermes, and Andie all stared expectantly, but the green splotches of forest stretched out across the maps were just green splotches. Nothing jumped out three-dimensionally. Nothing moved.

"I don't know what Athena thought would happen," said Cassandra. "That I'd see a miniaturized Artemis X-ing her way through the Congo?" She looked up at Hermes. "You're never going to find her. She's probably dead, and how would you even know where to start?"

Odysseus pushed the maps closer. "Just give it a minute."

She opened her mouth to say there was no point, but what came out was, "Taman Negara."

"What?"

Cassandra didn't know. The words meant nothing to her, but when she looked at the map again her finger struck the paper like a dart.

Hermes leaned in. "Malaysia." He groaned. "Damn you, Artemis. Why not Guatemala? It would've been so much closer."

"Have you ever been there?" Andie asked.

"I've been everywhere," Hermes replied. "Though not for some time. We'll have to fly into Kuala Lumpur. Get some guides. It'd be faster if I went by myself."

"Everything would be faster if you went by yourself," Odysseus said. "But you know how Athena feels about us going out on our own."

Only Athena went anywhere alone. The others were guarded and watched, paired up in a buddy system like children. Cassandra, Andie, and Henry most of all. Odysseus and Hermes couldn't leave until Athena returned to take over babysitting the mortals.

Cassandra watched Odysseus study the map. It was a wonder he was allowed to go anywhere. The way Athena looked at him when he wasn't watching . . . telling people he was her cousin from overseas had been an idiotic choice. The minute anyone saw them together, they must've thought the pair were incestuous perverts.

"When you get back," Andie said suddenly, "would you . . . I mean, do you think you could"—she nodded toward the sword—"teach me how to use that?"

"Since when do you want to learn?" Cassandra asked. "I thought you didn't want anything to do with your old life." *Your old life.* The words stuck to her tongue. Memories stuck in Cassandra's head from thousands of years ago. She hadn't had the choice to remember or not. Athena hadn't given her one. But Andie was different. And she'd decided to stay herself.

Resentment tightened Cassandra's throat, but she took a breath. What was done was done, and if she was honest, she wasn't sure what choice she would've made if she had been given one.

"It's not that I want to be another person. Or the old me," Andie said. "It's just that I feel different. Stronger. Almost like my arms remember"—she looked at the sword—"holding something like that."

"Rumor had it you were better with a bow," Odysseus said, and to Cassandra's disbelief, Andie blushed.

"And," Andie said, "I'm quitting hockey."

"What?"

"It just doesn't seem important."

"Before any of this happened, it was all you thought about."

Hermes and Odysseus traded a look, like they were about to be stuck in the middle of something uncomfortable that was none of their business. Only it *was* their business. It was their doing. Everything that had changed, and was changing, was their fault.

"Don't get dramatic," Andie said. "You're still you, and there's another *you* in you. All I want to do is learn to use a sword. What's the big deal?" She stood and gathered her bag and coat.

"Do you need a lift home?" Odysseus asked.

"Nah. You guys still have stuff to do here. I'll go to Cassandra's and catch a ride from Henry." She walked around the wooden partition and left without another word.

"I won't teach her anything, if you don't want me to," said Hermes quietly.

"Why not? It's her choice. I'm not her master." Cassandra crossed her arms. Hermes raised his brows and gave Odysseus the "someone-is-TESTY" expression before shoving more Chinese into his mouth and wandering into the kitchen.

"Have you heard any more from Athena?" Cassandra asked.

"Nope," said Odysseus. "It took me weeks to get her to carry the phone. But when she called she did say that Demeter sends her regards."

"Whatever that means," Hermes sang from the kitchen, apparently eavesdropping.

Cassandra looked down at the maps. The feeling she'd had about Taman Negara was gone, and they were just maps again. But if she did it for one goddess, she could do it for another.

Her palms tingled. She stared at the paper and thought hard.

Aphrodite.

Her fingers burned so hot she gasped, and the maps ignited. Orange fire shot up in a tower from the coffee table, inches from her face.

"Oh-kay!" Hermes shouted, there in a flash. He slapped the flames out and fanned away the smoke. "Let's not do whatever you just did again, yes?"

"I'm sorry," said Cassandra, eyes wide. "I don't know how I did that."

Hermes sniffed. "I smell burnt hair. It better not be mine."

"Come on." Odysseus pulled Cassandra off the couch and led her through the house until they stood on the rear porch that faced into the backyard. It was a bare rectangle of snow at the moment, but in the spring it would thaw and grow a pad of soft grass. With the privacy fence on all sides, it would make a perfect place to train Andie. And maybe Henry.

So they could die again. So someone could drive a spear through Henry's chest again, while she and Andie watched.

"Well," Odysseus said, "what was that about?"

"What do you think?" Cassandra asked sulkily.

"I think you were looking for Aphrodite, and you blew up the world."

Cassandra looked, into the trees, where an owl perched in the high branches, waiting for Athena.

"She'd better come back with news, Ody."

"Why?"

"Because she's kept me waiting long enough already." The backs of Cassandra's eyes stung; she clenched her teeth hard.

"Feels like you hate everyone on the planet right now, doesn't it?" Odysseus asked.

"Not quite everyone." But it was close. She hated. Over the past months she'd hated everyone and everything at some point, from her mother to the guy who made her coffee at the mall.

Odysseus sighed.

"I wish I'd had the chance to know him better, Cassandra."

Cassandra wiped her eyes. Already, Odysseus knew her well. He was the only other person on the planet like she was. The only one who remembered another life.

"Yeah," she said. "Me, too."

"I'm not going to say anything stupid, like how time heals all wounds."

"Good. Don't." She tucked her hands under her arms and tried to ignore the way he looked at her. But it was difficult. Odysseus had eyes that could make even unfeeling, bitchy goddesses blush.

"What?" she snapped.

"I was just remembering what they said you were like. Back then. In Troy."

"I don't care," she said. "But what did they say?"

"That you were full of fire. They talked about you like a prize horse to be tamed."

"Nice. Livestock. Very flattering." But horses weren't only livestock to the Trojans. They were revered partners. Her brother Hector carried them in his name. Hector, tamer of horses. Maybe that's why Henry had insisted on another Mustang after they'd totaled the last one.

Odysseus reached out and touched her hair. "It made me want to meet you."

"Stop it." She swatted him away. "I think you wanted to meet everyone. Weren't you married? You must've made a horrible husband."

"You're right," he said. "I think I did. But I only ever loved one girl at a time. Or at least, that's what it feels like now."

He looked so sad suddenly. Almost regretful, and Cassandra took a breath and relented.

"People change," she said. "They change in two years, let alone how many have passed since you and I were last alive. I didn't mean to make you feel guilty." She chewed her lip. "But I did mean what I said. I don't care what they thought of me then."

"But?"

She crossed her arms and tried to seem disinterested.

"But now that you've met me, are you disappointed?"

"Not sure yet," he said. "I do wonder what you were like before we came to town."

"I was ordinary," she said. "I blended in."

"Impossible. With Aidan? You can't blend in with something that pretty on your arm."

"Don't call him 'pretty.'" Her knee knocked into his. "And you weren't here. You didn't see how well he hid."

"Okay. But then why aren't you thanking us? If everything was so boring and ordinary."

"I *like* ordinary. People only wish for adventure until they're stuck in the middle of one. Haven't you ever seen *The Fellowship of the Ring?*"

"Sure. Lots of times. But I've been both hero and zero, and make no mistake—"

Cassandra exhaled. "Look. The difference between you and me is that you slid into your old life like it was a pair of old shoes. Mine has toes filled with razor blades."

Odysseus pushed off the wall.

"The difference between you and me, Cassandra, isn't our old lives," he said. "It's that I know who I am in this one."

"I know who I am in this one," Cassandra said. "The same as I was in the last one. A small fish caught in a big stream. Full of sharp rocks, gods, and assholes."

Odysseus laughed. "Assholes?" He pushed her hair off her shoulder, a gesture she was getting very used to. "But I cheered you up a bit, didn't I?"

"Distracted, maybe," she said. "But the fact remains. This is the only thing I can do now." She held up her hand. "What I was made for, Athena says. So she'd better not try to stop me from doing it."

"Just Aphrodite though, right?" Odysseus asked. "What about the others?"

"What?" Cassandra asked, and dropped her hand.

"Other gods," he said. "Major and minor. Ares and Hades. Hephaestus. Good old drunk Dionysus. Will you be able to point that thing in their direction, when they haven't murdered the love of your life?"

Cassandra looked down and said nothing.

"You hadn't thought that far ahead, had you?" he asked.

"I killed Hera."

"Because she was trying to kill you. You're not a murderer, Cassandra. You're not a hunter. And when it comes down to it, you might find it not so simple. Even with Aphrodite. When you look into her eyes. When you understand. It might not be so easy."

"Then I hope I'm too angry to hesitate," she snapped. But she wasn't angry now. Only exhausted, and more than a little scared to really think about what Odysseus said.

"I just want him back, Ody. There has to be a way, doesn't there? There has to be a way to go and bring him back."

Odysseus hugged her and rested his chin on her head.

"I don't know. But if you find a way, I'll be there. Right to the end of the earth and over it."

3

WORLDS

Henry had no taste. Andie lay upside down on his bed, scratching his German shepherd's neck. A poster for The Black Keys hung on his west wall, which wasn't too bad, but the rest of his room was a mishmash of crap.

"At least there aren't foldouts of naked women, eh, Lux?"

"Huh?" Henry asked. He was barely listening, sitting at his desk trying to finish a calc problem.

"I said your room is a mishmash of crap. You shouldn't let Lux lie in here so much. How's he ever going to learn that there are better bands than Linkin Park and better movies than *Avatar*?"

"Those are old. And Lux likes *Avatar*. Now will you shut up so I can finish this?"

"Is that a Vancouver Canucks commemorative puck? I swear if you don't die in this gods' war I'm going to kill you."

Henry scowled. "Don't you live somewhere else?"

Andie ruffled Lux's fur, unaffected. "If he really wanted me to leave," she said to the dog, "he'd have stopped doing that stupid math problem and taken me home a half hour ago."

"Why do you need a ride, anyway? Why didn't you let Odysseus take you?"

Andie eyed Henry slantwise. The keys of his calculator clicked, and he erased something, his head of black hair bent over the paper.

"I can't believe I used to be married to you," she said. "So rude."

"Yeah, well, thankfully that was in another life that neither of us remembers," Henry said, and erased something so hard he almost broke his pencil.

"I remember some things," Andie whispered. "Like holding a weapon."

"But not holding me?"

"Gross!" Andie shouted, and threw a pillow. "Don't say those words together. 'Holding' and 'me.' Makes my stomach want to crawl out through my ear."

Henry laughed and threw the pillow back.

"I think your sister is pissed at me," Andie said. She tossed the pillow into the air and caught it to her chest. "I asked Hermes to teach me to use a sword."

"Why would you do that?"

Because it felt like the natural thing to do. Because it felt like she needed to know. "And I'm quitting hockey."

"You're an idiot."

"Thanks for your input. I'll file that away under 'none of your business.'" Andie rolled over and sat up. "Don't you want to learn, too? Don't you want to remember, I don't know, some of the things?"

Henry shut his calculus text and reached for his hooded sweatshirt.

"I live in this century. I've got plenty of things to do here to keep me busy."

"But do you feel it?" she asked quietly.

"Do I feel what?"

"Don't tell me you don't," she said. "Don't lie. Whatever's happening to me has to be happening to you, too." Old instincts bled into her muscles and got stronger every day. The past was loose, and it lingered like an itch down deep. She didn't want to be Andromache. But she was becoming a new Andie all the same.

"I don't know what you're talking about." Henry stood, and Lux got off of the bed. "Come on. I'll drive you home."

"Liar," she said. The way he held his shoulders, the way he carried himself, was all subtly different. He looked stronger, more muscular. Maybe even taller. It was Hector, breaking the surface, the shadow of a thousands-of-years-dead soldier settling on Henry like dust.

"I don't know how you can stand it," Andie said. "I feel like I have to do something, or I'll explode. Like there's too much of me in my own body." She thought he tensed at that, but she wasn't sure. He was always so damn stoic. "You're not going to say anything?" She reached out and shoved him.

"Knock it off, Andie."

"Knock *you* off, maybe."

"Not in this life." Henry grinned in spite of himself. "And not in the last one, either."

She sprang up off the bed and got him in a headlock. Lux whined as they tried to hook into each others' legs. When they toppled onto the bed, he barked and quit the room with an unhappy groan. His tail thumped against the door.

It was nothing new, the way they wrestled. It felt normal

and natural. When she finally twisted loose, she felt Henry holding his breath, and his heart hammered in his chest. Maybe she really was stronger after all.

Athena stood in the driveway and looked up at her house. The house she'd bought to keep up the façade of a happy family: sick brother and concerned sister, taking time off from college. The house she'd bought so she could stay close to Cassandra.

On the walk back from the bus station, slush-water crept up the legs of her jeans almost to the knee. Her feet were soaked. Two days away from the desert and she could barely conjure a memory of its heat, though yellow dirt still clung to her jacket and rucksack.

"Hoot."

She looked up and saw yellow eyes and a clicking beak.

"Hoot yourself, little one," she said, but the weight of the bird's eyes got her moving and she walked toward the light thrown by the nighttime windows.

"I wondered how long you were going to stand in the driveway," Odysseus said from the sofa as she passed the living room.

"You didn't see me."

"No, but I knew you would stand, debating whether or not to come back. I'm right, aren't I? How long? A half hour?"

"Fifteen minutes."

"In your mind maybe. Gods are horrible judges of time."

She walked into the dining room and set her rucksack on a chair. She cringed at the sprinkling of sand it left on the up-holstery. Hermes would hiss like a goose. Odysseus walked in behind her and leaned against the table.

"How is he?" She looked down the hall toward Hermes' bedroom.

"Keeping the takeout restaurants in business," Odysseus said, but it wasn't hard to read between the lines. Hermes was no better. The food wasn't helping. "Did Demeter know where Aphrodite was?"

"Can we talk about it tomorrow? I just want a hot, hot shower." A bath would've been nicer, but with all the sand in her hair it would be like lounging in a mud puddle before she was through.

"A simple yes or no will do. Or I could join you in the shower, if you'd rather talk there."

"The punishment for watching a goddess bathe is to be eaten by hounds," she warned.

"Right," he said. "By your own hounds. And I'm distinctly houndless."

"I'm sure Henry would give Lux out on loan." She opened the refrigerator and grabbed a takeout box. Sesame chicken, and plenty of rice. "Why are there leftovers? He's supposed to eat—"

"Even he has limits." Odysseus grasped the back of Athena's neck. His fingers found their way into soreness she hadn't known she had. "Do you want him to burst?"

"I suppose not." She leaned back and closed her eyes. Let his fingers work their magic on the dozen or so knots in her neck, and down her back and shoulders. His touch had come to feel familiar and safe. Until he slipped one hand beneath her shirt and the other up into her hair.

"Odysseus. You don't know how to *not* put the moves on someone."

"Only you, goddess," he whispered, and then chuckled softly. "There's sand in your hair. You been sleeping on the desert floor again?"

"Under the stars," she said. "Scorpions and night spiders danced across my belly." Odysseus slid his fingers across her stomach and she felt it all the way down. A little more pressure, and she might've bent in two. She put her hand over his to stop him.

"How is Cassandra?" she asked.

Odysseus sighed and let go.

"Broken," he said. "And not healing. But she did do a nifty trick with the maps. Right before she set the maps on fire. You'd better deliver Aphrodite into her hands, and fast."

"Artemis first," Athena said. "What happened with the maps?"

"She says Artemis is somewhere in the Malaysian rain forest."

The Malaysian rain forest. So far away. Again. But their sister had to be found and saved. Artemis was clever, and a skilled hunter. Coolly indifferent, and quicker to rage than Athena, but so very protective of those she pledged to. She would make a fine soldier. She would avenge Aidan beside Cassandra, and that would be fitting.

"I'll shower, get a few hours' sleep, and repack for the climate. How fast do you think I can get a flight connecting to Kuala Lumpur?"

"Not so fast," said Odysseus. "You just got here. Why not let Hermes and me go?"

"I—"

"It'll do him good to roam out of Kincade a bit. And me. We're not children, you know."

"Please. When have I ever treated you like a child?" But she had, she supposed. In the old days. Odysseus had been her favorite, and she'd guarded him like treasure.

What will happen to you if I fail, hero? What will your destiny be, if I'm not around anymore to guide it?

She touched his face, and he grabbed her hand. Dried blood capped her index finger, where a feather had burst through on the return journey and torn most of the nail away.

"It's nothing," she said, as Odysseus dragged it under the kitchen light. "It barely stings anymore."

"Are there others?"

"None that I can feel. Not now."

"Not yet," he said.

"Don't worry about me." She tugged her hand away. "Worry about Hermes. He's fading, and hurting worse than a cracked fingernail." She paused. "I don't know if it's the best idea. The two of you going off on your own. To the middle of nowhere."

"It's a better idea than you going off again," he said. "You're away from Cassandra too much, Athena. You should know better than to leave your primary weapon unguarded for so long."

He had a point. The girl who killed gods was no secret. Every former immortal who didn't hold Athena's favor would try to eliminate Cassandra, that is if they couldn't convince her to jump into their pockets instead.

"Speaking of weapons," Athena said. "When are you going to tell me where Achilles is?"

"Never," he said. "You said he was no use to anyone, and you were right. He's my friend, but he follows his own mind. He's better off hidden."

"Someone else could find him."

"They won't."

"Tell me where he is."

His expression grew wary. She ought to lie. It would be easier if she lied. But she couldn't. Not to Odysseus.

"I don't want to use him," she said. "I want to kill him."

He didn't look away, or say she wasn't serious. It didn't even seem to surprise him that much.

"I'll never tell you," he said.

"He was the weapon Hera sought. Now that she's dead, others will seek him. Maybe even Aphrodite. He might lead us straight to Cassandra's vengeance."

For several beats of her heart, Odysseus stayed silent. "What are you up to?"

"The only thing I'm ever up to," Athena replied. "War."

"Hey."

Cassandra blinked at the suds on the end of her nose. Her mother had just flicked soap into her face. Almost into her eyes. Her own mother.

"The water's getting cold, space cadet."

"No one uses the word 'cadet' anymore." She wiped the bubbles off on her shoulder. "They're astronauts. Get with the space program."

"Well. Aren't we clever today." Her mom smiled. Cassandra knew that smile. It always showed up right before someone asked whether she was okay. But she seemed okay. Up to her elbows in lemon-scented dish soap or dutifully taking notes in class. Slogging her way through the million details that made up every single stupid day.

"How are you today, sweetheart?"

No one's eyes never stayed on her face when they asked. Except for maybe Odysseus'. Athena's would, too, if she ever bothered to inquire.

"My fingers are pruny."

"You know what I mean."

"Yeah. I know what you mean." Cassandra rinsed a plate and set it in the rack to dry. She thought she'd already scrubbed everything in the sink, and if she hadn't, so what? They were family germs.

"Hours go by without me thinking about anything," she said brightly. "Tasks pop up and keep my mind on other stuff." She frowned. "Life goes on."

"I wish you'd—talk to us more."

"You didn't raise me to talk. You raised me to figure things out for myself, which is what I'm doing." A snap crept into her voice, and she bit down. "Besides, Dad isn't the best at heavy-lifting emotional stuff, you know? He's been in the garage restoring the same armoire practically since Aidan died."

"He just doesn't know what to say, Cassie."

"Or maybe he doesn't know how to restore furniture."

Her mom laughed. "Who knows what he's doing out there? Stripping paint? Huffing fumes? I don't even want the damned thing."

"You will when I'm finished." The smell of paint thinner preceded her father into the kitchen. Cassandra didn't need to turn around to know he had goggles around his neck and was dressed like a walking drop cloth. "Or maybe we could put it in Cassie's room."

"I don't want it, either. Besides, you and Henry would break your backs getting it up the stairs."

Her father flexed, considering. He usually took her advice on these things. Even when it didn't come from a vision.

"Maybe if you got Ody to help," her mother said, and nudged her. "I'm sure you could convince him to come over."

"Sure." Cassandra smiled. "Why have two bodies at the foot of the stairs when you can have three?" The nudge was the most pointed attempt yet at pushing her and Odysseus together. At first, it had made her mad that they expected her to move on so soon. But her parents were ancient. Dinosaurs. Everything they'd learned about relationships they'd forgotten before she was born.

She sighed. That wasn't fair. Her parents just didn't know how much deeper and further she and Aidan went. Thousands of years further.

And they never would. This mother wasn't that mother. This father wasn't that father. Cassandra didn't know why that was. She only hoped that her other parents were at peace. And that these parents would never be touched by any god's madness.

"Maureen," her dad said, "I've got to run to the hardware store. You coming along?"

Her mom wrinkled her nose. "Only if you change out of that stuff and crack a window. And only if we can stop by the post office and the bakery. And the drugstore," she shouted after him. He was already headed up the stairs, muttering about wanting to be home before midnight.

"Is that Ody's car I hear?" Cassandra's mom asked. The Dodge buzzed and grumbled, audible from several streets over. Odysseus pulled into the driveway, killed the engine before it got really annoying, and bounded up the front steps.

"Knock knock," he said, and poked his head in.

"You have got to get a muffler," said Cassandra's mom.

"Really? I think it makes my entrance more dramatic. Like trumpeters." Odysseus smiled at Cassandra. "Ah. Dishes. Need help?"

"You wouldn't."

"I wouldn't. But it's gentlemanly to offer." He grunted

when Lux leaped up and pinned him to the door. Henry wasn't far behind, and he peeled the dog off.

"What brings you by?" Cassandra's mom asked.

"Aside from an uncontrollable desire to see your daughter?" Odysseus' constant flirting didn't help the matchmaking efforts. But it was just for fun. Anyone who saw the way he looked at Athena could tell you that. "My cousin's home," he said. "She was hoping Cassandra and Henry might come by for awhile."

"How is Hermes?"

Odysseus shifted his weight. It was a strange charade they kept up, an ailing student and his concerned relatives. And it wouldn't last forever. Someday soon, the truth would come rushing out to knock them all over.

"I thought I heard the car." Cassandra's dad returned, less paint-covered but still reeking of chemicals.

"Hey, Mr. Weaver. Working on the armoire?"

"What kind of a question is that?" Henry asked. "He's always working on the armoire."

"Except when I'm shuttling your mother from store to store. Let's go!" They exited in a turpentine-scented cloud. Cassandra's mom was right. They'd need to crack a window.

"What did she learn?" Cassandra asked. "What about Aphrodite?" A burst of heat jumped quickly into her hands, and she kept them carefully unclenched so Odysseus wouldn't notice.

Odysseus shrugged. Lux put a paw up on his knee and whined until there was more petting. "Lots of talk but no answers. From what Hermes says about Demeter, we shouldn't be surprised. I guess she's all riddles and wrinkly skin. But Athena's not giving up, Cassandra."

"She's not trying hard, either."

"So what do you need to see us about?" Henry interjected.

"Hermes and I are leaving soon. For the jungle Cassandra showed us in Malaysia. It'll just be you three and Athena for awhile."

Cassandra fumed. She should have held the information about Artemis ransom until Athena delivered Aphrodite.

"How long?" she snapped.

"Could be a few weeks. Maybe longer."

"But what about school?" Henry asked. "They'll hold you back."

"It'd be better if they did," Odysseus said. "I should keep getting held back. I could be in your year, and then Cassandra's."

"Well." Henry shrugged. "Good luck then." He turned and went back upstairs with his dog. A few seconds later, his door shut, and music turned on.

"I thought he would've warmed to us by now," Odysseus said.

"Really?"

"Well, to me at least." He walked into the kitchen and pulled out a chair. "Want to come by and see us off?"

Cassandra ground her teeth together. Malaysia wasn't where they should be going. They should be going after Aphrodite. But even though Cassandra was the god killer, Athena ran the show. Heat flared in Cassandra's palms, asking to be let out. Sooner or later, it would stop asking and demand.

Odysseus eyed her. She'd been unconsciously flexing her fingers.

"You okay with this?" he asked.

"I suppose," she said. "Aidan would want me to be."

"No," Odysseus said, a little sadly. "Aidan would want you to run. Far, far away. But I'm glad you haven't."

"What's that face for?" Cassandra asked, grudgingly. "Is Athena not well?"

Odysseus sat and put his elbows up on the table, slumped forward like he was exhausted.

"There was only one feather," he said. "Under her fingernail. She can't feel any more. Unless she's lying."

"I don't think she'd lie to you," Cassandra said, and was surprised she said it.

"She would if she thought it was for my own good. And she always thinks she knows what's for people's own good. Gods are controlling buggers."

"Why don't you just tell her," Cassandra said quietly. "How you feel." Even though Athena would break him like a toy. That was what gods did to mortals who loved them.

"She's not exactly the soul-baring type," Odysseus replied. "And besides. She knows."

"She does love you," Cassandra said. "Only, the way she loves isn't enough to sustain a rat. You deserve better."

"You don't know her like I do."

"I know that with everything she's taken from me, she still won't do me one favor."

"She's trying," Odysseus said.

He looked at Cassandra calmly. Fondly. But she knew she was pushing it. If anyone else had talked about Athena that way, they'd have found themselves flat on their backs.

"She's trying to let you grieve," he said. "Hate her for being a god, or hate her for trying to be human, but don't do both."

Cassandra's eyes dropped. "You know Artemis is probably dead, right?"

"I know. But she's their sister. If there was a chance for

Henry, no matter how slim, you'd have to take it, wouldn't you?"

She would. Of course she would.

"Don't be gone long," she said.

4

IN THE CAVERNS OF THE EARTH

Olympus didn't exist anymore. As far as Ares knew, it had cracked and crumbled into the sea. It dissolved into particles and was carried off in the mouths of birds. It disappeared the moment the gods left it, the moment they leaped or were thrown from it. The moment the humans forgot them.

But Aphrodite was dragging him to Olympus nevertheless.

"Olympus. Come home to Olympus," she said, and her teeth shone like pearls. "Mother waits."

"Olympus is gone, sweet one," Ares said, as she tugged and pulled, leading him through the trees, her pale, bruised fingers wrapped around his dark, bleeding wrist.

He had lingered with Aphrodite in the wood for days and nights, leaving blood streaks across her skin. Despite the bruises on her rib cage and hips, she was still beautiful. So he let himself be dragged toward whatever delusion she wanted. Her hair swayed down her back, bright as gold, as she picked her way through branches. Her tiny puppy wriggled happily in the crook of her arm.

"We shook Olympus down a millennium ago, pet. With our sadness and indifference."

"We don't have time for indifference anymore, Ares," she said, and turned to him with sane blue eyes. Her fingers bit into the bandage on his bicep, already soaked through with blood from a new cut. "I know what's happening to you."

"Aphrodite."

"And I know what's happening to me," she said. "I don't want to be mad. I remember who . . ." She paused and closed her eyes. "I remember sometimes."

Ares pressed his hand to her cheek. She remembered what she used to be, before her mind started to soften and burn. Her death was unfair and cruel, without dignity.

"I'm ashamed," she said, "of what I'm becoming."

He kissed her hair. "Let's go." His poor Aphrodite. It was difficult to keep his touch gentle when he wanted something to break. Something to cut. Something to crush.

The urge subsided when they reached the mouth of the cave, a modest opening dug into a rock wall and grown over with ferns and moss. They'd have to bend their heads to go inside.

"It isn't much," he said. The wind from inside was cold, and spoke of large, black caverns.

Aphrodite squeezed his hand, and they went in.

Ares knew exactly when it was that they left the cave on earth and entered the cave on Olympus. He felt the gravity change. The rock walls increased in luster and somehow in boldness, like a blurry curtain had suddenly been drawn back. It was hard and sharp and beautiful. It felt like home.

"How can this be?" he asked, and it was Hera who answered from somewhere in the shadows.

"It exists because we remade it," she said. "It exists because we have need."

"Mother." Ares couldn't see her. Even with immortal eyes, the dark was too complete. When he strained forward, he could barely make out her shape. She stood tall and proud, shoulders back, the curve of one hip thrust out, forming the perfect silhouette.

"My son."

Aphrodite stepped away to let them have their reunion.

"It's true then," he said. "You live."

"Is that disappointment I hear?"

"No," he said, but he heard something in his mother's voice: a soft grinding, like a heel twisting against gravel. "I thought Athena and the girl killed you."

"Rumors of my death were greatly exaggerated." Hera paused. "Well. Perhaps not greatly. I've missed you, Ares. The child of my husband." As she spoke she came into the light. It took everything he had to keep from shrinking back, not to recoil when she put her hands on his shoulders, her right fist heavy stone and the left warm flesh with fingers that squeezed him.

The perfect silhouette in the dark was a lie. It hid the awkward way her legs moved to compensate for the weight of stone across her shoulder and right side. Her body was a wreck of rock and fused flesh. But her face was the worst. Hera's beautiful ivory cheeks were all but gone. Most of her jaw and lower lip had turned to mottled stone. It ground against her teeth when she spoke. Bits of cracked marble and granite rolled in her cheek like joints or cogs in a grotesque clockwork.

"It's not so bad," she said, and tried to smile. "It barely

hurts." The stone pulled at the edges of her skin until Ares thought her lip would tear away and bleed.

"And how are you?" Hera touched her stone hand to his bandage. "Are you weak from lack of blood?"

"No. It's not bad. Not yet."

"He's strong," said Aphrodite. "Still strong. And I found him."

"You did," Hera said. Her eyes rested on Aphrodite and lost focus. "Death robs her of her mind, and me of my beauty." She shrugged. "We're lucky that it isn't the other way around."

"Don't be cruel," said Ares.

"I won't be. Not ever." Her expression softened as much as was possible. "For all of our past differences, I love her now. As much as if she really were my daughter."

Aphrodite wasn't listening anyway. She swayed slowly back and forth to unheard music.

"You sent her to find me," said Ares. "Why?"

"We're all we have left," Hera replied. "And Athena would see us dead."

"From what I understood, Athena was just protecting mortals."

"She places mortals above us," Hera said. "Above her family. Even though there are so few of us left, and billions of them."

"We're dying," Ares said. "And it doesn't surprise me that Athena'd spend her last days playing protector. It was always her favorite cape to wear."

"So you'll let her win?" Hera asked. "I thought you would fight."

"We're dying," he said. "What's the point?"

"Such a defeatist attitude," Hera clucked. "You're the god of war. If you're going to bleed to death, wouldn't you rather it be all at once?" Her jaw worked, and small stones clacked together like dice in a palm. "Wouldn't you rather not die at all?"

"What are you talking about?" Ares asked.

Hera turned away. Her movements were rough and crippled. Ashamed.

"That girl really did kill me," she said. "That day by that lake. When they killed your uncle Poseidon, they killed me, too. The rock crept over my lungs and into my heart. It felt like . . ." She paused and laughed. "It felt like turning to stone from the inside out. I saw the granite spread over my eye. I was inches away from death. Moments."

"But you're not dead."

"I didn't tell him," Aphrodite sang from the corner. "You said not to tell him, and I didn't."

"I know, my darling," Hera said. "We couldn't tell him until we knew whose side he would be on. But he's my son. And he's your lover. We can trust him."

"You can trust me, Mother. What are you saying?"

"I'm saying that if it hadn't been for them, I would be dead."

"If it hadn't been for whom?" he asked.

"They healed me. And if I please them, they'll heal me more. Until all this rock is gone."

"Who?" he asked. "Who could do that?"

Aphrodite slid behind Hera and wrapped bruised arms around her ribs. Her cheek pressed against Hera's stone shoulder.

"The Fates," Hera said. "The Moirae. The three sisters."

Ares stood aghast. He hoped wildly that she spoke in metaphor. That she spoke of miracles.

But she didn't. Hera meant the Moirae. Klotho, Lachesis, and Atropos. The sisters of Life, Destiny, and Death. The gods of the gods.

"What have you done?" he asked. "Not even Zeus would dare."

"It's not what I have done," she said, and fear quickened her eyes. "Come now. Don't be afraid. It will be fun. Don't you want to fight Athena one last time? Don't you want to find out which god of war will be left standing?"

"You're mad. You've called down the Fates—"

"I didn't call them," Hera hissed. "As if such a thing were even possible. They came to us. They sent us out to fight." Her voice dropped low. "They heal us and give us strength. And we serve them."

Aphrodite stuck a fingernail into her mouth and hugged Hera tighter.

"In the beginning, it seemed like a choice," Hera said. "They seemed like allies. But then I fell, and they dragged me back through worse pain than any god can imagine. They left me like this."

"Why did you send for me?"

"Because I'm a fallen soldier," Hera said. "I failed. *You*, my son, are my chance at redemption. I'll send you out in my place. You'll get what they want. And then they'll heal me."

Ares wanted to run. The Moirae had to be near, somewhere in Olympus. They could come crashing through the doors at any minute. He pointed at his mother.

"You put me under their eye," he said.

"They are the Fates, Ares. You were always under their eye. At least now you know. So make the most of it."

He looked at Aphrodite, sucking on her fingernail and hugging Hera tightly with her other arm. He had no choice.

"Don't be so glum," she said. "Aren't you happy to live? Aren't you happy to fight? Won't you enjoy putting that bitch in her place?"

That part, at least, truly was appealing. But the Moirae struck icicles of fear through his back.

"I'll—" he said, and swallowed. "I'll want to see them."

"Soon," Hera promised. "Once you have something to please them. Something they want."

"And what do they want?"

"They want their weapon," she said. "They want Achilles found."

5

GODS FLUNG TO THE FAR CORNERS

"I don't even think it's legal to bring this much food into a country. You're going to get us stopped at customs."

"So eat most of it on the way to the airport." Athena tossed Hermes a box of granola bars. She'd packed half his bag with protein mixes and canned meat. It hardly seemed enough. His shoulder blades stuck out of his back like wings. He was so very thin. At least the fever had abated, and he seemed strong. But questions filled Athena's lungs every time she took a breath. *Are you sure you're okay to go? Do you really know your way around? Do you know what to do? Maybe I should go instead.*

But he was a god, not some mortal to be babied. And Odysseus was right. She'd been away from Cassandra for too long, and you didn't leave your primary weapon unguarded.

"Why not send me to the airport with a dozen pizzas? I could make a pretty good dent in them by the time we hit security," Hermes said. "Or maybe a Crave Case from White Castle."

Athena smiled. He was disgusting. Her little brother. Until the gods had started dying, she hadn't seen him for hundreds of years. Now she sent him off to Malaysia to look for their dying sister, into the jungles where beasts chased her with razor teeth and lolling tongues.

"Tell me you can still outrun anything," she said.

"I can still outrun anything."

"This isn't all for nothing, Hermes. Cassandra's finger struck that map for a reason. Artemis is alive."

"If you say so," he said. "But if I get there and find some beasties sleeping off a full belly of goddess in a shady spot, what should we do? Kill them?"

Athena sighed.

"What?" Hermes asked.

"Nothing."

She coughed, and Hermes looked at her sharply. Her right lung had ached when she'd woken up that morning. A new feather, and a large one from the pain of it. She'd wanted to keep from coughing until Hermes and Odysseus had gone.

The front door opened; Odysseus and Cassandra tramped into the house loudly, in boots and coats. The change from the frigid winter of Kincade, New York, to the humid sweatbox of a Malaysian rain forest would be extreme. She hoped Odysseus wouldn't get sick.

"Athena?"

"We're in here," she called, and in moments they crowded into Hermes' bedroom.

"I thought we were packing light," said Odysseus. Hermes' black duffel bag was filled to the brim, stuffed with the odd shapes of boxes and cans.

"We were, until the grocery Nazi got back."

Athena gave in. "You're right. Lighter is better." She up-ended the bag and let half the contents spill out, along with several of Hermes' meticulously folded shirts and boxer shorts. He threw up his hands and made a "pth" sound with his tongue, even as she stuffed the clothes back in. "Just remember to buy plenty of food when you get there."

"You do know that we know how to hunt, right?" Odysseus asked.

Cassandra looked appalled. "You'll be in a rain forest. Most of those animals are endangered."

"*We're* endangered," Hermes said, and zipped up his bag before Athena could do any more damage.

The flight to Kuala Lumpur was booked, and Hermes had set up a guide for when they arrived. A car would take them as far as Kuala Tembeling, and then they'd plunge into Taman Negara on their own.

The room fell quiet. Athena hadn't said much to Odysseus since they'd spoken about Achilles. Odysseus said it wasn't fair. That it wasn't Achilles' fault. And it wasn't. Achilles didn't ask to be Achilles. But he was too dangerous to be allowed to run free. Some things were like that. The atom bomb. Ebola. And Achilles, son of Peleus.

In the drawn-out silence, Athena and Cassandra finally looked at each other.

"How was your trip?" Cassandra asked.

"No word on Aphrodite," Athena replied.

"No surprise there," said Cassandra.

"I'm sorry." For the thousandth time, Athena wished her weapon weren't a small, mortal girl. It would have been so much easier, so much simpler, if the primary weapon had been a god.

"You told them where to go? Exactly where to go?" Athena asked.

Cassandra shrugged. "There isn't really an 'exactly' in a

rain forest. I gave them as good a starting point as I could. There's a lot of ground to cover." She glanced at Odysseus. "Maybe they'll get lucky."

"How did you know? Could you see it? Could you see Artemis?"

"No. I didn't even think it would work. But then they put the maps out, and I just knew."

"Have you seen anything else?"

"If I had, I would have told you."

"What about your other power? Have you felt anything?"

Cassandra rubbed her hands along her legs. "Yes."

"Are you sure?"

"Do you want me to demonstrate?" Cassandra snapped, but if it was a threat, Athena didn't take it as one.

"Maybe. I think that's what we should do while Hermes and Odysseus are gone."

"No," said Odysseus, and moved between them. "Cassandra, don't."

Athena picked up Hermes' duffel and strode from the room. If they kept yakking for much longer they'd miss their flight.

"She can't go up against Aphrodite untested. She's got to learn sometime."

"Not on you." Odysseus walked as close to her shoulder as possible in the narrow hallway. "She's not ready."

"I shouldn't have said anything. Now you'll worry."

Odysseus gritted his teeth. "Don't make it sound like I'm worrying over nothing."

"I'm not." Athena knew what could happen. That one misplaced or careless touch from Cassandra could make feathers bloom in an instant, filling her heart and slicing through her blood vessels.

"If something goes wrong . . ." he said. "They need you."

Athena stopped. He meant that he needed her. But that wasn't true. He'd always been more than fine on his own.

"She won't hurt me. Will you, Cassandra?"

Cassandra looked at Odysseus. "I won't. If I can help it."

"You're both really pissing me off," Odysseus said.

"Would you rather I use her map trick to find Achilles, then?" Athena asked, and he scowled. She would, if it came to that. If he wouldn't tell her.

"Hermes, did you call the cab?"

He nodded. "Should be here—" An impatient honk sounded in the driveway. "Right now. So, table whatever argument this is, and let's go. I've got a goddess to find."

They stopped in the living room. Hermes took his bag from Athena and grasped the back of her head, pulling her forehead quickly to his.

"See you when I get back, big sister," he said, and let her go, leaving her more than a little surprised. "And when I get back, our little family will have grown." He winked at Cassandra and headed for the door, grabbing Odysseus' worn leather bag from the entryway as he went.

Odysseus eyed Athena. "You know we're not done with this conversation."

"I know."

He hugged Cassandra and kissed her on the head, told her to be careful, and whispered, "Don't kill her," into her ear.

"I won't."

He looked at Athena and said his fast and silent goodbye. It was nothing more than a soft encircling of his fingers around her wrist, and his eyes on hers, but it was somehow so intimate.

Don't let go.

Athena tugged herself away.

The door closed, and the cab pulled out of the drive. They were gone.

The wind smelled of ice. Athena breathed it in, walking back and forth on the porch that extended out from her second-story bedroom. She should put on a jacket, or wrap herself in a blanket. Anyone in a passing car might call the police, thinking she'd lost her mind out on the roof in the middle of winter in a t-shirt. But the air across her skin felt good, and when she sucked it in deep, the ache in her lung was still just a quiet burn. No ruffling vane had emerged to tickle and sting. It was buried. If she was lucky, it would stay that way.

She gripped the edge of the railing and thought of Odysseus and Hermes on the other side of the world. The house felt too big without them. Every sound she made announced itself loudly and died off with nothing to answer it. They could be gone for weeks. For a month. It had only been a day, and already she paced the rooms like a lonely ghost. Already she was out on the porch without a coat, like a crazy person.

A widow's walk. That's what they would call this, if it faced the sea. A place for anxious wives to watch the water and wait for their men to come home safe.

Athena's fingers tightened around the wood. One twist of her wrists and she could rip the whole thing apart. It wouldn't even be hard. She could splinter it and toss it down into the snow. Maybe then she'd feel better.

And I could rebuild it afterward. Give me something to do until they get back.

The hum of a familiar engine caught her attention. Andie's silver Saturn came into view and pulled into the driveway amidst a cloud of pounding music. The girl was alone inside, her face through the window a pale orb with big eyes.

"I see the car's running again," Athena said, as she got out.

"Better than ever." Andie stood before the front steps, looking up. "Aren't you cold?"

"No."

"Right. Gods don't feel cold. Neither snow, nor heat, nor gloom of night will keep a goddess off her porch."

Athena leaned down. "I recognize that, you know. The creed of the U.S. Postal Service. I've been in America for most of the time it's been America. And you got it wrong."

"I'm sure I did," Andie said. She looked over her shoulder at her car, and at the road. A worried gesture, like she was doing something illicit. "Can I come in?"

"Door's open," Athena said. By the time she got downstairs Andie had taken off her coat and was toasting her fingers over the fireplace. Athena joined her, spreading her hands close to the flames.

"I thought you said you weren't cold."

"I wasn't. Cold doesn't really affect me." She turned her hands. Currents of heat flickered against her skin. "But I feel it."

Andie seemed uncomfortable there without Cassandra, and with Odysseus and Hermes gone. It was no secret that she and Henry thought Athena the strangest of the three, and the most godlike.

"Cassandra doesn't know you're here," Athena said, because it was obvious. "So why are you?"

"Didn't Hermes tell you?"

"Hermes didn't have a chance to tell me much. It was a scramble to get all the travel arrangements made, and then they left."

"Oh." Andie cleared her throat and gestured to the

sword, mounted inches above their heads. "Hermes said he would teach me to use that. But he's gone now, and Cassandra said he might be gone for a while. So I was wondering if you would teach me. Or at least start, until he gets back."

Athena didn't answer, and after a minute, Andie started to babble.

"I mean, maybe it would be better learning from you anyway. You're, like, the battle goddess, right? Or are you really as big a jackass as Cassandra says, and coming here was a huge mistake?"

Athena snorted.

"Flattery's not necessary," she said. "I'll teach you. Come downstairs."

"Now?" asked Andie.

"Why not?"

"I—" Andie's mouth closed slowly. "I hadn't figured on starting so soon. Honestly, I didn't think you'd say yes."

"Well, I did. So do you want to learn, or not?"

"Yeah. I do. It feels like I should."

Athena raised her brow. "No matter what Cassandra and Henry think?"

Andie pushed past her toward the basement.

The basement was floored in sealed concrete, the walls bare aside from a few other swords and knives. It wasn't much more than a large open space and a partially finished laundry room. A speed bag and a black heavy bag hung in the eastern corner beside a set of free weights and a bench.

Andie whistled. "I don't know what I expected, but it wasn't anything so humble."

"We'll have to get some mats," Athena said. "We can't be slamming you down onto concrete."

"What is this?" Andie asked. She ran her hand over the

black leather surface of the heavy bag. "Don't tell me you use a punching bag. Or free weights."

"Please," said Athena. "I could juggle every one of those weights with my fingertips. This is for Odysseus."

Andie walked to the speed bag and gave it a gentle push.

"He was some great warrior, wasn't he?"

"He was." In her memory, Athena could still hear his scream and see the flash of bronze as he charged into swords and arrows. "One of the best. He still is."

"Better than Henry used to be? Better than Hector, I mean?"

Athena cocked her head. In a fair fight, Hector would have won. But Odysseus had never been bound by the rules of a fair fight.

"It would depend on the day," she answered finally. "Why are you doing this?"

"I don't know." Andie shrugged. "Because it feels like I should. It feels like who I am."

They still are what they were. That's what Demeter had told her. So was this black-haired girl really a warrior? Even without her memories? Athena'd be lying if she said she wasn't curious to find out.

"Cassandra doesn't want me to," Andie went on. "She says she wants to kill Aphrodite, but what she really wants is for all of you to go away. For everything to go back to the way it was. She wants Aidan back. But none of those things are going to happen. Are they?"

"No."

"That's why I want to learn." She rubbed her hands together. "So let's go. Do you have some wooden swords or something? Maybe a shield?"

Athena walked to the closet and disappeared inside.

When she returned she held two long staffs, like walking sticks.

"What're those?"

Athena tossed one to her. "It's a *bō*. You use it like an extension of your arms."

Andie's face fell as she turned the staff back and forth. She'd wanted the sword. But she already held it correctly, right palm away and left palm in, so maybe her hands did remember.

Andie sighed. "I feel like the lame Ninja Turtle. Don't you have any *sai*?"

"You can do more with this," Athena said, and quickly used the *bō* to pop Andie in the chest. Lightly, very lightly, but the girl nearly buckled.

"Ow!" Andie rubbed her sternum.

"There's an easier way, you know," Athena said.

"There is?"

"I could just choke you to death." Andie took a hasty step back, and Athena laughed. "Take it easy. I'm kidding."

"Well don't. You're not very good at it."

Athena spun the *bō*. Maybe time wouldn't pass so slowly after all.

"We're never going to find her."

Odysseus stared up into the trees of Taman Negara and felt small. The rain forest canopy stretched up and out and on forever; or at least that was how it seemed. And they were going to plunge into it, headfirst, to try to pick up the months-cold trail of one dying goddess.

Hermes didn't agree or disagree with Odysseus' declaration; he was too busy trying to explain to their boat guide that they didn't have a hotel to get to and didn't need transport to one. He knew enough of the local language to keep things civil, and he'd gotten them this far, but his vocabulary failed in the face of the guide's good-natured insistence. He had to resort to a lot of wild hand gestures.

Odysseus adjusted his pack on his shoulders. They'd stopped off at a hostel near the airport to shower, but it hardly made a difference. Hours and a very long boat ride later, the humid air felt like a second, very amphibian skin.

"Okay, okay, so we'll die," Hermes said loudly, and both he and the guide threw up their hands. He picked up his duffel and affixed it like an improvised backpack. When he met Odysseus' eyes, the look they shared spoke volumes. They were already tired and felt like shit, and it was only going to get worse.

"How did I let Athena get me into this?" Hermes grumbled. He picked an arbitrary spot in the forest and stepped in.

"I thought you were excited for the chance to get out of Kincade, mate."

"Yeah? Well, you were excited to tag along." Soft ferns brushed against their legs as Hermes picked his way through a patch of dense green leaves to a space where the ground was clearer, coated with dark soil and dead plant scraps. "So who's laughing now?"

Odysseus didn't think either one of them was laughing, but he knew why they'd come. Athena's determination to murder Achilles left little doubt. Gathering forces and destroying arsenals. His Athena. She'd never stop fighting. Keeping her off Achilles' scent was going to be the battle of his life.

"I know it's early to be asking, but do you feel anything? Can you feel Artemis anywhere?"

Hermes lifted his head and scanned the trees. "Nothing yet. Maybe nothing ever. My god-dar was never as good as Athena's. Even before we started dying. Probably not the answer you were hoping for. Now that we're here, this place certainly seems a lot bigger than Cassandra's fingerprint, doesn't it?"

They walked for a few moments, listening to the sounds of rustling leaves and insects. The jungle did seem larger than Odysseus had imagined. Everything was a wonder; the heaviness of the air, the span of the leaves. And if the noise was any indication, they were surrounded by at least three million bugs.

"Maybe we should've brought Cassandra with us."

"Ha," Hermes said. "And risk her falling to a snakebite or a poisonous insect? Risk her tripping down a ravine?" He veered around the curve of a large trunk. "Athena would have your tongue just for suggesting it."

"Maybe," Odysseus said. "But she might've made this go a lot faster."

They found a spot to camp when the light began to fade, and Odysseus channeled his inner Boy Scout to start a serviceable fire. Hermes disappeared into the trees to hunt but returned carrying a large, gutted fish.

"Cassandra's speech about endangered animals get to you?" Odysseus asked while Hermes scaled the fish and put it on a spit.

"Shut up. Fish just cook faster." He rinsed his hands with water from his canteen and rummaged in his bag for a can of potatoes, which he opened and shoved down into the coals. "Athena should've packed herbs and butter," he grumbled, but it wasn't long before the fish skin was crackling, and the savory smell made their mouths water.

They ate in relative quiet, just a few muttered comments about how surprisingly good the food was. Odysseus ate only a small portion of the nearly two-foot-long fillet, allowing Hermes to polish off the rest, along with most of the potatoes and a chocolate chip granola bar for dessert. Athena still would have wanted him to eat more.

"So," Odysseus said. "Is there anything I should know about sleeping on the rain forest floor?"

"Hm?" Hermes asked, even though he'd probably heard. He'd been looking up through the canopy, catching a glimpse of stars above the smoky orange glow of the fire. "Oh, uh, not that I can think of. You might want to check yourself for leeches every once in a while."

"Leeches." Odysseus grimaced. "Fantastic. And then what? I just yank them off? I think I saw that in a movie once." He glanced downward, trying to detect any movement or sliminess in his shorts.

Hermes laughed. "Right. *Stand By Me*. The leech in the kid's tighty-whities. But don't just yank it. I packed salt. They'll drop off." His smile faded, and he looked back up into the sky.

"Hey. You all right?"

"As all right as a dying god can be, I suppose."

Odysseus prodded the coals with a stick and sent up a whirl of sparks. "You're not going to die," he said. "Athena's going to win this war."

The words came easily and sounded confident. But Odysseus couldn't meet Hermes' eyes, and he couldn't stop his jaw from clenching. He needed to believe what he said, that they would win, and that Hermes would live, because it meant that *she* would live. But he didn't really know.

"I don't want to take that hope away from you," said Hermes. "And I'll admit, she seems pretty sure. Just in case, though . . . I don't know how long I want to do this."

"Do what?"

"This." He kept his voice cheerful and gestured around to the trees and sky. "I mean, it's scenic and everything. A once-in-a-millennium commune with nature. But that's about how often I'd like to keep it. Even if I weren't thin as a sack of sticks, I'm not cut out for all this . . . labor."

Odysseus grinned. "Got someplace else you'd rather be? Leading a caravan of glitterati across the cities of Europe, maybe?"

Hermes lowered his eyes. "You have to admit, there are things . . . that one would wish to do once . . . or several more times, before dying."

"Like what?" Odysseus asked softly. Hermes looked so tired. Let him daydream for a while. Let him out of the sweltering trees, and into someplace bright, and gilded, and marble.

"Like walking midday through the Piazza della Signoria. Like spending hours on a winter bridge over the Seine. Eating a meal that doesn't show up at my door in a cardboard box." He laughed. "And other things, too. It would be nice to feel things." He cocked his eyebrow. "Like one last, sweaty fling with a beautiful boy. Under a canopy of stars, perhaps? In the Taman Negara rain forest?"

Odysseus' eyes widened. "Believe me, mate. If boys were my fancy, I would be the luckiest bloke on earth."

Hermes waved him off. "Straight or gay, I'm irresistible. We both know why you and I won't be tumbling through the leaves. It's the same reason that we're here, in the middle of a sweltering, rotten jungle. The same reason I won't see the piazza ever again."

"What's that?" Odysseus asked, even though he knew.

"We both love my sister."

6

CIVILIAN RELATIONS

Andie and Cassandra cut a slow, straight, limping path through the crowded halls on the way to Algebra. Faster students edged around them like rocks in a stream, grumbling as they passed. But Andie could go no faster. She'd trained with Athena almost every day for a week. There wasn't much left of her besides a patchwork of bruises, held tenuously together by frayed muscles.

"I play hockey year round," Andie said. "Dry land practice, calisthenics, three ice practices a day during summer camp. And I've never felt this much like shit."

"It's because they're muscles you don't normally use." Cassandra shifted their books in her arms as a frustrated freshman pushed by and knocked them loose.

"Muscles I don't normally use," Andie repeated. "Yeah. For like two thousand years."

"You're overdoing it. She's going to injure you."

"She knows what she's doing."

Cassandra narrowed her eyes. Athena probably did know

what she was doing. But that didn't mean she had any consideration for Andie's well-being while doing it.

"Look at you," she said. "Look how you're walking. You're like the Tin Man after a good bout of weeping."

"Jerk," Andie said. "She has a plan, okay? And I think that plan is to use up my body's entire reserve of lactic acid."

Cassandra sighed. "Brace yourself. Here come the stairs."

"I want to take the ramp."

"We don't have time to take the ramp." She let Andie put a hand on her shoulder like an old woman and listened to her bitch and moan her way up the first flight.

"You could take the heat off me, you know, if you'd let her train you, too."

"Not a chance."

"It wouldn't even be hard for you," said Andie. "You have all your memories already. It would be like riding a bike. It would all come back."

Cassandra shook her head. There was still another long flight of stairs to go, and then two long hallways to the classroom.

"You and I had very different past lives, Andie. You were an Amazon married to a warrior. I was a crazy princess they locked in a basket."

"You mean you don't remember anything useful? You can't shoot an arrow, or drive a chariot?"

Cassandra's memories of Troy sat in the back of her mind like something she'd done in childhood rather than thousands of years ago. She didn't like to think about it. Not only because of how it ended, in blood and despair. But because it felt normal to think about it, when it should've felt strange.

She shrugged.

"I'm pretty sure I can work a loom," she said.

"Yuck. Boring."

"Just be glad Athena didn't choke you, too. You used to do it with me. We'd sit all day in a room and weave, talking about the menfolk. They were riveting times."

"Hey. You guys are going to be late." Henry walked toward them from the direction of his locker, looking strangely naked without a notebook in his hand.

"We're late already," said Andie. "Aren't you?"

"I've got a free study hall period. I told Coach Baker I'd go clean up the weight room." He nodded at Andie. "You look like hell. You've got to rub out the lactic acid. Strip the muscle." He moved toward her, and she growled. "Fine. Later maybe. So are you learning anything, or just getting your ass kicked?"

"I'm learning everything," Andie replied. "I could kill you with my pinkie finger. If only I could bend it." She told him what she and Athena were working on, and the excitement in her voice was plain. And something else, too, that Cassandra didn't like: eyes like stars when she said Athena's name. The goddess' glamour, getting to her. Henry didn't like it, either. But there wasn't anything they could do about it.

"You should let her train you, too," Andie said.

"No." Henry was firm.

"Is it just because it's her? If Aidan was here, would you let him?"

"No," said Henry. "I just want them all to die." He looked sheepishly at Cassandra, but she knew what he meant. He hit Cassandra in the shoulder and walked away.

"How can he say that?" Andie asked. "How can he mean it? I know you guys blame Athena for Aidan dying, and frankly, that's twisted, but what about Hermes? He's our friend. And Aidan was. It's not all of them."

Cassandra stared after Henry. He looked more like Hector

now, even without his memories. One life bled onto the other. Why? Out of necessity? Because he was needed? She'd often wondered why fate had chosen to plant the three of them in Kincade and no others from Troy. Where were Paris and Helen? Where were Troilus and beastly Agamemnon? Were they waiting somewhere? Would she see them again? Or had the Fates finally finished with them?

If they have, they should count themselves lucky.

"It's not all of them," Cassandra said to Andie quietly. "But their problems become our problems. Their problems are going to change our lives."

Cassandra had been standing in front of Aidan's headstone for an hour. Another Friday in front of his grave, not knowing what to say. Her throat hurt from the urge to cry, from backed-up tears and stopped-up words. If she opened her mouth, she would only scream.

He couldn't be dead. Not really. He was a god. But Cassandra looked at the ground and felt nothing. No lingering spirit. No connection.

If only he were there. If only she could speak to him and have him speak back.

"Where do gods go?" she wondered aloud. To Hades? To the underworld? Or somewhere else entirely?

Behind her, Athena stood in the trees, feeding owls or something and waiting to take her home. Cassandra turned to see her guardian at her post, but Athena didn't seem to be guarding. She was restless, pacing and kicking her toes into the snow like a deer after grass. Maybe she was missing Odysseus.

Cassandra walked quietly out of the cemetery, and waited for Athena's head to rise, for her to notice. But she didn't. She didn't notice until Cassandra was practically on top of her.

"Your feet are freezing." Athena glanced at Cassandra's shoes, soaked through. Her toes curled inward and lifted as they walked to the street, trying to keep them off the cold ground. "I should've been warming up the car."

"It's fine," Cassandra said. They got into the Dodge, and Athena blasted the floor heater to no avail. It was basically shot; by the time they got home, the air coming out of it would be almost lukewarm.

"How's it going with Andie?" Cassandra asked.

"It's going well. She's strong. Mindful of her balance."

"But none of that will make any difference if she comes up against a god," Cassandra said. Andie was strong. Tough. Smart. But against a god she could swing a sword with a razor edge and it might as well be made out of Nerf plastic.

"Against a god, the only thing she could do is die well," said Athena.

"Do you think that's funny?"

"Am I laughing?"

"Why are you training her, then, if she can't fight what we're fighting?" Cassandra asked.

"Because she's afraid. And because she will have to fight, and Henry, too, before this is over."

"Your war," Cassandra said. "But what about my war? When are we going to find Aphrodite?" Heat flooded her hands, right down to the fingertips.

"No one seems to know where she is, Cassandra. And I heard about your maps. How well that worked out."

"I could try again."

"Great," said Athena. "I'll keep the fire extinguisher handy."

"You're an ass."

"Cassandra. Aphrodite will die. In time. Let me fight the war and help me win, and she'll die right and proper."

Cassandra clenched her fists.

"Then let's get going. You want help to find Achilles? You got it."

Athena glanced at her, surprised.

"Do you think it'll work?" she asked. "I didn't think you'd want to help. You know I'm going to find and destroy him."

"He murdered my brother," Cassandra said.

"In another life."

True enough. In this life, Achilles was probably no different than Henry. Just as innocent. In this life, they could be friends.

Athena pursed her lips.

"No," she said. "Not yet. I told Odysseus I would wait."

Cassandra groaned through her teeth.

"If you were half the god you're supposed to be," she said, "Aidan would still be alive."

Athena didn't react. Whenever Cassandra lashed out, she took it, like Cassandra's pain was her burden. Athena reached for the heater controls and tried to push them farther into the red, as if that would make a difference.

"Are your feet getting warmer?" she asked.

"Shut up. You don't give a shit about my feet." Cassandra tucked them up closer, away from the blowing vents. "You just want to use me to kill the other gods, like Hera did. So you can live. You'll probably find Achilles and decide to use him, too. You didn't listen when Aidan asked you to leave us alone and fight your own battles."

"They were coming for you."

"They followed *you* here!" Cassandra shouted.

"Of course it must seem that way. But they would have

found you eventually. And Ap—" Athena sighed. "And Aidan wouldn't have been able to protect you on his own."

"Don't talk about him." Fire rushed into Cassandra's chest, intense as an itch, but clouded and red, not clear like it had been with Hera that day on the road. "Don't tell me what he could and couldn't do. He could've done anything. He might've done a thousand things if you'd never come here."

"All right. I'm sorry."

"I want you to go."

Athena nodded. "I will. And I won't come here with you Tuesday if you don't want me to."

"No. Not just the cemetery. I want you gone. Out of Kincade," Cassandra said. "Hundreds of people died in the explosions in Chicago and Philadelphia, from bombs that Hera planted. Hundreds of people! Can't you go and pretend to protect other cities?"

"No."

"Why not?" Cassandra asked. "I haven't had a vision of a dying god in months. I haven't had a vision of anything since we killed Hera. Since *I* killed Hera. And I'll kill Aphrodite, too, all on my own." Cassandra's heart thumped, and the heat in her hands flickered. She heard Odysseus in her head. Big talk. Big, tough talk, but talking isn't the real thing.

"I promised my brother I would take care of you," Athena said quietly. "It's the only promise I made to him that I intend to keep."

"Shut up. He wasn't really your brother."

"He was my brother long before he was your love," Athena said, showing anger for the first time. But she couldn't sell it. She shook her head guiltily.

"I shouldn't have said that. You were the most important thing to him. But he died for you, and I'm not about to—"

"Shut up, I said," Cassandra screeched. "You want me to

do this, and you want me to do that, but you don't care what I want. You don't give me Aphrodite and you don't give me a way to find Aidan and bring him back!"

For a second, they both sat silent, struck dumb by the request.

"Is there a way?" Cassandra asked quietly. "Where do gods go? To the underworld? Somewhere else? Is there a way to go there, and bring him back? People used to. And gods could. I remember that. So is there? Is that where he is?"

Athena's eyes went glassy.

"We're not those kinds of gods, Cassandra."

"What kind?"

"The kind who know everything."

Cassandra closed her eyes. As usual, Athena was no damn use. All at once Cassandra's frustration reared up in her chest and ran hot to her hands. She had to let it go or she would burst. She reached across the seat and grabbed Athena's wrist.

Athena jerked the wheel hard. Someone screamed, and Cassandra wasn't sure if it was Athena or her as the Dodge jumped the curb and narrowly missed a signpost. She rocked forward into the dash as Athena hit the brakes.

The burning in her hands was gone. It had disappeared and left them cold and clammy. Beside her, Athena pulled up the sleeve of her coat and held her wrist up to her face. A broken red ring, cracked and enflamed, marred the skin where Cassandra had grabbed her. Small, speckled feathers protruded in a grotesque bracelet, pushing through the flesh like blossoming seeds. As they watched, a few more tore through the surface and twisted outward, tinged with blood.

"I'm sorry," Cassandra blurted. The anger that had seemed so fresh a second ago felt a million miles away. "I didn't mean to . . . I don't know why—are you—" She took a hitching breath and opened the door. "I think I'm gonna throw up."

"It's all right. It's all right. It's stopping." Athena stared at the wound as the feathers took over her wrist. A trickle of blood ran; one of the quills must've nicked a vein. It had to hurt like a bitch, too, like a thousand bee stings, but she watched it as if it were happening under glass. "There's a first aid kit in the trunk," she said, popping it, and Cassandra took wobbling steps around the back of the car and brought it back.

"I'm sorry."

"It's all right, I said." Athena rolled gauze around the wound and tore the strip to tie it with her teeth. Her movements were brutal and efficient. It was that, and the lack of feeling on her face, that made Cassandra start to cry.

"What?" Athena asked. "It's fine. I'll just pluck them out with tweezers later." She took a deep breath. "The one in my lung isn't any worse. Whatever you did, it was localized." Cassandra exhaled, relieved to have the wound covered. Seeing it even for those few moments had made her nauseous. Athena patted her back awkwardly. "It's all right."

"It's not all right. And you're an idiot." Cassandra wiped her eyes. "Odysseus made me promise not to turn you into a feather pillow. But I almost did. And I didn't mean to. I really didn't mean to."

"He said that? A feather pillow?"

"Will you shut up?" Cassandra asked. How could she make a god understand? Until just recently, they were creatures without consequences. And even now, the way Athena studied the feathers in her arm, more curious than scared, as if it were a science experiment. As if it weren't real.

"Aphrodite killed Aidan, do you understand? She *killed*

him. And Hera almost killed me." Cassandra remembered the stretch of road beside Seneca Lake. The blackness behind her eyes after her head struck the pavement. "I'm sixteen years old. And I'm two thousand. But none of that means anything to you."

Athena paused a moment. "You can kill gods with your bare hands," she said. "A prophetess who died at the end of an axe. But you're also a brown-haired girl in a red wool coat, with flushed cheeks and frozen toes. I see you, Cassandra. I see that you're young."

"But it doesn't mean anything to you."

"Yes it does." Athena hesitated. "I know what it means, to be too young to die. Whether you believe it or not. And I am sorry about all of this. I wish I didn't have to use you. But I do."

Cassandra watched her carefully.

"What did Demeter tell you, in the desert?"

"That it wouldn't really be over until I'm dead," Athena said. "So I have to survive the longest, do you understand? And then I'll go. And it will be over."

Cassandra wiped her face. Athena gripped the wheel hard with her unspoiled hand.

"You think you're going to win, don't you?" Cassandra asked.

"I think we are. Yes."

"I just want all of this to go away."

Athena sighed. "It will. After."

"I am sorry about your arm."

Athena tucked the bandage under her sleeve.

"Don't be," she said. "It's what you're supposed to do. If you can't stomach giving me a feather rash, how do you expect to kill Aphrodite?"

"That's different," Cassandra muttered.

"Maybe," Athena said thoughtfully. "But it would be better if you had more control."

"I can't control it," Cassandra snapped, angry again in an instant. It came and went, ebbed and flared, all on its own. "Every time I think of Aphrodite I want to watch her burn." She paused. "And sometimes when I see you."

"It wasn't like that on the road, with Hera."

"No. But that's what it's become." Cassandra let out a long, shaky breath, scared by her own words. Her own thoughts. One second she didn't want to be a killer, and the next, rage flooded her heart and mind, washing everything red.

"What it's become," Athena repeated softly, and to Cassandra it sounded like a warning. What it had become. And what she was becoming.

"This place is a constant facial," Hermes said, and pushed aside a vine. "The heat, the mist, the aromatics."

"I wouldn't know," said Odysseus. They were deep into the rain forest, far from worn paths and tourist excursions. He couldn't tell how far they'd traveled. Their pace had been fast and uneven. Hermes led by choosing directions seemingly at random. He'd walk for miles steadily, and then reach back and grasp Odysseus under the arm to take off at breakneck speed, so fast Odysseus had to huddle close to Hermes' neck for fear of catching a tree in the face. When he stopped, it was just as quickly as he started, and he never gave an explanation.

"I don't believe you," Hermes said, and peered at Odysseus' face. "No mortal has pores that small naturally."

Odysseus took a deep breath as he stepped over a rotting log. The smell of decaying meat and blood filled his nose in a cloud, so strong he almost puked.

"What is that?" he asked. He scanned the ground for a corpse, hoping to see half a rotted monkey, or a gutted tapir. Anything but a tanned leg and long silvery hair. Anything but Artemis.

Hermes took a whiff. "No need to panic. There's nothing dead. It's the rafflesia. Corpse flowers." He pointed to an obscenely large blossom, fat red petals speckled with white. It looked more like a fungus than a flower. He sniffed again. "It doesn't smell anything like death, really."

"Smells exactly like it to me." Odysseus walked carefully around the plant, like it might bite. It was oddly beautiful. He wouldn't have touched it for all the tea in China.

"Not to my immortal nose." Hermes sniffed the air again. Odysseus ran up against his back. He had his hand over most of his face to filter the smell.

"Can we get going?"

"Hang on. We're coming up on something else, and it won't do to startle them."

"Them?" He couldn't see or hear anything living, except for the constant chorus of insect chirps.

Hermes took off again, slightly to the right. "People. A village. There's a little bit of smoke and something cooking."

"Are you sure we should approach them? Are they safe?" Odysseus asked, and Hermes gave him a look. What group of natives could stand against the god of thieves? Odysseus shrugged. "Right."

They walked through the trees, Hermes following his nose until the village became visible through the dense growth. It was an oblong stretch of cleared land, crowded through with huts that reminded Odysseus of "The Three Little Pigs": small, rounded, and made from sticks, reeds, and woven plants. Smoke rose from several fires, and the smell of roasting meat drove the memory of the reeking corpse flower far away.

A group of children huddled in the dirt, playing some kind of game with stones. At their approach, the children raised their heads. Odysseus paused, but Hermes smiled broadly and opened his palms. The children smiled unabashedly back.

"Are you using some kind of god trick?" Odysseus asked. "To make them unafraid?"

"That'd be a pretty good trick," Hermes answered. "But no. Look at them. At their fat bellies and rounded arms. Listen to the quiet of this forest. What reason do they have to be afraid?"

"Instinct. You know. Fear of the unknown. Of the strange."

"If we had fangs and claws, they'd scream soon enough. But we don't. We walk on two. Like them." They emerged from the trees and were greeted by a grizzled black and gray dog, who thumped her tail and snuffled their pants pockets. One of the children raised an arm and said something too fast for Odysseus to make out, but Hermes said it right back.

"A greeting," he explained, as the children surrounded them.

Curious hands tugged at Odysseus' sleeves and tried to get into his rucksack. Two of the children ran for the center of the village. "Should we go? Are they—?"

"Relax, will you? Look around." Hermes gestured toward the huts and their wide open doorways. "Do you see any bones? Any trophies? Look at their clothing. As much woven from plants and bartered cloth as leather. These people hunt for sustenance. It's not like we've stumbled into an Aztec city. Believe me, I could tell you stories."

The two children were on their way back, with several equally curious adults. A woman with long black hair and rosy cheeks came up close and pushed a green, rounded fruit into Odysseus' palm.

"Smile. Show your appreciation. If we play our cards right we can get a cooked meal and a cozy straw bed."

Odysseus did as he was told; the woman blushed and grinned behind her hand. It was a sweet and bashful gesture, and his stomach started to relax.

Beside him, Hermes nodded at the people and spoke in their language.

"You speak this? What'd you say?"

"Always ask for the oldest woman. If she likes you, you're golden."

They were herded through the village, past curious faces sitting in huts or beside fires.

The oldest woman in the village had to be the oldest by about fifty years. She wore a shift beaded with blue and yellow, and her hair flowed around her rickety shoulders in a peppered curtain. But the hand that held her machete had an iron grip.

Hermes said the greeting and waited. The old woman was slower to smile than the others, and when she spoke her voice was cautious.

"We can rest here," Hermes said when she was through. "And eat. They're roasting a monkey."

"I don't know about that," Odysseus said. He looked up into the canopy, at the slanting light. "But the resting part sounds fantastic."

They ate communally, sharing between fires. And even though he doubted Cassandra would approve, Odysseus ate plenty of the monkey. The villagers glazed the meat with some kind of fruit juice, and it tasted a little like rich pork. Beside him, Hermes tried to show restraint, but the village children kept bringing him bits of roasted yam and nuts, amazed at how much he could put away.

"How do you know this language?" Odysseus asked. He dragged a woven straw mat beneath the shelter of a lean-to, a short distance from the main fire.

"I don't know all of it. Their dialect is a little different. But I've been to this part of the world before. And I'm good with languages." Hermes crunched through some kind of root, sitting on his own mat. "She said she dreamed of me." He gestured toward the old woman, who sat watching and not watching them from across the flames. "She said she dreamed of me long ago, and today, and tomorrow."

"What does that mean?"

Hermes shrugged. "I don't know. She's the tribe's shaman. Maybe nothing. But it was nice. And she said something else."

"What?"

"She said she heard the ravening beasts. Not long ago. That way." He pointed across the village, to the east.

"The ravening beasts? You mean—?"

Hermes nodded. "Artemis. We're close."

7

RUNNING RED

The carpeted stairs that curled around from the library were just far enough from the clanging of plastic trays in the cafeteria to feel private and separate, though it was anything but. Voices echoed down the hall like it was a megaphone, unless you were the ones tucked farthest back into the stairs. That honor went to Andie and Sam, who sat sharing a pair of earbuds.

"Cassandra, you want some of my chips?" Megan asked, holding out a plastic baggie. "Dill pickle."

"Sure."

Megan plopped down beside her and stretched her striped stocking–clad legs. Underneath a few shades of blue eye shadow and thick black liner, her eyes were tired.

"You look rough," Cassandra said, and crunched a chip.

"I got zero sleep last night." Megan jerked her head up toward a boy in a too-tight Abercrombie t-shirt. "Jeremy kept me on the phone until three."

"Talking about what?"

Megan rolled her eyes. "Isabelle, as usual."

"You're half-dead because you lost sleep listening to him moan about his ex-girlfriend? There's a lesson in there somewhere."

"What? That I should stop letting him bounce around on me when Isabelle isn't feeling generous?" Megan blew her bangs out of her face. "I know. But it's hard, when he needs someone to talk to. When she's being a bitch."

"It's still a crappy deal, Megan."

"I guess," she said, and stared into her chip bag. "You were really lucky, you know? To have Aidan. A real, decent guy. Even if it *was* only for a little while." She stopped and looked at Cassandra, horrified. "I'm so sorry. I don't know why I said that."

"No," said Cassandra. "You're right. It's true. I was really lucky. For a little while." He should've been there next to her on the stairs. She tried to imagine him there, and it was just that close. Like if she closed her eyes and fell asleep, she might wake against his shoulder.

"I shouldn't have said anything. I made you sad."

"No. It's okay. I—" She paused. Blood soaked Megan's shoulders and dripped down her knees. Finger tracks of red smeared and streaked across her face. Cassandra held her breath as buckets covered them both, hot and heavy as a cloak. The carpet squished beneath her shoes.

"I think I need to get some air. Andie?" She kept her voice calm and stood. It wasn't even hard. Blood and terror had become like milk and cookies. Even through the coppery taste. Even through the smell.

"What's up?" Andie asked, and Cassandra glanced back at Megan's bloody face.

Only it wasn't Megan's. It was Odysseus'. And it was Hermes'.

"We've got to skip class," Cassandra said.

"No arguments here," Andie said. "But why?"

Cassandra wiped at her lips. The blood was gone, but the flavor coated her mouth as if she'd swallowed a gallon.

"Hey, are you okay? Should we get Henry?"

"No. Yes. I don't know." Hermes and Odysseus were in trouble. But the distance between Kincade and Malaysia was an impossible jump. How would they get there? How would they find them? She slammed a fist into the lockers. Stupid, useless visions.

"Cassandra, what's going on?"

"Odysseus and Hermes," she muttered.

"What? What about them?"

She took a breath, spat blood onto the floor, and saw only saliva.

"I think they're dead."

Athena knew something was wrong the moment she heard the growl of Henry's engine and the squeal of his tires. But Cassandra, Andie, and Henry were all safe when they pushed past her into the entryway: no blood, no scrapes, no broken bones. Good.

She closed the door against the wind and it ruffled their coats like soft sails.

"What happened?"

The three looked at each other. Pale, frightened mortals. For the hundredth time she thought what strange soldiers they made.

"I saw Odysseus and Hermes covered in blood," Cassandra said.

Athena went still. "How much blood?"

"Buckets. Like they'd been dipped in it."

"Buckets of blood." Athena wandered past them, into the living room. "What could that mean?"

Cassandra and Andie exchanged a look. "I think it means they're dead," said Cassandra after a moment.

"No. That can't be what it means." The Fates couldn't expect her to win a war without her brother and her hero.

"It might not have been their blood," Andie suggested. "Maybe they were in a fight. Or hunting."

"Hunting what?" Henry asked.

"Athena," said Cassandra. "Maybe you should sit down."

"Why would I need to—?" Athena shook her head. "I don't need to sit. I need to figure out what it means. And I think better when I pace." But she stopped, as a small compromise. Odysseus and Hermes were in danger. But not true danger. The Fates wouldn't let them die. Not now. Not yet.

What if I'm wrong?

She closed her eyes. She wasn't wrong. But what, then, did the vision mean? Why had her prophetess seen what she'd seen?

"I told you what it means," Cassandra said. And a minute later, "Hey! Are you listening?"

"Cassandra." Andie grabbed her arm.

"She's not even upset. Why? Did you send them out there as bait? Did you know this was going to happen?"

"You and your conspiracy theories," Athena muttered. "I wasn't the one who sent them. They wanted to go." And now she had to go after them. Why else would the Moirae have sent Cassandra that vision? She slid past Andie and Henry and flew upstairs to her bedroom. She'd pack fast, fast as Hermes, and light. "They'll be fine," she whispered to no one. "You'll be fine, both of you. Just hold on. I'm coming."

She ransacked drawers, paying no mind to what she threw into her bag. It hardly seemed to matter. She wouldn't take a bag at all if not for TSA snoops getting suspicious at the airport. Questions flicked through her mind as she zipped up: how long did she have? Were they injured? Had their mission cost them a soldier? Had they lost Artemis?

You'll be all right. My brother and my Odysseus. You have to be.

She snatched up the bag and flew downstairs.

"Go home. Pack a bag," she said as she passed them en route to the kitchen. Cans of food and cereal bars went in on top of her clothes.

"What?" Henry asked. "You can't take her with you. You said there were things in that rain forest."

"Nothing I can't protect her from."

"This is ridiculous. She's not going. Cassie. You're not going."

"Well, I'm going," Athena said. She closed the fastenings on her bag. "And I'm not leaving her here unguarded, to be snapped up or killed by who knows what god. Besides—" She looked at Cassandra's hands. "She might come in handy."

"Cassandra," Henry said, and took her arm.

"I'll be okay, Henry," said Cassandra. She turned to Athena. "I have a bag packed in Henry's trunk. We all do. Just in case."

"Your passport in there?"

"Yeah."

"Clever girl. Let's go." She ushered Cassandra out the door and waited as she ran to Henry's Mustang for her bag. He squawked the whole time, trying to get Cassandra to stay. He was going to be a tough nut to crack. But when the time came, he would fight. He would, because Hector had. Reason carried him pretty far, but if someone pushed, he pushed back. For now though, the big brother/mother hen routine was getting on Athena's last nerve. She stuffed Cassandra quickly into the cold Dodge before Henry could really work up a guilt trip.

"What am I supposed to tell Mom and Dad?" he shouted.

"Lie," Athena shouted back. "You ought to be getting pretty good at it by now."

"I'm sick of the jungle. And I could really use another serving of monkey." Odysseus kicked through an enormous leaf and was rewarded with a long streak of wet across his shin.

"Don't tell Cassandra that," Hermes said. "She'll never speak to you again."

They'd walked all day since leaving the peace of the village at dawn. Now the sun dipped low, and Odysseus had passed tired about three days and a dozen or so miles ago.

"She heard the ravening beasts," he said loudly, referring to the tribal elder. He raised his brows. "But maybe they weren't *our* ravening beasts. There's got to be more than one beast that ravens in a jungle this size, eh?"

"She knew what she was talking about."

"Did she? But your ears are ten thousand times the ears that she's got, and you didn't hear anything." He ducked a vine that Hermes intentionally flapped back into his face.

"Maybe I would if you'd stop yammering. Besides, she didn't hear them with her ears." Hermes slowed and took a breath. "I'm sorry. I keep trying to remember you're only human, but we're so close. And I don't know how I know that, before you ask.

"You're not the only one who's tired. Or sick of all this wet." He looked back. "I want to go home, too."

[97]

"Home," Odysseus said. "Is that what Kincade is now? Home?"

Hermes smiled. "I guess it is. I didn't think I'd ever have one of those again. And certainly not Kincade, New York, a piddly town with no decent shopping mall and not a single museum to speak of."

"But it's where we all are," said Odysseus.

"Yes. Where we all are." Hermes turned back in the direction they'd been heading all day. "But we can't leave until we find my other sister. So get a move on. I miss my pot stickers."

8

STRANGER FORESTS

Lux ran back and forth between Henry's and Cassandra's rooms, searching for someone to play ball with. In the end he wound up playing by himself, letting the ball drop and bounce and chasing it down with stomping paws. The sound of dog toenails skittering across the bathroom tile was so loud it broke through the music in Henry's headphones.

He leaned back from his desk and called the dog. Lux was restless. So was he. Cassandra had been gone for three days already, and the house felt empty. Especially since no one else knew she was gone. He'd told their parents she was at Athena's, keeping her company until Hermes got back from having treatments in Arizona. They kept asking how Athena was, and how she was doing. Their mom talked about the whole thing like a girly sleepover.

Lux put his head on Henry's leg and chewed his soggy tennis ball, hoping to have it thrown. It was so much better when people did it.

"This is nasty," Henry said. "Where's your tug rope?"

Lux whined and rolled the ball into Henry's lap. Despite the plea in the dog's brown eyes, he had no time to play. A half-finished history paper glowed on his laptop, due fourth period. His phone buzzed on the desk, and Lux snatched his ball back and whined.

It was Andie.

"Hey," he said. "What's up?"

"Nothing, I guess, from the tone of your voice."

"Yeah. I haven't heard anything. I didn't really expect to."

"Me neither." The line went quiet for a few seconds. "Maybe we shouldn't have let her go. So far, and so cut off from everything."

"Like we had a choice? *She* dragged Cassandra out of here. And *she* said she'd take care of everything."

"*She* has a name," Andie said. "And that doesn't really make me feel better. I can't focus on anything. I can't sit still." She paused again. "Do you . . . want to hang out or something?"

Henry looked at his unfinished paper and closed the laptop.

"Sure."

"Good. Because I'm just pulling into your driveway."

Henry leaned over his desk and looked out the window. Andie's silver Saturn flashed in the sunlight.

"Park behind the Mustang," he said. "My parents took the Jeep to the movies."

Andie chuckled. "Aww, that's cute. Was it a drive-in? Think they'll go parking after and make out in the back-seat?"

"Why don't you just turn around and go home," Henry said.

Andie scoffed and hung up on him. Lux could barely

contain himself, watching her approach through the window. When the front door opened he almost knocked Henry off his chair in his haste to get to the entryway.

"Lux, calm down," Andie said, then shouted, "Your dog's trying to kill me!" Moments later, she slung herself into his doorway, cheeks flushed from the cold and from wrestling her way up the stairs. "Whatcha doing?"

"Homework." Henry jerked his head toward his shut laptop.

"Oh. It's a good thing I called, then."

Henry snorted.

"So, what do you want to do?" he asked. "We could watch a movie."

Andie's eyes glittered. "Gave you ideas about making out, did I?"

"Shut up." He swiveled in his chair and unplugged his computer.

"I don't think I could sit through a movie. All week I've felt like I should be doing something. Can't we do something that'll help me work off this jittery energy?"

Since they'd learned of their shared, married past, Andie never missed a chance to be a smartass about it. Asking if he knew how she could work off jittery energy was the perfect opportunity to get her back. Or get her on her back. Henry closed his eyes and rubbed them hard. She was his kid sister's best friend, and she was annoying. What was wrong with him?

"What'd you have in mind?" he asked.

Andie searched the room for an answer, settling on the dog. "It's not bad out. We could go for a walk. Throw the ball for Lux a little. Back through the woods?"

———

They were here. They are here. Somewhere. I can feel them.

Athena paused in the jungle. She felt them, but what was she feeling? Not their heartbeats. She couldn't hear their footsteps or sense the weight of their thoughts. Hermes' presence registered as a dull flicker in her chest, barely strong enough to home in on. They were still too far away.

Or they were dead, and what she felt was the ebb of a bloody ramshackle of bones and not much flesh.

"No," she whispered. "That's not possible."

"What?" Cassandra asked from behind her.

"Nothing." Rain slipped into Athena's eyes and she wiped at them. Salt from her forearm stung her. Her whole body was dirty, sweaty, and coated with plant slime from tearing through leaves and vines. The dry season of a rain forest was still wet. They'd been under a light drizzle since morning, and Cassandra shivered despite the warm temperature. They needed to find a sheltered place and make a fire.

"What are you doing?" Cassandra asked. "Why are you stopping?"

They'd been moving at a steady jog, occasionally at a sprint when Athena thought she heard or felt something, or when Hermes' light shone brighter in her chest. She'd kept Cassandra plastered to her side or on her back piggyback style, but now she set her down.

"We've been moving too long," she said. "You need to sleep. And get dry."

"I didn't come to slow you down. I'm fine. Let's keep going."

Athena paid no attention. "There." She pointed toward three close-growing trees. "I can pull those leaves together like a canopy. It won't be much, but it's the best we've got."

"We can't afford this," Cassandra muttered, but Athena was already at the trees, drawing the leaves down and lashing their stems with strips of torn-away vine. When she was finished, it amounted to an impressive leaf lean-to, but the ground was soggy beneath her shoes. Everything in sight was slick with rain. Building a fire was a pipe dream. A change into dry clothes and a canned meal would have to do.

"We should keep going," Cassandra said, standing stubbornly in the rain. "I'm not tired, and I'm not hungry."

Athena walked back out into the wet. Cassandra was more than tired. She was exhausted. Dark circles loomed beneath her eyes, and the draw of her breath was heavy. If she sat for a minute and got something into her stomach, she'd pass out and sleep for weeks. Athena snatched her rucksack and returned to the makeshift shelter, where she pulled out a can of ham and a small loaf of bread they'd bought at a market on the way to Kuala Tembeling. She cut slices of each with her pocketknife and fashioned two crude sandwiches.

"Listen, I might need you. What good will you be to Hermes and Odysseus if you're dead on your feet? Come under here and rest. Eat."

Cassandra wiped water and sweat from her forehead and looked around at the trees like she might go on by herself. But then she ducked under the lean-to and took a sandwich.

"Stop scowling at me so hard," said Athena. "You'll forget to chew and choke to death. Here. Spread this out to sit on." She handed over a bundle of shirts.

"But that's most of your clothes."

"I don't need them. I can stay wet. But you should change."

"Fine." Cassandra held out her sandwich. "Hold this. And turn around."

Athena turned and ate her own ham while the girl dug in her bag.

"Okay."

Athena handed the sandwich back. In a fresh pair of khaki shorts and a long-sleeved t-shirt, Cassandra looked better already. She'd almost stopped shivering.

"Do you think we'll find them?" Cassandra asked.

"Yes." Athena stuffed down the last of her sandwich. Cassandra's was already gone, and she had three fingers in the can of ham, breaking off chunks and stuffing them in her mouth. So much for not being hungry.

"You seem pretty sure," Cassandra said. "You don't seem that scared."

"It doesn't do anyone any good to panic."

Cassandra's mouth twisted. "Just so you know, your brother dying is more than enough reason to panic. One might say it's almost mandatory."

"Then one would be an idiot," Athena snapped. "The line between fear and fucking up is very thin, and I can't afford to cross it. There's too much at stake." Too many things depended on her having everything in hand. The thought that Hermes and Odysseus were already hurt sat on her chest like a cold stone, but it couldn't be her only thought.

"We shouldn't lose too much time," Cassandra said.

Athena nodded. "I won't let you sleep long. I don't want to lose them, either. But I can't lose you."

"Right. I'm the ace in the hole."

Athena's eyes narrowed. "That's right, sweetheart." And then, softer, "Besides. Somewhere in the after, the god of the sun would never forgive me."

"Whatever." Cassandra twisted around like a cranky cat, trying to get comfortable on the hard, damp surface.

"Do you ever dream of him?" Athena asked.

"No," said Cassandra. "I wish I did. But I don't. He's just gone."

Athena looked out into the drizzle. It took less than a minute for Cassandra to pass out cold.

The smell of rotting meat hit Odysseus square in the face, strong enough to stop him in his tracks.

"Where is it?" He waved his hand in front of his nose.

"Where's what?" Hermes whispered.

"The bloody corpse flower. This one's worse than the last. It must be a bunch of them. A bouquet of the buggers."

"No. There are no flowers."

Hermes' flat voice made Odysseus forget the stench. For the last few minutes, their walk had been silent. He'd thought that Hermes had just gotten tired of talking. God knew they'd had plenty of dead air between them on their trek. But it hadn't been that. Hermes had smelled it hundreds of yards ago. The scent of death. Real death.

"It might be a rotting animal. A big snake maybe."

"Maybe," Hermes said in his toneless voice. "Maybe." Hermes' legs moved on autopilot, propelling him mindlessly toward the source of the smell, because he'd come this far, and because he'd said he would do it. He had to see her for himself.

"Hey, mate. Maybe you shouldn't."

But it was too late. The trees opened up on a clearing painted red.

"Oh, god." Odysseus tried to catch Hermes before he went to his knees but didn't make it in time.

The space where Artemis had lost the chase was a glory of blood. Bits of her littered the clearing like the discarded pieces of a doll. Streaks of red shone on leaves and across the trunks of trees. There was so much of it, like she'd been filled to the brim, like buckets had been dashed across the ground. And it was still wet. Still fresh, as if they'd been only seconds too late to stop whatever had chased her from tearing her apart. But that was a lie. They could come back a week from now and find it the same. The blood would stay. Rain wouldn't cleanse it. Animals wouldn't consume it. Perhaps time would, if enough time still existed.

Odysseus surveyed the scene, mostly frozen. It wasn't until his eyes set on a bloody pile of brown cloth that he gagged. It was part of Artemis' shoulder and neck. Strands of silver-brown hair lay nearby, as if someone had torn them out of a brush.

"Hermes," he said. "Don't look."

Hermes' shoulders shook, and Odysseus put a hand down to steady him.

"I have to look!" he screeched, and jerked away. "Don't you understand? Someone has to *see*." His weeping was loud and unashamed, breath ripping through him like a storm through sailcloth. Raw enough to make Odysseus wince.

"They're dead!"

"I know."

"Do you?" Hermes spat. "Do you know? Because no one else does. No one knew who they were, or what they'd done. The sun and the moon *went out* and no one fucking noticed!"

Odysseus put an arm around his friend. Hermes wept for Artemis and Apollo. But he also wept for himself. These were Hermes' fears. The fear of dying alone. The fear of ceasing to exist.

"We noticed," Odysseus said quietly. "We'll notice."

"It's not enough. How do you stand it?"

"I don't know."

Hermes gestured numbly to the blood surrounding them. "I haven't seen her in a thousand years."

"A thousand? That's a long time. Even by an immortal's standards."

Hermes scoffed sadly. "You talk like you haven't been stumbling around in a jungle for days on end. She wasn't exactly easy to find. She never was." He sobbed. "But I loved her."

As the silence stretched out, Odysseus began to feel like an interloper, an unwelcome witness to this strange thing that no other human in the world might see. The blood splashed across the fallen leaves and rotting vegetation was a god's blood. Artemis had been reduced to waste, when she'd been so strong, and young, and free.

"We should get back to Athena," he said, so suddenly that Hermes flinched. "She'll want to know."

"What am I supposed to tell her?"

A voice came from behind them. "Tell her anything you want."

Odysseus looked up. For an instant it was like hallucinating; seeing another person in the middle of the jungle made so little sense that it jarred his brain. Then a hand clamped around his throat and jerked him up to stare into a face he barely remembered. He'd only glimpsed it for brief moments, on a battlefield thousands of years ago.

Hermes shuffled backward. His feet slid in Artemis' blood, the knees of his jeans soaked red from kneeling in it.

"Ares. Let him go."

But Ares had no intention of doing that. The grip on Odysseus' throat tightened and the world began to fade.

Lux ate snowballs, snapping each one out of the air and chomping down on it as it was lobbed at him.

"He's so funny," Andie said.

Henry threw another snowball. It fell just short of Lux's reach, so he chased it into the rest of the snow, digging with his snout like he could pick it out of the rest. Some secret smell distracted him, and he snuffled around in a broad circle. Then he lifted his head and sneezed.

With Athena out of town, the winter trees stood quiet, their bare branches mercifully free of owls. Henry had come to hate the owls over the past months. Their yellow dish-plate eyes. Their swiveling necks. It felt as if Athena could see out of every skull, and he didn't believe Odysseus when he said she couldn't.

He took a deep breath and let it out in a wandering cloud, listening to the whisper of snow over their boots and Lux's familiar whine. It was too good a day. Something was bound to screw it up. What would it be? News of his sister dying halfway across the globe? Or something more mundane, like frostbite. Maybe just a disturbing urge to kiss his sister's best friend.

Andie chased Lux through the snow, hair flying around her face like a flash of black feathers. She was all grown up. And she was beautiful, in a rough, extremely annoying way.

"How do you think Cassandra's been doing?" she asked. "About Aidan, I mean."

Henry shrugged. "I don't know. Same as before. She doesn't talk about it much."

"Have you tried?"

"Have you?"

Andie frowned. "Not really. I'm not that kind of friend, you know? I don't know what to say. She seems like she's working it out. But I half think she's faking."

"Yeah, well. Haven't you ever heard of 'fake it 'til you make it'?"

"As your former wife, I bet I'm very familiar with that."

"What are you? Twelve?" Henry packed a snowball and chucked it at her. She threw one back, twice as hard.

"Have you been to the cemetery lately?" she asked.

"Not since the funeral. Have you?"

"I was thinking of going. I mean, I really miss him. Everybody's supposed to be so careful about Cassandra and her feelings, but he was our friend, too." She looked at him. "You probably think we didn't know him at all."

"I don't think that."

Andie wiped at her eyes.

"Are you crying?"

"No," she said, but she clearly was. "It's just that I do miss him. And I don't know about you, but *I* really wish he was here." She sniffed. "I really wish he was here." Lux slipped up and licked her face.

"Maybe we could go together," Henry heard himself say. "To the cemetery."

"Yeah?"

He nodded, and she set Lux back on four paws.

"Tell anybody I cried, and you're dead."

"Please. Who would believe me?"

Andie laughed. "Henry. Sometimes I can really see why I married you."

"Not to ruin your romantic notions," he said, "but our marriage was probably arranged."

She wiped her face again. "I bet you're right. Huh. Guess that takes a lot of pressure off of us, then, doesn't it?"

"Guess so." But people fell in love in arranged marriages all the time. And Henry was more and more certain that it had happened to Hector. "Come on. Let's go back. My fingers are cold, and I've got a paper to finish."

When she tackled him from behind, he went down easily.

Her training with Athena was paying off. He spit snow and rolled backward, and she laughed as Lux tried to help and grabbed her by the coat.

In the midst of shuffling bodies and barking, they didn't notice four sets of paws make their way closer. They didn't hear the strange growls until Lux broke away with a yip, his tail tucked low between his legs. But by then the wolves had made their way around to all sides.

They were already surrounded.

9

THE DOGS OF WAR

Ares held Odysseus a foot off the ground. He slapped his cheek, one and then the other, trying to get him to come around.

"Did you squeeze too hard, you big oaf?" Hermes hissed. "Did you kill him?"

"He's breathing. Don't you hear that desperate whistle of air pulled over his lips?"

So smug. But Ares hadn't meant to choke Odysseus unconscious. Why bother? If Ares wanted him dead, one twist of his wrist would take his head clean off. Blood would splash across Ares' fist. And Ares loved blood above all things.

"What are you doing?" Hermes asked.

"I'm looking for something."

"That's how you look for something?" Hermes watched the muscle in his dark brother's arm. He had to be careful. If Ares lost his temper, Odysseus' poor, mortal neck would pay the price. "What do you want?" Hermes asked. "Why don't you ask me?"

"Because you don't know," Ares said lazily. He kept on slapping until Odysseus jerked awake. "There he is. Good morning, sunshine. Do you know who I am?"

"Ares," Odysseus croaked.

"Good. Feel this?" Ares dug his fingers into the back of Odysseus' skull, and he kicked like a snared rabbit.

"You don't want to do that," Hermes said. "Big sister won't like it."

"She's not *my* big sister, little brother. I don't care what she likes and doesn't like." He slapped Odysseus again. Despite everything, Odysseus' jaw clenched with anger. No fear.

"Listen close, boy of many ways. I'm only going to ask once. You know what I'm after, don't you?" Ares shook him lightly, and Odysseus grabbed onto the hand around his throat.

"Yes."

"Good. Then where is he?"

He. Achilles. Ares had taken up his fallen mother's cause.

"Just tell him," Hermes said quickly. "Tell him and be done with it. Let Athena deal with the fallout."

Odysseus sucked air down deep. "No. I won't tell him, or her either."

"Isn't that too bad. Hera says you're the only one who knows where to find him."

"Hera?" Hermes asked. "What are you talking about? Hera's dead."

Ares smiled, lazily, in a way that made the skin scrunch up between Hermes' shoulder blades.

Ares shrugged. "Whatever you say, brother. And anyway, I don't believe her." Ares' fingers tightened. "There's always more than one way to skin . . . well, anything." A few notches tighter, and they'd hear the sound of bones breaking.

Hermes' pulse quickened. If he could get to Ares' fingers fast enough, he could make him drop Odysseus.

But how fast could he get there? He wasn't as quick as he used to be. And he couldn't afford any telltale gauging of muscles. No flexing or tensing. If he was too slow, or if he missed, Odysseus wouldn't survive the impact. He had one chance.

Hermes sprang like a twitch. Like a beam of light. His fingers twisted around Ares' fist, and Odysseus fell to the ground. Hermes heaved hard and pushed the other god back so fast he would have laughed with joy had Ares' elbow not connected with his face and sent the side of his skull cracking off the trunk of a tree.

Hermes pushed his arms out blindly, trying to get a solid hold and keep Ares at bay. But the god of war was strong. Hermes tasted blood and wondered whose it was. Had he bitten his lip? His eyes cleared just in time to see Ares' bared teeth inches from his face.

"I used to clothe my throne in the skins of men," said Ares. "But times have changed. Perhaps the skin of gods will prove more durable."

"Times have changed," replied Hermes. "Nothing about gods is 'durable' anymore." The blood on his lips did belong to Ares, forced into his mouth from a seeping cut on the god's forearm. It was gross. He'd rather have bitten his lip. "Is that what's happening to you?" Hermes asked. "The god of blood will die slathered in it. Seems fitting." He braced himself and shoved. "Ha," he said. "Still strong enough to send the god of war skidding backward."

Backward, through Artemis' remains. Did Ares even know what it was, all that red beneath his feet?

Hermes didn't have much time to wonder. Ares crashed back into him, his weight like lead. All the air left Hermes' lungs in a rush. Spots and stars flooded his eyes as his spine ground against a tree, and the roots began to give way.

"Odysseus! Run!" he groaned, but he didn't even know if Odysseus was conscious. But he'd have to get up. Hermes couldn't keep this up for long. Grappling with Ares, he could almost feel the point when his arms would break.

Then, as if he'd wished her into existence, Athena slammed into Ares with full force. The impact tore him off of Hermes and sent him sprawling, tumbling like a pile of expensive clothes. Athena's hands were on Hermes' shoulders, keeping him on his feet.

"Stay up," she said, and he did. Her voice brought his senses back from whatever scared corner they'd run to. It was even and strong, and more than a little angry.

"As you wish, big sister."

Odysseus lay in a heap beside the broad trunk of a tree. Cassandra ran through the clearing, splashing through what had to be the last of Artemis, and knelt beside him.

"Is he all right?" Athena asked, her eyes on Ares, who had rolled to a sitting position and stayed there, looking amused and not at all in a hurry to flee.

"He's awake. His throat is black with bruises," Cassandra said. She whispered to Odysseus, and he nodded. "He's breathing. He's okay."

Ares got to his feet and made a show of brushing himself

off, but he'd rolled twenty feet in blood. It soaked into his clothing and streaked across his bare forearms and cheeks. It was terrible to see him so, covered in his sister's death. Yet it was right. Ares wore blood like armor. In it, he looked like himself.

"Is that her?" he asked.

"Never mind her," Athena replied.

"But it is her, isn't it? The prophetess. The girl who kills gods."

Cassandra pulled Odysseus into her lap. She glared but said nothing.

"It is," Athena said. "Is that why you've come? Want her to put you out of your misery?"

Ares laughed. But he didn't charge in like he had with Hermes. Athena was a different game altogether. No one really knew which of them was stronger.

"Hera said you were infested with owl feathers," Ares said. "Seems like she exaggerated. I can't see a single one."

"When did she tell you that?"

Athena flexed her fist, annoyed at the small bandage wrapped around her wrist. The only visible blemish. The rest of her was long mahogany hair and smooth skin. Healthy, and without weakness. She hoped it irritated the shit out of him.

"And what about you?" she asked. "What death waits for the god of war?"

"Who says I'm dying?"

"You're dying," Athena said. "I'm not blind. Not all of that blood belonged to Artemis." She gestured to a long, shallow cut running along his elbow. "Unless Hermes did that to you."

"Hermes? Not on his best day. And this is nowhere near his best day."

"Screw off," Hermes muttered.

"Brave now, aren't we?" Ares said. "Brave, once Athena is here to hide behind." He made a fist and squeezed a few drops of blood back onto the forest floor. "So this is Artemis?" He looked at his gore-streaked hand. "I don't know whether to feel dirty or comforted. Like she's a blanket."

"She's dead, you asshole." Athena kept still, uncomfortably aware of her sister's blood, and worse than blood, beneath her shoes in a grotesque carpet. The sight of it, and the smell, made her stomach tighten. She should've known. She never should have let Hermes and Odysseus come. But they were there. A vision had led them there, straight to her handsome, grinning brother. Ares, just like she remembered him. His face full of blood.

"She's dead," Ares mused. "And I'm dead. And you're dead. Spitting out feathers like a cat in a canary cage." He snorted. "That's funny. Can you do it now? I'd like to see."

"It is funny, I suppose." Athena kept her breath shallow. She didn't need him to know how spot on he really was. The feather that had wormed its way into her lung was starting to tear loose. It was a maddening tickle every time she breathed, a gristle-coated fan, waving back and forth. "As funny as the god of war bleeding to death without taking a single blow. As funny as your bitch mother turned into a statue."

The insult didn't touch Ares. Maybe he didn't care. He wiped a little more of Artemis onto his pants. Something was wrong. In the corner of Athena's eye, Hermes tensed like he was trying to tell her something, and a familiar feeling ran through her frame. The same feeling she'd had when Hera had tracked them so effortlessly that fall. But Hera was dead. Cassandra had killed her.

Odysseus coughed, a raw sound, and got to his feet. Ares had a lot of balls, coming after him.

"What the hell is going on?" she asked. "What are you doing here?"

"These days, sister, I do what I'm told. And I was sent"—he pointed at Odysseus—"for him."

Only not really for Odysseus. For what he could lead them to—Achilles. The other weapon. What was it about Achilles that made him so special? If Cassandra was the girl who killed gods, what could he do?

"Who sent you?" Athena asked.

Ares walked to the right, nonchalant and closer. Athena moved, too, staying in his path, and in her shadow Hermes did the same. It was a lovely little conversation they were having, but of the three of them, only Ares allowed himself to blink.

"You wouldn't believe me if I told you," he said.

"Try me."

He sighed and looked up at the sky. After a few long moments, he said, "My mother sent me."

"That's impossible," said Athena. "Try again. Hera's dead."

"It's true." Cassandra spoke suddenly. "I killed her."

"Yes, but unfortunately for you, it didn't stick."

"I turned her into a freaking rock," said Cassandra. "Half of her face was granite."

Athena looked from Cassandra to Ares. She'd seen Hera's face half-fused to stone. Hera had lost the ability to work her jaw. Most of her chest and shoulder had solidified. Her cheek, even her hair on the right side, was statue. It should have killed her.

"You're lying. I was there, Ares. She couldn't speak. She's dead."

"You should have stayed longer and made sure the job was done," he said. "She can speak now. Mostly about your foolishness. She's being healed. You never used to be this sloppy, sister."

"It's not possible for her to be alive," Hermes said.

"Don't talk about possible and impossible. You have no idea. You're on the wrong side, little brother."

"What side is that? The side that hasn't gone insane?" Hermes asked. "The side that doesn't want to blow up buildings with innocent witches in them?"

"Innocent witches. And innocent mortals," Athena said. What Ares said couldn't be. Hera couldn't be healing. Yet Ares wasn't lying.

"You've always been so fond of saving mortals," Ares said. He looked at Cassandra and Odysseus, standing near a thick trunk. "You curried their favor and accepted their accolades. Had cities named for you. You had their love, and I had their fear.

"Hera says it's you or us. I don't know if that's true. I don't get bogged down in the politics. All I know is that you'll try to save these people, and I will try to kill them."

The words came so easy. Life to him was a shrug of the shoulders, even when his was ending.

"Why, Ares? Do you even know?"

"I know better than you do. What we are. Why we're here. We are two sides of a coin. You save and I kill, but blood runs because of us both. We are the dogs of war, Athena, and we always have been."

"No," Odysseus said, his voice ragged. "Don't put yourself in the same sentence with her. War isn't battle. It's not the same."

Ares smiled smugly. War, battle. Semantics.

"Hermes," Athena said. "Are you well? Can you take them to a safe distance?"

"What are you doing?" Hermes asked. His eyes shifted from Cassandra and Odysseus to Ares and back again.

"Take them and stay with them. Don't leave them alone." She clenched her fists. "The gods of war are about to bleed."

Wild dogs, was the first thought in Henry's head. Then *wolves*. Then something exponentially worse. One was white, but not like snow. It was white like bone, with a long, thin snout and lips a size too small, stretched back and dried out past its purple gums. Another was red, and it moved faster than the others. The sound of its fangs snapping was like something trapped in a box. Then a slow gray one came, hunched and panting. Blood dripped from its mouth and ran down its chest, into the sores matting its fur. But the worst one was the last, so black it didn't appear to have eyes.

"Henry," Andie whispered. They huddled back to back, with Lux between them. "What are they?"

Dogs, he almost said, but couldn't quite manage it. They weren't dogs any more than they were ponies. What they were was something that Henry couldn't quite see, as if what he was looking at were just skins taken from some other animal. A sheepskin tossed over a wolf's back. But what could be so horrible that it would use a wolf's skin to hide under?

Between them, Lux whined and leaned into Henry's leg. Whatever they were, they were closing in fast. Henry looked each one in the eye, except for the black one whose eyes he couldn't find. He couldn't remember if that was the right thing, making eye contact, or if he should've been appearing submissive. Somehow he didn't think it was going to matter.

The creatures around them stopped. They rose up on two legs, and their forelegs stretched until they hung like arms. Their torsos shifted until they were upright, and Henry could barely imagine them on all fours.

"What are you?" Andie asked angrily.

Pain.

Said the gray with the matted fur. It hadn't spoken with its mouth. Its tongue hung out, mute, bleeding drops onto its chest.

Panic.

Said the one with red fur and fierce yellow eyes.

Famine.

That was the white. Flecks of something dropped from its dingy fur: dry skin or parasites.

Oblivion.

The black wolf. Its voice was deeper than the others, and more terrible. Hearing it, and looking into the utter blackness where its eyes should have been, made Henry sick to his stomach.

Pain, Panic, Famine, and Oblivion. The names felt familiar. But Henry couldn't think. He couldn't do anything besides stare, and breathe, and move closer to Andie.

"What do you want?"

Is this the boy? asked the wolf called Pain. *The boy he said to kill? Who they said must be killed?*

This can't be the boy. Famine sniffed and snapped its jaws. *He smells like ordinary meat to me.*

Oblivion snarled, and the other three whined and stepped sideways.

He smells like blood. And a job to be done. As does the girl. As does the pup.

Andie, Henry thought feebly.

The wolves attacked together. Pain collided with him with the force of a small truck, Henry's nose stuck deep into sick-smelling fur. Claws tore into his coat, down to the skin and straight through. Henry shouted and twisted his head away, and saw the red wolf sprawled in the snow like it had tripped. It snarled and kicked, and he refused to blink, terrified that the snow would turn red, that he'd see black hair and hear Andie screaming. Blood dripped onto his face from Pain's tongue, and he pushed back hard, on instinct, so the teeth missed his throat and sliced through his cheek instead.

The gray wolf was heavy and incredibly strong. Cold snow worked into Henry's coat, and claws dug deep into his shoulders.

Lux growled loud, and in the corner of his eye Henry saw the brave dog up on two legs, biting the neck of the thin, white wolf. He bit and held, until Oblivion came at him in a flash of black. Then he yipped, and flew, and lay still.

"No! Get away from my dog! Andie! Run!"

Henry wrenched himself hard, as hard as he could, and Pain wheezed as his knee crunched the wolf's ribs. Fear and surprise washed away. He looked at his dog, and the wolves, and the fear washed away red.

"Get away from him!" Andie shouted. She swung a thick branch across Oblivion's back, coming out of nowhere, running into the clearing from the trees. Henry wanted to scream for her to *run, run, you idiot,* but he couldn't. She looked so damn brave. She'd gotten out, somehow gotten away, but she'd come back. For him and his dead dog, when she might have lived.

"Lux, get up! Henry!" She swung the branch between herself and Panic. Famine edged around behind her. And Oblivion wouldn't stay down in the snow for long.

Andie adjusted her grip, and her balance. She ducked fluidly when the white wolf jumped, and then looped the branch at Famine's feet to send it rolling. The other end she thrust into Oblivion's chest, popping it back. Watching her, Henry could almost believe she could win. He watched so close he didn't notice Pain regaining its feet in the snow beside him.

"Andie, run!"

"Not without you," she shouted, and Henry barely dodged left as Pain sprang again. He caught the wolf's jaw in his hands and its fangs slid into his palm. *Don't let go. Tear its head clean off.* But it was the wolf who pulled, jerking on his arm like Lux at the end of his tug rope.

He didn't know how, but he caught the creature's shoulders and lifted it, his hand coated in hot blood and spit, and threw the wolf away. He ran to Andie, his eyes on the wolves and not on the motionless bit of black and silver fur at her feet.

Henry leaked blood from his hand and cheek. The wounds on his shoulders were hot and wet. The wolves hadn't taken much worse than a couple of tosses into soft snow.

"We have to move together," Andie said.

"Right." But it wouldn't matter. They were going to die. Torn apart, red and steaming in the snow. Pain would slice them open. Panic would spread them out. Oblivion would swallow their hearts and eyes, and Famine would eat the rest. All their families would find was red snow. Red snow, and the body of a discarded German shepherd.

Andie swung the branch out and it raked across Panic's skull. Henry felt the warm press of her against his back. He tried to fight alongside her, but his vision began to blur. He was losing too much blood. The whole world went white, like the clearing was filling with fog.

"Andie, you have to go. I'm not going to make it."

"What is that?" she asked. "What's happening?"

Henry blinked as Andie staggered and rubbed her eyes. The clearing really was filling with fog. The wolves whined and snapped their jaws on empty air.

"A song?" Andie asked, and Henry heard it, too. Low and sweet, a song he knew in a language he didn't. The wind smelled like salt and burnt sugar. He felt arms around him, and lips soft beside his ear.

"Keep quiet, hero, and let me sing." Her voice was beautiful. So he closed his mouth and let himself be taken away.

"Are you sure you want to do this?" Ares asked.

Athena watched Ares across the clearing. It was obvious that *he* wasn't sure he wanted to do it, and that more than anything convinced her that yes, she did. For just a second, she tried to see beyond the blood, to the boy-god Ares hid down deep. The one who'd had his pride hurt the most of all the gods. The subject of Olympus' ridicule. Their father, Zeus, had hated him. Ares' own father. And sometimes Athena had hated him, too.

If they had ever been on the same side, Athena couldn't remember it. But Ares was right when he said they were alike. When she looked at him, she saw one side of herself. A side she neglected, preferring to box rather than brawl.

But a brawl is what lay before her. Diplomacy didn't work with gods. They were ancient, with ancient sensibilities. War, they understood. War, she could do.

"Are you really going to make me kill you, brother?" she asked.

"Is there a choice, sister? If I opened my hands now and said I would come to your side, would you let me?"

She looked at those hands, and into his dark, clean-shaven face, so civilized with his cut hair and expensive clothes. He could've walked out of a Calvin Klein ad. But the centuries hadn't changed him that much. His eyes were still a wolf's eyes.

"No," she said.

Something like disappointment flashed across his face and disappeared just as quickly.

"It's fitting, isn't it," he said, "that this should happen here. On Artemis' grave. In her blood. Do you think she sees? Do you think she'll feel it, when one of us joins her?"

"I think you're disgusting," Athena replied. "Father always said you were the most hateful, the most wretched of all his children."

That got through, as she'd known it would. Ares' face crumpled, and he charged, not as fast as Hermes but with ten times the force. The impact sent them both into a slim tree, overwhelming the strength of the shallow roots. It fell, and Athena's foot skidded backward to keep from going over with it. The sound of the tree cracking and crashing would have reached Hermes and the others, and she imagined them stopping short and looking back.

Balance recovered, she twisted Ares around and slammed him into the diagonal fallen trunk, then rolled him onto the ground, back through the blood. He'd sop up all that was left of their fallen sister, before she was done. Penance for his disrespect.

"You fight like I remember," she said. "Poorly, and without brains." But with bluster and bronze, too. With rage and heart, like a bellowing bull. When his fist connected with her jaw, and then her stomach, it doubled her over, and he tossed her easily into another tree. Artemis' blood splashed when she dropped into it.

"You're still strong," he said.

"Bother you, does it?" She got up and shook blood drops from her arm.

He bared his teeth and clenched his fists. But he didn't charge. And there was something in his eyes like pity. It couldn't *be* pity, but whatever it was, it made her angry. Ares, pity her? Never.

She jumped for him, and they fought like forces of nature, like blunt instruments, with no regard for pain or damage. His fist split her lip and hers broke his nose. Athena didn't bother dodging; she didn't feign and slip like she had with Hera to avoid her stone fist. With Ares it wasn't about skill or tricks. It was all about strength.

And speed. The feathers in her lungs sapped her wind. Strong or not, she couldn't keep it up forever. Already her breath came too fast. She didn't have long.

Her elbow rose up and caught him under the chin. It pushed him back a few steps.

"How do you want to die, Ares?" she asked. "Want me to take your head off, like Aidan and Hermes did to Poseidon? Or should I just poke twenty holes through your chest with a sharp stick?"

"Familiar threats," said Ares.

"Yes. Only in the old days you'd have gone home and bitched to all of Olympus. Now Olympus is gone."

"For the goddess of wisdom, the things you don't know could fill a book." Ares reached behind himself and pulled a short-bladed knife from his pocket. In the filtered light it looked dull, even less impressive than it already was. Ares shrugged. "It's not much," he said. "But anything bigger seems less than sporting."

Athena almost laughed. She wouldn't have been surprised if he'd pulled a gun. Ares had never cared about rules or fair play, or being *sporting*.

She let Ares advance, dodging the small knife a few times before dodging not quite enough. It sank into her shoulder, and she grabbed his hands and twisted his fingers loose. Then she yanked it out of her own shoulder.

"Got your knife."

Ares grinned. "Got another one." And true to his nature, the one he drew from his other pocket was bigger. They both struck, but she was faster. The tiny blade thrust up under his ribs and kept on going until her hand was buried to the first knuckle. He roared and stepped back to lean against a tree with his hands pressed to his stomach.

"A knife wound for a knife wound," he said. "Enough for today."

"What's your hurry?"

"They didn't send me to take care of you," he said.

"They?" She thought a moment. "Of course. Aphrodite. Where is she? I have a girl who wants to boil her brains inside her head."

Ares' eyes went black as pitch. He lurched forward and knocked Athena sideways. She brought her knife down into his back, but not before his sank into the side of her knee. It cut through something taut, and all at once her leg went loose at the joint. She crumpled with a growl.

"That girl won't get within a mile of Aphrodite," he shouted, and looked wildly into the trees. "I wonder how far little brother managed to take them."

"No, Ares—"

He bolted too fast. The tip of her knife sank into the

ground inches behind him and left her sprawled on her stomach, chin coated with their sister's blood.

"Ares!" Athena drew her good leg under her and rose with a grimace, dragging her useless one and forcing it to work. She braced it with her hand, wrapped around the knee.

"Don't touch them!"

10

OUT OF THE PAST

The girl who saved them was not from Kincade. She was far too beautiful, for one, and for another, she wasn't human. She had flawless beige skin and enough grace to make a jungle cat jealous. Braids of differing width and length fought their way through brown hair, and her eyes were flecked green and brown, sea glass and sand.

"They won't find us here," she said, the last of the song she'd sung to disorient the wolves still leaking out of her voice. "The beasts won't follow. They'll return to their master."

Henry looked over his shoulder anyway. Whatever the girl had done, whatever spell she'd cast to conceal them, was gone. The air was clear. Only the scent of burnt sugar and salt remained. Her scent.

"What were they?" he asked. He sat in the snow with his dog on his lap. Even though Lux was a bag of broken bones, the girl hadn't left him behind.

"Ares' pests," the girl answered.

"Pests?" Andie asked. "Those were more than pests." She pressed a mitten into Henry's good hand. "For your face," she said, and he wiped his eyes. He hadn't realized he was crying.

"No," she said. "Not for that." She pressed the mitten to his torn cheek. Then she shoved her fingers into Lux's fur, and started to cry, too.

"Don't weep yet," the girl said. "Your dog will live. If we can get him to a good veterinarian fast enough."

Henry clamped his hand over the largest of Lux's cuts. He was warm, and a weak pulse fluttered under his fingers.

"Come on," Andie shouted, and pulled the dog's hind-quarters into her arms.

"Let me," said the girl. "I'm stronger." She lifted him smoothly, without heaving or effort.

They ran for the cars, and the jostling shook Lux out of his stupor; by the time they got him into the backseat of the Mustang he was conscious again, and whining.

When they burst through the doors of the emergency vet on 142nd, it was easy enough to cobble together a story about wild dogs, and in the confusion no one noticed the gash on Henry's cheek until they were in the exam room.

"Is that a bite?" The vet tech asked. The veterinarian looked up from Lux.

"My god, your face. And your hand. You should be at a hospital."

"Later," Henry said. "Is he going to be okay?"

"Listen, kid, you've got to get to a doctor yourself."

"I'll drag him there right after you answer his question," Andie snapped. "Promise."

The vet put his stethoscope buds back in his ears and pressed it to Lux's abdomen and chest.

"The cuts I can stitch. The bleeding's not bad." He paused. "This was a dogfight?"

"Yes. Why?"

The vet looked at the tech doubtfully. "Because there's fluid in the chest. Maybe blood. You're sure he wasn't hit by a car?"

"It was a big dog," Andie said. "A bunch of big dogs."

Lux whined and shoved his muzzle into Henry's hand. "Just fix him, please? I don't want to leave him."

The doctor sighed and scratched Lux between the ears. "All right. But go to the hospital. Leave your cell number at the front desk, and I'll call as soon as I know what he needs. It's probably going to be surgery—"

"Just do it," Henry said. "Please. Don't worry about what it costs. I've got savings." He gave Lux one last scratch and let Andie pull him out the exam room door.

The girl who had saved them waited patiently in the lobby. She stood by the windows, humming another song and twisting a brown braid around and around her finger.

"Will he live?" she asked.

"They don't know yet. But if he does it's thanks to you."

"He'll live," she said. "He's strong. I felt it through my arms when I carried him." She raised a hand to hover over Henry's cheek. "This is going to scar. And it needs to be cleaned. Stitched. It's very bad. Almost grotesque."

"So he looks pretty much the same as usual," Andie said, and grinned weakly. She stood beside Henry and cupped his wounded arm, forming a human sling. Adrenaline and shock were wearing off, and frightened exhaustion crept in behind. In the lobby mirror, the cut on Henry's face made him want to pass out. A flap of flesh hung from his cheek and wobbled. His coat was torn and mostly covered in blood. He didn't even want to look down at his hand.

He stepped close to Andie. She was alive and miraculously uninjured. When the wolves had surrounded her, he was more scared than he'd ever been in his life. He wanted to grab her and shake her, tell her what an idiot she was for coming back, for not running when she had the chance. He wanted to hug her until she ran out of oxygen.

Andie didn't notice. She stared at the girl, who was wearing an unseasonably light jacket and no boots, jeans soaked to the knees. Not a day over seventeen, except in the depths of her eyes.

"How did you do that?" Andie asked. "I mean, thank you, but what was that?"

"I have a way of hiding things," she replied. "You might call it a talent."

"Do you also have a way of finding things? Because you showed up at just the right moment."

"That was an accident. A lucky one, but still an accident. I was looking for someone else. Odysseus."

"Why are you looking for him?" Henry asked.

"Because I miss him," she said. "My name is Calypso. I suppose you could say I'm his girlfriend."

Athena shoved herself past trees, through ferns. She dragged herself along by vines. In the corner of her eye, she could see her blood streaking across shiny green leaves in a pathetic parody of Artemis. Limping and wounded. If Artemis were alive, she'd have laughed in Athena's face.

Every injury sang: the feather in her lung, the holes in her shoulder and leg, even her split lip. She'd pushed Ares one step too far. But Hermes' light still blinked in her chest, and Ares didn't have the nerve to go after Cassandra. Cassandra was the weapon that killed gods. If what Ares said was true and she hadn't finished the job with Hera, she would have if they'd stayed even a moment longer. Ares would know that, and deep down he was a coward.

Faint screams of grief reached Athena's ears. Someone was dead.

She propelled herself faster. It wouldn't be Ares. The screams were women's screams, and no one would grieve so loudly if he'd been the one to fall.

When she burst into the village, she expected panic. But there was none. No smoke except for the small trail rising up from the cooking fire. And all around, dead bodies. Sun-browned bodies of well-fed, happy men and boys. A few had mercifully crushed skulls. Others had gotten Ares' blade and died sliced open. Women and children wept and yelled, but no one took up weapons and swore vengeance. They were people of peace. Hunters. Farmers. A little boy sat beside his dead father with dry, empty eyes. He didn't understand. He wouldn't until they took away the body.

"Athena!" Odysseus ran to her, and she leaned on his shoulder.

"I thought—when he came and you weren't there—" His hand pressed against her cheek, and he glanced down. "Your leg."

"What happened here? What is this?" she asked. Several huts had caved in or been flattened altogether. It was all so small. So fragile. Ruined. Hermes and Cassandra stood in the center. Hermes had his hand over his eyes.

"Come on," said Odysseus. "Let's get you somewhere you can rest."

He tugged her, but she resisted. She wouldn't embrace him, or even look him in the eye, though his heart beat against her and she wanted to. Odysseus was alive. As much as she had believed he would be, she was still grateful.

"What happened here?" she asked again, louder.

"They tried to help," Hermes shouted. Tears tracked in clear lines through the dirt and dust on his thin cheeks. "They tried to help, and when they did, he ignored us and went after them." He turned his palms up, turned his arms so she could see the cuts he'd taken trying to defend them. Then he let them drop. It hadn't done any good.

"Where is he?" Athena asked. "Where did he go?"

"I don't know," Hermes said. Somewhere, someone wailed louder, and he grimaced. "They didn't understand. When they picked up their weapons they didn't understand that they'd become soldiers to him."

"These weren't soldiers," Athena snapped. "These weren't warriors." Ares would have known that. He just didn't care. He'd turned on the villagers because he was too afraid to do what he'd threatened. He'd killed a dozen because he feared one girl.

"Cassandra stopped him," Odysseus whispered.

Cassandra had her arms crossed over her chest, her shoulders hunched, her cheeks pale. She was afraid. Less of Ares than of herself.

"Tell me what happened."

"She—" Odysseus swallowed. His throat had to hurt, but she needed to hear. "I tried to hold her back. I tried, but—she kicked me. And then she ran up from behind and put her hands on his back like she was going to jump on him. Where she touched him, his back popped like a burst mosquito."

"And then he ran away," Athena finished.

"She didn't kill him. But she was close."

Athena watched Cassandra, standing mute and shell-shocked in the middle of the massacre. She really had needed the girl, after all.

"Come on." Athena still held Odysseus' shoulder, but

her knee already felt better. A few hours off of it and she'd be able to walk on her own.

Cassandra looked up as they approached.

"You're hurt," she said.

"You're not," Athena said. "Good."

"I should've done something sooner."

Athena had nothing to say to that. The bodies of strangers lay strewn at their feet. Strangers who had taken it upon themselves to stand between them and a god.

"We should go," said Hermes. "Before we bring anything else down on their heads."

"Isn't there anything we can do for them?" Cassandra asked.

"No," Athena sighed. "Aside from help them bury or burn their dead. And I don't think they'd want our help."

A voice sounded from their right, paper thin but strong. The white-haired elder walked toward them on stiff knees, her woven dress splashed with blood. She looked at Athena and spoke.

"She says she dreamed of you," Hermes translated. "Like silver fire. She dreamed your pain. She—" He stopped.

"What? What did she say?"

"She said she dreamed of you, the dog of war. The dogs of war are your home. Or something." Hermes shook his head. "I'm sorry, lady. I'm a poor and rusty translator."

The elder drew closer, a tall woman hunched over and become small. An illusion of curved back and stiff knees to hide strength like steel wire. Athena took comfort in that, at least. With this woman at their head, the people would recover. The elder's hand shot out like a whip and grasped Cassandra's arm, too fast even for Hermes, and Cassandra flinched, frightened. The elder let go and muttered something into Hermes' ear. Then she patted his arm, almost tenderly, and touched his face.

"God," she said, and walked away.

"What was that?" Cassandra asked. "What did she say to you? Was it about me?"

"I don't think I understood. She said that you were without dreams. Or that she dreamed of you without dreams. It didn't make sense."

Athena looked after the elder and frowned. Two thousand years ago, she could've protected these people. "Let's just go home."

At the airport, they changed clothes and cleaned up as best they could to hide the blood. Odysseus tied a scarf around his neck to cover Ares' handprint of bruises. It looked ridiculous. But the effort was wasted anyway. Aside from a few uncomfortable glances, no one paid them any attention. Their boat guide back upriver had asked if Athena needed help getting to her seat with an air of careful politeness: your business is your business.

"I like these people," Athena said to Cassandra as they took advantage of hot water and soap in one of the airport bathrooms.

Cassandra arched her brow.

"You're in a good mood," she said.

"I am," Athena replied, even as the smile died on her face. "The village. It shouldn't have happened. That was my fault."

"Normally I'd agree with you. Everything's your fault. But he got around you. Even the goddess of battle has to have a hard time against the god of war."

"No, she doesn't," Athena said. "And she won't. At least you're safe. And Odysseus. And Hermes."

"It's my fault as much as yours," said Cassandra. "I should have stopped him."

"He'd have crushed you with one hit. You were smart to stay back."

"No," Cassandra said. "There were lots of times. Lots of chances when he wouldn't have seen me coming. I could have saved them. Some of them at least. But I was scared." She paused. "I suppose you think that's stupid. That I should have killed him."

"You almost did," Athena said. "Burst his back like a blood balloon."

Cassandra scrubbed her hands under the hot water. She scrubbed hard, like she was soiled.

"What about Hera?" she asked. "Do you really think she's alive?"

"I do," Athena replied. "But it doesn't matter. Hera lost once, and she'll lose again."

"How did she lose if she's not dead?"

"She lost because I beat her to you." Athena shook water off her hands and stared at their reflections in the mirror. "Next time, though, we stay until it's finished. Until she's dead. There's no healing from dead." Next time they would check with a stethoscope and heart monitors. They'd get an official certificate from a munchkin MD with a funny mustache. Cassandra didn't reply, and Athena grabbed a few paper towels and handed them to her. "You got some sun. Are we going to have to tell your parents that part of our girls' week included a tanning bed?"

"I don't know if they'd buy that," Cassandra said. "I don't even know how they buy that we're friends. I'm just glad to be going home. That we're all going home." She dried her hands and looked at Athena in the mirror. "And I'm a little glad you got stabbed."

Athena snorted.

"One good thing about Ares showing up," she said.

"What's that?"

"He and Aphrodite are always thick as thieves. He's sure to lead us to her." She gave Cassandra a small smile, and left before she saw the girl's eyes turn black with hate.

They boarded the plane after a short wait. Athena buckled her seatbelt and took quick stock of the magazines and movies available in-flight. The trip would be long.

"You must've been really worried about him," said Odysseus, from the seat beside her.

"What?" Athena asked.

"Hermes. You must've been really worried about him."

"What are you talking about?"

"You let him book us first class."

She looked at her brother, sitting a row ahead across the aisle, with Cassandra next to him in the window seat. He'd already charmed the entire cabin crew, and they hadn't even pulled back from the gate. As soon as they reached cruising altitude, he'd be head-to-toe hot towels and champagne. He looked so happy. Her throat tightened, but she swallowed it down angrily. It shouldn't mean so much just to see him smile on an airplane.

"Maybe I thought we all deserved some pampering," she said.

Odysseus laughed. "Bollocks. And stop doing"—he pointed at her face—"what you're doing there."

"What's wrong with my face?"

"You saved our lives. Got us out of the bleeding rain forest and home in first class. So until we land, don't think about the rest of it. It'll still be there when we're back on the ground."

Athena frowned.

"It feels wrong to forget about it. Even for five minutes." And it felt dangerous, too, to allow her mind to wander away from the objective. At least when she was waging a war, she had something to do. She looked down at their hands, at their arms almost touching. At least when she fought, she knew what she was doing.

"Besides," she said. "We still have so much to do. Achilles, for a start—"

"Don't," he said. "We're not having that conversation at thirty thousand feet. Especially when I can think of other things to do at thirty thousand feet. Have you heard of this club? Something about mile high—"

"Shut up, hero," she said, but she couldn't keep from smiling. When Cassandra had told her she'd seen his face covered in blood, it didn't matter that she thought he'd survive. Part of Athena's heart had stopped beating. "Sometimes I think the cleverest thing about you is your ability to manage me."

"The cleverest?" he said. "No. Not the cleverest. Not by a mile. And speaking of miles, back to this club—"

"Shut up and help me order the entire in-flight menu for Hermes."

"Come on." He leaned in and brushed his fingertips across her arm. "When are you going to let me kiss you again? In the back of that truck I was half-asleep. I'm so much better when I'm awake. I promise."

Athena's cheeks flushed hot. She thought of Odysseus' kisses in the sleeper of that truck more often than she cared to admit. The way his lips had made her tingle. It was hard to imagine it could be any better.

"Not on a plane, in front of a flight crew, with my brother four feet away and the ligaments in my knee held together with one of your socks," she said, and tugged away.

Odysseus chuckled and put up the armrest. So gently, he pulled her injured leg onto his lap.

"As you wish," he said. His fingers walked up her calf and over her knee. "But I don't know how you stand it."

"So sure of yourself," she said, and her voice came out breathless. She grabbed his hand and held it tight, safe and sound, inside her fist.

II

THE WOUNDED AND THE DYING

Ares' blood-soaked return sent Aphrodite into hysterics. Her wailing rang off the walls, from the caverns of Olympus to the peak.

"Calm, calm," Hera said. She hugged Aphrodite, pinning her arms to her body to stop her flailing. Aphrodite moaned and went limp. Her slender form was no match for granite. "Go now, pet." Hera kissed her. "Lie down and rest. Let Mother tend to her boy."

"It's not bad," Ares whispered, and watched Aphrodite go. The way she'd screamed, one would have thought he was spraying arteries instead of slowly leaking.

"Not that bad?" Hera asked when Aphrodite was out of earshot. "You're wet from the neck down. It's soaking into our silk rug."

"Not all of it is mine. Some of it is Artemis'. We fought in her remains. And some of it's Athena's."

A shadow crossed Hera's face when Ares spoke of Artemis' remains. Another god gone. It didn't matter that she would have joined Athena's side. Artemis had been one of them. Hera cleared her throat and bowed her head.

"A fitting tribute," she said softly. "The huntress would approve."

"I hope so."

"Show me your back," Hera said, and gestured with her good arm. Ares pulled at his buttons sheepishly.

"It was the girl," he said.

"I know it was the girl. I can smell the stink of her hands." Her face crumpled as his exploded flesh came into view. Rock rolled through her half-flesh cheek. "You weren't supposed to let her touch you. You said you'd be safe."

"I got carried away."

"Carried away doing what?"

"Killing."

Hera made an exasperated sound in her nose, but she didn't scold him. Instead she wrapped an arm around him and squeezed. Not a word about his being careless or stupid. She knew what he was, and how he was when he killed. He was the god of war. Her terrible son.

Looking at his wounds, Hera gritted her teeth, and the granite of her lower molars scraped against the regular enamel of her uppers. Ares would have rather taken another knife to the gut than listened to that sound. The motion made the rocks and cracks in her face tremble.

"Come and sit." She motioned toward a pair of brocade-covered chairs.

"But the blood."

"I've got other chairs. Two thousand years of collecting mortal finery. We'll never want for new rugs, or art for the walls, or fine clothes. But you'll want for blood, if you don't sit down and slow your heart. I'll bring some food."

Ares sat in one of the chairs, and his blood sank hotly

into the fabric. Hera set down a tray piled high with fruit and cheeses and some sliced cured ham.

"When this war is over," she said, spreading cheese on crusty bread, domestic as he'd ever seen her, "Olympus will return in gold. No more caves. It'll be a palace again. And we'll come out from underground. Except for Hades, I suppose. But he likes it that way." She turned her cheek, and for a second only her beautiful side showed. Ageless. Light blond hair and cream skin. Second only to Aphrodite. Then she turned back, a monster cobbled together out of drying clay.

"Will they heal you more now?" he asked. "Since we've tried to do as they asked? Will they heal me?"

"The Moirae do as they will. Don't presume to guess. You know better." She thumped her stone fist against the tabletop. "But perhaps they will. Tell me about your wayward half sister. About the damage you did. Tell me where Achilles is."

Ares hesitated. When the Moirae realized he had failed, would they crumble his mother to dust before his eyes?

"I stabbed Athena," he said. "A few times. Nearly cut her leg off. She's still—" *A force,* he almost said. *Still the goddess of battle. Still more than a match for me.* But Hera looked as eager as Aphrodite's puppy, and he didn't have the heart to disappoint her. "She's just as much of a bitch as I remember."

Hera laughed. "Some things are hard to forget. And what of Achilles?" She ground her teeth again and moved her heavy stone hip to rest more comfortably.

"Let me tell them myself," he said. "I want to see them."

Hera blinked, like his words made no sense. "But they haven't asked for you."

"I'm asking for them."

"You can't . . . do . . ." she trailed off and looked everywhere but into his eyes. She stood, with effort, dragging her stone parts. She had to be in constant pain, and the Moirae didn't fix it. Why? As punishment? Or was the job too much for them? Ares had to know for sure. What they were. What they could do. He would see it for himself before he bent his head to their whims.

"I'll settle for one of them," he said. "Take me to Clotho. I want to see if her hair is really as red as they say. I want to know if the Moirae of life and birth remembers mine."

"One of them," Hera said, and made a mad sound. "One of them. Of course they remember your birth. As I do. The god of war. You bit through your own umbilical cord. I was so proud of you."

"Don't try to charm me," he said. "And don't change the subject."

She made a fist and her nails dug into her palm until they drew blood. When she spoke, her voice was hesitant, and careful.

"Ares. I want you to listen. I want you to try and understand. Can you do that?"

"I should think so," he said.

"I wasn't . . ." she started, and stopped. "I was never truly a mother. I was your mother, but you were a god." She rubbed her fingers over her stone fist. "What did I know about fear? Or about worry? I never had to watch you bleed and wonder if it would heal. I never had to understand that you could die." She pressed her hand to his cheek. "But I know that now."

"Mother—"

"So don't ask me to take you before them. Don't ask to look upon them before you are forced to. Just trust me when I tell you that they are terrible."

———

Cassandra walked into her house quietly. If she was lucky, no one would see her and she could sneak up to the shower before her dirty hair and the strangely identifiable odor of jungle raised questions. All she had to do was clean up, stash her bag, guzzle a pot of coffee, and she'd be good to go.

Her luck held. The house was silent.

"Lux?" she whispered, and waited for his cover-blowing woof, or the click-clack scramble of his toenails on the floor. Nothing. Henry must've taken him out. But the lack of clamoring dog wasn't the only thing missing. "Mom?" she called. "Dad?"

The clock on the kitchen wall read six thirty. On a Wednesday. They should have been sitting around the table eating dinner. Maybe they had gone to a movie, she supposed, but then where was the dog? She pulled her phone out of her bag, but it was dead. No outlets in the rain forest. "Dammit." She fished her charger out of the front pocket and plugged in her phone, then called her mom.

"Cassandra? Where have you been? I've been trying to call since yesterday, and your phone's been off. Why weren't you at school today?"

"Athena was having a bad day," she said quickly. "Got bad news about Hermes. So we sort of took a spa day." Not the best lie. Athena at a spa was more than a stretch. But she could've done worse after getting off a very long, exhausting, international flight.

"That's not—" Her mother sighed. "We'll deal with that later. Call Andie and get a ride to the hospital. Your brother was attacked by wild dogs yesterday."

"What?"

"And don't go into the woods! Animal control hasn't found them yet."

"Is Henry okay?"

"He's fine. We were supposed to take him home today, but he's having a reaction to the rabies vaccine. They're keeping him one more night, to be safe. Get here soon, all right? I bet Andie will give you a lift."

"Okay, Mom," she said, and hung up. Wild dogs and Henry in the hospital. She dialed Andie, hoping that Kincade truly did have a roving dog problem, and it was nothing god-related. But come on.

"Oh, thank god you're home," Andie said. "Are you okay? We walked into a world of crap while you were gone."

"What? What happened?"

"Four little wolf *things*, that's what. Friends of Ares, Cally says. I didn't even know Ares was around. They attacked us in the woods behind your house and almost killed us. And Lux."

Cassandra looked around the kitchen like the dog might come padding in at any second.

"Where's Lux? And who's Cally?"

"Still at the vet. But he's going to be okay. And so is Henry."

Cassandra waited. "And Cally?"

On the other end, Andie took a deep breath.

"That, my friend, is an even more interesting story."

Athena looked up at her house, at their house, at the quaint brown siding and wood rail of the widow's walk. They were home.

"First thing I'm doing," said Hermes as he extricated himself from the backseat, "is calling in an order at Stanley's Wok. Pot stickers and a few dozen chicken wings."

"How can you be hungry?" Odysseus asked. "You just ate out the entire plane."

"Look, I know you're British, but you should really rephrase that." Hermes thumped his fist on the trunk.

"It only opens with the key." Odysseus tossed it, and Hermes opened the trunk and threw the others their bags.

"Let's go in," Hermes said. "I want a fire, and a hot cup of something."

The sensation of coming home was magic: silence broken by stomping feet and brushing fabric. Athena breathed in a mingled smell of cleaning products and ash from the fireplace, and just a whisper of Hermes' sandalwood incense. It was so poignant and comforting that it took her a minute to notice the house wasn't empty.

"Wait," she said, and put her hand on her brother's shoulder.

"Wait for what?"

The girl came around the corner from the living room, wearing a cream-colored sweater and camel skirt over dark leggings. Her sand-and-sea eyes lit up at the sight of Odysseus.

"Odysseus!" She ran and threw her arms around his neck. He had half a second to glance at Athena in shock before they were kissing.

It was long and drawn out in the utter silence of Athena's stony eyes and Hermes' open mouth. But it did eventually break, and Odysseus wiped his lips.

"Athena." He looked between her and the girl in his arms. "This is—"

"I know who this is," she said. Of course she did. As if she would ever forget such a beautiful face. "Hello, Calypso."

Athena stood silent on her widow's walk, fully aware of Hermes creeping up behind her. No doubt he wanted to make sure she was all right, after Calypso's brazen announcement. It was almost funny, how afraid they'd been of her reaction. You'd have thought Hermes and Odysseus had turned to statues. She couldn't tell which one was more terrified. But she knew who wasn't. Calypso hadn't budged. Hadn't flinched. She'd just happily nuzzled Odysseus' neck. Nuzzled his neck with her stupid, lovely face.

"Hermes," Athena said. "Stop creeping."

"You're right," he said, and held out his arms. "Bring it in. Weep. Hug it out. I won't tell anyone."

She snorted. "Just because you're my baby brother doesn't mean I won't smack you around."

"Indeed you could," he said, his eyes on her hands where they gripped the railing. "No telltale white around your knuckles. But we both know you could crumble that wood as easily as a mortal crumbles a cookie." He walked closer and gave her a nudge. "Want to throw me over the edge? It wouldn't hurt, but I'd take it if it'd make you feel better."

"I don't need to toss you to feel better. Bring me that little waif inside. Bet I could make her fly a country mile." She smiled softly. Absurd. The words out of her mouth were as bitter and jilted as any love-sick puppy dog. "And to think, it was so nice to be home. Is Stanley's Wok on the way? I could use an order of chicken wings."

"I haven't ordered yet. Thought I should come up and face the rumbling volcano first."

"I'm no rumbling volcano," Athena said. But Calypso's lips plastered all over Odysseus seemed to be burned onto her eyeballs. Calypso, the sea nymph, who had been Odysseus' lover for seven years after the Trojan War. She'd had the guts then to tell Athena she was keeping him, even when Athena had demanded she let him go.

And now she had the nerve to squat in Athena's house.

"Maybe not," said Hermes. "But you can't be happy. I remember how mad you got, when she wouldn't let him off of that island. Hissing and stomping, until I had to go down there myself. I could do it again, you know. If you want."

"I didn't hiss and stomp," she said. But she had asked Zeus. Begged him to make Calypso let Odysseus go. She remembered what she'd said, too: that it was wrong for any immortal nymph or goddess to have an affair with a mortal man. "Do you believe what she says?" she asked Hermes.

"That she saved Andie and Henry from Ares' wolves?" Hermes shrugged. "I called Andie, and she confirmed it. Guess we shouldn't have left them behind."

We, he said. But it was Athena who'd done it. And Calypso had saved them. Hell, she'd even saved their dog.

"She's here to fight," Athena said. "Another soldier. And we owe her, for Andie and Henry. Just—" She waved her hand and pressed her lips together in a firm line. "Move her into Odysseus' room."

"Just like that," Hermes said. "You're going to give him up to her."

"He's not mine to give up."

Hermes rolled his eyes. Then he raised his brows.

"She doesn't even look like she's dying," he said. "Did you notice that? Those sea-green eyes, that perfect skin, and the shine off her hair was bright as a lens flare."

"It's an illusion," said Athena. "She's dying. Her death just isn't as grand as ours. She's a nymph, not a god. She's just aging. She's just mortal. She looks older than she did the last time I saw her."

"For sure," Hermes scoffed. "Seventeen, definitely, instead of sixteen."

"Shut up." It was sweet, how he tried to make her resentful. Resentful, and jealous enough to snatch her toy back. But Odysseus wasn't a toy. And he was better off with Calypso.

Calypso would die with beautiful silver hair, in a soft bed. Not in an explosion of bloody feathers.

"He tried to tell me about her," Athena said. "In the alley behind the Three Sisters. He told me that she came for him. She. I guess I should have known who he meant."

Hermes put his hand on hers. "But he left her, to find you. Back then, and now, he always wanted to leave her. For you."

"For his wife, back then."

"Yeah, yeah, yeah. But to do what *you* wanted."

Athena's chest grew heavy. "Can we not do this? Can we focus on the fact that we have a war to fight? Ares is coming at us from two fronts, and we need to find Achilles. Hera is alive." They had more than enough problems, without throwing unrequited love into the mix. "Who else would side with them? Hades, surely. But Hephaestus and Dionysus are probably ours, assuming Dionysus hasn't died of cirrhosis already."

"You're going to start a war, to forget about a boy."

"I'm not starting a war," she said. "I'm finishing one. And when it's over, we'll stand the victors, and live out the rest of our lives in peace."

"You really think we'll win?" he asked.

"We won Cassandra," she said. "And we're closer to Achilles. Don't you see? The cards are falling our way. Wherever they are, the Moirae are with us. Fate favors us. That has to be true, Hermes. We have to have another chance." She looked back toward the house, where Calypso and Odysseus were doing god only knew what. "Because I've already missed this one."

He squeezed her shoulder. "Are you going to stay out here?"

"Awhile."

He went into her bedroom and came back with a blanket.

"Put this around yourself at least. Before someone sees you and thinks you're nuts. I'll bring up the wings when they get here."

"Thanks, Hermes."

"Anytime, big sister." He turned to go, and said, "He'll always love you best."

"Yes." She nodded. "He'll always love me best. But he'll love Calypso for real."

12

MURDEROUS HANDS

"Hey, are you going to get something or what?"

Andie's voice startled Cassandra in front of the hospital vending machine, and she hit buttons without thinking. Out dropped a bottle of unsweetened iced tea. Gross. Maybe her mom would drink it.

"Iced tea? What's wrong with you? Did it give you the wrong thing?"

"No," Cassandra said. "You just scared me."

"Sorry. You were standing there like a zombie. What were you thinking about?"

Cassandra twisted off the cap of the iced tea. It was bitter, and watery, and so not the Orange Crush she wanted. But she was thirsty, and she didn't have any more dollar bills, which was all the ridiculous machine would take.

"I was thinking of . . ." she said, and stopped. She'd been thinking of touching Ares in the rain forest. The heat in her hands when she did it, and the feeling she got, when his blood burst under her fingers. Joy. Flat-out, powerful joy.

Ares had it coming, for sure. Murdering those people. Those plump, happy men who ran at him but didn't quite attack. They shook flimsy spears at the god of war, and he bashed their brains in. But as monstrous as Ares was, she couldn't stop thinking of his face. His handsome, too human face. He had black hair and dark eyes, like Henry. And he looked a little like Aidan, too, if Aidan had been stretched taller and more muscular. If his jaw were more square and the line of his mouth were cruel. She could still feel Ares' blood sliding down her wrists. Athena said Cassandra was a killer. She hadn't said anything about Cassandra liking it so much.

"Earth to Cassandra," Andie said. "Thinking of what?"

"Nothing." She wrapped her hands around the cold bottle and wondered if she could make it boil. What if she couldn't really kill gods? Ares said that Hera was alive. That Cassandra hadn't finished the job.

But she knew she could. Down deep in her gut and in the dark part of her mind, she knew. Her touch could kill.

"Nothing?" Andie asked. "It clearly wasn't nothing. Come on. Are you worried about Henry? Or what happened in the jungle? You didn't tell me any details—"

"Andie, will you shut up!"

Cassandra's hand shot out and grasped Andie's wrist, red hot, ready to reduce it to ash. To paste. She wanted to burn everyone who chattered in her ear about school, or doing the dishes, or going out to dinner. How she hated the way they filled time. How she hated that they thought they knew her, and all the things they thought mattered.

"Is that supposed to hurt?" Andie asked. "Because honestly, you've never had much upper-body strength."

Cassandra dropped her friend's hand.

"Sorry," she said quickly.

"What was that about?"

"Nothing. Let's just go see Henry."

"No wait," Andie said, her brow clouding. "That wasn't nothing, was it? You were trying to do something to me like you do to them." Andie rubbed her wrist.

"Oh god, are you okay?" Cassandra held out her hands, but Andie took a step back, and then one big angry step forward.

"It doesn't work on me, Cassandra," she half-shouted. "But my fist will work on you just fine if you ever try that again. What are you thinking? I'm your friend!"

"My *best* friend," Cassandra half-shouted back. Hot, angry tears backed up in her throat so fast. In a blink she was angry. Angry and sorry all at once.

"That sounds weird when you say it through clenched teeth," Andie spat.

Cassandra tried to swallow it down, to relax her jaw and breathe cold air, to say anything with a calm, gentle voice. But she didn't sound much different when she said, "I don't know how to make it go away."

They stood eye to eye. For as long as she'd known Andie, Cassandra had never seen her back down from a fight. So she loved Andie a little bit more when she growled and shivered all over, letting it go. Giving in, because Cassandra needed her to.

All at once, the heat in Cassandra disappeared.

"Look, it'll be okay," Andie said. "I'd be angry too. I am angry. It's normal, to feel this way because he's gone." She turned to lead the way to Henry's room, but Cassandra grabbed her and hugged her tight. Andie tensed immediately, never the touchy-feely type, but Cassandra hugged her tighter.

" I really am sorry I tried to murder you," Cassandra said.

A tear slid out of her eye, but Andie only chuckled. She patted Cassandra's back with stiff fingers.

"I forgive you. Just let go." She tugged loose and held Cassandra at arms' length. "Look," she said. "Don't worry about it. You'll . . . find Aphrodite soon, and burn her up, and then you'll start to feel better."

Cassandra watched her walk down the hall. Andie needed to believe that, to think that Aphrodite would somehow fix everything, and the old Cassandra would return. Cassandra used to think so, too. But now it didn't seem so simple.

They'd been at the hospital for the last hour with Cassandra's parents, trying to figure out if Henry could go home. The doctors said there were problems with his wounds. Cassandra heard one of them whisper that it was almost like they were *trying* to be infected. Too bad they couldn't tell the doctors that the bites weren't really from dogs. That they were from immortal, humanoid wolves owned by the Greek god of war. Would have cleared things right up.

"They're going to let him go," Andie said. "He's a horrible patient. They were half-ready to kick him out yesterday. He keeps asking about Lux and trying to pull out his IV." She stuffed a handful of M&M's into her mouth. "I hate hospitals. They smell weird. And I feel like I should trust everyone who works here, but why should I?"

"I wish this hadn't happened," Cassandra said suddenly. "We shouldn't have left you here. I should've thought."

"It would have been hard to get us all out of school," Andie said. "Besides, we held our own, Cassandra. You should've seen us out there. We would have gone down fighting."

"That doesn't make me feel better."

"Maybe not, but that's how it is."

They turned the corner toward Henry's room. Athena stood in the hall, talking to their mother. Both wore broad smiles. Cassandra's mother put a hand to her chest and shook her head sympathetically, and Athena nodded. Cassandra lip-read Athena say, "Thank you."

Athena. Since the day they'd met her, both of her parents swallowed everything she said and asked for seconds. So easy. But it wasn't real charm. It was a goddess's trick. A stretched mask of humanity to help them smooth their lies.

As they approached, Athena disengaged herself. She touched Cassandra's shoulder as she passed. To her watching mother, it must've looked like a sympathetic, familiar gesture. The fond gesture of a friend. But Athena hadn't even looked at Cassandra when she did it. The text message arrived a few moments later.

HENRYS GETTING OUT TODAY. I WANT ALL OF
YOU AT THE HOUSE TOMORROW MORNING.
EARLY.

Cassandra hit delete. Hard.

Gods. Goddamn gods.

The girl sitting across the table from Cassandra was beautiful, just like Andie and Henry said. Braided, brown hair was gathered with ribbons down her back. And she had the most incredible eyes, like the beach glass they'd found on a family vacation in Florida. She seemed at ease, too, even as the others sat and stood, leaned against counters and walls like refugees with arms in slings and bandaged knees. Black bruises ringed around necks. Calypso, the girl's name was. Cally. Odysseus' girlfriend, shown up out of nowhere to change everything they knew about him.

Poor Athena. Whether Cassandra liked her or not, to have someone blow in and claim the boy she loved had to be hard. Especially when the girl looked like Calypso. Say what you would about Aidan, but at least he never had secret girlfriends popping out of the woodwork. If he had, Cassandra would have turned them to leather.

Hermes whispered something to Athena so quiet that only gods could hear. It was irritating. They'd gathered at the butt crack of dawn at Athena's whim, and for what? To watch her sigh and look out the window? Hermes glanced their way and shrugged, thinner and thinner in a red t-shirt emblazoned with a snowboarding logo. His methane-torch eyes shone large and worried in his face.

"Someone has to start," Odysseus said. "Hera's back. What are we supposed to do about it? Find out how weak she still is? Bait Ares and follow him until we find where they hide?"

"What does it matter about Hera?" asked Andie. "Ares is the one sending wolves after us and stabbing Athena in the jungle."

"But he's taking orders from her."

"So what? Immediate threats first. Let's kill the wolves. They said Henry has to die."

"They must've made a mistake," Odysseus said. "Thought he was me or something."

Athena dragged her hand across the countertop.

"None of this matters now," she said. Her voice cut through all the others. "We need to find Achilles. That's what Ares was after in the jungle. That's what he wanted to choke out of your throat. We handle him"—she looked at Cassandra—"and then we focus on Ares, Hera, and Aphrodite."

"Look, we can't ignore the wolves," Andie said. "Especially if you're going off again after Achilles."

Achilles. The name sliced through Cassandra's ears like a knife. For once she didn't mind Athena pushing the hunt for Aphrodite aside. Achilles was the greatest warrior Greece had ever seen. He'd been the terror of her people. He'd murdered dozens of them. Hundreds. But none with more hatred than Hector.

"We're not going off after Achilles," said Odysseus. He looked at Athena gravely. "Not when all she wants is to find him and kill him."

"What's wrong with that?" Andie asked. "Eliminate the weapon. Makes sense to me. If we can't use him, neither can they." Across the kitchen, Athena stifled a smile. "Let's vote on it."

"We're not going to vote on it," Odysseus said. "It wouldn't be fair. Hermes votes with his sister." Hermes shrugged. It was true enough. "And we know which way she'd vote."

"So the gods won't vote." Andie looked around the table at Cassandra, Henry, Calypso, and Odysseus. "Who votes for letting Achilles stay hidden?"

Odysseus raised his hand. Calypso raised hers.

"And who votes for killing him?" Andie asked, and raised her hand. Cassandra raised hers as well. Both looked at Henry, who drew his brows together and clenched his jaw.

"Who votes for killing him?" Andie asked again. "Who votes for killing Achilles, the monster who jammed a spear through Henry and dragged him around Troy behind his chariot." She narrowed her eyes. "And fed him to his dogs.

Henry, so help me, if you don't get your good hand up I will re-kill you myself."

"Well, Cally's vote didn't really count," Cassandra said. "She might have lost her immortality, but she's still sort of a god."

"How cavalier you all sound," said Odysseus, "talking about killing when you're not the ones doing it. When you won't even see the deed done. And also, fuck the vote. When Greece wanted war with Troy, I was the only one who knew where Achilles was, and I was the only one who could convince him to fight. It's the same now. Nobody gets him without my help."

Only sooner or later, Ares, or someone like him, would get the answer out of Odysseus. They'd pull it right through his skin if they had to. Cassandra knew it, and from the look on her face, so did Athena.

"I've had enough of this." Athena shoved off the counter-top hard enough to rattle the cupboards. "Tell me," she said. Hermes and Andie scattered from her path, and Henry, too. Even Cassandra stood and backed off a few steps. With stony focus, Athena upended their empty chairs and dashed them against the walls. She flipped the table from under Odysseus' arms, and he stood to meet her nose to nose. The room held its collective breath. She would never hurt him. But she made a damn good show of it.

"No more special treatment, hero," she said. "I asked nicely. I won't do it twice."

"Do what you have to do, love," he said softly. "I'll tell you I'm sorry as many times as you like. That I didn't mean for us to be here, like this." He gestured subtly toward Calypso, but not so subtly that Calypso didn't notice, and her face fell. It wasn't helping, either. If anything, it made Athena angrier.

"Just tell her," Hermes said, a little nervously. "She'll get her way in the end."

"Can't do that," said Odysseus.

"I don't see what the big deal is," said Henry. "He's just one person."

"That's what everyone says," Hermes replied. "Until their city burns. That's what you said, Hector. That's probably what you thought, right until he killed you."

Henry set his jaw. "Is that really how it was? They said Hector was the best in all of Troy."

"The best," Hermes agreed. "And Achilles killed you without breaking a sweat."

"Everyone shut up," Athena shouted. She wrapped her fist around Odysseus' shirt, to shove him or throw him. "Tell me where he is."

"Let go," Calypso said. She stood calmly and smoothed her clothes. "You don't need to harm Odysseus. I'll tell you where he is."

"Cally, don't," Odysseus started, but Athena shushed him with a jerk of her head.

"How do *you* know where he is?" she asked.

"I know because I was there, with Ody. Really, I am the one who hid him."

Athena dropped Odysseus like a hot biscuit and stared at Calypso.

"Come with me."

Odysseus almost followed them into the backyard, but there was little point. Beans were spilling. He swore and stalked past Cassandra.

"Where are you going?"

"Plan B."

Cassandra, Andie, Henry, and Hermes stood, half of them trying to hear what was being said in the yard and the other half listening to Odysseus ransack his bedroom. It didn't take long for Athena and Calypso to come back in. Athena didn't say a word to anyone, and she was up the stairs in a flash.

"She'll be after him soon," said Hermes. "I'll stay with the lot of you. Not that I can do much against Ares and his wolves besides throw you on my back and run."

"We should think about leaving Kincade," Cassandra said.

"Because it worked so well last time?" Andie asked. "No. If we're going to get attacked, home ice advantage sounds pretty good to me."

"If we go, they might follow us," said Cassandra.

"And what then? We try to hide?"

"Hiding from gods," Henry muttered. "That doesn't feel possible."

"I don't understand," said Calypso, in her soft, musical voice. "If you run, they will find you. People will die. People you know, or people you don't. Is one more important than the other?"

Cassandra crossed her arms. "Well, yeah. Sort of."

"I don't want to run, Cassie," Henry said. "I can't give up everything."

"Say that the next time there's a wolf on your throat," she said, and walked out after Odysseus. "Or on Mom and Dad's throats."

Cassandra peered into Odysseus' room. The room he shared now with Calypso? It was impossible to tell. Clothes hung out of halfway open drawers and everything looked like a t-shirt. She certainly didn't see anything frilly, or lacy, or bra-like. But maybe Calypso packed light. And she was probably cleaner and more organized, and didn't leave everything in wrinkled piles on the floor.

"So, do you always have a Plan B?" she asked.

"Always," he said. His duffel was open on the bed, and he stuffed clothes in it from the closet, drawers, and floor. "But they suck. I never need to use them. My Plan A's usually work."

"I guess you're going with her," Cassandra said. He had already changed into boots fit to hike in and a jacket too light for Kincade winter.

"Well, she's not bloody going without me."

"If she doesn't want you to go, do you think you can make her let you?"

Odysseus smiled ruefully. "Don't let her fool you. There are any number of things I can get her to do."

"Dirty."

He chuckled. His manic packing slowed, then stopped. He swatted his duffel.

"Damn. I didn't fancy getting on another plane so soon."

"Another plane? So it's far? You didn't just hide him right under our noses or something?"

"No, but remind me to next time."

Cassandra stepped into the room. It smelled of fabric softener and whatever cologne Odysseus wore. Or maybe not cologne at all. Maybe just deodorant.

"Why would Calypso tell Athena where he is?" Cassandra asked. "She just got here, and she's your girlfriend—"

"She's not my girlfriend. I mean, she is. She was." He groaned into his hands. "I am in so much trouble."

"Doesn't seem like the smartest thing," Cassandra agreed, "pissing off two girls who can kill you with a flick of their wrists. And they say you're so clever."

"Look, I have a weakness, all right? Always have. Circe,

Calypso, the witches at the Three Sisters . . . Athena should know this."

"You didn't seriously just say that."

"I did, actually, but listen. It's all right. Cally told Athena because Cally is almost as clever as I am. She wants me to think she let the cat out of the bag to kiss up to Athena, because she needs a place here. When really she did it to drive a wedge between Athena and me." He looked around for anything he needed, anything he was forgetting. Then he closed his duffel and slapped his hand down on top.

"Will it?" Cassandra asked. "Drive a wedge, I mean."

He took a breath, and for a second he looked so sad she almost hugged him.

"I don't know," he said. "Maybe there was already a wedge there to begin with." He touched her shoulder. "Will you be all right? With Hermes and Cally here, I think you will be, but if you don't feel safe—"

"We'll be fine." She punched him lightly. "And it's really cute, the way you call her Cally."

He rolled his eyes. "Don't you start."

"Where are you going, anyway?" she asked.

He shouldered his bag.

"Australia."

13

KILLER OF MEN

Cassandra turned her head right and left in front of the mirror, looking for changes in her reflection. But there were none. Same straight brown hair, same big brown eyes. No smile. She looked like she'd always looked. Maybe it really was true what they say, and homicidal maniacs looked just like everyone else.

With Athena and Odysseus gone, she'd had plenty of time to think. And the thought that kept coming back was the sensation of Ares' warm blood on her hands. How right it felt. And how disturbingly good.

She turned on the faucet and cool water ran over her fingers, nowhere near as satisfying.

"I am what I always was," she whispered. That's what Demeter had said. A killer of gods. Hadn't she killed Aidan all those years ago, by loving him and putting everything into motion?

That couldn't be what it meant. She looked hard into the mirror, until she could see Aidan there, behind her.

One more step and he'd wrap his arms around her. If only it were so easy. One thin piece of silver mirror between them. Then she'd know what to break. What to cross over into.

If only I knew where you were.

She put her hand against the mirror and pushed.

Just one more time. A day. An hour. You're a god. There has to be a way. You can't just be gone.

The glass shuddered under her palm.

"Knock knock."

Henry poked his head in, and Cassandra jerked her arm down to her side, and Aidan vanished. She almost slammed the door on Henry's face. But it was his day. Lux was finally coming home from the vet.

"You going to pick him up after school?" she asked.

"What do you mean, 'you'?" he asked. "Aren't you coming?" Then he saw the look on her face and winced. "Right. It's Friday. I'm sorry; it slipped my mind."

"It's okay. It's not your job to keep up with my cemetery schedule. Besides, maybe I'll skip a day." But as soon as the words came out of her mouth, she knew she wouldn't.

"It's cool."

"I could go earlier. Maybe Andie'll drive me out at lunch. Or Hermes."

"It's okay," he said. "It's important."

"Lux is important," she said, and Henry nodded. He didn't look anywhere near as happy as he should. "What's the matter?"

"Nothing," he said. "Just thinking."

"About?"

"Lux," he said. "He fought. That day in the woods. Those . . . things. They didn't attack him. *He* attacked *them*.

For us." Cassandra imagined how Lux would have growled and leaped. Henry's foolish, brave dog, so outclassed by Ares' wolves.

"I knew they'd kill him," Henry said. "That he would die for me. And all I could think was how much I didn't want him to. I wanted him to be a coward and run away." He swallowed. "Is that how you felt . . . back then . . . when you watched me walk out of Troy to face him?"

Him. Achilles. The memory made her sick. How did he think it had felt, to watch her brother walk out to his death? To know he was going to die. And all because Achilles challenged him, and he had too much honor, or pride, to be smart and stay safe inside the city walls.

"Yes," she said. "I wanted you to be a coward. I hated you for not being a coward."

Henry picked at the paint on the bathroom door. He seemed ashamed, and Cassandra's heart sank. She'd seen that look before, a lifetime ago. She knew what came next.

"Maybe that's why I've been a coward now," he said. "To make it up to you. I lay in that snow like a baby. I would've died if Cally hadn't saved my ass. I couldn't protect Lux. Or Andie."

"Andie would say she doesn't need protecting."

"Don't I know it," Henry said. He touched the wrapping on his wounded arm. "When this sling comes off, I'm going to ask Hermes to train me."

Athena loved Australia. The ruggedness and the wild. It was so many things at once, and easy to get lost in. She hadn't been there in decades. She should have come back sooner.

"I hate airplanes," Odysseus grumbled from behind aviator sunglasses as they walked toward the Rent-A-Car in the Sydney Airport.

"Would you have preferred a boat?" she asked.

"Not with you around. The trip might've taken ten years." There was an edge to Odysseus' voice, and it was more than just travel crankiness. The closer they got to Achilles, the angrier he became.

"A plane or a boat. Scylla or Charybdis. Feel familiar?" Athena asked, and smiled.

He dropped his duffel into a plastic chair. "Just shut up and go rent us a car. Something decent. Something with four-by-four." He waved her off, and she ground her teeth. But fine. Let him have his mood. What she would do to Achilles later would rankle him worse.

Ten minutes later they were on the road, headed for the Hume and Monaro Highways in a rented Land Rover. Odysseus insisted on being behind the wheel, no doubt to feel more in control, and Athena turned on the AC. It was early March, but the temps were still high. They'd come too soon for falling leaves and dying foliage. Pity. It might've made spotting Achilles easier, if what Calypso said was true and he lived half-wild in the mountains past Jindabyne.

Athena watched the land pass through the window. Buildings and metal and roads and people. So many cars. She'd stayed away too long. When she'd been there last, it had been another world.

Another world, in sixty years. Everything changes. Even gods.

Athena glanced at her wrist, bare now, the gauze gone. The feathers had all been plucked, and the scabs healed to faint curling scars that would disappear in a week. There hadn't been any feathers since, except for the one she'd coughed out of her lung.

"No new feathers?" Odysseus asked, reading her mind.

"No. I must've used up my feather quota for the month. Maybe I should have Cassandra zap me more often. Feathers through the wrists aren't so bad. I could bear an eternity of them, if it meant they'd stay out of my lungs."

"That was stupid," he said. "I should never have left you alone with her."

"Don't be such a dad," she said, and set her foot up on the dash. "You're not the boss of me."

"Hmph." Odysseus snorted. "You're looking awfully chipper for someone who's about to kill a boy."

"I've killed lots of boys. And none of them were so wicked as the one I'm about to."

"You don't know him. He's just a kid caught up in your mess like the rest of us. He went mad with grief, and you called him evil."

"He behaved like a god, but he wasn't one," Athena said, annoyed. "Maybe it was you who didn't know him."

She looked back out the window and tried to relax, focus on the changing scenery. All that sunlight and wind in the brush. After the war was over, maybe she'd come back. She and Hermes could stand on top of mountains. But no. Hermes would want somewhere with satin and wine. Shirtless boys and roast meat on silver platters.

Still, Australia was a country she wanted more of. If they were wrong, and the war didn't save them, it would be an excellent place to die.

"What are you thinking about?" Odysseus asked.

Athena blinked. "Shirtless boys," she said. "No. Not really. I was thinking of the time I was here last. Has to be more than sixty years ago. When there was more wild."

"I'm sure there are plenty of bits of Australia that are still as wild as you remember."

"I'm sure there are," she said. "I loved it here. The quiet. I swam for days in the Adelaide River with the crocodiles."

"I've never heard you sound so nostalgic," Odysseus said. "Maybe back in Chicago, when we talked about my travels. About the old days."

"Well. Swimming with crocodiles is a strong memory."

"I bet." He glanced at her and shifted in his seat. "Of course you know I'm imagining it nude." She reached across and slugged him. "Ow. They never tried to bite?"

"Never," she said. "I think they sensed that I couldn't be touched. Or maybe they thought I was one of them." She peered at the speedometer to make sure Odysseus wasn't stalling, and he cleared his throat and signaled to change lanes.

"I should have told you about Calypso," he said.

Athena chewed the inside of her cheek. She wished they weren't stuck together in the car.

"You tried," she said. "When I found you at the Three Sisters, you said that 'she' came to you in London. She. I remember that. I just didn't think any more on it. There've been other things for me to think about."

"We've been busy, I know. But not always. I should've said—"

"Why should you have said? It's none of my business."

His fingers clenched on the steering wheel. "I thought you might say something like that. Despite the tattoos and holey jeans, you haven't changed. The bronze helmet and shield are still there in spirit."

"In more than spirit. They're in a safe in Zurich."

"Damn it," he said. "I'm being serious."

"So am I. Anyone robs that safe, they'll have me to deal with."

"She's not in my room," Odysseus said loudly, and Athena's mouth clamped shut. "She's in the guest room. And that's where she'll stay, if you'll just—" He paused. "When I saw her in London, it was like on that island. She was beautiful, and she has that voice. And there's so much history between us. When I left her to find you, I didn't know. I didn't know how I was going to feel when I saw you." He paused guiltily. "But I think she knew. That's why she came. She knew I was never going back."

Athena's heart pounded. Joy raced through her all the way to her fingertips, hearing the words come out of his mouth. He loved her best.

"Calypso is a good girl," she said softly. "She cares for you. And she can give you things that I can't. That I can never."

"Athena."

"Odysseus. I don't want you to think of me like this anymore."

The Snowy Mountains loomed in the windshield of the Land Rover. Since Athena had turned Odysseus away, they hadn't spoken. Nothing about a love that could never be made real. Nothing about why she shouldn't kill an innocent boy, already living in exile. Odysseus eased up on the accelerator, but it was no use. Athena did what she said she would, without exception. So Odysseus didn't say stupid things like, "You won't be able to, when you see him." And

[169]

she hoped he wasn't entertaining the notion that if he threw himself in front of Achilles, he could stop her.

They pulled off the highway, into the town of Jindabyne at the base of the mountains and drove straight through, to a Jeep trail he and Calypso had found. He drove up the winding path until it thinned out and cut off, then killed the engine.

"I know you're going to try to stop me," she said. "I know you feel like you have to."

"That's how it is, isn't it? You and I, we both do what we feel we have to." He opened the door and got out. Athena followed, and the sun warmed her cheeks against the mountain air, cooler than in the lowland. Odysseus walked slowly into the trees.

"But you understand, don't you?" he asked. "I dragged him into this, back then. Dragged him off to war. I won't do it again."

Athena slammed her door. "Don't beat yourself up about it. Down deep, he wanted to go." She gestured up the thinning trail. Somewhere overhead, some kind of squirrel or glider shook the leaves of the low, broad branches of a gum tree. It was a skittering sound. The sound of prey.

Today I am a huntress, like my sister Artemis.

"Let's go."

They'd hidden him well, far up the mountain and off the trail. Athena and Odysseus walked miles through the trees. Achilles must be so alone, living on wallaby meat and talking to birds.

Athena closed her eyes. Pity was for later. After it was done.

"You're not doing something stupid, are you?" she asked Odysseus' back as he led her through the trees.

"Something stupid like what?"

"Like taking me the wrong way."

"I'd only be able to stall you for so long. I'd starve before you would." He grasped the twisting gray bark of an alpine ash, digging his fingers in and dragging himself by. He was tired. And he was right. He could only stall her for so long.

Finally, a faint hint of smoke and cooked meat touched Athena's nose. Dull, chemical smells from cleaners and plastics. A few more steps and she saw it: a tiny house in the trees. Barely large enough to be called a cabin. Chairs fashioned from whittled wood sat in the yard around a small table. A boy sat in one with his back bent over, reading a book. Long, hanging blond hair obscured most of his face.

Athena moved behind a tree and let Odysseus go ahead. She didn't recognize Achilles like she'd thought she would. And there was something peculiarly sad about the extra chairs. Like he was always expecting friends who might never show up.

Athena saw the exact moment Achilles realized someone was coming. Just a slight tensing of muscle and an almost imperceptible turn of his head. No other tells, and no fear. He didn't turn until Odysseus called out his name, and then the smile on his face was broad. She noted the power in his stride and his sharp green eyes. The joy on his face at seeing his friend.

Don't let him fool you. He's an atom bomb. He's got to go.

"Ody!" He held out his arms, and for a minute Athena thought she wouldn't have to do much of anything, that

Odysseus might fall in line. But then Achilles' face changed from happy to wary.

"Run, Achilles," Odysseus shouted. "Run!"

Achilles saw her before she sprang, before she burst out from behind the ash tree like a flushed bird. He spun and ran, dodging the table and chairs. He dashed around the corner of his shelter and sprinted farther up the mountain, lightning fast.

Her pupils zeroed in on his fleeing back. The scent of blood in her nose was so strong she didn't see Odysseus throw the chair. It struck her shoulder, and she glared at him.

"Don't!" he yelled. "Talk to him at least!"

But Odysseus was behind her already. She ran, following the glimpse of Achilles' blond hair as it darted through the ashes. The first trap was a total surprise. Her foot landed square in the steel jaws, and it snapped closed on her ankle. She barely had time to inhale before the snare engaged and dragged her onto her back and into the air.

"Athena!" Odysseus stopped short below her. There was no pain in her foot yet, but blood was traveling the wrong way up her leg, soaking hot through her sock. She gritted her teeth, gripped the trap's jaws, and pried them open. Then she swung her legs under her and dropped to the ground.

"Are you all right?" Odysseus asked.

"Don't follow." She knelt and assessed her foot. Not broken.

"What?"

"Don't follow!" She stood and pushed him backward. "He's rigged the path with traps, don't you understand?"

"I can watch for traps as well as you can," he said stubbornly.

There was no time to argue. Who knew where Achilles was headed, or how far ahead he was already. But she didn't want to watch for traps. She wanted to run right through them. Only with Odysseus there, she couldn't take the chance.

"Stay with me," she barked, and took off again, slower this time. Achilles had built his traps well. It must've taken him countless days to dig the pits and sharpen the poles to line them, to figure out the ideal branches to lay his pulleys across. And he was clever. She jumped over a poorly hidden tripwire and nearly fell into a covered pit of skewers.

"Watch it," she called to Odysseus. "He let that one show on purpose." She nodded toward the concealed pit and held out her hand to pull him across. She evaded three more traps before a thin, half-buried tripwire caught on her foot. When the hundred-pound log fell toward them like a swooping hawk there was nothing she could do but take it, catch it, and keep it away from Odysseus. Her shoulder crunched and popped out of its joint. If it wasn't broken, she'd put it back in later.

By the time she made it to the clearing, she was panting, bloodied, and pissed. But Achilles hadn't lost them. The look on his face as she walked toward him was somewhere between surprised and disappointed.

"You're not afraid," she called.

"Not then and not now," he called back. So he remembered the old days, and who he was. Achilles. Manslayer. That should have made it easier. But Odysseus' voice rang through her ears. *He's my friend, Athena. He's just a kid, caught up in your mess.*

"How did you die?" she asked curiously. "How did you get your old memories?"

[173]

"An accident," he said. "A fall. A long time ago. I was seven."

Seven. He would've been a skinny towheaded kid with big green eyes. Dirt on his nose. Maybe a lizard in his pocket. A boy she would've liked. Damn it.

But the traps. He knew why she'd come. He was no deer in the headlights.

Odysseus grabbed her arm.

"I found him last year in Brisbane. I don't know how. I just knew where he was. He took one look at me and laughed. Hugged me like we'd never been apart. When I told him about the war, he wanted to hide. So just . . . let him stay hidden."

Her maimed shoulder and foot throbbed dully, like beacons on a far-off shore, and she'd be hurt worse before it was done. *Let him stay hidden.* But if she did, they would pay for it. Cassandra would pay for it. Hermes. Weapons like Achilles never stayed quiet. And the regret of that wasn't something she could live with.

She pushed Odysseus away gently. Achilles wouldn't die easy. Not the best of the Greeks. He held something in his hand. A hammer.

He ran at her and swung. The end of the hammer breezed inches shy of her cheek as she turned her head. He brought it back fast, and it caught her in the shoulder. The already dislocated bone cracked.

A mortal, cracking my bones. Am I getting weaker, or was he always so strong?

She wasn't sure. She'd never fought him. But she'd watched him cut down men like wheat in a field. The hammer pulled back, and she could have grabbed it. Should have grabbed it and made him face her hand to hand. But he was still a mortal. Letting him keep his weapon felt fair.

She dodged the next strike, meant to bust into her rib cage, and kicked out, but what should have dropped him only knocked him backward. Not even off-balance. And he still wasn't afraid. The light in his eyes was the same mad light she'd seen on the battlefield in Troy. Hector must've been terrified, looking into them.

She caught Achilles by the arm and threw him around her in a circle. He rolled to his feet unharmed, and so damned fast. He sprang forward and struck, his fist against her jaw. The clack of her teeth was loud and embarrassing. But he'd overplayed his hand. She reached around the back of his head and threw him to the ground, on him before he could regain his feet, her one good arm wrapped around his head. With brutal grace, she snapped his neck.

The body slumped to the side and rolled onto its back. Odysseus shouted, and the clearing went silent. It was over. Athena rose and closed her eyes. She didn't want to see the body, or Odysseus' face. But when he tried to go past her, she caught him across the chest.

"I knew you would do it," he said. "I knew. But I didn't believe it." He threw her arm off and turned back the way they'd come.

"Where are you going?"

"To get a shovel. To bury him."

"I don't have any shovels, actually."

Athena spun around at the impossible voice. Achilles' head rolled toward her and smiled.

"I broke the last one digging that bloody pit," he said. "Haven't made it down to buy any replacements." He pushed himself up onto his elbows and twisted his neck. Broken bones popped back together with a hideous sound. "But I appreciate the sentiment."

"I broke your neck," Athena said.

He shrugged. "Been broken before."

She looked at Odysseus, but he hadn't known. His eyes were round as one of her owls'. Achilles stood up and dusted himself off, none the worse for wear. He didn't even seem angry. The way his green eyes flickered from Athena to Odysseus, he seemed mostly embarrassed to have been killed. Except he hadn't died.

"You still are what you were," Athena said softly.

Invincible.

14

WEAPONS

Odysseus checked Achilles over as if he were assessing a horse. He lifted the boy's arms and moved his chin back and forth. Another minute, and he'd open his mouth and look at his teeth.

"I don't believe it," Odysseus muttered. "You bloody can't be killed. Unless"—he cocked his head—"what about your heel? Did your mum really dip you headfirst in the Styx and miss that part? If I cut it, would you die?"

Achilles smiled. "The legend's not that literal. Not quite."

"So you can be killed," Athena said. "You're not immortal."

"The whole world knows my name," he said, and shrugged. "If I'm not immortal, I'm damn close."

"What if I pulled you apart?" she asked.

"What if you could?" He nodded toward her ruined shoulder and foot, then turned back to Odysseus. "What're you doing here, anyway? Why's she all . . . after my hide?"

"Haven't you heard? You're the weapon of the gods. Or

at least, you're one of them." Athena waited while Odysseus filled him in.

"Mm," Achilles said. "Well, since killing me is out, why don't I come back with you? Then you'd have both weapons instead of one." He cocked his eyebrow at Athena. "Might've saved us all a broken neck if you'd just asked that in the first place."

Athena glowered. Since killing him was out. What a thing to assume. But she was in no condition to try again. And the idea of Achilles dying and popping up over and over like some macabre prairie dog was just too awful.

Her eyes took in his wild blond hair and gray-blue t-shirt. He was built sort of like Henry, with broad, muscular shoulders and fast, narrow hips. But he was taller. And much more lethal.

"I would have been content to stay on the mountain," said Achilles. "But you found me. And this is what I was made for. So make your choice, goddess. The side who has me lives forever."

"He'll be a help, I promise," said Odysseus.

Athena sighed. "Shit." Was he going to promise to feed and walk him next? "Fine. Never let it be said I'm not flexible." He would come back to Kincade. And they could use Hera's own weapon to cut her throat.

"Do you know how much alcohol it takes to get a god good and drunk?" Hermes swallowed beer from a red plastic cup. "Not as much as you'd think."

But still, a lot. It was his twentieth cup.

"I'm out," he said, and eyeballed the plastic bottom.

"Take mine." Cassandra handed him her cup. The mortals, it seemed, didn't feel like drinking. Not even amidst the whoops and laughter of what seemed to be half the school. An impromptu party jammed the bonfires at Abbott Park to near capacity, celebrating the suddenly rising temperatures. The mercury had risen above sixty that day, and the forecast said it would go as high as seventy for the remainder of the week. A strawberry spring. One little glimpse of paradise before winter's fist closed back up.

The air smelled of warming dirt, wet leaves, and smoke. Organic smells. Nostalgic smells of past fires where Aidan had kept her warm. Now she stood by herself, watching Hermes laugh with Sam and Megan, both of them smitten with him to varying degrees. He told them stories about his fictitious dorm at his fictitious college. Or maybe it wasn't so fictitious. He'd been alive a long time. He'd probably gone to lots of colleges.

Behind him, Calypso spoke when spoken to. Hermes seemed annoyed to have her there and ignored her. Most of the girls were too intimidated to say hello, and the boys just stared. She looked alone. Alone, but not lonely. There was a difference.

"Should Hermes really be getting drunk?" Henry asked. "When he's supposed to be watching out for Ares?"

Cassandra smiled. Maybe not, but who had the heart to tell him so?

"Don't worry." Andie gestured toward Calypso. "She's here. If those wolves come back, she'll just sing them stupid, like last time. Do you need anything?" She tugged at Henry's jacket, carefully arranging it around his sling. The shoulder was healing well. The sling would be off soon, and he'd start to train. Start to use a sword. Start to learn how to kill.

"It's going to be a hell of a scar," Andie said.

"Yeah," Henry replied. The scar on his face was brutal

and ugly, a red, stitched stripe just below his cheekbone. "The docs did a real Frankenstein job of it."

"Makes you look like a warrior," Andie said.

"Don't say that," Cassandra said. "You wouldn't say that if you remembered what it was like to watch a spear go through his chest. And stop . . . touching him all the time."

"What? Gross, I'm not touching him all the time," Andie protested, but Cassandra turned and walked away.

"It will all happen again," she muttered. "They'll get together. Henry will die. I'll swallow an axe, and Andie might live just long enough to wish she hadn't."

"That's no prophecy. That's only your fear."

Cassandra turned. Calypso blinked innocently and sipped from her cup.

"How do you know?" Cassandra asked.

"I don't. It was just a guess."

Just a guess. But it did make Cassandra feel better somehow.

"You're thinking about him," said Calypso. "Your Aidan."

"How can you tell?"

"I've seen that face on lots of girls. And in the mirror, when Odysseus is gone, and I'd give anything for him to walk through my door." She shook her head, and pretty braids fell across her shoulder. "It must be difficult to believe. That someone eternal as Aidan could be truly dead and gone forever."

"I don't believe it," Cassandra said. "But no one knows where he went. Not even Athena."

"Athena doesn't know everything. I've guided my share of mortals to the underworld. Almost as many as she."

Cassandra stared at Calypso intently. With the fire reflected in her sea-glass eyes, she appeared entranced.

"Is that where he is? Is there a way to get there?"

Calypso blinked away the fire and turned her face to the shadows.

"I don't want to give you false hope," she said. "The way to the underworld has been closed for more than a thousand years. And I don't know if your Aidan is there. But if he is, it doesn't matter. Because we can't reach him."

"False hope," Cassandra whispered. But if it was false, it didn't stop her head from filling with possibilities.

Athena sat on Achilles' lonely cot while Odysseus knelt on the floor, tending her crushed ankle. The shack was extremely well fortified. Shelves warped beneath the weight of canned food and bottles of water. He had plenty of first aid supplies, too. And, of course, weapons. Nothing so rudimentary as his hammer, either. He had blades of all kinds. He had a longsword, for Pete's sake.

"The boot's ruined," Odysseus said. The steel trap had bitten all the way through the leather. It flopped sadly when he pulled it off her foot. "Might as well cut it down and make a bootie."

"As if I'd ever wear a bootie." Under the boot, Athena's sock was all blood from lower leg to heel. When Odysseus plucked the fabric away and rolled it down, dark holes in her ankle and foot were plainly visible.

"Sheesh," he said. "You should probably have stitches."

"Do you know how to stitch?"

"Not really."

"Then just bind it up. Either they'll close, or feathers will pop out of them."

Odysseus turned slightly pale at that.

"Hey." She toed him. "No time to get queasy." She glanced out the door at Achilles, who had put all the clothes he owned in a rucksack, along with a couple of his favorite books, and waited for them in the yard. "Are you sure about him?"

"As sure as I was the first twenty times I told you to leave him alone," Odysseus snapped, and tugged the bandage just a bit too tight.

"If you're waiting for me to say you were right—"

"I'd never wait for that."

"I'm still not sure that you *were* right," she snapped back. "What about Henry? How can we bring Achilles face-to-face with Hector?"

"Henry isn't Hector," Odysseus said. "But I'll talk to him about it. Make sure he understands that Henry isn't the enemy."

Athena chewed her lip and watched the progress on her foot.

"Make sure you use enough bandage so the blood won't show through at the airport."

"You're the boss." Odysseus poured water into a bowl and sponged most of the blood off, but the wounds still bled, and in no time the water was thick and crimson. "I'm going to clean it a bit, all right? I know you don't have to worry about infection, but—it's nice to be tidy."

He lifted and turned her foot with gentle fingers, dabbing the gaping holes with iodine. It stung like hell, but it was the kind of pain she could take. The kind she knew she'd heal from. Not like the feathers.

"Odysseus?"

"Yeah?"

"That thing you said—that you kept saying. Being a kid caught up in our shit," she said. "I never believed you meant it. I didn't see how you could. You were always *my* Odysseus."

"I am your Odysseus."

Only he wasn't. Despite the same wavy dark hair and mischievous eyes, the same crooked smile, this Odysseus wasn't *that* Odysseus. This Odysseus had a future and choices the other hadn't had.

"I think oaths expire when you die," she said softly.

"Then you don't know much about oaths. There." He set her ankle on the ground and reached for the padding and bandage. "Hold this." She bent and pressed the white pad to her foot. Where her fingers touched, blood seeped through immediately. "I didn't mean it, right?" He wrapped gauze round and round. "I mean, not for me. It was just something to say to keep you from killing Achilles. Not one of my most successful lies."

"Well," Athena said. "Not everyone's as stupid as a Cyclops."

"Not everyone's as hardheaded as you." He rubbed his hands together and eyed the sheets of the cot. "Now, how to get that shoulder back in the socket? Maybe we can tie off some of those sheets."

"Just pull it."

"Even with the bone broken?"

"Just pull it, or I'll jam it in myself, on the wall."

He blew breath out, but he stood and grasped her arm between the elbow and wrist. "Bloody stubborn," he whispered, and yanked hard. The cracked bone in her arm sang a friggin' aria, and fire burned up the whole side of her body as the joint popped back in. But it went in. The bone was only cracked, after all. It wasn't like it was sticking out of the skin.

"Okay?" He touched her shoulder gently.

"Okay." She took a breath. The adrenaline had begun to fade. It would be an extremely uncomfortable flight home, followed by perhaps a few days off her feet. But just the same, she couldn't help feeling excited. She'd found the other weapon. She looked again at Achilles, where he stood waiting patiently. He was a sharp new knife indeed. Sharp enough to cut her stepmother's head off. The invincible brute would plow a path straight through to the gods, and Cassandra would walk unharmed in his wake.

"The Fates are still with me," she whispered.

"What?" Odysseus asked.

"Nothing. Just taking stock."

"And you're pleased?"

"Yes," she said. "And that's as close to an apology as you're going to get."

"Well. It's shitty, but it'll do." He hadn't moved away. He stayed close, half-kneeling, bent toward her. "What you said in the car. About Calypso. About us. Is that really what you want?"

Her eyes moved over his familiar form. The muscles in his shoulders. The way his hair fell across his cheek.

"Yes," she said.

"But what if I can't?"

"Don't be difficult. You can do—" She stopped. He'd picked up the bowl of water and blood and stared down into it. Something floated in the center, small and dark and speckled. A feather. There'd been a feather in her blood.

I don't like to be dying. I don't think I'll like to be dead.

"Athena," Odysseus said.

"Sorry." Achilles walked abruptly back in and headed to the corner of the shelter to dig through his stacks of books. "I didn't want to forget this." He held up a thin white volume and flashed it at Odysseus. A book on trap building. "Best book you ever got me. Did you get her patched up?"

"Could you give us a minute, Achilles?" Odysseus asked, but Athena grabbed him by the arm.

"Hang on. You got him that book? The book that taught him how to make the traps?"

Achilles ignored them and flipped through pages.

"I thought it'd come in handy, and it did."

"You knew there would be traps, and you didn't warn me."

"I didn't know for sure," Odysseus said. "And besides, you wouldn't have been killed."

"I might've been maimed."

"You could've been maimed; he could've stayed dead. All that's in the past. Let it go." Odysseus stood and rolled his shoulders back.

"Come on," he said. "Let's get him home."

Odysseus wanted a beer before the flight, so they pulled up at the first bar they found along the concourse and wedged their way into a corner table. Odysseus ordered a round of Guinness, and all three flipped open their passports for the waiter.

"It must be strange," Achilles said to Athena. "Getting carded. You're what, five thousand? That's got to be legal everywhere."

"It's the purple streaks," Athena said, and pulled a few locks over her shoulder. The last of her punk highlights. "I should cut them out."

"Don't," Achilles said. "It looks good. Wild. Besides, it isn't your hair. They'd card you anyway."

Athena didn't know, really, how old she was. Passing years weren't something immortals paid attention to. Or at least they hadn't been.

She watched Achilles as he waited for his beer, talking to Odysseus amiably about cricket, of all things. His eyes darted this way and that, taking people in. All the harried travelers speed walking down the concourse. It was probably more people than he'd seen in a year.

Athena tried to remember what he'd been like, in his other life, but she didn't know. The only thing that mattered was the way he fought. Achilles had been able to take down twenty, thirty armed and trained soldiers by himself. She couldn't wait to find out what he could do now that he was truly invincible.

But Henry and Cassandra. It felt wrong to ask them to see the sense of it.

It was a lot to ask.

"How long until we get to Kincade?" Achilles asked.

"Too long," Odysseus muttered.

"About twenty hours to Philadelphia, and then we connect to the Kincade Airport." Athena stretched her back. A full day of travel, with a torn-up foot and a cracked arm.

"I hope they have a good in-flight movie," Achilles said.

"I hope they have *eight* good in-flight movies," Odysseus said, and took a long drink. If he kept drinking like that, he'd be passed out for most of the trip. Which was probably his plan in the first place.

"What did you do, Achilles," Athena asked, "in the middle of nowhere for so long?"

"What do you mean?" he asked. "Clearly, I made traps."

"I'm serious."

"Athena," Odysseus said.

"I'm just making sure he didn't go Unabomber out there. A year's a long time to spend whittling and playing the harmonica."

"What's a 'unabomber'? Never mind. I get what you mean. And I assure you, I'm sane." Achilles looked around awkwardly. "Not sure how I'm supposed to prove it, though."

"You put up all those traps," Athena said. "And you hid. So why join us now?"

He took a drink and nodded thoughtfully. "I hid. I did. I thought it was the best thing, and so did Ody. He can be right convincing, I'm sure you've noticed. But a year is a long time, and I know what I can do. What I'm supposed to do. So when you made it through the traps, I figured, she must be the one. She must be the side to fight for."

"You're not angry at me for killing you?"

"Not at all. I guess it doesn't bother me as much as it would someone else."

She snorted. "I suppose it wouldn't." She watched him closely. "What about Hector?"

He swallowed and set his glass down, hard. "What *about* Hector? I ran a spear through him a few thousand years ago. He burned on a pyre."

"Listen, mate—" Odysseus started.

"Hector is with us," Athena said. "In Kincade. He fights with us." She waited for the glass to break, for Achilles to launch across the table. Thousands of years and a lifetime later, Hector's name still made his blood boil.

"It can't be," he said. "Why would he be brought back? Why would fate put him here? He was nothing. Less than nothing."

"He was second only to you," Athena said.

"Patroclus was second to me," Achilles spat, referring to his best friend who had meant more to him than a brother. The one Hector had killed.

"Hector killed Patroclus. That makes Hector second."

Achilles scowled, and veins stood purple in his forehead. Odysseus was seconds away from punching Athena in the face to shut her up. But she had learned what she needed to. The old wound still bled. Long ago in Troy, a warrior named Patroclus had shown too much pride. He'd disguised himself in Achilles' armor and tried to run up the walls of Troy. But Hector threw him down and killed him in the dirt.

"This won't work," Athena said. "How will we keep them apart?"

"You won't," Achilles growled. "You need me more than you need him."

"Hey," Odysseus said, and grabbed his shoulder. "This isn't about you and Hector anymore."

Athena pushed her beer away. "We'll leave him here and go back on our own. Move Henry first. For all we know, Henry would want to kill him, too." But that would be a sorry attempt. A fly attacking a tarantula.

"Who the hell is Henry?" Achilles asked.

"Henry is Hector," Odysseus replied. "Only he isn't. Not really. He's not like you and me. He doesn't remember anything. He's not the same person. He's just a seventeen-year-old kid with bad skin and too much homework."

Henry didn't have bad skin. But Athena didn't correct him. Across the table, Achilles tried to get a hold of himself. He didn't want to be left behind. And maybe he didn't want to be so angry.

"Things aren't the way they used to be," Odysseus said.

"How do you forgive?" Achilles whispered.

"You just do. Hey, they forgave me, and I'm the one who thought up the Trojan Horse."

"They've forgiven me, too," Athena said. "And I helped Hera tear their city down because a Trojan said I wasn't pretty. We all made mistakes."

"He really doesn't remember?" Achilles asked.

"He doesn't," said Odysseus.

"Then he isn't Hector."

Athena took a breath. "Okay, then."

Ares trailed blood wherever he went. He ruined furniture as fast as Hera could replace it, and his wolves followed behind, trying to lick up the mess. Damn that girl. Cassandra. He didn't understand how a formerly useless prophet could touch him and make his blood burst from his skin like a filled balloon.

"Ares," Aphrodite whispered, and pressed into his back. Wetness soaked into the front of her dress, mostly crusted over crimson now instead of blue and green. "Does it hurt?"

"No," Ares lied. It did hurt. But the weakness was worse. Blood flowed out and took his strength with it. At night he could barely keep from shivering, and he felt so weak and anxious.

He looked at his wolves, lounging on all fours. Pain, its gray tail twitching as its infected tongue lapped Ares' blood from the floor. Famine with its skinny snout resting on its bare paws. Panic pacing a red line through the room. And Oblivion, barely visible in the shadows. They didn't look half as ashamed as they should be for failing him. He'd sent them on an easy job. Kill the boy hero as the Moirae ordered. And they'd failed. They hadn't even managed to kill the dog.

"I failed the Moirae on two fronts," he said. "Is that why they let me bleed out?"

"They won't let you bleed," Aphrodite said. "Mother won't let you bleed."

Ares clenched his fists. It was hard to be with Aphrodite sometimes, because of the madness. Her voice wasn't her voice. It was vacant. Nonsense. And he wished she'd clean his blood out of her dress. Not out of her hair, though. It raced through her gold hair like ribbons. That he liked.

"Hera's not your mother," he said. "She's mine. Like Athena is my sister."

Aphrodite threw her arms around his neck.

"Your most irritating sister," she said.

"When did she become so terrible? She wasn't always so bad." He pulled Aphrodite into his lap. "She defended me once, to our father. When he said I was his most hated child. And then she goes and says the same thing to me."

"Words, words, words," Aphrodite said. "Sticks, sticks, sticks. Stones, stones, stones."

Ares snorted. Yes. Athena had said it to get a rise out of him, and it worked.

"You're really in there today, aren't you," he said, and tapped Aphrodite's temple. She smiled, but her eyes were glazed as donuts. "I still understand you, through your babble."

Her brows knit, and she tensed, trying to concentrate. Sometimes she'd be herself for hours at a time. Sometimes she was nowhere to be found. And other times Aphrodite skated just below the surface, her beautiful, intelligent face drowning under the ice.

"It's all right," Ares said. Only he was beginning to suspect it wasn't. If the Moirae were truly the gods of gods, they would heal Aphrodite's mind. They would heal Hera's stone fist, or at least the stone parts that were less useful. But they didn't. And Hera still refused to let him see them, instead keeping them secreted in the heart of the mountain.

He kissed Aphrodite gently and pushed her hair behind her ear.

"Don't tell Mother," he said, "but I don't really want Athena to die. I don't really want to kill her." Gods shouldn't kill one another. They'd become desperate, grasping leeches, cracking each other open like the Titans had.

"Ares," Aphrodite whispered, "I know what's happening to me."

He wiped tears from her cheeks. "I know." Aphrodite was trapped inside her own rotting mind. "Don't worry. I said I didn't want to kill Athena. I didn't say I wouldn't." He called for Oblivion, and the wolf came on silent paws.

"Take the others," he said. "Go out hunting again. Don't come back without pieces of heroes."

The boy? Oblivion asked.

Blood leaked from Ares' back.

"No," he said. "The hell with the boy. The hell with the Moirae." Aphrodite hissed. "I want you to take a piece out of the prophetess. The so-called god killer."

He watched the wolves go, snapping at each other, standing up on hind legs, forelegs stretching in their sockets.

"You and I, Aphrodite, are going to see the Moirae. Right now."

15

HOMECOMING

Hermes finally let Andie use a sword. Sure, it was blunted, wooden, and designed for kendo, but when she held the weapon aloft, her grin took up half her face. Cassandra sat on the back patio, and watched them practice, listening to every "Ow!" and "Hey!" and "Not so hard!" She watched Andie feint and dodge. Even bogged down with protective gear, she was fluid and strong. Fast, sure, and well balanced. Nowhere near a beginner. Bruises painted her face, and streaks of early spring mud made her ponytail filthy. She looked at home in her skin.

Lux pressed his nose into Cassandra's thigh. Henry'd brought him along that afternoon, unable to bear leaving him behind, barred off on the ground floor. The poor dog couldn't climb stairs for another week, when his last stitches came out. Henry'd been sleeping on the downstairs couch with him.

But Henry wasn't by Lux's side now. He was in the mud with Andie. He and Calypso practiced one-armed moves and blocks. Like Andie, he learned faster than a normal student. He was stronger than an ordinary high school senior, too, and had better instincts. Like Andie, his muscles remembered.

In the yard, Calypso ducked Henry's arm and smacked him around a little, just for fun. He laughed.

"It's all games to you," Cassandra whispered. "All games, until the swords are real. Until Athena gets back, and gods come hunting."

Lux whined.

"What?" she asked the dog. "You don't think I'm being fair?"

But she wasn't, she supposed. Because it hadn't been a game to either Andie or Henry, since the wolf attack. Really, not since Aidan died. So what if they laughed? So what if they enjoyed themselves? She couldn't ask everyone to be as glum as she was. Heat tingled in her palm, and she drew her hand away from Lux fast. Not everyone could be as angry as she was, either.

Tires crunched up the thawing driveway, and Lux barked.

"Pizza's here," Cassandra said. Hermes blocked one of Andie's blows and snatched her sword away without any effort. Andie squeaked and rubbed her wrist. A lesson within a lesson: they were training to fight, but not to fight gods.

"Finally," Hermes said. "I'm literally starving."

Andie laughed. "Athena would say that's not funny."

"You guys get un . . . armored." Cassandra waved at them. "I'll go tip the driver." She opened the sliding glass door and went into the house, grabbing a small stack of cash off the table. She looked over the fives and tens a moment, wondering how much to tip. Was it a standard percentage of the bill, or based on the number of pizzas? Because the guy had to carry six.

When the front door clicked open, at first she thought she was hearing things. The clomping footsteps and sounds of bags dropped onto the floor didn't make sense until she heard Odysseus' voice. She tucked the money into her back pocket and walked into the entryway.

"You're back."

Odysseus smiled. "Don't sound so surprised."

"It's just—sooner—" she said, and stopped. Athena was there, dusty and robotic as usual. But behind her—

She'd never seen him up close. They'd never been on the same level, or looked at each other eye to eye. His face she remembered, and the wild blond hair. But not his eyes—so bright green and curious.

"I thought you were going to kill him," she said.

"Well I did, sort of," Athena said. "I need to talk to my brother." She slid around Odysseus, and Cassandra noted the limp. The sliding door whirred open and shut, and the sound of Hermes clapping her in an embrace was loud and happy. But Cassandra couldn't take her eyes off of Achilles.

"What happened?" she asked Odysseus.

"She couldn't kill him."

She couldn't kill him? What, did she have an attack of conscience? Impossible.

Odysseus read her expression and laughed.

"It wasn't like that," he said. "She didn't change her mind."

"Was she limping just now?"

"That's my fault," said Achilles. His voice was as surprising as his eyes: low and reasonable, laced with an Australian accent. "I'm harder to kill than she thought." He smiled, and she wished it reminded her of a wolverine, but it was only a smile. "Nice to see you again, Cassandra. It *is* just Cassandra now, right? You don't still go by Princess Cassandra?"

She glanced at Odysseus, and he raised his brows. So he was like them. He remembered their old lives.

"It's Cassandra, God Killer Great and Terrible now," she said. "What about you?"

"That's a mouthful. I'm just Achilles still. Or Achilles of the Swift Feet, if you want to get Homeric."

Odysseus clapped him on the shoulder.

"Try Achilles the Invincible," he said. "Athena tried her damnedest. But he just won't stay dead."

Achilles the Invincible. Cassandra the God Killer. The two weapons of fate stared each other in the eye.

"No wonder she brought him back."

Hermes peeked around the corner from the kitchen, staring slack-jawed at Achilles.

"Knock it off, will you," Athena said. "It's not like I brought home a bearded lady or a Fiji mermaid."

Hermes gave her a look and squared his shoulders before going to inspect Achilles up close. As he circled, he puffed up like a cockerel, bumping into Achilles a little and looking him up and down. Hermes. Alpha male.

"He's thinner," Calypso said, rubbernecking over her shoulder. "Hermes, I mean. We've been trying to feed him. But his clothes are looser and looser."

Athena breathed in vanilla and flowers. "Why don't you let *me* worry about my brother."

Calypso shrugged.

"I thought you were going to kill Achilles," she said.

"Why does everyone keep saying that?" Athena pushed

past Calypso. She rolled her cracked shoulder and felt pain in her foot, full of clotted, closing holes. At least it was the same shoulder Ares had stabbed. Small blessings.

"How are you?" Calypso asked. "You don't look well."

"That's a rude thing to say," Athena said. But Calypso hadn't meant anything by it. Besides, it was true. Athena looked like walking shit. She sucked air into her lungs. No feathers, but a suspicious, warm throb in her side told her they were up to something new. Her eyes zeroed in on the refrigerator. There had to be a beer in there.

"You brought him here."

Athena winced at Henry's voice. Of course he would be there. That's how her luck was going. Maybe she could wedge herself into the crisper drawer until he left. Behind her, Lux whined, and his black muzzle poked into the fridge to sniff at the cold cuts.

"He looks better," she said. She stroked the dog's ears. A growl rumbled through her fingers even as she fed him a slice of roast beef. "He doesn't trust me. Because you don't trust me." She looked up at Henry. "Sign of a good dog."

Footsteps sounded behind them, and Henry stiffened. Achilles. She tensed and got ready to intervene in case they decided to go for each other's throats. Henry wouldn't remember Achilles' face, of course. And Achilles hadn't seen Hector since the night he'd ransomed the body outside Troy. And by then it wasn't so much Hector's body as a ragged slab of meat, no matter what the poets said.

Achilles broke the silence. The corner of his mouth curled up.

"Ody was right," he said. "You're not him. You don't look a thing like him."

Athena narrowed her eyes. Henry was the spitting image

of Hector. Maybe Achilles was lying. Or maybe he was lying to himself. Either way, it seemed like a good thing.

"I don't remember anything," Henry said, and for a second Athena was ashamed of him. He sounded like a coward. But that wasn't fair.

"I know," Achilles said. "And that's good."

"I guess so."

Hector and Achilles in her kitchen. Their fates had twined together so tightly. And now they maneuvered them face-to-face again. Why? To bury old hatchets? Maybe in each other's backs.

The sliding door opened and closed around Andie. Her hair stuck to her forehead in sweaty black streaks.

"You're back so soon," she said. "We thought you were pizza. Who's this guy?"

"Andie, Achilles. Achilles, Andie." *You remember her. You killed her husband once.*

Andie stiffened and turned white. "What is he doing here?"

Cassandra and Hermes edged past Achilles, Hermes to linger near the wall, Cassandra to stand by her brother. Beads of sweat crept down the back of Athena's neck. Had the kitchen always been so small? She wanted to blow out the walls, let the late winter wind rush in and distract them with shivering. Where was Odysseus? And Calypso? Hermes caught her eye and made a face. *Tension in the mortal ranks,* that look said. *What are we going to do about it?*

But she'd just gotten off of a plane. Couldn't he think of something for once?

"Look." Achilles put his hands in his pockets. "I don't know what I'm doing here. I think I'm here to help you."

Andie stepped beside Henry. "We don't want your help."

"I've heard that before. But you need it."

"Why didn't you kill him?" Andie hissed.

Athena rolled her eyes. "Why don't you give it a try? He can't be killed. At least, not easily."

"He can't be killed?" Hermes snorted. "Great. Now even mortals are more immortal than we are." He sighed. "Well, he's pretty enough. What are we going to do with him?"

"He broke my arm," Athena said. "He can do worse to Hera and Ares. I figure, we use him like a bulldozer. It'll keep Cassandra a hell of a lot safer." Athena shifted her weight and caught sight of Odysseus and Calypso still in the entryway. Their heads were bent together intimately.

"A bulldozer?" Achilles said, and shrugged. "I've been called worse."

"Athena," said Andie. "He can't stay. He killed Henry."

"You don't remember that."

"But I know it."

"Hey," said Achilles. "I didn't kill any Henry. I killed Hector." He bared his teeth. "And Hector killed my friend. I should've killed him twice."

Hermes winced and raised skeptical eyebrows, but Athena waved him off. Yeah, yeah, it was a mess. Henry and Achilles would never be pals. But both weapons were there, in the same room. She had them both. Why couldn't anyone else see how everything was going according to plan? Why couldn't they see that it would be over soon? The war would be won.

She wished Odysseus were paying attention. He could defuse things when no one else could. But he was still lingering in the entryway with Calypso, her hand pressed to his chest.

"This might not work, big sister."

"It has to, little brother. It's *meant* to." And if Odysseus didn't get his ass into the kitchen soon, she'd be reduced to stomping her feet.

Achilles pulled his hands from his pockets.

"If you don't want me, you're welcome to die. Again. I'm an instrument of battle, but I don't need it. I sat out half a war in Troy and would've sat out all of it, had Hector not murdered Patroclus."

"That's a lie," Henry said.

"A lie on lots of counts." Odysseus walked in with Calypso behind him and threw an arm around Achilles' shoulders. "Your pride would've dragged you back sooner or later. And in war, there's no such thing as murder."

"We can't trust him," Andie said. "You know we can't. We should put him in a block of cement or something."

Achilles laughed. "You're brutal, girl," he said. "I like you. But I'd like to see you try."

Odysseus stood between them. "We can trust him. And we will. We're not on opposite sides anymore. This isn't Troy." He looked at Achilles, who nodded.

"This isn't Troy."

"Knock knock."

"Go away."

"But I saved you a slice of pizza." Hermes pushed a plate through the cracked open door and waggled it. Athena had been hiding in the darkness of her room for hours, not bothering to turn on a lamp when the sun went down, just trying to keep from hearing mortal drama and ignoring the throbbing of her mangled foot. Hermes flipped the light on and sat on the bed. He eyed her shoulder and leg, elevated on a pillow.

"You look rough," he said.

If she looked rough, he looked worse. Skin stretched across his wrist as he passed her the plate. She couldn't tell if the extra eating was helping at all.

But it might be slowing it down. Please, let it slow down.

"Here," he said. "Eat up. Sausage, bacon, and onion. I don't waste space with low-calorie veg."

She snorted and picked it up. "Hermes. There's a bite taken out of it."

"Well what did you expect?" He swooped in and stole another bite. "I only ordered six, and you brought home two extra mouths."

"This house is getting crowded."

"Well." Hermes lay back beside her. "We've got the space for one more boy. And such a pretty boy." A low fever radiated off him. He hadn't had it when she'd left, but they'd come and gone before.

"How are you feeling, brother?"

"Fine and finer," he said. "Don't worry about me." He gestured to the plate. "Eat that before I do."

She took a bite but barely tasted it.

"It'll be over soon, Hermes. The war. I promise."

He put an arm around her. "Why so blue? Suburban life getting you down?"

She rested her head against him. What had he said to her on the banks of the Green River, camped out on their way to find Circe's witches in Chicago? They were obsolete gods in a dying world. He wanted peace. Comfort in his final days. If she'd left him there by the river, he might've accepted dying and had months of wine and beauty and decadence. But they would win, and he would live. So there would be plenty of time for that.

When she looked at him, her eyes burned.

"What should we do, after it's over?" she asked. "Where

should we go? Rome? Firenze? Amsterdam? Anywhere. You name it, and we'll go. We'll drink it dry. Throw money in the air. Roll around in satin."

He laughed softly. "Someone's been watching too many music videos. Not that it doesn't sound nice." He stole a bite of crust. "First things first. We have the weapons. What now?"

"I don't know," she said. "Train them. Get them ready. It won't be long before Hera comes for Achilles. Her pride won't let me have him, too."

"Was that your plan all along?" he asked.

"No. My plan was that she'd come for us once she knew I'd killed him. But one is just as good as the other."

There was a knock, and Odysseus poked his head in.

"Am I interrupting?" he asked.

"Only if you have bad news."

"Just looking for blankets and an extra pillow." He walked in and opened the door to Athena's closet. Several quilts and a comforter still in the plastic sat on the top shelf, but there were no extra pillows. He grabbed a quilt and the comforter.

"For Achilles?" Athena asked.

"For me. I gave up my room to Achilles, and Calypso's already in the extra room. I'm riding the comfy couch."

"The couch?" Hermes asked, and made a face. "Why the couch? Athena's bed's more than big enough for two."

She shoved the plate of pizza into her brother's stomach. "So's yours," she said. "Get out."

Hermes rolled off the bed and paused at the door. "Alas, Odysseus and I already tried that in the rain forest." Odysseus laughed, and Hermes ducked out before Athena could throw a pillow.

"Here." She tossed it at Odysseus instead. "Take one of mine. I only have the one head anyway."

"Thanks." He headed for the door then stopped. "Fancy some company? I'm not really that tired."

"That's because you passed out cold most of the way from Sydney." She jerked her head toward the other side of the bed.

"Plane sleep isn't good sleep," he said, and got in beside her. After fluffing the pillows, he leaned back and yawned. So much for not being tired. "What's on the docket for tomorrow?" he asked.

"I want to see what Achilles can do. He broke my bone easy as looking at it. That impresses me. And he was so fast. . . ."

Odysseus narrowed his eyes. "Right. He's a real wunderkind. Oughtn't you better pay attention to the norms instead? You know, the ones who might actually get their heads cracked?"

"You and Andie and Henry will be ready," she said.

"I wasn't talking about me. I'm no weapon of fate, but I know how to handle myself."

"Fine. Andie and Henry, then. I think they'll be all right. Between me, Achilles, Hermes, and Calypso, we should be able to keep them covered. Maybe I'll put them on Ares' mutts and let them get a little payback."

"You're not the slightest bit worried?"

"What good does it do?" she asked. "Mostly I'm looking forward to setting Cassandra on Hera. Helping her drown Aphrodite for good measure. I wish Hermes had brought me something to drink with that pizza."

"Want me to go get something?"

"No. It's all right. It's not like I need it. Godly constitution and all." She laced her fingers behind her head. Underneath them, the house felt full to bursting with power. Gods and heroes, stuffed inside. And she lay atop it, ready to wield them.

"Did you know there's a desert mouse that produces its own water internally?" she asked. "Never has to drink a drop."

"Fascinating," Odysseus said. "Do they call it the God Mouse?"

"I don't think so. But they should." They sat quietly for a few moments. "I thought you were going to stay with Calypso."

"Why?" he asked. "Because you told me to? You can't tell me who to be with, Athena. Come to think of it, you can't tell me how to feel, either. But it was right godly of you to try."

"You're so difficult. Ever since you thought of that stupid Trojan Horse and became convinced of your own cleverness."

"Yeah, well. I am clever."

"Pride goeth before the fall, hero," she said. His eyes closed, and she let hers close, too.

"Where will you go, after the war is over?" she asked. "Back to London? I'd give you money, if you wanted to open a pub or buy Manchester United or something."

"Try Arsenal," he muttered. "I don't know. Thought I'd see what you were up to. We could wander the world again. Odysseus and gray-eyed Athene. Like old times."

Old times. Good times.

"I'd like that," she said.

"And sooner or later," he whispered, "I'll wear you down."

She let him drift off to sleep, and she lay there for a long time before going out onto the widow's walk. The night air was good and cold on her cheeks as she looked at him through the windows of her French doors.

"You'll never wear me down, Odysseus," she said. But as long as they were together, he would try. He would have no other love, and no other life. It was a nice dream to have, wandering the world with her favorite hero. But it couldn't be.

After the war was over, she would have to disappear.

16

THE DAYS OF HEROES

Athena twisted in front of the bathroom mirror and prodded the dark, reddening spot under her ribs. The feather buried inside hurt like an open wound. She pressed, and the quill rolled beneath her finger, down deep. It itched.

"You'll take your time, too, won't you, fucker."

She could cut it out and sew the hole closed. It would heal faster that way than letting it emerge on its own. But there was another, fluttering against the back of her tongue, and there'd be another after that. If she started plucking and cutting, she might never stop.

She wiped fog from the mirror and toweled her hair. Somewhere in the backyard, Achilles had already started training with Hermes and Calypso. Andie, Henry, and Odysseus would join them after school. Athena slipped her shirt over her head and gave the dark spot one last look. Would it turn into a disgusting, weeping sore? Probably. She only hoped it wouldn't hinder her in the fight to come.

When she went downstairs, Calypso was in the kitchen

drinking a glass of lemonade. A long, black bruise marred her right cheek. Achilles' work. She smiled at Athena through a cracked lip, and the blemishes didn't make her any less beautiful. How irritating.

"Taking a break?" Athena asked.

"I needed one. Achilles is quick, and stronger than me. How are you healing?"

"Fast."

Calypso raised her glass. "Can I get you something to drink before you start?"

"You're the guest here," Athena said. She ducked into the refrigerator and grabbed the milk. "Can I get *you* anything before I start?"

"I'm not a guest."

The urge to drink from the carton was strong. But that was stupid. She wouldn't mark her territory with milk drinking. She grabbed a glass from the cabinet.

"Your name's not on the mortgage, and you're not family."

"But if you asked me to leave, I wouldn't," said Calypso.

"So you're a squatter."

Calypso shook her head. "Why do I try to argue? I remember that day, on my island, when Hermes came and ordered me to give up Odysseus. Never mind that it was *my* island. Never mind that I loved him."

"He wasn't yours, Calypso. He had to go home."

"Excuses, excuses. You hate me even though I'm on your side. There's no winning with you."

"I don't hate you," Athena said. "I resent you. It's completely different." She drained her glass and wondered why she'd said that. Why she'd let Calypso bait her.

"You resent me," Calypso said quietly. "Because of Odysseus. Because I found him. Because I was with him." She paused, and her voice slipped lower. "Because you can't be."

What was that tone? Compassion? Or pity? Athena looked into Calypso's eyes, ready to knock them through the back of her pretty head. But she saw no malice. Had there ever been any there? She glanced over the nymph's brown, braided waves, her narrow waist and feminine curves. She was more beautiful than most goddesses, certainly more beautiful than Athena. But more miserable, too. She'd come so far for a boy who had left her with embraces, maybe with promises. And when she'd found him, he'd turned her away for someone else.

None of it was Calypso's fault. It hadn't been on the island, and it wasn't now. She only loved him, and try as she might, Athena couldn't despise her for that.

"I don't have any right to Odysseus," Athena said. "Do what you want." She walked past Calypso, gently, and that was it. The words hadn't choked her after all.

As Henry had predicted, the school held Odysseus back. The principal called him down to the office in the middle of first period and explained that he'd missed too many days to graduate. It was not, they made clear, an expulsion. They even offered to let him audit the rest of his classes.

"At least I can still keep an eye on you," Odysseus said. "Which was the whole point anyway." He tucked the official letter into his shirt pocket. "I can't believe they expelled me! Did you see this coming? With your—" He whirled his hand around at Cassandra's head.

"They didn't expel you," she said. "And no, I didn't foresee it. I didn't have to. But I did know you were going to wear that shirt today." She crunched through an apple on their way to her last class, Algebra III.

"Damned good thing I already finished school in London,"

he grumbled as they pulled up next to the door. "You coming along tonight? To watch Achilles train?"

"I want to see him," she said through her teeth. "And I never want to see him."

Odysseus flashed his most charming smile.

"Give it a month," he said. "You'll love him. And even if you don't, at least you can watch Hermes punch him in the face a bunch of times."

"I'll never love him."

"Come on. He might save your life." Odysseus touched her shoulder, and she shrugged away. No need for him to feel the hate-filled heat coursing all the way up her arms.

"Okay, okay," he said. "But remember. He died in the war, too."

"Yeah," Cassandra said. "But he liked it. It made him a legend."

Odysseus looked at her funny. Sort of cockeyed. "Huh," he said. "You just reminded me of someone."

"Who?"

"You. The old you."

Cassandra rolled her eyes.

"You're just pissed because I don't automatically take your word for it like everyone else does," she said.

"No, that's not it," he said, and peered at her close. "You haven't been quite right since that day in the jungle with Ares. It got to you, didn't it? All that blood under your fingers."

"I had to do it," she said.

He glanced down at her hands. She hadn't realized they were clenched into fists.

"And maybe it felt a little good, too," he said softly. "For all that anger to finally have somewhere to go."

Cassandra stared past him, at the wall. She didn't dare move, or make a face. Not in front of Odysseus, who always saw the truth behind her eyes.

"You been to see Aidan lately?" he asked.

"He's not really there."

"Where do you think he is, then?" Odysseus asked.

The question made her blink, too fast, wondering if Cally had told him about their conversation in Abbott Park.

"Gone," she said in a flat voice. "Timbuktu. The other side of the rainbow. Maybe he's not dead at all and living in Cleveland under an assumed name."

"Why Cleveland?"

"Because Cleveland rocks."

"Is that a joke? If it is I don't get it."

"Look," she said, "he's gone. I know he's gone." She stood her ground, and looked straight into Odysseus' eyes. After a moment, he stepped aside and let her into the classroom.

Hermes breathed hard, bent over with his hands on his knees. Sweat sparkled on his brow and dripped onto the thawing ground. He'd sparred with Achilles for an hour, about fifty-eight minutes too long for his liking. The boy was too fast and brutally strong. His reflexes and his balance were impossibly good, and not just for a mortal. The kid still stood, arms flexed. Small patches of sweat showed through his borrowed hooded sweatshirt, but that was it. He could go another ten rounds. Another twenty.

Of course, Hermes hadn't hit him. He hadn't even tried.

"I forget," Hermes said as he plunked down on the patio furniture opposite Athena, "is breaking this kid's arms or killing him on the menu? Because short of that, I'm not going to be able to put him down."

"I'm not sure," Athena said. "I guess you can if you want to. It's not like it would stick."

"Oi," Achilles shouted. "What are you two clucking about?"

"Breaking your arms and dismembering you," Hermes shouted back. "Got a problem with that?"

Achilles shrugged. "Won't be pleasant."

Hermes groaned and mimed choking him. "Care to tag in, big sister?"

"My foot and shoulder are only at eighty percent," she said. The foot and shoulder were an easy excuse. Really, she wasn't ready to tangle with Achilles again. "What are you belly-aching about anyway, Hermes? He hasn't even managed to hit you yet."

"Yeah, but if he does you'll be picking pieces of my pretty cheekbones out of the fence."

"It's only the first day." She supposed it wasn't fair, him out there dodging and walloping while she sat comfortably on patio furniture. She nodded at Calypso. "Help my poor brother out, would you?"

"Of course." Calypso stood and brushed dirt from her lap. On her last turn, Achilles had tossed her into the bare flower beds where she had landed on her belly. "But I don't know why you think two of us are going to fare any better."

"No," Hermes said. "No, no, no, no, NO! I need a break, and food." He stripped his sweatshirt off over his head and let his t-shirt ride up just far enough to give Athena a glimpse of his prominent ribs. She didn't say a word when he went inside to order.

The sun was high and bright in the sky that day; Aidan was helping them along by warming the joint into the low seventies. The strawberry spring threatened to become not so strawberry at all. Every last bit of snow had melted, even in the shadows at the corners of the privacy fence, and the thawed dirt made a nice soft place for Achilles to throw Calypso around. She made a grab for him and yipped like a surprised pooch when he tossed her through the air. Athena didn't stop smiling until Calypso landed and skidded into the side of the house.

"Nice one, Calypso," Athena said. She got up and hobbled exaggeratedly to the sliding door. "Keep at it."

"No doubt why Hera wanted him now, is there?" she said to Hermes after she closed the glass. "So strong, and he can't be killed—"

"He can probably be killed."

"No easier than we could be. And maybe he can't. Maybe if you tore off his head he'd sprout a new one. Or his body would resurrect itself and join the stumps back together."

Hermes lowered his phone in the middle of dialing Stanley's Wok. "You're disgusting. How many orders of chicken wings should I get?"

"Four. And get extra egg rolls for Cassandra. Sesame beef sounds good. Maybe pork skewers with lemon and vegetables."

"Got it." Hermes dialed. "The left half of the menu and extra egg rolls."

Athena listened to the first few minutes of the order before zoning out. Stanley's Wok would be in a rough spot in a few weeks, after Hermes was healed and had no more use for double orders of Double Happiness. Oh well. All good things came to an end. She glanced at the digital clock on the microwave. Almost time for the others to arrive.

"Keep them apart," she said.

"Keep who apart?" Hermes asked, clicking off with Mr. Hong.

"You know who. Achilles and Henry. I don't want them fighting each other. Not ever."

Hermes glanced out the window at the beast in the backyard. "It wouldn't be much of a fight."

By the time Odysseus, Cassandra, Andie, and Henry arrived, the food had been delivered. Of the four, only Odysseus filled his plate. The others picked at chicken wings and took tiny scoops of rice, afraid to train on full stomachs.

Across the table, Achilles ate most of the sesame beef.

"Dinner break's over," said Athena. She clapped her hands and got them up. "Back outside. Hermes, take Achilles again."

"Come on, are you serious?" he moaned.

"Don't whine. You're the one who can make him faster. He's more use to us if he learns not to take so much damage." Both muttered as they went out, Achilles about being glad to be of use and Hermes about what damage? But they both went. Calypso and Odysseus took Andie. Athena stepped subtly in front of Henry.

"You," she said. "You're the one I want."

"Me?" Henry asked. "Why me?"

"Because I want to see what you can do. You're here, when your other Trojan brothers aren't. There must be a reason."

Henry swallowed. "What, am I supposed to be honored or something?"

"Cut the attitude." She reached down, scooped up a bō, and tossed it into his chest. "Makes you sound like a boy, instead of a hero."

"I am a boy," he said. He adjusted the bō in his hands and held it like a long spear. Yeah, he was a boy, all right. But he was a boy-hero. She mock charged him, and he used the end to pop her in the chest. He glanced at Achilles.

"Don't be distracted," Athena said. "Not by your hatred of him. Or your dislike of me."

"That's not it. I mean, I do dislike you. Him, I don't even know. Not really."

"So what is it?" she asked.

"I don't want him to think of me as Hector," Henry said. "I don't want him to decide he wants a rematch. Maybe you think that's cowardly."

Achilles hadn't stopped watching since Henry touched the *bō*.

"I think that's sensible," she said, "in a way that Hector of Troy never was. But, Henry, your remembering how to fight won't make him think of you as Hector any more than he already does." How could it, when Henry already looked exactly like Hector, from his height, to his stance, to his black hair and careful eyes?

"How do you know?" he asked.

"Because he's trying," she said. "He not the way he used to be. Consumed by glory and the hunt for immortality. Blinded by loss. It took a lot for him to not tear your head off in the kitchen that first night. But he didn't."

"Well, bully for him."

"Come on, Henry. It's a start. Now try to hit me in the face."

He exhaled and narrowed his eyes in concentration. But he didn't hesitate. She didn't know how to take that. The *bō* whirred past her left ear as she dodged.

"Again," she said, and he moved to strike. His body knew where to put its feet. His arms knew when to tense and when to give. "Keep at it. Show me how much you hate me. Hit me!"

He moved laterally and whacked her across the hip.

"I never said I hated you," he said, and went for her head again. "I don't."

"I know," she said.

"How do you know?"

"Easy." She grabbed the *bō* and shoved him back hard enough to roll him through the damp grass. "Because you let me pet your dog."

Henry regained his feet and smiled, just a little. When he came at her again she couldn't help being impressed. He was steady and strong. But it didn't matter how fast he learned or how much he remembered.

Achilles was fire and knives, rage and poetry. Achilles was slaughter. And Henry would never be his equal.

After a shower, Hermes shut himself inside his room and blasted music Athena didn't recognize, some kind of re-mixed electronica. He was pissed, she supposed, that he'd gotten stuck with Achilles all day. The hardest job. The only job that could really be called a job.

Athena stood over the stove. The steam from a massive pot of noodles basted her face. A decent vat of linguine with clam sauce would do for a peace offering. She didn't really know how to make it, but she'd lived in Italy long enough. She'd seen it prepared a thousand times. She stirred, trying to make her fingers cooperate. Even now they were too used to scavenging, or being served.

"I didn't know goddesses could cook." Achilles walked up behind her and peered into the sauce. He took a deep sniff of the white wine.

"I'm not sure this one can," she said, and glanced at her sink, which was full of hostile clams.

Achilles stretched.

"It feels good here," he said. "Like a camp. Or a compound. I can't wait to do it again tomorrow."

"And you could, couldn't you? You could do this every day."

"Of course. Can't the others?" His blond hair was wet from his shower, slicked back and hanging down his neck. His t-shirt clung to the muscles of his chest. He looked like a rogue or a male model.

"How old are you, Achilles?"

He ran his eyes over her body and stepped closer.

"Almost as old as you, Athena."

"Careful."

He chuckled. "Sorry. All the fighting makes me . . . amorous." He jumped onto the countertop. "I'll aim my affections elsewhere. No shortage of beauties here. Even that big girl, Cassandra's friend."

"Andie?" Athena asked. "You stay away from Andie. She's a biter."

"I could win her over. And wouldn't that be something, if I killed the boy in one life and stole his girl in the next. What would they say?"

Athena sighed. "How old are you, I said."

"I'm seventeen."

Seventeen. Two years younger than Odysseus. Four years younger than she and Hermes pretended to be.

"Have you always been this way?" she asked. "So strong?"

"I don't think so," he said. "Of course, you don't exactly jump off a building until you know you can. After I was killed that first time, I pushed it. There's not a lot you can't do, without that limit." He smiled. "But you know that."

"I used to know that."

"That's the last time you shower first," Odysseus said.

He walked into the kitchen with a towel around his shoulders. "Ran out of bloody hot water." He sniffed the air. "What's going on here?"

"Clam sauce," said Athena. "Well, probably."

"Right. Can you give us a second?" Odysseus said to Achilles. "I need to talk to her."

"Sure." Achilles hopped off the counter. "I'd be willing to give that sauce a try," he said. "Assuming there's any leftovers." He winked and headed for his bedroom.

"He really does get flirty," she said.

"What?" Odysseus asked.

"Nothing. What did you need to talk to me about?"

Odysseus stared suspiciously down the hallway. "Cassandra," he said. "She should train, like the others do. Learn how to defend herself if she has to."

"Anything she fights she can burn up with a touch. Besides, she doesn't want to."

"But—"

Athena shook her head quickly. "Never mind. You're right." Cassandra's powers weren't instantaneous. To use them she had to put herself in harm's way. She'd almost died facing Hera the last time, and this time would be worse. This time Hera knew their tricks. "She'll have to be convinced."

"No problem. I'll start with her tomorrow, after school. Which, by the way, I was expelled from." There was a surprising amount of heat in his voice, considering he'd never been seriously enrolled.

"Poor hero. Did the principal wound your pride?"

"Shut up."

"How soon can you have Cassandra ready?" she asked.

"Inside of a month, I'd say. She's no warrior, but if we focus on dodging . . ." He walked to the sink and poked at a clam. "You know you might lose some of them. Even with all this training."

"I don't know any such thing," said Athena. "You want to chop those tomatoes?"

"I know you have a plan," he said. "And I know you can lead an army. But even the best-laid plans can unravel."

Athena handed Odysseus a knife. "Don't worry so much. It will all fall into place." A chill ran down her back as she spoke. He could be right. Even if the Fates were on their side, that didn't mean they would all make it. Their first victory had cost them Aidan. And when she'd faced Ares in the jungle it had cost a tribe of men.

But that was my fault. My mistake. I won't make another one.

"What smells so delicious?" Calypso asked. She walked into the kitchen, clean and freshly dressed in dark jeans and a light, form-hugging sweater.

"You going somewhere?" Athena asked.

"Cassandra and the others invited me over to watch a movie. Are you coming, Ody?"

"Yeah." He handed the knife to Athena and left without a backward look. Athena listened to the Dodge kick to life. Tires rolled down the driveway, and the house felt suddenly empty.

Calypso had been there less than a month, and already they welcomed her into their group as a friend. Already they trusted her. Because she'd saved them? Or because she wasn't a god?

"It doesn't matter," Athena whispered. She wouldn't have gone anyway, even if they had asked.

She stood for a few moments and let the pasta steam her face. Then she walked to Hermes' bedroom.

"Hermes, I'm making . . . something." She knocked on

his door. "Will you come out and pretend to eat it?" She waited, trying to discern sounds of movement above the techno thump. He couldn't be giving her the silent treatment. Hermes didn't even know how the silent treatment worked.

Farther down the hall, light shone through the crack of the bathroom door. The shower was on. She smiled. Any moment he'd come flying out, bitching up a storm about the lack of hot water.

Something in the bathroom crashed to the floor. It sounded like a bag of baseball bats dropped onto cement. Or a thin body tumbling against hard tile.

"Hermes," Athena gasped. The bathroom hinges and lock didn't stand a chance. The door cracked and gave way. She stood in the frame and moaned, hands clapped over her mouth.

"Get out. Get out!" He scrambled to get his legs underneath him, not much more than bruises and bones. Dark marks covered his stretched skin. She could see every rib. Every bump of his sternum.

"Get out!" he shouted. "Don't look at me!"

She took half a step back, to mind her own business, to hide behind useless noodles. But then he crossed his arms over his face. Her brother feared her eyes like a vampire feared daylight. She wrenched his robe off the wall hook. When she draped it over his shoulders she braced for an elbow to the face, but instead he leaned into her and let her hold him tight. Heat from his fever bled into her cheek and chest.

Hermes cried, naked and shivering on the floor. Footsteps sounded across the carpet: Achilles, coming to investigate. Athena leaned and turned the broken door closed before he could see in.

"Everything all right in there?" he asked.

"It's fine," she said, and squeezed Hermes tight while he held his breath. "Trying to figure out the hot water."

"Okay. Well . . ." Achilles didn't say anything else. After a moment his footsteps moved back down the hall.

"Trying to figure out the hot water?" Hermes sniffled.

"I didn't hear you coming up with anything." She spoke through her teeth, her chin resting against the top of his head. "How did you hide this?" she asked. "How did I not know how bad you were?"

"I know how to dress. I've always known how to dress." His voice sounded better already. Clearer. She shut her eyes.

I make every excuse, use all the right words, to make him seem fine. How his fever is lower. How his eyes are bright. I stuff him full of food. Like it helps. Like it matters. Like he isn't going to die.

He tried to gather himself up, and adjusted the robe to slide his thin arms into the sleeves.

"This is humiliating," he said. "I look disgusting."

"No you don't. You could never."

He *hmph*ed. "I think they call this phenomenon 'sister goggles.' What are you doing in here, anyway? Ruining my ice-cold bath?"

"I made you something to eat." The words barely made it out before she broke, and tears streamed down her face. She clung to him, and he stroked her hair and let her cry, even though her weight had to hurt him, thin as he was. He hurt all the time, every day. She didn't know what she would do, when his skin started to tear. Would it be in one place? Or all over?

"I don't have much longer, sister," he said.

"No." Athena shook her head, furious, and wiped her

eyes. "You do. If Hera can heal, then so can you. If she has a way, I'll take it. I'll take it and pour it down your throat. You'll live, and she'll die."

He hugged her tighter. "Don't hope too much." He brushed her hair back, and she looked into his face, handsome despite everything. Like his vanity was strong enough to force his illness to stay below his chin.

"You should have told me," she said.

"So you could worry more than you already do?" he asked. "No. I just wanted time. Normal time."

"Why did you let me pit you against Achilles all day? You idiot."

"Bah," he said. "I can still take that kid."

But he couldn't. Not anymore. His time was up. She had to make her move, and make it fast.

17

NEVER LOOK A GIFT WOLF IN THE MOUTH

Cassandra's shoes crunched through the receding snow of the cemetery. She pressed her heel down, and it sank an easy two inches into mud. She thought of the coffins, all buried beneath the thawing ground, and wondered if they were waterproof, or if the water seeped through the weaker ones and dripped onto the decaying bodies inside.

"Do you have anything to drink?" she asked Calypso. "I suddenly feel like retching."

Calypso handed her a bottle of cherry vitamin water. It coated her throat and swished away the grave dirt. Across the cemetery, workers labored with shovels and a small Bobcat. The edges of their spades cut through the earth like butter. What a good day to bury someone.

"Thanks for coming with me," Cassandra said. Aidan's grave wasn't too far ahead, a few headstones away from a large tree. "It keeps Athena off my back."

"You really don't like her," Calypso said.

"You do?"

"No. But I understand her."

Cassandra eyed Calypso quietly. She was so beautiful, and there was a sweetness to her that made the beauty impossible to resent. Odysseus thought she was maybe a bit manipulative, but Cassandra didn't see it. Cally was dying, like the others were, but she didn't carry any of the desperation that they did. Though maybe she would, when her hair turned gray and her forehead wrinkled.

No. Calypso wasn't there to live forever. She was there for Odysseus. That much was plain.

They stopped in front of Aidan's grave, and Calypso put her hand on the stone.

"It's warm," she said. "Aidan. A good, modern name. Maybe I should choose one for myself."

"Odysseus calls you 'Cally.'"

She smiled. "He does." She gestured over Cassandra's shoulder at the bare branches of the broad tree. "That tree will never bear leaves again. The buds will fall dead to the ground this spring. I wonder if it knew."

The tree looked fine. No signs of rot or disease.

"How can you tell?" Cassandra asked.

"I can't tell," Calypso replied. "But I know. Aidan won't allow the shade. The same way he won't allow snow on this stone."

"Don't say that."

"Why not?"

"Because I don't like to think of him . . ." Cassandra paused. "As being under the ground. As being there."

"He isn't there. He is somewhere else. I didn't mean that he was in that box. Only that some things are strong enough to leave pieces behind."

"Pieces." Cassandra frowned. "You're not good at saying comforting things."

Calypso's laugh dragged a smile out of Cassandra from somewhere down deep.

"I know," she said. "I haven't lived with humans as long as Athena and Hermes have. I think it's made me strange. If I wasn't strange to begin with."

"I don't think you're strange," Cassandra said. "I start training today. Hand-to-hand stuff. I'd like you to be the one to do it, if you're willing."

"I think Odysseus wants to train you."

"You or him, then," said Cassandra. "Or Hermes."

"So, just not Athena."

"Not Athena, and not—"

"Achilles!" The way she said it, Cassandra knew Calypso wasn't just finishing a sentence. His shoes squelched as he walked the last yards to where they stood.

"What are you doing here?" Cassandra asked.

"I wanted to see him," he said. "The god beneath the ground." He stared at the headstone as if it were a museum exhibit, and it made Cassandra want to tear her skin off. Her palms began to tingle and itch, but the tingle couldn't do anything to Achilles besides make him nice and toasty warm.

"It doesn't seem right," he said. "This small marker when he used to have temples."

"We should have brought wine," Calypso agreed. "To pour out a proper libation."

Achilles gestured to the bottle in Cassandra's hands. "Maybe he accepts libations of vitamin water now."

Libations. Godly talk from a godly hero and a nymph. They didn't really know whose grave they stood at. They didn't know Aidan at all.

"Stop it," Cassandra said. "He's not a god. He doesn't accept offerings of anything anymore."

Achilles stuffed his hands into his pockets.

"You should have come another time," Calypso whispered to him.

"I wasn't sure what the right thing was," he said. "What seemed more respectful. To come when she was here, to show I cared—"

"You don't care," Cassandra said. "Everyone else is fooled by you, but not me. Even though they know I'm the prophet, no one listens. My curse is still at work all these years later. You'd think I'd be used to it."

"I don't blame you," Achilles said. "My face is the face you remember killing your brother. Just like Henry's is the one I remember killing Patroclus."

"You didn't—" she said, and shut her mouth. She'd been about to say, *You didn't actually see that*, but she stopped herself. That was an assy thing to say, even to Achilles.

"We only do what the Fates ask of us, princess," he said. "You and me both."

"Don't put us in the same sent—" she said, and Calypso screamed.

Cassandra barely had time to whirl before the black wolf sprang and took Calypso down to the ground. Then Achilles had Cassandra around the waist, half-dragging and half-carrying her through the cemetery.

"Stop," she shouted. "Let go!" She pushed at his hands, but he might as well have been made of steel for all the good it did. The ground whipped by so fast. They were beside the family Jeep in less than a minute.

"What was that?" she asked. "Cally . . ." She remembered a flat sound as Calypso had collapsed: her head striking Aidan's gravestone. "You have to go help her!"

"I can't leave you," Achilles said. Snarls echoed through the cemetery. Calypso shrieked. "That was one of Ares' wolves. Just one. They travel in four."

"Take me back there, damn it! I stripped Ares' back down to bones, what do you think I can do to four puppies?" She took a surprised breath. She'd been so angry she'd been screaming through her teeth.

"Shit," he muttered. "If anything happens to the other weapon . . ." He took her by the shoulders. "Get in the car and stay there, do you understand? And get Athena here. Now."

He opened the door and stuffed her inside. She pulled out her phone and texted Athena with trembling fingers.

She peered through the rows of headstones, trying to see Achilles and Calypso. Cally would be okay. The wolves wouldn't give Achilles any trouble. Even if they managed to kill him, he'd just get back up again.

A few minutes passed. Exactly how long she couldn't say. She remained in the Jeep, clinging to the steering wheel with hands hot enough to hurt, trying to fight off waves of rage so strong they felt like nausea. And then Achilles jogged through the cemetery with Calypso in his arms.

"Cally," Cassandra said, and opened her door.

"Stay inside!" Athena shouted through the window of the Dodge as she and Odysseus squealed into the parking lot. She jumped out before the car stopped and pointed at Cassandra with a stern finger.

"Geez!" Cassandra said. "Odysseus, what did you do, drive through yards? I just texted like four minutes ago."

"Yeah, it was fast," he said. "Cally, Jesus!" He ran over

and took her from Achilles. Blood streaked her jacket and sweater, bright red. The wolves had slashed at her cheeks and bitten her shoulders and hands.

"I'll heal," she said, leaning against him. "It won't scar."

"Of course it won't," Athena said, her voice equal parts comforting and bitter. "The wolves. Where are they?"

"They ran," Achilles said. "When I threw the white one into a tree."

"They ran," Athena said, and grabbed him by the arm. "So we chase." Without another word, they took off together, and they didn't stop no matter how loudly Odysseus called.

"What are you up to?" Achilles asked, but Athena didn't answer. If he wasn't an idiot, he'd figure it out.

She sniffed the air, scanning the larger grave markers, and the trees, anywhere a pack of wolves might hide. Then again, they might scatter. But that was all right. She only needed one.

Ares, Ares, Ares. My idiot brother. What were you thinking, sending them after us when you knew I was here?

But she really didn't care. The wolves were a gift, and much like gift horses, you didn't look them in the mouth. A flash of red fur, flicking fast like a fox tail, darted toward a copse of trees on their left.

Excellent.

"Go!" she shouted to Achilles, and he took off, cutting off the wolf's path of escape so she could come in from behind. As they closed in, she noted that it was the twitchy one. Panic. Maybe the most annoying wolf, but no matter. She wasn't picky. The other wolves would sing like canaries to Ares and Hera. They'd tell them all about Achilles. She hoped it drove fear deep into their bellies. Fear, like icing on her cake. But, it didn't really matter what they felt. Because while the other wolves sang, this one would lead them right back to its master.

"Take it alive," she said.

18

EXHIBITION

They kept the wolf chained in the basement. It refused to talk. It refused even to stand up on two stretched hind legs and pace. Panic quivered and twitched and looked as sad as any wild animal on an eight-foot leash.

"Talking wolves," Andie said. "Just another fine day in godland." She stepped closer to Henry, and he put an awkward hand on her shoulder.

"It's weird knowing one of those things is right underneath our feet," he said.

According to Odysseus, Athena had brought the wolf home in a sack, like a huntsman. He said that she and Achilles had looked positively triumphant.

"What's the rush all of a sudden?" Henry asked. "None of us are ready."

"She won't say," Odysseus replied.

Across the room, Hermes fidgeted and cleared his throat. "Maybe she just sees an opportunity," he said quietly.

"For what? A new pet?" asked Cassandra. "Someone needs to talk to her."

"Why not you?" Achilles asked. He came out of the kitchen with a metal bowl and held it out. "Here. You can take this down for me."

"What is it?" she asked.

"Raw, room-temperature hamburger."

"Gross."

Cassandra walked down the hall and opened the door to the basement. The red wolf's growl reached most of the way up the stairs, a jittery, unearthly sound that made her shudder. But when she saw it chained in the corner, crouched down on all fours and shaking, she almost felt sorry for it.

"Staring contest?" she asked Athena, and the goddess turned, surprised.

"Something like that," Athena said. "You might not want to get too close."

"Is it dangerous?"

"Not right now. Can I have that?"

Cassandra handed over the bowl. It sort of smelled, a little bit bloody, rotten, and unpleasant. Or maybe that was the wolf. There wasn't much ventilation in the basement.

"Are you hungry, Panic?" Athena asked. "Of course you are. You're always hungry. So tell me where your dad is, and you can have some uncooked burgers." She wafted the meat under Panic's nose and waited.

Nothing. Not even a whine. She tossed the bowl onto the floor, and the wolf dove on it, swallowing the meat in huge, mushy chunks.

"I think you're supposed to withhold the food longer," Cassandra said.

Athena sighed.

"I don't want to torture it," she said. "I'll figure something else out. But it will lead us to Hera and Ares, one way or another."

Panic finished eating and began to pace back and forth, fast. Its red brush tail twitched with a maddening lack of rhythm.

"Why don't we just let it go and follow it?" Cassandra asked.

Athena glanced at her.

"You're in as big a hurry as I am," she said.

"Well, yeah. You think I don't know that where we find Ares, we find Aphrodite?"

Cassandra cocked her head at Panic.

"It looks plenty scared," she said. "It'd probably run right home."

"Yeah," said Athena. "It looks pretty scared. Except it knows exactly what you're saying and can stand up on two feet and talk. It's not a regular wolf, Cassandra. It'd be more than happy to lead us on a merry chase all the way to Indonesia."

They'd held the wolf hostage for two days. Long enough for Calypso's cuts to almost completely disappear, and long enough for Athena to run out of patience.

"Speaking of hurries," Cassandra said, "why *are* you in such a hurry all of—" She paused. Her nose tingled, like she was about to sneeze. But instead the tingle turned to a burn. Smoke rushed into Cassandra's eyes, and she doubled over, coughing, her eyes watering buckets. The basement cement burned up in flames and ash. All the walls. Even the floor. Someone screamed. Not her. Not Athena, either. The voice was raw and full of panic. On fire. Cassandra whimpered, and Athena caught her as the flames ate the last of the oxygen in the room.

Cassandra woke up on the living room sofa smelling like a campfire, and underneath that, like burnt human flesh. Her clothes were ruined. All the Febreze in the world wouldn't take that stench out.

"Here," Hermes said to Athena, and handed her a steaming mug.

"Cassandra," Athena said. "Sit up. Take a few sips of this."

The heat of the tea burned over Cassandra's lips and down her throat, nowhere near as hot as the smoke. Athena touched her cheek with the backs of her fingers and brushed her hair over her shoulder, the way Odysseus sometimes did.

"Tell us what you saw."

A vision. Like so many others. Death and destruction. People in flames. Vague, maddening flashes full of blood and smoke and never once any useful detail.

"A fire," she said. "Something's going to burn. And someone. Lots of someones."

"Someone?" Andie asked. "Who?"

"Just go over it from the beginning," Athena said.

Go over it from the beginning. Athena sounded so calm. Like she really thought it would make a difference.

In one fast, sweeping motion, Cassandra threw the mug of tea into the opposite wall. It shattered, and Athena jumped backward, dragging Hermes and Calypso back with her. Beware, beware, the tantrums of a god killer.

"Sorry," Cassandra muttered. "The tea tasted like burnt people."

"Hey," Odysseus said. He moved closer and put his hands on her shoulders. "Easy. Take a few minutes. It's okay."

"I don't need a few minutes," Cassandra spat. "Why

aren't we training? Or interrogating the red dog some more?"

"Cassie," Henry said.

"Don't fucking *Cassie* me, Henry."

"But why won't you tell us what you saw? Was it that bad? Was it one of us?"

"I don't know," she said. "And it doesn't matter. I saw it, so it is. You, or me, or Andie, I don't know. But if it was us then we burn. Let's go." She stalked toward the backyard.

"We could try," Athena said, without much enthusiasm.

"We can't, and you know it. The only way to stop more of this is to stop all of it. To stop the source. So come on."

Calypso volunteered to babysit Panic.

"See if you can charm some secrets out of its head while you're at it," Athena said.

"And don't get too close," said Odysseus. He touched her arm and her cheek, all but healed. Jealousy and bitterness balled up in Athena's throat.

"Tastes like shit," she whispered, so quietly that only Hermes heard. He squeezed her shoulder as she led them outside. The light was fading, the air heavy and chilled with mist. They didn't have long. The mortals would catch a cold.

"Come on then, Hermes," Achilles said, and stretched his arms like a lazy cat.

"No." Athena tossed him a *bō*. "You're with me." There would be no more marks on her brother's limbs. No more bruises, if she could help it. "Hermes, coach Henry and Andie. Odysseus, you're with Cassandra."

Hermes tossed Andie her wooden kendo sword. But as they walked into the yard, every eye lingered on Athena and Achilles.

"You and me?" Achilles smiled. "I'm flattered. Honored."
He dropped the *bō* and let it clatter against the cement patio.

"Pick that up," she said.

"I don't want the distance between us."

Athena circled. "We've done that before. I broke your neck."

"Right. And if you do it again, it'll cause a three-second delay in the action." He sprang and struck her in the face.

Odysseus said they should practice the only thing Cassandra would find useful against a god: dodging. For several minutes he stood across from her and threw punches at half-speed, all the while listening to Athena's and Achilles' fists.

"I'm fine, you know," Cassandra said. "You don't have to treat me with kid gloves."

"I'm not treating you with kid gloves," he said. "But that vision had to take a little wind out of your sails."

"Not all the wind. These punches are pathetic." Even when she didn't dodge fast enough, the blows landed with as much authority as a tossed pair of socks.

"Fine. How about some holds, then?"

He twisted to demonstrate, and she elbowed him in the nose.

"Ow."

"How about you pay attention?" she asked.

"I am."

"To me. Not to Athena and Achilles."

It was a lot to ask. Athena and Achilles slammed into the side of the house, and it shook to the foundation.

"They're pulling their punches," Odysseus said.

"How do you know?"

"If they weren't, that wall would've caved."

He was probably right. They should keep away from the house altogether before they cracked something important. Achilles pulled Athena in close, her back to his chest. He whispered something into her ear, and she smiled.

"He's been pulling her in like that a lot," Cassandra whispered to Odysseus.

"I've noticed."

"Jealous?" she asked. "Threatened?"

The storm clouds vanished from Odysseus' face. He flashed his typical Odysseus smile, and went for weapons.

Athena shifted her feet. The boy kept her on her toes. So much power, encased in mortal skin. A human being who could stand against gods. But she would save the philosophical questions for later. Achilles demanded all of her concentration. Even when he held back.

Of course, she held back, too.

"So, what do you think?" he asked.

"That your tale hasn't grown much in the telling," she said.

"Would you be angry if I made you bleed?" He wiped at his mouth with the back of his hand and left a wet, red streak.

"No. But you aren't likely to."

He looped an arm around her neck and twisted her close. The muscles of his forearm squeezed her throat like a constricting snake.

"Your bones are steel," he said admiringly. "Fat chance of me breaking your neck like you did mine." He let her go a fraction of an inch and placed his free hand on her hip. "But I think I've found a weak spot." His fingers slipped up her waist, underneath her shirt.

"Enough!"

Athena jerked loose as Odysseus shouted. Achilles had been going for the feather working its way out underneath her ribs.

"It is," she said. "I want to see how Cassandra's progressing."

"Not so fast," said Odysseus. In his hands he carried two swords: thick and short bladed, like the ones they'd used in their last life. He tossed one to Achilles. "It's been awhile."

Achilles shook back his blond hair. The sword flipped in his palm. "Feels familiar."

"Those aren't practice swords," Hermes said. "They're sharp enough to dice a tomato."

But of course Odysseus would know that.

"It's okay, Hermes," said Athena. "It's only play. Two old friends sparring. Right?"

"Like we used to," Odysseus said. Except back then Achilles hadn't been truly invincible. Back then he'd been just a boy.

"Blunt swords would be just as good," Hermes said, but Athena shushed him. She wanted to know who would swing first. What tricks Odysseus would use.

The swords clashed once, hard. Andie flinched at the sound, and Henry nudged closer to her. The two fighters grinned. Achilles slashed and drove Odysseus back; Odysseus parried and spun away to give himself fresh space.

"Careful," Achilles said. "No armor."

Odysseus laughed. "What? Afraid of a few scars?"

They fought, and talked, and never drew the slightest blood. It was all for show, but Andie gasped and held Henry's arm so tight it was about to turn purple. Achilles cut the air inches from Odysseus' face, and Odysseus arched backward just right.

"They look good together," Hermes said. "Your heroes."

"Yes," Athena agreed. "They do."

Odysseus' lines were beautiful. He kept his pacing erratic to keep his opponent off-balance, and even though it was Achilles he fought, Athena couldn't keep her eyes off him. He could've been fighting the Chimera. To her, Odysseus was always the only thing worth watching.

If this is how Aphrodite feels every day, I envy her.

"Lose the shirts!" Hermes catcalled, and Odysseus glanced over. Achilles didn't, and Odysseus jerked quickly to maintain his block.

Too quickly. The block was twenty times as fast as Henry or Andie could have done it. It was closer to Hermes' speed.

Athena's eyes narrowed.

"All right," she said. "That's enough. Exhibition over." The swords lowered, and they clapped each other on the shoulders. Odysseus returned to Cassandra.

"That was impressive," Cassandra said. "But next time why not save the sweat and just pee around her in a circle?"

Athena's skin crackled. Pee around her in a circle? Like she was a tree a dog could claim? Exhibition, indeed. A show for Achilles, so he knew how things stood.

"What time do we start tomorrow?" Hermes asked.

"We don't."

Everyone paused.

"That's it," she said. "You know what you know. You're as ready as you need to be."

"But couldn't we be, I don't know, readier?" Andie asked.

Athena looked at Achilles. Then Cassandra. Two weapons, fully loaded. Surely she wasn't the only one who saw that.

Hermes crossed his arms, and the bones moved beneath his clothes. His lovely bones. Ready to tear through the skin.

"Time grows short," Athena said. "I'll crack that wolf soon, and then we go. There's nothing more you can learn here."

She bent to pick up their equipment as the first fat drops of rain fell. Polite weather, to wait until they'd finished.

"Well, I'm not sleeping tonight," Andie said. "Anybody want to rewatch all of the Harry Potter movies?"

"I'm down," said Henry.

"I'll get Cally," said Odysseus.

"Let me." Hermes walked into the house. "I'll relieve her wolf-watching duty."

Andie, Henry, and Cassandra started to follow, and Henry stopped short at the sliding door.

"Achilles," he said, and paused. "Did you . . ."

"No, he didn't," Cassandra said. She grabbed Henry by the arm and dragged him inside.

Achilles chuckled and leaned down to help Athena with the weapons.

"She's a tough one," he said.

"No, she's not," said Athena. "But she's getting there. Pretty damn big of Henry to invite you over for popcorn. Don't you think?"

He flashed a killer smile. "A bit bigger than I am, yet."

"Why's that? I killed you not a month ago, and you don't hate me."

"I would, if you'd killed someone I loved."

Fair enough. But given enough time, blood enemies may yet become friends. It was on her, she supposed, to give them the time.

She looked through the glass as Calypso came upstairs and grabbed Odysseus by the hand, smiling and tugging him toward the door. So damn pretty. So maddeningly sweet. Odysseus dragged his feet half a second and looked back at

Athena, who bent quickly to pick up an imaginary practice sword.

She let the cold rain run down her back in icy rivers as their cars drove away. Let it make her feel wild, instead of chained. Defiant, instead of foolish and love-struck. Instead of so heavy with sadness and plain old dumb loneliness that she couldn't breathe.

"Don't let them bother you," Achilles said. He shouldered the weapons. "They can watch their movies and have their laughs. They're not like us. They never will be."

"Not like us." Athena took a breath. The world smelled like it wanted to freeze again.

"I like Odysseus," he said. "Always have. But he never understood the point of it all. The glory."

"He understood it," she said. "His glory just wasn't the same as yours." And Odysseus understood something else, too. Strategy. Secrets. That speed he hid in his arms. And strength, too, probably. Achilles hadn't noticed, but she had. That one little move. That one mistake.

"Nah," Achilles said. "Ody's only a man. Not like me. Not a demigod, half-divine and growing by the minute."

"True," Athena whispered.

So how does he have that speed?

19

MOIRAE IN THE MOUNTAIN

Ares hesitated with his hand on the doorknob. But he'd made it this far, so deep into Olympus that he could no longer tell whether they were nearer the summit or the belly. Right up to the Fates' door. The Moirae. Clotho, the spinner of life. Lachesis, the weaver of destiny. Atropos, the shears of death.

Aphrodite placed a hand on his.

"I won't stop you," she said. "But take care. They're weakened. But they're still our gods."

"Hera's inside," he said. Half-question and half-deduction. He hadn't seen her in almost a day. And Olympus, despite its endless size, had few places where a god could truly disappear.

He pushed the door open, and a strong draft of herbal smoke hit him in the face. Braziers. Hera must've burnt herbs of offering. Or maybe she'd burnt them to cover the smell. Decay, sweet and sinister, clung to the walls, and not the smell of a rotting battlefield, the kind Ares enjoyed. This was the scent of sickness.

His eyes swept over the marble floor. Hera lay near one of the gold braziers, her eyes open, sweat on her chest and face.

"Mother!"

"Ares?" she asked. Her arms trembled against the stone floor. He picked up her granite fist to stop the rattling.

"What happened?"

"Healing me," she whispered. Stone molars clacked against her upper teeth as she shivered. "Trying."

They must not have tried that hard. Aside from a slight softening on her neck, she seemed worse: in more pain, feverish, and exhausted. Silk rustled behind them. He thought it was Aphrodite, finally brave enough to come inside, but Hera braced herself and pushed up onto her elbow, her eyes wide and terrified.

"Smile," she whispered.

"What?"

"Smile," she hissed. Her lips stretched as well as they could, pulled taut against her stone jaw. "They like it when we smile."

"I don't smile," Ares said. "I look ridiculous."

(ARES)

The voices hit the center of his brain like a truck. Hera cupped her hand under his chin to catch the blood that fell from his nose. He put his palms to his ears, but it didn't matter. The voices weren't in his ears.

(JUST FOR YOU)

The voices backed off by decibels. Because they could. Now that he knew what they were capable of.

(WE WOULD BE GENTLE, BUT WE KNOW YOU LOVE THE BLOOD)

"Not my own blood," he said. "Or at least not as much." He licked a little of it, strong and salty, and pressed his mother's hands together. The Moirae stood at his back, and suddenly he wanted to keep them there. To never, ever lay eyes on them, and rewind straight out of this hot, firelit room. He would forever lie happily wounded with Aphrodite on their ruined bed.

But it was too late for that. The Fates put their hands on his back, and an electric shock passed through his skin and through the blisters of blood Cassandra had burst. It burned. It sliced with more pain than when the girl had done it in the first place. Their fingers dug like insects, sharp legs burrowing and embedding into the muscle. No wonder Hera lay panting on the floor. If he hadn't been the god of war, he would have cried like a tiny baby.

"This is your healing?" he gasped.

(PRICES FOR EVERYTHING. THAT IS THE WAY. THAT IS THE LAW)

"The law is for me to feel every scrap and fiber stitching itself together?"

"Ares," Hera whispered, and he shut up. Because they could always make it worse. They could make it worse, and they could stretch it out. They could refuse to help him at all.

Sweat beaded on his lip, but he sat silent as a biker in a tattooist's chair. It would be over soon, and then he could wear shirts again without the fabric sticking to him the minute he put them on.

The Moirae worked for a long time. Twice he almost passed out from the pain. Every now and again he heard something sharp and metallic, like razors rubbed together: the shears of the Moirae, opening and closing. Not on his skin. They opened and closed in their idle hands, just an absent habit. Hera stayed with him as they worked, her flesh hand on his knee. Aphrodite hummed a soothing tune from the open doorway.

(THERE. ENOUGH)

He stretched his mostly healed back, reformed from ribbons into one piece. Yes. They were his gods. They decided what was enough. Even though his godhood called for more, for all, like it always did.

"Turn," Hera whispered. "Turn and thank them."

He didn't want to. He wanted to wave and jet the hell out of there. Leave a fifty on the brazier and promise to call them sometime.

"Yes, Mother," he said. At least the Moirae had moved away, receded to wherever they'd snuck up on him from. Better than turning around and finding his nose stuffed into their silk dresses. He imagined they smelled half-rotten.

The Moirae sat in a puddle of stitched-together fabric. Red, silver, and black merged in a sadly extravagant patchwork quilt to cover them up like old ladies. To hear Zeus tell it, the Moirae were three beautiful girls. Ivory cheeks and sparkling eyes. Curves and temptation along with wisdom and war. Clotho, the spinner of life, had red hair that flowed over her shoulders. Lachesis, the weaver of destiny, tantalized with silver-blond hair down her back. And Atropos wore her black braid long and thick.

At least Zeus had gotten the hair part right.

Lovely red hair hung down Clotho's back, and a mop of silver stuck to Lachesis. But they were wigs glued onto mummies. Clotho and Lachesis themselves were pale, withered husks, so thin and limp he would've thought them dead had the shears in their hands not opened and closed.

(WHAT DO YOU SAY)

Ares swallowed. He fixed his eyes on Atropos, the Moirae of death, the only sister who was still beautiful.

"Thank you."

(YOU ARE WELCOME, GOD OF WAR)

"You're ill," he said. Hera grasped his ankle, but he ignored her. The Moirae's illness was obvious. Clotho and Lachesis barely functioned. Their eyelids and lips drooped. Their shoulders slumped into Atropos. They breathed, and that was about it.

"Forgive him," Hera said, dragging herself half-upright. "He is in awe of you."

But to Ares' surprise, Atropos smiled. It was lovely and horrid, and he hid his shudder.

Atropos brushed her sisters' hands aside and tugged at the cloth that covered them until it fell away.

In the hall, Aphrodite began to cry. Ares could only stare.

Three voices melded into one. As three bodies melded into one. Five of six arms remained mobile. The fifth, one of Lachesis', had grown into Atropos' stomach. Clotho and Lachesis' hips and legs had merged with Atropos' and seemed to have broken, as if sucked inward, or as if pulled and knotted with string. Clotho and Lachesis were on the outside, with Atropos in the middle, and the sickness worked its way inward.

Ares looked into Atropos' eyes, black as ink and hungry, and wondered if it didn't work outward.

Clotho's head jerked. Her milky eye swiveled and fixed on his face, and all at once, he knew. The Moirae were the source.

The source of their deaths. Gods died as their gods fell ill.

"What do you want?" he asked.

(THE WEAPONS OF FATE. BRING THEM. NOW)

"The weapons of fate. Achilles and that girl. Athena has them both."

(BRING THEM)

"Easier said than done," he said, and the Moirae pierced

his mind hard in punishment. Fresh blood gushed down his chin, and a vessel in his right eye popped. Aphrodite and Hera whimpered. Oblivion whimpered, too.

"Oblivion!" Ares squinted at the wolf through the blood. It cowered on all fours. Behind it, Pain and Famine cowered as well. At the wolves' entrance, the Moirae backed off again and tugged their silk back into place. What a relief.

"Where's Panic?" Ares asked.

Took Panic, the black wolf answered. *Your warlike sister. And the boy killer of men.*

So Athena was already putting Achilles to good use. The bitch. He clenched his fists.

"They took Panic. But is Panic—?"

Alive. Yes. They torture Panic. They mean to be led here.

"Fools," he muttered. The red wolf would never talk. Never betray him. It would hold its tongue until they lost their temper and cut it out. Until they killed it. And if she killed it, Athena would pay. She would pay already.

Reluctantly, he turned back to the Moirae. They'd listened to Oblivion and become incensed or excited, writhing like snakes beneath the silk. Clotho's and Lachesis' pale heads jerked back and forth.

"I'll go," he said. "I'll get my wolf, and your weapons."

(YOU CANNOT. YOU HAVE FAILED)

"I haven't," he said. Though he had. Twice. "I won't. But I'm going to get my wolf." He thought of Panic, constantly agitated. Constantly afraid. "My sister," he said through gritted teeth, "needs a lesson on what she can and can't touch."

(NO. SHE HAS THEM BOTH. LET THEM COME)

"Not at the cost of my—" he said, and Hera rose and grabbed his shoulder.

"We will be ready," she said, and hauled him out like any mother might. She stopped just short of taking him by the ear. Aphrodite and the wolves trailed them, through doors and down hallways, until the Moirae were left far behind.

"Get off me!" He shrugged loose and called the wolves to him. Athena wouldn't get away with this. Even if the Moirae wanted her and their precious weapons for themselves. There was a price for offending the god of war. There was a price for everything. They'd just said so.

"Ares! Where are you going?" Hera hobbled after him. "Have you gone mad? You heard what they said!"

"I heard, Mother. And I saw. And I'm thinking that even *they* have limits now. So I'm going. Athena's earned herself some bloodshed."

20

BLOOD AND SMOKE

A late winter storm covered Kincade in eight inches of wet, white fluff overnight. Kincade High closed for the day, and Cassandra sat on the couch in the den, flipping through channels. Any minute, a special report would break through about a building blown up and gone down in flames. People dead and bodies to bury. But at least it would be over, and the uneasy feeling in her guts would go away.

She craned her head, trying to keep the screen in view as her mom dusted it for the umpteenth time.

"Mom, seriously. You've got, like, a cleaning complex today. And you're blocking the remote."

Her mom turned around and blocked as much of the TV as possible.

"I remember when snow days meant you and Henry would put on snowsuits and go make angels and snowmen in the yard. Now they mean two teenage slugs underfoot, saying, *What's for lunch,* and *I'm bored,* and *When are we going to get a snowblower.* Can't you go make me an angel or something?"

"I outgrew my snowsuit when I was nine."

"So use your dad's Carhartts."

"They smell like turpentine. Also, he's in 'em." Cassandra jerked her head toward the garage, where her dad continued work on the armoire. Now sanding, or maybe varnishing.

"Well," her mom sighed. "Talk to me while I clean, then. How's school?"

"Fine. They're holding Ody back."

"What? But he's so smart."

"Maybe he just doesn't apply himself."

"Or maybe he helps himself to extra days off with Athena, like you do," her mom said. Cassandra flipped the channel fast. "I still think we should've grounded you for your little spa day."

"You don't know how to ground me," said Cassandra. "I've been too good for too long. Henry, too."

Her mother started off on a tirade about what was and wasn't within her powers of punishment. It was easy, these days, to change the subject. To talk without really talking. She'd gotten good at it, so fast.

But it was better than the truth. The truth involved too many things no one would understand.

"I wish I could make you an angel," Cassandra said quietly.

"What?"

"I wish I could do anything that would make me feel not so powerless."

Her mom sighed and dropped the dust rag.

"You have a lot of strength in you, Cassie," she said. "All the strength in the world."

Cassandra flexed her fingers. "Yeah. All the strength in the world. But I still get dragged around like a"—she gestured broadly—"thing in a current."

"What are you talking about, honey?"

Her mom blinked big, open eyes. How Cassandra wanted to tell her. She wished for that magical mom-telepathy to kick in. *You're my mother, don't you know? Don't you know just by looking at my face?* But of course she didn't. It wasn't the kind of thing someone guessed.

On the TV, a special report broke in.

"Mom. The TV."

"Oh." Her mother reached down for the remote and turned up the volume. "What's happened now?"

The cameras panned over blackened, smoking buildings, some still in flames.

"A fire claimed at least three dozen lives in the early hours of the morning," said the news anchor. "At approximately seven oh five AM, firefighters responded to an emergency call in Bryn Mawr, Pennsylvania. They arrived to find the entire block engulfed in flames. It is unknown yet what caused the fire, and the names of the victims have not been released. Several houses were involved in the blaze. Most were fraternity houses."

"Henry." Cassandra pushed her hands into the hair at her temples. "Henry!"

His and Lux's footsteps pounded down the stairs. "What, Cassie?"

Their mother shook her head. "All those kids. Asleep in their beds, probably."

Asleep in their beds. Only if they were very, very lucky. Henry put his hand on Cassandra's shoulder. The news would get a lot more interesting as the day went on. Investigators would wonder how a fire removed victims' limbs. How it could bash in a skull or leave half a body in the kitchen and the other half in the dining room. They would wonder why none of the fraternity members had managed to make it out of the house, despite unlocked doors and ground-level windows. They would puzzle over a pile of bodies, neatly stacked eight deep, in an upstairs hall.

Athena met them at the door.

"Why'd you walk?" she asked.

"The Mustang's snowed in," said Henry.

"You saw?" Cassandra asked, and went inside. Odysseus, Calypso, and Achilles stood in the living room in front of the TV. "Where's Hermes?"

"In the basement with the wolf."

Cassandra gestured to the TV. "What is this? And who?"

Athena glared in disgust. "This is a message for me. From Ares. Killing young men. Athletes and scholars. Modern-day heroes I would have favored."

"Why?" Cassandra asked, and then eyed the basement. "Because you took his dog." She advanced on Athena, and Odysseus stepped into her path. "You didn't think of that?" she spat over his shoulder. "You didn't figure your psychotic brother would want payback?"

"I don't know anything he'll do," Athena said. "But last I heard, he preferred combat. Wars in Central America. Not this Ted Bundy shit."

"She thought he'd come at her directly," Odysseus said. "I thought so, too."

"Some excuse," Cassandra said.

They watched in silence for a few moments as reporters commented on the actions of emergency crews. How unfavorable road conditions might have hindered their response time.

Cassandra's fists burned. She turned to demand that Athena do something, but the goddess' eyes were already black.

"Get the wolf out of the basement," Athena said. "He wants it, so we'll bring it. Achilles, you're coming with me." She looked at Cassandra. "And so are you."

Getting the Dodge out of the snow-filled driveway wasn't a problem. Athena simply picked the back end up and dragged it until it was clear. She wiped ice off her fingers against the sides of her jeans.

Achilles waited in the doorway with the massive, chained red wolf, its jaws taped shut. Athena grabbed it, lugged it down to the car, and shoved it into the trunk. It looked up with questioning eyes.

"Yes, your daddy called. Now, stay." She slammed the trunk hard and waved to Achilles and Cassandra. "Come on!"

"Wait," Odysseus shouted. "What if the Dodge breaks down? How do you even know he'll be there?"

Athena listened with half an ear.

"Hurry," she barked at Achilles as he got in. "It's a long drive. We don't want our passenger suffocating in the trunk."

"We don't?" he asked, and smiled.

Cassandra came after, slogging through drifts.

"Cassie!" Henry yelled from the door. "Don't go!"

"Make my excuses for me," she yelled back.

"The rest of you stay on guard," Athena said. "Someone go check on Andie." She ducked inside the Dodge and started it up. Odysseus continued to shout concerns from the door. When no one responded, he started down the driveway.

"Better get moving," Achilles said, "or he'll grab onto the roof."

Athena hit the gas. The tires spun for a second before grabbing exposed asphalt and jerking forward. Odysseus started to jog, and then run, shouting as they drove away.

"What's he saying, anyhow?" Achilles asked.

Athena glanced into the rearview mirror.

"What if it's a trap," she said.

Cassandra frowned. She and Achilles belted themselves in tight. The roads hadn't been plowed in hours, and Athena's foot was heavy on the accelerator. Their journey might be short lived. They might careen into a ditch before even hitting the freeway.

"Don't go so fast," Cassandra said.

"I know how to drive," Athena said.

"Oh god, you're one of *those*," Cassandra groaned. "It's not the driving, it's *physics*. Traction and the lack thereof. Don't flip the car. Not all of us are impervious to twisted metal and broken glass."

Athena smiled.

"What's so funny?"

"You. You're afraid of the ice but not of my brother."

"Why should I be afraid of him?" Cassandra asked. "He's just a bag of blood to me, right? Isn't that why you brought me?"

"Yes. That's why."

They turned onto the southbound interstate, toward Bryn Mawr, Pennsylvania, where the fires were. Ares, the prick, would've known there was a statue of Athena at the college there.

"Not so fast, I said," Cassandra cautioned, eyeballing the speedometer. Athena reluctantly let the Dodge slow to a molasseslike fifty-five.

"At this rate, it'll be dark by the time we get there."

"All the better," Achilles said. "We can't go around killing gods and talking wolves downtown in the daylight."

In addition to providing good cover, the dark made it easier to spot the flashing lights of the last lingering fire crews. They drove past the burned-out buildings and stared at them in angry silence before parking a few streets over.

"How close do you think we'll be able to get without attracting attention?" Achilles asked.

"I don't think we'll have to get close at all," Athena said. Above the houses smoke puffed skyward, still visible in the well-lit night of a normally safe, civilized neighborhood.

"I hope they partied hard the night before," Cassandra said. "Is that weird to say? I hope they togaed the shit out of this town. Had the time of their lives."

It didn't matter now.

"No," said Athena. "It's not weird to say." She opened her door and stepped out; Cassandra and Achilles did the same. The wind carried burnt wood and chemicals to their noses, scorched flesh and smoke. Death and shock hung heavy in the air as well. But that wasn't what Athena focused on.

Ares was there. She felt his darkness and rage, smoldering like the fires he had started. Her legs itched to head for the trees, for the shadowy sides of buildings, but she waited long enough to listen, to feel for anything else. Any other god. But he was alone.

"Is he here?" Achilles asked.

"Yes."

Cassandra moved to Athena's side.

"Stay close," Athena said. "And let me know if you get any kind of updated vision, okay?"

"Okay."

Their words registered as puffs of air. Ares would be able to see that and know when they spoke even if he was out of earshot. But weather was weather.

"Achilles," Athena said, "get the mutt." She tossed him

the trunk key and listened to the squeak and scuffle as he opened it and grabbed the wolf. It lay docile in his arms, four paws dangling like an oversized red calf.

"Good. Now let's get somewhere dark, where we'll have some privacy."

They crossed the street, Cassandra keeping close, as she'd been told, Achilles following behind. Athena listened for movement and paid attention to the angry heat in her consciousness. But it didn't move.

She scanned the houses and the shadows of large, bare trees. One spot seemed darker than the rest, under better cover, isolated from streaks of yellow light thrown from streetlamps and windows.

"There," Athena said, and pointed. Their feet moved silently through powder-light snow. When they reached the cover of trees, Athena put her hand across Cassandra's chest.

"What? Do you see him?"

"No. Not yet."

"What are we going to do?" Cassandra asked.

Athena studied Cassandra's face. In the darkness, Cassandra didn't bother hiding her expression like she did in the light. She was afraid, yes, and a little reluctant. But she was also angry, and hungry. Part of it was vengeance, justice for those boys. But it wasn't all. Cassandra's eyes moved through the dark like a hunter's eyes.

"I want to hear what he has to say," said Athena. "I want the message."

"What if it was just a challenge?" Achilles asked.

"No. It was a message."

Cassandra turned her face toward the smoke and red flashing lights, her face a grimace of disgust.

"There are better ways to send one," she said.

Before Athena could reply, the smell of Ares' blood drifted toward them, along with the darker, richer scent of wolf fur.

The black wolf walked out from between the trees before Ares, watching them with silent eyes, on legs long and thin as sticks. Pain, the sick-smelling gray one, slunk out from behind a tree to the left. Famine came last, with its master, blending into the snow. And just like that, they were outnumbered.

Doesn't matter. Achilles can take the wolves. I can handle Ares.

But if a wolf got hold of Cassandra, it could tear her throat out in a flash.

Ares' black hair ruffled in the night air. He looked well. Whatever Cassandra had done to him in the rain forest hadn't stuck to him any better than it had to Hera.

"Ares," Athena said. "I see you've brought your best attack dogs."

"So did you."

She clenched her jaw. He always said they were alike. Two sides of the same coin, and she kept proving him right.

"What the hell is this, Ares?" she asked. "Killing college students?"

He shrugged. "College students. Tribesmen. All your fault. You shouldn't have taken my wolf. You shouldn't have goaded me." He fixed his eyes on Achilles. "Give me Panic."

"Not so fast," Athena said. She yanked the wolf out of Achilles' arms and squeezed its scruff hard enough to make it whine. "Questions first. Where's Hera hiding?"

"Let Panic go, and I'll tell you."

Athena huffed. "Sure, I trust you."

Ares said nothing. He stood casually, seemingly unafraid

and slightly somber. Anyone else would think him a beautiful boy, there to mourn his fallen frat brothers. Under the circumstances, the way he looked seemed particularly wicked.

"You can trust me," he said. "I was sent to tell you, anyway."

"Don't you ever get tired of obeying mummy dearest?" Achilles asked. "Aren't you a little old to be tied to a set of apron strings?"

"I look forward to tearing your head off," Ares said.

"I look forward to stickin' it back on."

Athena gave Achilles an irritated glance.

"Let him say what he came to say," she said, and tightened her grip on Panic again. "Don't piss him off so soon."

Ares tensed as Panic whimpered.

"I'm not pissed off," he said. "I'm glad you're here. Sister."

"Why's that exactly?" Cassandra asked.

"Athena," Ares said, ignoring her, "if I offered you a deal, would you take it?"

"A deal?" Athena asked. "Hera must really be afraid."

"Not from her. From me."

"From you?"

"If I agreed to stand down," he said, "if I told you all of the plans and secrets, would you let us walk away? Me and Aphrodite?"

"No." Cassandra stepped forward. "Not you after this, and definitely not her. Aphrodite dies, one way or another."

Oblivion raised its hackles and growled. Ares spoke through clenched teeth.

"You won't get within fifty feet of Aphrodite."

"Wanna bet?" Achilles asked.

Athena frowned. Ares' dogs were better trained. Another five minutes and they'd have a real fight on their hands. Gods' blood, wolves' blood, and mortal blood in the snow.

"Sometimes I wonder," Ares said to her, "whether I'll cease to exist when you're gone. Whether we need each other to survive. These two arms of war. Then again, maybe your death means I'll just burn brighter." He paused. "I'm not sure if I'm ready for you to die. I want it, and I don't want it. But it doesn't matter. Because you will."

He looked Athena straight in the eye, and the sadness she saw shocked her so much she loosened her grip on Panic. The wolf snapped the tape around its jaws and bit her hand. She barely had time to drop it before it scampered safely back to Ares.

"Goddamn it!" Cassandra shouted, and Athena couldn't tell if she was more frightened or angry. "What did you let it go for?"

"Wait," Athena said, and put her arm out to block Cassandra's path. "Ares. You have your wolf. Tell me where she is!"

"She's on Olympus," he said softly.

"Olympus," Athena said. Achilles' face filled with awe. The gods' home. Returned.

"I've never given you any good advice," said Ares. "But you should listen to me now. Don't go. Turn around and run."

Athena shook her head. "We can't spare her, Ares. However she's managed to heal herself . . . however you have . . . that belongs to us now."

He barked sad laughter, and the wolves cringed.

"You have no idea what's waiting for you inside that mountain."

"You always give Hera too much credit," said Athena. "She has no idea what I have. None of you know. What these weapons can do. What I still can. You're the one who should run."

"Run?" Achilles asked. "After all this? All this burning and murder and wolves? We're going to let him go?" He nodded to Cassandra. "This might be your best chance. You should take him and take him now. I'll handle the dogs."

"I—" Cassandra stuttered. But after a moment her eyes changed.

"No," Athena said. "There's too much risk."

But they darted forward anyway. Achilles moved first, going after Pain. It twitched and jumped away from his grip. Cassandra took a quick step forward, and Famine leaped for her face. Athena pulled her back by the coat collar just in time. The white wolf's teeth snapped inches from her nose.

"Stand down, damn you," she hissed. "Ares, get out of here!"

"What? What are you doing?" Cassandra asked, her voice full of rage. She struggled in Athena's grip, and grabbed Athena's shoulder. Pain flared bright and wet inside her jacket as fresh feathers exploded through her skin and muscle. Athena grimaced and let Cassandra go. Ares and the wolves had run anyway. Cassandra and Achilles gave chase a few feet in the dark, but soon slowed.

"Why did you stop me?" Cassandra shouted. "I could've done it this time. I felt it. I should have done it, for those boys. For those people in the jungle."

"Maybe," Athena said. "Or maybe you'd have gotten yourself killed. And you," she said to Achilles. "I never gave the order."

Achilles shrugged. "In the heat of battle, my orders come from right here." He struck his chest and his guts. "Always have."

"Damn it," Cassandra said.

"The odds weren't good, Cassandra."

"How much better do you think the odds are going to get?" she asked, angrier and angrier. "When I face him next time he'll be side by side with Hera."

"It wasn't the right time," Athena muttered. The shoulder of her jacket soaked through with hot blood, mocking her like Cassandra's words. She wasn't sure why she hadn't let the girl try. If they'd succeeded, their chances in Olympus would've been measurably better.

It was something in his eyes that I hadn't seen in a long time. Cassandra stalked past her and kicked snow on the way back to the car. *And it was something in hers that I didn't want to see.*

21

PLANS

"You should stay with me," Athena said. "With us. It'll look less suspicious if you go home in the morning. And then you can check in with Henry. See what load of BS he told them."

Light from Cassandra's den and kitchen blared yellow into the snow. At two in the morning on a weeknight. One or both of her parents were sitting up waiting. Whatever BS Henry had told them, they hadn't bought it.

"It won't make a difference," said Cassandra. "And I don't want to stay with you."

"What will you tell them?"

"How's your shoulder?" Cassandra didn't spare Athena a glance as she got out, didn't look back as she walked up the driveway. She was overjoyed thinking that Athena would be plucking feathers for hours.

When she walked into the house, she shed her coat and boots and went into the den, where both her parents waited as expected.

"Where were you?" her mother asked, sitting on the couch. A glass of brandy trembled in her fingers.

In Pennsylvania, on the trail of a god. On a school night. Cassandra frowned. She couldn't very well tell them *that*.

"I was with Athena."

"With Athena where?" her dad asked.

"Just out. Snowstorms make her sort of claustrophobic. We didn't mean to come back so late." Their shoulders relaxed. And to think, she'd always figured she'd be terrible at lying from lack of practice.

"Snowstorm claustrophobia or not," her dad said, "you can't just disappear until two AM on a school night. And when Henry got bitten—you ran off with her then, too . . . to the . . . spa, or whatever."

Cassandra clenched her back teeth down on a laugh. Her dad pronounced "spa" as if it were exotic as an alien spaceship.

"We like Athena. And we know it's hard for her, with her brother sick. But you're in high school. There are limits."

"I know."

Her mom put the brandy glass down. "You're not acting like you know."

"I know. But I do." Except limits didn't matter. She had to break the rules, to fight a war that raged on under their noses. She had to lie, because they didn't know who she was. And they might never. They could lose both of their children; she and Henry could be buried shallow in a ditch, and they would never know why. They'd wonder what they'd done wrong.

"I'm really sorry," Cassandra said. "That I cost you sleep. That I give you headaches." That they were so very, very in the dark. She bent and hugged them. "I'm sorry that you worry. You don't have to."

Athena breathed a sigh of relief when she and Achilles pulled up to a dark and silent house.

"Looks like they didn't wait up," Achilles said. He studied her wounded arm. Blood had run all the way down the sleeve and coated her hand in a red glove. "Good thing, I guess. But I expected a little fanfare."

"Tomorrow," she said. "We'll make you a hero's breakfast. You can fight Hermes for it." She parked the Dodge on the street and killed the engine. "Lazy a-holes. Didn't even shovel the driveway. Now I'll have to drag the Dodge back up when no one's looking."

"Or you could shovel it yourself."

"Not likely."

"Why not let me drag the car up, then?" Achilles offered. "You're not in the best shape."

"Fine. But tomorrow. Now, let's not wake anyone up."

Inside, she headed for her bedroom on quiet feet. But when she tried to close her door, she almost shut it on Hermes' face. He gasped at the dark stain on the shoulder of her jacket.

"Is that yours?" he asked. "What happened?"

"Nothing," she said. "Well, something. But it's only good. How's your stomach? Strong?"

"Why?"

"Because I think this is going to be gross."

She ground her teeth and skinned out of her jacket sleeves. The fabric of her shirt bloused out wetly where the feathers protruded, like she'd taken a wound and then stuffed it with something. Only the wound *was* the stuffing.

She chuckled, once. It wasn't going to be funny, when

the shirt was off. She started unbuttoning and glanced at her brother.

"We're going to need towels, and something to pull them."

He went to the bathroom for towels and tweezers. She moved the chair from her vanity to the middle of the room, and after a second rolled the rug out from underneath. Wood would be easier to clean.

She slipped her good shoulder free and winced as the extra weight of the shirt hit the feathers. It didn't hurt. Not compared to other things. But the pain of the feathers was special. It made her stomach turn. It scared her.

One good breath, and she pulled the shirt all the way off.

Brown and white feathers stuck out of her shoulder. She'd hoped it would look like a wing. Just a wing, attached to her skin. But it didn't. The feathers pushed through at all angles, in all sizes, nothing like natural growth. It was a wound of cracked, broken skin and bloody bits of tissue. Athena stared at it, scared to look away, afraid that she'd feel them move, or that another one would break through, even though there hadn't been any new pain since leaving Pennsylvania.

"Oh," Hermes whispered. He stood in her open door, his pair of tweezers looking tiny and grossly inadequate. What they needed was a weed whacker, or some way to tear them out by the handful. Hermes wavered on his feet, and she darted forward and steadied him.

"It's okay," she said. "I can do it myself."

He set her on the chair. The burn of the first feather being removed felt almost good. The hot trickle of blood down her arm felt less so. As he plucked, the burning and stinging melded together. Ten, then fifteen feathers fell to the towel on the floor.

"Maybe I shouldn't pluck all of them now." Hermes swallowed. "Your shoulder is coming apart."

"They can't stay," she said. Not one more minute. "Don't worry. We'll bind it up tight."

"Oh my god."

Athena looked up. Odysseus stood in the doorway.

"Dammit," she muttered. She turned her face away as if she could distance herself from her own wound. Hermes stopped plucking and backed off to give Odysseus a better view.

"Cassandra," Odysseus growled. "She's so fucking careless!"

"It was an accident," Athena said.

"This doesn't look like an accident."

She allowed herself a peek at Hermes' progress. The feathers didn't leave neat bleeding pinpricks. They cut through to the surface like razors and left jagged, deep crevices. Where two sprouted too close together, the cuts joined and gaped open, enormous and long. Hermes was right. The meat of her shoulder looked like it had hit something and shattered.

"Disgusting, isn't it," she said softly.

"What's happened?" Calypso came down the hall, smelling like vanilla, no doubt gorgeous fresh off her pillow. Athena wiped her eyes with the back of her arm.

"Jesus. Not Calypso."

"Hey," Odysseus said. He moved fast and blocked the door. "Not now, okay, Cally? Give us a minute. Everyone." He stared at the floor as Hermes walked by and handed off the tweezers.

"You ordering gods around now?" Athena asked as Odysseus shut the door. She tugged a towel over the feathers and sucked air across her teeth. "That's bold, even for—"

She stopped talking when he pushed his fingers into her hair.

"Uncover that," he said.

"No."

"Uncover it."

"It's ugly."

"It's ugly," he said. "You're not."

Her eyes burned again. "Why don't you get out of here? Hermes was doing a fine enough job."

"I want to do it."

"Why?" she asked.

"Because I know they scare you. Because you're not so scared when I'm around." He gently moved the towel away. But his other hand stayed in her hair, his thumb softly touching her jawline. He removed the feathers slowly, with short, steady pulls. "Cassandra and I are going to have words," he said.

"Guess we're lucky she didn't slap me in the face this time."

"Wouldn't have mattered," he said. "You'd still be you. Shining, larger than life."

"Yes," she said. "Shining goddess of battle, in silver and bronze. That's what I am."

"Idiot, that's what you are," he said. "You shouldn't have gone in the first place. And it isn't the armor that makes you shine."

She flexed her shoulder, squeezed her own muscle like an orange to ooze fresh blood. He looked up at her, fondly irritated. His dark hair hung in his eyes and he blew it out of the way, then removed his hand from her neck and used it to hold her fast.

"It was worth it to go," she said. "Because now I know."

"Now you know what?"

"About Olympus," she said, and he paused. "Olympus has returned. And Hera's hiding inside of it."

A statue of Hera sat heavy in the trunk of the Dodge—heavy enough to sag the rear suspension and take the muffler nearly to the ground. Athena had searched for the statue the better part of the morning, and paid cash. Then she drove home, careful not to chip its stone ass.

Dragging the statue to the backyard was nearly cathartic, even if it was only a statue. Athena stared into Hera's stone face and studied the curve of the cheek, the locks of hair escaping the headband. But the blank, pupil-less eyes were her favorite part.

"Is this what you'll look like when Cassandra's really done with you?"

No. In fact, it didn't look like Hera at all. Just a generic representation, made to look like the other sculptures artists had chiseled over the centuries. Thousands of stone gods and goddesses, with the same face. The only way to tell the statue was supposed to be Hera was the peacock twined around her feet.

The sliding door opened, and the smell of fried chicken and buttered biscuits wafted out of the kitchen.

"I would've voted for a lawn jockey," Odysseus said. He closed the door behind him. "Or some of them pink flamingos."

Athena smiled. "She's for Achilles. Stone he can hone his fists on."

"You never bring me any presents."

"I would, if you'd show me something worth rewarding."

She glanced at him slyly. He looked briefly insulted, then puzzled. He was such a good liar. Good enough to almost make her doubt what she'd seen: that he was faster and stronger than he'd shown.

"You really think he's something, don't you," he said.

"Don't get jealous. He *is* something. A weapon of fate, and all ours. And to think I wanted to kill him."

Achilles' strength grew by the day. It would be he who got them their victory as much as Cassandra. As much as Athena.

"I don't get jealous," Odysseus said. "How's your shoulder?"

"It's fine." It still bled when she flexed her arm, and bled more when she dragged the statue, bouncing, from the trunk to the backyard. The throb reached hotly all the way to her fingers. "Thank you. For last night."

"I wouldn't have been anywhere else."

"You'd better get some chicken before Hermes and Achilles eat it all," she said.

"Okay. Can I bring you something? A biscuit? A bucket?"

Athena smiled. He'd never pry an entire bucket out of Hermes' paws.

"Maybe a leg," she said.

The growl of Henry's Mustang preceded it down the street.

"Never mind," she said. "No time."

"Anybody care for some chicken?" Hermes tilted the bucket of original recipe and passed it around the circle in the backyard where they'd gathered with Hera's statue in the center.

"This is weird," Andie said. "KFC in the cold backyard, talking about Olympus. *Olympus*. You guys I can handle.

You're real. In front of me. In the flesh. But Olympus? That's a stretch."

"I had the same reaction," Hermes said around most of a leg.

Athena eyed the statue of Hera. She had to give her step-mother credit. Retaking Olympus was no small feat. She'd become a god again, in the gods' home, and it seemed that the gods' home healed those who resided there.

"I should have thought of it myself," Athena said. "But what's done is done. We'll claim Olympus and turn them out."

"What do you mean, 'turn them out?'" Cassandra asked. "You mean kill them. The war doesn't end until they're dead. You said so."

"No, it isn't over until *I* am dead. That's what Demeter said."

"Whatever," said Cassandra. "Hera dies. Aphrodite dies. They killed Aidan, and you promised."

"I did. To give you comfort. Hera will be killed. Aphrodite might be. But vengeance isn't . . ." Athena paused. "As rewarding as you might think."

Henry and Andie exchanged glances.

"Is it right what Cassandra said, then?" Henry asked. "That you lost your nerve? You let Ares go."

"To keep your sister safe," said Athena.

"To keep *her brother* safe," Cassandra muttered, and the mutter worked its way around the circle as if following the bucket of chicken.

"Dissention in the ranks," Odysseus whispered into Athena's ear. "Not the best time to mount an offensive."

She brushed him away.

"As soon as my shoulder heals, we go," she said. "It won't be long. And the trip won't be far."

Cassandra crossed her arms. "So you remember the way?"

"Of course I do."

"Oi." Odysseus stepped forward. "Why are we talking like it's decided? This doesn't feel like much of a plan. We rush into Olympus with nothing but guts and bravado, ready to be put on spits?"

"We've got more than just guts and bravado, friend," Achilles said. "And it sounds plenty fine to me."

"Yeah, it would," said Odysseus. "But how about some good old-fashioned recon? Maybe find out why they suddenly laid out the red carpet."

"Hera overestimates herself," said Athena. "Like she always does."

"Maybe she's not the only one."

"Enough," Athena said, glaring at Odysseus. The nerve. The balls. She'd have been impressed if it didn't piss her off so much. "We go, and we go now."

"Athena," said Hermes quietly, "you don't need to go so fast."

His collarbones peeked out of his shirt. The fever radiated off him from across the circle.

"Don't you say that to me," she said. "You know I do." Her mouth twitched downward. "I shouldn't have taken so long . . . it feels late already."

"Athena—"

"Save your breath, Ody," Cassandra said. "It doesn't matter that we have no plan. She doesn't think we need one." Her fingers twitched into fists. "Honestly, I don't think we do, either."

"Finally," Athena said. "The oracle says something I know is true."

"You really think we can win?" Odysseus asked.

As an answer, Achilles drew a hidden sword from behind his back. He swung hard, and the stone statue of Hera fell, cleaved clean in two.

22

THE SPACE THAT GODS INHABIT

"Olympus can be reached from the mouth of any cave. Just like the underworld can be reached from any lake or river."

"There's a . . . cave . . . up at the state park," Andie said. Her face was white as a sheet. "We went camping up there sometimes before my dad left. And I can't believe I'm saying anything to help you." She looked at Henry like she was nuts, and he offered no arguments. "It's not very big," she said.

"It won't matter. It'll do. Thank you, Andie."

"No problem. I guess."

"So," Henry said, "all caves lead to Olympus? How come nobody's ever accidentally spelunked into it, then?"

"All caves lead to Olympus for gods," Hermes replied. "As all bodies of water lead to the underworld for us. At least, when Olympus and the underworld exist."

Cassandra could barely believe it. Olympus. The underworld. Unreal places made real, as if she could look out her bedroom window and see a floating castle in a cloud. As if she could look into the river at Abbott Park and see Aidan waving up at her. Her brows knit as she realized. If Olympus had returned, perhaps the way to the underworld had opened as well.

Sudden hope ignited in her chest.

"The underworld," she said. "Has it returned with Olympus?"

Athena and Hermes traded an uneasy glance.

"If we can get to Olympus, can we get there, too?"

"I don't know," Athena said.

"Bullshit."

"I really don't," Athena said gently. "I suppose it's possible." She took a deep breath. "I know why you're asking."

"Take me there."

"Cassandra—"

"Look," Cassandra said, doing her best to keep from trembling, "I'm not mad, okay? I know you couldn't before, you didn't know. Maybe it wasn't even possible before." But it was possible now. She knew the legends. The myths. Orpheus and Eurydice. The Cyclops being freed. *Freed*. You could pull someone out of the underworld if you loved them and had a god or two on your side. She'd sing Aidan out of that hole if she had to do it belting "The Star-Spangled Banner." And she wouldn't be a fool and look back too soon.

"A trip like that," Athena said, "we don't know how long it would take."

"Don't you want him back?" Cassandra goaded. "Don't you want another *soldier* to help keep the mortals alive on that mountain?"

Athena gritted her teeth.

"We don't have time."

"Time? What are you talking about? Olympus isn't going anywhere, is it?" Cassandra dug her nails into her palms.

Nobody said a word. Andie held tight to Henry's arm. Achilles and Calypso barely blinked. Even Odysseus, the great butter-inner, remained silent, curious to see how it played out. Or maybe he was as crazily hopeful as she suddenly was. That she could have him back.

Athena looked nearly ready to pop when Hermes pulled her close and whispered into her ear.

"No," she said softly. "You can't wait."

"I can. I promise I can. And if it might be possible?"

"If it's possible now, it'll be possible after," Athena hissed.

"There won't be an after," Cassandra said. "If someone doesn't take me, then I'm not going with you to Olympus. Good luck with Hera. She'll turn you to feathery paste."

"You're making threats now?" Athena asked. "Giving orders?"

"Stop." Calypso stepped in between them. "You don't need to do this. I'll take Cassandra, if you won't."

Cassandra smiled triumphantly; Athena looked as if she'd swallowed a rock.

"Don't be ridiculous. We have no idea what condition the underworld is in," Athena said. "And it's no picnic on a good day."

"I don't care," said Cassandra.

Athena glared at her, every muscle in her jaw clenching. But Cassandra wouldn't give in. She couldn't. Not if it meant Aidan.

"Go home and pack," Athena muttered and turned her back. "Get an hour of sleep if you can. We leave before dawn."

Odysseus went with Cassandra to her house, along with Andie and Henry. After the growl of the Mustang faded, Athena went back into the yard and kicked the stone statue of Hera in half of its face over, and over, and over. In five minutes, the toes of her favorite boots were ruined, and chunks of Hera lay scattered across the grass.

"Dress rehearsal?"Achilles asked.

Athena smiled ruefully. "Maybe."

"We could do it all ourselves, you know. Walk in there. Blow up the place. Walk back out. Just you and me."

He sounded so confident. Very *Crocodile Dundee*. But it wouldn't work.

"No," she said. "We need her. We need Cassandra."

"The other weapon of fate." He nodded. "Right. You think that's why we'll win. Because if you have us, you have the Fates."

"Why do you think we'll win, Achilles?"

He walked to her and picked up half of the statue, as easily as she could have.

"Because you're the goddess of war." He blew dust off the cracked stump of Hera's neck. "That's why I joined up. What could be mightier than you?"

Andie didn't look like herself, sitting on the corner of Henry's bed, her knees up and her hands pressed against the blankets. She looked afraid. Like a backward-scuttling crab.

"Lux," Henry said, and gestured with his head. The dog bounced up onto the bed and curled into her lap.

"Dog therapy," Andie said.

Henry shrugged. "It usually works for me."

Her phone buzzed, and she reached into her pocket then texted something fast and furious.

"Who's that?" Henry asked.

Andie made a face.

"It's Megan, nosy. We were supposed to go to a movie."

"Not anymore?"

"What do you think?"

Henry sighed. She'd probably be this snappy until the moment they left for Olympus.

Olympus. They were going to real, live, legendary, mother-effing Olympus. The only thing that could make it feel larger and more ridiculous was if they got there on Pegasus.

"This is what we trained for," he heard himself say.

"I guess."

"You're the one who wanted to start using swords."

She squinted at him. "What's that supposed to mean? It's a good thing I did, or we'd both be in Ares' wolves' stomachs right now."

"That was weeks ago," Henry said. "We'd actually be in little piles of Ares' wolves' poop right now."

She cracked a smile, but just barely. "Big piles, you mean."

Around Henry's room, nary a piece of wall was visible for all his posters. Childish, outdated relics. Andie had made fun of him for it once. But the big blue *Avatar* face sure felt comforting now, when his sister was packing for the underworld across the hall. They would go and sit with her soon, he supposed. After she and Odysseus finished discussing whatever secret reincarnated-handshake crap they were discussing.

"Henry?"

"Yeah?"

"Do you think it's done any good? The training, I mean."

"Sure," he said. He flexed his arm. "Check out my bicep. It's almost doubled."

She smacked him. "I mean, do you think it's made a difference? Do you think we can stand against gods?"

"Hermes won't let us face gods," he said. "We'll handle

[274]

the wolves. We've faced off against them before." He didn't look her in the eye. He didn't look Lux in the eye either. The deep red scar on his cheek said enough. "And we have you-know-who. What's-his-ass. Achilles. Besides, I don't want my sister to go alone."

"Me, neither." Andie stuffed her hands into Lux's fur, and his tail thumped. "I don't know what I'm saying, anyway. They killed Aidan. Hurt Cassandra. Hurt Lux. It's our fight."

"Hey," he said, and pointed to his cheek. "And me."

"Yeah," she said. "And you." She moved Lux's head from her lap and stood up, looking at the posters like Henry had just done. "I spend more time in here with you than I do with Cassandra these days," she said. "Must be annoying. Bet you never counted on your kid sister's friend always hanging around." She crossed her arms. "I don't remember you dying. But it feels like I do. And that almost feels like a premonition." She looked back at him. "Or an omen? I don't know what the word is."

Henry swallowed. He'd never seen Andie so small and scared and nervous. He didn't know what to do, so he didn't do anything.

"When the wolves said that you were the boy who had to die, everyone thought that they made a mistake," Andie went on. "That they thought you were Odysseus, or somehow Achilles. But what if they knew you were you?" Her voice grew quieter, but more breathy, more intense. Her cheeks flushed rosy, and she shook from shoulders to wrists. "What if Hector has to die?"

"I'm not Hector."

"It doesn't matter to them!" She turned on him with big, scared eyes and rushed him, hugging him hard and fierce, like he always guessed her hugs would be—part affection, part cutting off circulation.

"I'm not going to die, Andie," he whispered.

"I think you are," she said.

Henry slipped his arms around her. He could feel her curves through her clothes, and all her hard muscle, from years of hockey as much as from bashing shields and swinging swords. Her black hair lay soft against his cheek and smelled like herbs. The dirt-smeared tomboy had grown into a pretty girl when he wasn't looking. And she hadn't been just his "kid sister's friend" in a long time.

Henry's heart pounded in his ears. It was weird to think that he could kiss her. Shove Lux off onto the floor and press her back on his bed. No time like the present to play the Last Night on Earth card. He cleared his throat.

"I guess it's a good thing you're not psychic," he croaked.

"Oh." She pulled away. "It's not a joke!" But she laughed a little and punched him in the liver, almost hard enough to make him buckle. The moment was over, and he tried to laugh with her, hugging his internal organs and kicking himself.

Henry Weaver, chickenshit of the ages.

Pack light, Athena had said. For the underworld. When Cassandra didn't even know what she was packing for, or what the weather was like, or if there was even weather at all. The open mouth of her suitcase yawned. Most of her clothes had gone into it already, only to be taken out again. Pack light. She nixed the suitcase and reached for her schoolbag, then dumped her books and notebooks onto the floor to make room for a few shirts and a spare pair of jeans.

"This is an impossible trip to pack for," she said to Odysseus. "You've been there before, haven't you? How about some advice?"

He leaned over the bed and surveyed the choices.

"Here." He grabbed a few t-shirts and a zip-up hoodie. "That should do it. Just don't forget your goat's blood and honey."

"What?"

He waved his hand. "Hermes will take care of it."

Cassandra peered down into her mostly empty backpack. "So that's it?"

"Yeah, that's it. You won't be gone long. She won't let you be." His voice turned bitter at the end, and his normally easygoing eyes sat hard as stones.

"You think we're making a mistake, going into Olympus," Cassandra said.

"I think *she* is."

"Why?" Cassandra asked.

"Because she's too bloody sure she's going to win." He exhaled sharply. "Doesn't matter anyway. She won't listen to me. Not when she gets like this. She didn't listen to me when I said not to kill Achilles—"

"And that turned out okay."

Odysseus shrugged. The outcome wasn't the point, she supposed. He ran his hands through his unruly brown hair. He was tense and scared for Athena. Probably scared for all of them.

"I don't think she likes you doubting her," said Cassandra.

"Yeah, well, I don't care. I care about keeping her alive. And telling her the truth."

Cassandra frowned and thought of Calypso, how she must feel, knowing that Odysseus cared for Athena first.

"Ody, are you and Cally . . . ?"

He shook his head. "No. And yes. And before you say anything, I know how shitty that is. What a bleeding mess I've made. It would have been better for us all if Athena had never showed a scrap of humanity. If she'd stayed a goddess, and I'd never been able to touch her."

Cassandra rested her chin on her hand thoughtfully.

"I don't know how to respond first. 'What the hell scrap of humanity are you talking about?' or 'So, you've actually touched her?'"

"My gods, did I touch her. In the back of a truck on the way to Kincade." He groaned and made fists. "The memory of it keeps me up nights."

"You. Are. Really gross." Cassandra zipped her bag. "And really unfair to Cally. She's so sweet. And beautiful."

"Cally's wonderful," Odysseus said. "Amazing. Lovely. She deserves better than me." He sat down on Cassandra's bed, wrinkling most of her wardrobe still spread out on it. He reached under his leg and pulled out a sweater, a blue one Aidan had bought for her. He folded it and held it out.

"What?" she asked. "In case I need something dressy?"

"Hades can be quite a particular bastard. He might want you formal. Listen. When you're down there, Athena's going to bait you. She doesn't want to go, so she's going to rush you along, piss you off. But you can't touch her, do you hear me? You can't touch her when you're angry."

Cassandra lowered her eyes.

"The thing that happened in Pennsylvania," she said, "when I grabbed her, I only meant to make her let go—"

Odysseus didn't blink.

"You knew what you were doing," he said.

The feathers in her shoulder. He's right. It was easy. I barely thought. I just let it out.

"Cassandra? What's that look for?"

"Just thinking," she said. "A few months ago, I would've run miles to keep Athena safe for you, even though I hated her. Because you're my friend."

"And now?"

Now I kill gods.

"Now everything's different."

He lay back on the bed and patted the pillow beside him. A few hours' sleep was a good idea. But she didn't see how it was possible, when she was leaving for the underworld and Aidan when she woke. She lay down and closed her eyes. Reviving dead boyfriends was worse than waiting for Christmas morning. Her heart pounded, and blood raced through her limbs. In a few hours, she would see him. She would touch him. And she and Athena would pull him out of the underworld, or die trying.

"Thank the stars for Athena," she said.

"Never thought I'd hear you say that."

"Don't get me wrong. I do basically despise her. But you have to admit she has a knack for getting things done."

Odysseus switched her lamp off and lay with her in the dark.

"What will you say to him, when you see him?" he asked.

Maybe nothing. It could be like it was at his grave. No words. But it wouldn't matter. She'd have him back, and whatever she had to say, she'd have all the time she needed to say it.

"Well?"

"I'll tell him I love him," she said finally. "And that I'm glad he's dead. I'll tell him I'm grateful he protected me, and that he deserved what he got." She breathed out, and to her surprise, began to feel sleepy. "And then I'll bring him home."

23

TRIP TO THE UNDERWORLD

Some hours later, Odysseus woke her. It was still full dark, but she came awake immediately and grabbed her backpack. Together they put on their jackets and crept to the door. A folded note was taped to the other side.

"It's from Andie and Henry," Cassandra said.

"What's it say?"

"It says, 'We hope you find him. We miss him a lot. Good luck, and be careful.'"

"Real poets, those two," Odysseus said, and looked at Henry's closed door. "Do you think they're in there?" He waggled his brows. "You know."

"What? Gross. No." Cassandra tiptoed down the hall and down the stairs, then slipped into her shoes in the entryway. It was lucky that Lux was no longer a stellar guard dog, or they'd have been busted for sure. After the wolf attack he'd become timid and a much deeper sleeper.

They closed the door quietly and jogged through yards to Athena's.

"You're so going to get packed off to boarding school for this," said Odysseus.

"No way. I can distract them with my boyfriend, suddenly back from the dead," said Cassandra, and realized she was smiling.

"Right. Maybe try the long-lost twin brother angle. That always works."

"Hey!"

Henry, Andie, and Lux ran to catch up.

"What are you doing?" Cassandra asked. "Go back, or you'll get us all caught."

"*You're* going to get us caught." Henry scowled. "You didn't even make up a story for Mom and Dad. I told you to before you went to bed."

"If you wanted me to listen to you," she said, "you should have bossed me around more when we were younger."

"I tried," said Henry. "You were a brat."

"You're covered staying at my house until Friday," Andie said. "Assuming you're back before then, Tom and Maureen will never know a thing."

"Thanks, Andie."

"Cassandra?" Andie asked. "If you . . . can't bring him back. Would you tell him . . ." She paused. "That I miss his stupid face. And thanks for . . . you know. Dying for us."

Cassandra steeled her jaw.

"We'll be back soon."

Athena met them at the door in boots, jeans, and a jacket. A burlap sack that looked mostly empty hung in her right hand. When she said pack light, she meant it. She poked Cassandra's backpack.

"Whatever you've got in there, clear it out by half and let Hermes repack it with food."

"Okay." She nodded at Odysseus. "Thanks for staying with me."

"Anytime," he said, but he was already distracted, his eyes on Athena. Cassandra had barely walked down the hall toward the kitchen before they started to whisper.

"Will you at least think about what I said?" Odysseus hissed. "You don't know how to fight this war!"

"I know how to fight *every* war!"

Cassandra turned the corner and heard no more. Hermes' clattering around in cupboards made sure of that.

"All right," he said. "I've got granola bars, beef jerky, bottled water, a few apples, some canned meat, and bread." He touched each lightly. "And, of course, a bear-shaped bottle of honey. Everything you need for a trip to the underworld."

"Okay," said Cassandra. "What's with the honey? Odysseus mentioned it, too."

"Well, it's pretty good on the granola bars. Or, if the dead surround you, you can take the cap off and throw it in the other direction."

Cassandra's brow knit. "The dead can eat?"

"They can taste," said Hermes. "They can drink. Hell, I don't know, maybe they just like to roll around in the stuff. It's been awhile since I've been down there." Underneath the jovial tone he was tense and nervous. On his overthin frame it gave an impression of constant vibration.

"Are you okay, Hermes?"

"Haven't been for over a year," he said. "But a few more days won't hurt. And I understand why you're going. Half of me wants to go with you. He was my brother, too."

"I know. And we'll hurry." Maybe she did understand Athena's rush. Hermes was so thin he looked fake, like a wax figure or a mannequin. Far too thin to be alive and talking.

He ran a shaky hand through his hair, still chestnut and shiny despite the failure of his muscles and tightening skin.

"Just, when you get back, I don't want to see any new feathers coming out of my sister's ass, okay?"

Cassandra nudged him. "You know you're making me pass up a great joke about ass plumage, don't you?"

"Yes, I know. But now's not the time."

An hour and a half later, Cassandra followed Athena through the dark, over rocks and boulders still half-covered with snow and ice. She couldn't see two feet in front of her face. They could have been going anywhere. But she bit her lip and didn't ask. She felt enough like a child already, scrambling along, without whining and wanting to know if they were there yet. Since leaving the house, they hadn't spoken much aside from the usual questions about whether it was warm enough in the Dodge and if she needed to stop to go to the bathroom. Which was fine by Cassandra. She wasn't there to bond.

But she wasn't particularly angry, either. Mostly she was nervous and afraid. If Athena had any sense of how to deal with mortals, she would have seen the fear leaking straight through the bottom of Cassandra's wet shoes. But Athena didn't notice. She parked the car on a side road in the middle of nowhere, mumbled that it was adjacent to a state park, and plunged onto the trails.

They crested a hill, and the barest glimmer of predawn light showed a dull wooden building lit poorly by pale fluorescent lights. Beside it, a large lake lay choppy and slate gray.

"Where are we?" Cassandra asked finally.

"Boathouse."

"What are we doing here?"

"Stealing a boat."

Of course. They would need one to get across the river to the underworld. She remembered that much from her life in Troy. They had to cross over either the river Styx or the river Acheron to reach the shores of the dead.

"We're not going to portage, are we?" she asked. "Because I can guarantee my slowness will piss you off."

Athena didn't look back. "We don't need to portage." She walked straight for the deserted boathouse, across the nicely plowed dirt road and very empty parking lot. Cassandra smacked her lightly on the back.

"Why didn't we park here?"

"I didn't want the Dodge here," Athena replied.

"Or maybe you just wanted to make me hike three miles over frozen rocks."

Athena sighed. "Not everything I do is expressly designed to make your life harder, Cassandra."

"Sure."

Inside the boathouse, Athena chose a light wooden skiff and pulled it down as easily as if it were an empty nutshell. She set it into the water, and Cassandra grabbed oars off the wall. Athena knelt and gripped the sides.

"Get in."

Cassandra lowered herself in carefully. The skiff rocked and bobbed. Below the sides, the water looked black and very cold.

"How far do we have to row?" she asked.

"We're not rowing anywhere." Athena stood and let go of the boat, and Cassandra made a mad grab for the dock.

"Hey, jerk! How about a warning?" She flexed her arms and tugged the boat close to the side. "What are you doing?"

"Well, I was thinking torches, but that might be a bad idea. Plus—" Athena looked back the way they'd come in. A large flashlight was affixed near the door. "I'm not sure about the batteries, though. We should probably bring both."

"Both?"

Athena shrugged and went for the flashlight. "You're right. This should be plenty."

"Have I mentioned that I love the way you explain things?" Cassandra asked. She looked out across the lake. Daylight had begun to leak through the clouds, showing them low and gray. It wouldn't be dark much longer. Athena handed her the flashlight.

As Athena got into the skiff, something shifted. The boat and the water, normal, everyday things a moment before, turned strange and out of context. The air went stagnant, and despite the motion of the skiff, the black water didn't ripple. The flashlight was just a flashlight, but right then it felt about as familiar as a goat's head.

Athena crouched and reached into the pocket of her jacket. What she pulled out looked like a bunch of sticks mixed with small, dried flowers. She flicked a lighter and set them on fire, burning orange against her cheeks, her lips whispering words Cassandra couldn't hear.

"Turn the flashlight on," Athena said.

"What?" Cassandra asked, an instant before Athena dropped the flaming bundle into the water, and the world around them went pitch dark.

"What's happening?!" She fumbled with the switch on the flashlight, terrified it would slip out of her hands and be lost in the water. "I can't find the button!" But in the next second she did, and the beam fell yellow on Athena's calm face. "Why is it so dark?"

"The way down is always dark."

But this was more than dark. The beam of the flashlight felt heavy trying to cut through it.

"What did you do?" Cassandra asked. "Are we still in the boathouse?"

"Not exactly."

Cassandra's heart pounded, bobbing on top of the inky water. Water that might very well have reached the center of the earth.

"Athena?" Her voice trembled. "I think I've had enough cryptic. Would you tell me what's going to happen, please?" She pointed the beam of the flashlight back toward the dock, and it hit nothing. Just blackness, in all directions. Nothing to be seen except for the boat they sat in and Athena's un-ruffled face. She'd never been so grateful for Athena's unruffled face.

Athena looked into the flashlight beam a moment.

"Don't be scared," she said, and her voice was softer. "This is how it happens. I'm opening the way. Now we just have to find the river."

"How do we do that?"

"Hold the flashlight steady. And look away, if your stom-ach's feeling weak." She reached into her pocket and pulled out a short-bladed knife.

"What's that for?" Cassandra asked.

"Not for you. But we have to pay the fare. And the fare is blood."

Cassandra swallowed. As Athena talked, she felt less cold, and less scared.

"I thought it was just coins," Cassandra said. "We used to put coins on their eyes, for the boatman. For Charon." Charon, the ferryman of the dead, who transported souls across the river to Hades for a price. "Don't tell me that didn't work."

Athena smiled. "Sometimes I forget what you are. That you were with us back then, when we were real."

"You're still real to me, if you haven't noticed. Irritatingly real."

"Well," Athena said softly, "no Charon this time. It seems I lost his number a few thousand years ago. This time it's blood. I just hope the blood of a god is payment enough, since I couldn't fit a sheep in this boat." She reached out and handed Cassandra the burlap sack she'd brought from the house. "But just in case mine doesn't work, I brought a snake."

"A snake?" Cassandra shone the light on the burlap and saw slow movement inside. "There's been a snake in here the whole time?"

"Mm-hmm. The cold keeps her still."

"So." Cassandra turned the bag. "If you're not sure your blood will work, why don't we just start with the snake?"

Athena snatched the bag back. "I like this snake."

Once the snake was safely in the belly of the boat, Athena put the knife to the palm of her hand and nudged one of the oars toward Cassandra. Cassandra grabbed it as the blade dug deep into the meat of Athena's palm. The blood pooled for a few seconds, and then she tipped it over the side in a steady stream as if from a chalice. Her lips moved in a soundless prayer or incantation, and she plunged her hand into the water.

"Push us out, Captain."

They moved off into the dark, slowly at first, and then faster. The water against Athena's wrist stung like blades of ice. She fought the urge to pull her hand out, had to force herself to leave it below the surface, trailing like chum to the sharks, to every monster and beast that lurked in the water below the paper-thin belly of the boat. Some hideous child of Keto might twist out of the depths and tear her hand off with rows of triangular teeth. Or worse, they could drag her down to be crushed in the dark between scaly coils.

But no matter how her teeth threatened to chatter, she kept her voice calm. Cassandra was still afraid.

"That's good," Athena said. "Good. Don't worry about direction. I can feel the current now. It's taking us."

Cassandra nodded, and Athena realized she could see her outside of the flashlight beam. The dark wasn't so complete. The current grew stronger against her fingers, and she detected a hint of warmth, separate from the steady stream of blood pulsing from her palm.

"Athena? I think it's working."

Light came up slowly, light the likes of which only existed in one place. Orange and rosy red at once, it cast no shadows. The light of the underworld. Athena pulled her hand out of the water: a sad, pale, empty thing that throbbed and ached. She wiped it on her jeans and balled it into a fist.

"Here." Cassandra nudged her and handed her a long white sock. "For your hand. And it's not off my foot; it's out of my bag."

"Thanks." Athena tied it around her palm. "We're almost there." Banks of black rocks and sand appeared on both sides of the broad waterway. She almost told Cassandra not to look up. The expanse over their heads would make her dizzy to the point of vomiting. But it was better not to. If she told Cassandra not to do it, she'd do it for sure.

"What river are we on?" Cassandra asked. "Acheron, or Styx?"

Acheron or Styx. The river of pain or the river of hate. Not much to choose from, but no rivers of dancing ponies led into the underworld. Athena leaned over the side and scooped up water. She pushed it into her mouth, swished it around, and spat.

"Styx." She spat again.

"How do you know?"

"Don't you know what hate tastes like?" She glanced back. Cassandra's face darkened. Silly question. She knew better than most people. "I'm sorry," Athena said. "It's making my voice harsh." She spat more. "Don't drink it. Don't even smell it."

Below them and on all sides, the Styx glittered like a malevolent jewel. Achilles' mother had dipped him in up to his heel to make him a killer of men, to make him invincible. The lengths of a mother's love. Athena supposed it had worked. But it was difficult to imagine dunking an infant into so much hateful water.

Behind her, Cassandra looked from shore to shore with fearful fascination.

"Where do we go? It all looks the same. Which side is the one we want?"

"Probably best to ask the dog," Athena said.

Cassandra frowned. "Cerberus?"

"Ding, ding, ding! Ten points for the princess of Troy."

"Is this the river of hate, or the river of smartass?"

"Sorry," said Athena. "Let's just hope Hades' three-headed Fido is still alive and kicking."

Athena put her fingers to her lips and whistled. After a few seconds of tense silence, Cerberus howled back. Twice. *Twice?*

They waited, but no third howl followed. Then the river turned and they saw why, as he bounded down the bank.

Two of his heads were alive and well. The third was not. It dangled from his black shoulder, a grotesque marionette of bloodstained bone and sinew that rattled as he pawed the sand.

"Land the boat," Athena said.

"Where? Near that?"

"He's not a 'that.' He's a dog." She pointed toward him again, and Cassandra reluctantly maneuvered the boat toward shore.

"Dog," Cassandra muttered. "He's the size of an elk."

And a large elk at that. Cerberus was two thousand pounds of muscle and shining black fur, with fangs just a size too large for his mouth.

"He doesn't seem dangerous," said Athena. "His tail's wagging, for Pete's sake."

"Yeah," Cassandra said. "But wagging why? Maybe he's happy to see us because it's been a long time between meals."

The belly of the boat scraped against the rock and sand bed of the river. Athena used the other oar to push them in hard, and wedged the bow in deep. As they landed, Cerberus stayed back, watching with alert black eyes in both heads, tail still wagging softly.

"Cerberus." Athena held one hand out and slipped her other, sock-wrapped hand into her pocket, for her knife. Just in case. The dog's heads bobbed and licked their jaws. If he decided to bite with both sets of teeth, she'd lose most of an arm.

"Well," she said, "will you sniff? Or strike?"

He did neither. The left head darted forward and ducked under her hand. She grinned and let go of the knife to pet the other head.

"Is it safe for me, too?" Cassandra asked.

"I should think so." Athena scratched Cerberus' ears as Cassandra got out of the boat, careful to keep her feet dry. In seconds she was also stroking and patting the dog's massive shoulder.

"He's sort of . . . monstrously cute." Cassandra leaned away from his teeth and looked at the fallen head, lying limp and furless in a string of bones. "That's either disgusting or the saddest thing I've ever seen."

Maybe it was both. Athena couldn't help noticing the meticulous cleanliness of the bones, as if they'd been picked clean of meat, skin, and fur. She looked at the remaining heads suspiciously, but he was a dog. That was what dogs did.

She turned the left head back and forth. The fur was smooth and the eyes bright, the gums and tongue pink and wet. The middle head looked much the same, except for a little cloudiness in one of the eyes. Even sadder than the thought of two heads eating the remains of the third was the thought of one head, the last head, doing it alone.

"Is he going to die, too?" Cassandra asked.

"Not after we take back Olympus," said Athena. "I've always liked Cerberus. And who knows? He's Hades' dog, the dog of the lord of the dead. Maybe this is as far as it goes for him." She scratched his chins thoughtfully. "One dead head."

"This is . . . interesting and everything," Cassandra said. "But what now? Where is Aidan?"

Athena patted both heads and tried to look into both sets of eyes.

"Cerberus. Be a good boy and take us to Mommy and Daddy."

24

CORPSE ROYALTY

They walked behind the massive black dog through the caverns of the Underworld to the gates of Hades. Cassandra barely blinked, taking in the mass and fire of the place. The starkness of it, the lack of change. She had thought that it would smell like decay or sulfur, that there'd be tiny, dancing demons. But the only smell was the faint metallic scent of the river behind them.

The underworld. So few living mortals had seen it. She couldn't believe she wanted to be there.

She walked closer to Athena, who was as usual solid and steady as stone, and so familiar compared to everything else. She wanted to take Athena's arm. But of course she didn't actually do it.

"Where are the dead?" she asked. "Where's Aidan?" She tried not to sound so disappointed. But her heart had hoped she'd be able to sense him the moment they arrived. Her foolish heart had hoped he'd be there to meet the boat.

"They're everywhere and nowhere," said Athena. "They

barely exist unless someone has need of them. Like dusty books in a boarded-up library. Like stuffing in the walls."

Cassandra stopped in her tracks. She didn't want to see him that way. A shade, no more substantial than a hologram.

Athena touched her shoulder.

"I didn't mean that's what happened to Aidan," she said. "He's my brother. He's different. To get him out, we first need to speak to Hades. My uncle. This is his turf, and you don't take anything without permission."

"Will he give us permission?"

"For a price, maybe."

"And if he doesn't?" she asked.

"I'll figure something out. We won't leave here without him, unless . . ." Athena slowed.

"Unless what?"

"I don't know what a dead god is like, Cassandra. He could be awful. A monster. Or worse. We're close now," she said. "But we can still turn back."

Cassandra stared at Cerberus' massive heads and at the dark tunnel before them. A monster. Or worse. If she looked into Aidan's eyes and didn't see him, she didn't know what she'd do.

"No," she said. "It's worth it, whatever the answers. It has to be."

Cerberus barked and darted around a corner. Athena put her arm out protectively.

"Whatever we find, don't be scared," Athena said. "He might be fine. Maybe it won't be just me protecting you here, but both of us."

It was a nice thought.

They turned the corner.

Cerberus stood with both heads bowed before a young dead woman, her profile gray, her yellow hair dry as straw.

A black dress, dusted with her own decay, hung from her bony frame. She turned to greet them, and Cassandra almost yelped.

One half of her was dead. The other was rotten. Rotten and run through with small rips and tears from flesh that had swollen, burst, and receded again. Her left eye was clear and bloodless. Her right was yellow, milky, and softening. Most of her hair had fallen out on the right side, and most of the scalp skin had gone with it.

"It's been a long time, sister-cousin," the dead woman said. Her black tongue moved across her lips.

"It has, Persephone," said Athena.

Persephone. The goddess of the underworld, who was once so beautiful that all gods wooed her. So beautiful that Hades kidnapped her to be his eternal bride.

"May I offer you something to eat or drink?" Persephone gestured behind her, to a golden table piled with sweet fruit and roasted meat, golden chalices filled with sparkling liquid. Cassandra hadn't noticed it before, too distracted by the horror in front of them.

Or perhaps it just hadn't been there. The scent of the food and particularly the drink drifted toward their noses, the first real smells since they'd arrived. All at once she was parched and starving. Athena gripped her arm.

"Not a good idea," she said out of the corner of her mouth. She nodded politely at Persephone.

"You may offer, cousin. But we must refuse. We're here to visit, not to stay."

Persephone smiled. Or she mostly smiled. The rotted side of her mouth refused to obey. It stretched and tore instead. Cassandra stifled a heave.

"Tell me," Persephone asked, "what news of my brothers and sisters?"

Athena shrugged. "Dying. Or killing each other. Where is my uncle? Your husband, Hades?"

"Venice, last I heard," Persephone said. "But he could be anywhere, in any city rife with decay. Rife with disease and rot. He has forever been a collector, you know, of dead things and pestilence. He keeps massive houses all over the world, stockpiled with powdered poisons and plague victims in jars. All manner of freak and fancy, every abomination and flesh-eating bacteria. Each one is a treasure in petri dishes and formaldehyde. Precious as leaves pressed in a book."

"Is he well?" Athena asked. "Is he ailing?"

"He may be ailing, but he isn't dead. If he were, you would know. He'd have exploded in a cloud of viruses. A city would lie dead around him. One last tribute." Persephone touched her hair, and it fell out onto the ground. "Hades doesn't come here for me anymore, Athena. In case you hadn't noticed, I'm not the golden flower he once plucked from my mother's grasp."

"The god of death understands decay," Athena replied. "Your dead half was always his favorite."

"We'll see when I fade further. When I am one half bone and dust." She toyed with Cerberus' dead head. Her fingers twisted the bones like the heavy jewels of a necklace. "How is my mother?"

"Missing you. She mourns your passing."

"I'm sorry for that. My last summer above was four years ago. Since then I've been too dead to move with the spring."

"But you won't be apart long," Cassandra blurted, and Persephone's dead eyes settled on her face. "When Demeter . . . dies . . . you'll see her again. You'll be together again."

Persephone looked from Cassandra to Athena with a mix of amusement and hunger. She stepped away from Cerberus and walked closer. "Why have you come?"

"We've come for—"

"Aidan! Apollo. Your cousin," Cassandra blurted again. Athena pursed her lips, but Cassandra couldn't help it. He was here. So close.

"My cousin," Persephone said. Her black tongue rolled in her mouth, dry and granular in the quiet. "Have you paid the fare?"

"I paid it," Athena said. "She doesn't have to pay."

Persephone's head twitched, so much like a zombie that Cassandra was sure she'd charge them any minute, biting.

"I make the rules here, cousin," Persephone said. "And a little blood is not too much to ask."

"Back off, Persephone."

"How much blood?" Cassandra asked. She held her hand out for Athena's knife. "How much to pay his passage back?"

"Cassandra, don't," Athena said, but Persephone started to laugh.

"His passage back?" She cackled. "You can't take him back! He's dead. This is his home!"

"Mortals have left here before," Athena said. "Surely a god is allowed special favors."

Persephone licked her lips, her eyes marking the path of Cassandra's veins.

"Pay the fare," she said. "Perhaps there will be special favors."

"Give me the knife, Athena." Cassandra held her hand out, but Athena didn't move. She only stared deep into Persephone's eyes.

"He's not here," Athena said.

"No," said Cassandra. "He has to be. Where else would he go?"

"Where dead gods go," Athena said. "No one knows. Including her."

Persephone slid toward them, her rotten eyes so wide they threatened to fall out.

"No, no," she hissed. "He is here. He is. Let me taste the girl, and you'll see. Let me drain the girl, and I'll bring him."

The idea of those teeth on her skin, of that dead girl anywhere near her, was terrifying. But it was for Aidan. She'd do it for Aidan.

"It's okay, Athena," she said.

"It would be," the goddess agreed. "If she wasn't lying."

"You don't know that," Cassandra said. She tried to tug the knife closer, but it was useless. She pulled on Athena's arm, and her feet skidded in the dirt. "Just let me have it!"

"Wait," Athena said gently. "Persephone. What's his last name?"

Persephone's head twitched to the side.

"Apollo has no last name. He is Apollo. Sun-lord."

"And he uses a last name now. Like you must've done, during your time above. So what is it?"

"He hasn't said."

"Go ask," said Athena. "We'll wait."

Cassandra let go of Athena as Persephone trembled. She didn't know. She couldn't ask. He wasn't here. Cassandra's heart fell down hard and took her body with it.

Athena tried to catch Cassandra as she crumpled, but the girl hit the ground.

"Dammit." Athena scowled at her cousin. "Where is he? Is he not here? Tell the truth! I'll pay your stupid fare." She tore the sock off her hand and used the knife to cut through the clots. Blood ran into the dirt. Cerberus sniffed the air.

"I don't want your filth," Persephone said. "Vile blood, infested with feathers."

"Well, it's what you get. You certainly don't get Cassandra. You don't even get my snake." She reached into Cassandra's backpack and uncapped the honey. It flowed into her palm and pooled with her blood, sweet and golden with salty and red. She drew back and threw the whole mix into Persephone's face.

"Tell the truth!" she shouted.

Persephone grimaced and growled, but her black tongue stole out and licked the mess from her cheeks in spite of herself.

"He is not here," she said after she'd swallowed. "He never was."

"If you're lying, I'll slice you down the middle. Dead half separate from deader half." Athena stepped in front of Cassandra where she'd buckled, her hands dangling in the dirt.

"Why would I lie?" Persephone asked. "And if he were here, do you think I could control him?"

"Where is he, then? Where are they? Where do they go?"

"I don't know."

Athena jumped forward and brought the knife against Persephone's throat. The dead goddess's gray skin parted like paper but didn't bleed.

"Queen of the dead, and you don't know? You're lying. Down!" she shouted at Cerberus, who growled. "Why are you here and they aren't? They have to be here."

"I'm here because I'm tied to this place. I have been since Hades took me from the autumn. I'm here because I'm dead, but I'm not finished dying." Persephone pushed her throat farther onto the blade and showed teeth smeared red with Athena's blood. Her hands shoved against Athena's chest and sent her flying backward. Athena stumbled over a stone and landed on her hip in the dirt beside Cassandra.

She scrambled onto her feet and crouched. Persephone's

hands against her ribs and sternum hadn't felt like dead hands, or even dying hands. They were elastic, hard, and fast. Cerberus had both sets of hackles raised beside his mistress. And Cassandra had collapsed slack, in no shape to run or fight.

But Persephone didn't advance. The black dress hung on her bones like a sack, and she sighed.

"I wish they were here," she said. "I felt it when he died his mortal's death. And I dreamed of Artemis set upon by dogs. Torn to pieces. Her screams echoed off these walls. We smelled her blood soak into this dirt. But she never came." She looked at Athena. "I'll wait for you, too, when Hera crushes your bones. But you won't come, either. I'll be here, alone with my rotting dog, until this place fades. Or perhaps until Hades coughs his final plague.

"Get out. Take her back where she came from. Offer her some comfort."

Athena's hands balled into fists.

"She doesn't want my comfort."

Cassandra let Athena get her up and guide her back through the catacomb caves of the underworld. She let her load her back into the skiff and push off the shore. They'd come so far. Crossed worlds. She'd been so sure she would see him. Only hours ago, she'd been sure they would bring him back.

"Take care," Athena said. "Don't fall out."

Aidan wasn't there. Not in the boat beside her or in all of the underworld. He was nowhere. Not even a shade of him remained to wander. He had been blotted out with no stain left behind. But that couldn't be. Aidan was too bright, too bold, too beautiful to disappear. He was too much a part of everything she was.

"I love him," she said.

"I know," Athena replied. She paddled slowly, sadly. Mournful paddling.

Cassandra's hands began to burn.

Before they were through, the gods would take everything. They would spear Henry and Andie onto wooden pikes to buy themselves another ten minutes. They blew up buildings full of people and burned homes to the ground. All to extend lives that had gone on for too long already.

Aidan. She loved him as much as she ever had. As much as she hated his family.

"We're almost there, Cassandra. The light's returning."

Yes. She could see that. Athena said such stupid things. Dying bitch, taking too many others down with her. Hades' death alone would cost a city. Thousands of innocents dead, choking on phlegm or full of sores.

Once, a long time ago, the gods had murdered her whole family. All of her people.

The Styx disappeared, replaced by the steel blue of the lake. Cold wind slipped down her collar.

"We're home, Cassandra."

She was supposed to kill them.

Cassandra turned and stared at Athena. Shadows crawled across her face.

She was supposed to kill them all.

25

ALL THE HOURS THAT REMAIN

On the drive back to Kincade, Athena treated her carefully. A gentle touch here, a soft word there. No pushing. No questions. Stupid goddess, playing at sympathy. But Cassandra took it, so she wouldn't have to talk. So she wouldn't have to scream. She didn't say a word until they passed the Motel 6 where Athena, Hermes, and Odysseus had stayed when they first hit town that fall.

"What day is it?" Cassandra asked.

"Still Thursday, I think."

"If you don't know, don't guess. Just drive me to school." But Athena was right. Almost no time had passed. They'd gone so far, and it had been nothing. Been nothing, and for nothing.

"What time is it?" she asked. She glanced around the Dodge, but there was no clock display on the radio. She pulled her phone out of her backpack and looked at the dead screen, then tried to power it off and back on again. It did neither. The fucking underworld had fried her phone.

She squeezed it hard in her fist, to no effect. She could kill a god but lacked the strength to crack a Samsung.

"There's only one thing I'm good for," she whispered. "Only one thing I can change." And it was a good thing. An important thing. It would save the lives of strangers and those she loved.

"Cassandra," Athena said.

Cassandra ground her teeth and threw the phone hard against the dash.

"Don't touch me!" she shouted when Athena pulled over. "If you touch me now, you'll be feathers to the elbow. And I still need you to get me onto Olympus."

"It's 'into' mostly, rather than 'onto.'"

"Are you still talking?"

Athena stared straight ahead, both hands on the steering wheel. Her fingers twitched, and her throat worked like she might say something about the brother she'd lost, the one her war had gotten killed. If she did, Cassandra would go for her face. She'd spear long feathers though her eyes. Through her tongue.

"Listen," Athena said, "you don't have to go to school if you don't want to."

"Where else would I go?" Cassandra opened the door. "When do we leave?"

"When you're ready to," Athena said.

"I'm ready now."

The goddess of war never slept the night before a battle. As the rest of the house slumbered, storing strength for the fight to come, Athena stood in her quiet kitchen, peeling an apple with a paring knife and feeling all the blood in her veins. She was full of blood and life, her lingering death forgotten in the face of a more immediate, and much more violent, end.

It felt wonderful.

She was nervous, of course, and she always felt a small measure of fear. But that was secondary. Leaving Cassandra in the school parking lot that afternoon, she'd never felt such power. Clear, pure force, radiating off Cassandra steady as a beam of light. The girl was ready. Somewhere across the trees and yards, Cassandra was lying in her bed. But Athena doubted that she was sleeping, either.

She bit into the apple and swallowed the juice, sweet and sour. This was the fight of her life. It would save her brother and retake their home. It would make them gods again.

And all it would cost were the lives of other gods.

She set the knife on the counter. War came with a price. There was nothing she could do about that. All day long, she had waited for doubt to creep in, to tell her there was another way, some other destiny hanging in the stars. But it didn't, and there wasn't. No matter what Odysseus said.

He was there somewhere, in the house. She took her apple and sought him out, needing his voice suddenly. She walked down the basement steps.

"Odysseus?"

The basement was empty, the heavy bag still, weapons in their place. Even Achilles took the last night to rest, or to revel. She had no idea where he was, either.

She walked back up the stairs, finished the apple, and tossed the core. Every inch of her hummed and vibrated like a taut bowstring. Her body was ready to fight, ready to kill, but it would have to wait until morning.

As she passed by the sliding doors, she saw Odysseus standing in the backyard. He was alone, in the breeze, under the moon and the yellow light cast into the grass from the porch. Stubbornly freezing without a jacket on. He had half of Hera's statue propped on top of the other half and balanced on the ends like a skateboarder. Just watching him calmed her. Only not enough.

He could, if she let him. He could make her sleep the sleep of the dead, like he had in the back of that truck, in his arms.

The muscles of his back flexed as he adjusted his balance, and her lips parted, remembering what he felt like pressed against her. The long, lean hardness of his body. His hands on her hips and the heat of his mouth. Odysseus was a boy whom girls devoured, and he looked at Athena a way no one had ever looked at her. Like he wanted to make her lose her mind. Like he could.

Inside the house, beside the table, she imagined walking up behind him. He would be confused at first. Surprised. But then she'd hold out her hand, and her fingers would stop trembling when they touched. He'd say her name in that way he had, and his fingers would push into her hair. His lips against her neck. All of him at once, making her dizzy, so fast she could never change her mind.

Her heart pounded into her fingertips, and she reached for the sliding door.

"What are you doing?" Calypso asked.

Athena spun, her cheeks red hot.

"Calypso, what the hell?" She checked to make sure Odysseus hadn't seen them and pulled the other girl farther into the kitchen. "You creep like a cat."

"What are you doing?" Calypso asked again.

"Nothing. I . . . I need to talk to Odysseus."

"Talk. About what?"

Athena squinted at her.

"None of your business," she said.

"None of *your* business, you mean," said Calypso. "What do you think you can do for him in the middle of the night? Goddess of battle. You'd use up these hours talking in circles."

"You caught me," Athena said wickedly. "Talking isn't what I'm after."

If she meant to shock, it didn't work. Calypso didn't budge. But she did shift her hip, such an easy, naturally seductive motion that Athena blushed darker.

"What kind of comfort can you offer?" Calypso asked. "Awkward embraces and frustration?"

Athena looked back out through the sliding door. Even balanced ridiculously on a broken statue, Odysseus was the best thing she'd ever seen. The lines between them had blurred once. She'd told herself she wouldn't do it again. Yet here she stood.

"Tell me I'm wrong," said Calypso. "Tell me the virgin goddess of war is finally ready to take him into her bed, and I'll get out of your way."

"If I were, it wouldn't matter if you stood in my way or not," Athena said. She refused to blink, to acknowledge the way her eyes stung and watered. Calypso would never see her cry.

"But you aren't," Calypso said. "I am. I love him, like you do. Only I can say it out loud. And I can give him everything you can't." Calypso's hair fell in a perfect frame of her face. The curves encased in her clothes outpaced Athena's by miles. Even Aphrodite would be jealous.

"Shut up, Calypso," Athena said. She stared at Odysseus, wishing she still had the godly will to make him turn and see them. But who would he choose? Calypso was right. He would go with her, back to her room, and Athena would be left standing alone.

"You want him, you don't want him. You tease him, but you won't take him," Calypso said. "Just go away, goddess. Stop being so unfair."

Athena tore her eyes away from Odysseus and shoved past the table. She grabbed her jacket off the hook and threw open the front door.

"Calypso."

"Yes?"

"Tomorrow, after this is over, you are out of my fucking house."

Cassandra left Andie sleeping in her room and snuck out through the backyard, into the woods. There was a special thrill to it, and not just the chilly night air and stealthy movements, but because Athena would have been furious. Cassandra out alone, unprotected, the night before the goddess' big battle. She looked up into the barely visible branches of the trees, but there were no owls. No yellow eyes tracking her. It was nice.

For a while.

But after the first half mile, Cassandra started to wish Andie and Henry hadn't needed their rest. The woods were lonely and too quiet. If only one of Ares' wolves would pop out from behind a trunk, so she could blow it up into blood and fur and wolf bits. If only she'd brought Lux to throw his ball around.

A branch cracked to her left, and leaves rustled with unmistakable footsteps. Achilles came through the trees, moonlight and stars on his bright blond head.

"What's this?" he asked. "The other weapon of fate? Fancy meeting you here."

"What are you doing out?" Cassandra asked.

He stretched his shoulder, rolled his neck back and forth.

"Same thing you are, I imagine. There isn't a lot of sleep to be had the night before you storm Olympus."

"I didn't figure you'd be nervous."

"I'm not," he said. "Not exactly. But even a hero as great as me has never been inside Olympus before." He nodded back toward her house. "The other two sleeping?"

"Finally."

"Good. They'll need it. Athena said you didn't find what you were looking for."

Of course she hadn't. Did he see Aidan standing next to her? Anger balled fast in her throat, and she swallowed hard.

"I don't want to talk about it."

"Fair enough," he said, and shrugged.

He seemed so easygoing. Not unlike Odysseus. But there was more ego to Achilles, and less reason. And of course the rage, bubbling beneath his skin. There was always that. Cassandra supposed she could relate.

They walked together a while without talking, and her dislike of him faded in the face of her hatred of the gods. He hadn't harmed Henry yet. He hadn't even threatened him. And he was going to be her human shield on Olympus. They were a team, the pair of them. He was the brawler, and she was the finisher.

"It's going to be an interesting day tomorrow," he said. "All that glory."

"Yes," she agreed. "And so many dead gods."

Athena walked out of her neighborhood and into the outskirts of Kincade. She'd have liked to go miles away, until the house was little more than memory. Until she stopped imagining what was going on inside it, in Calypso's borrowed bedroom.

She swore loudly, and the night was cold enough that it appeared in front of her as a little cloud. Except for her cursing and the sad, steady scrape of her boots against the gravel shoulder, it was quiet. She hadn't seen a car for miles.

She stopped. She had no idea where she was. Tree-lined pastures surrounded her on all sides, some fenced in with white boards. Crusted patches of snow clung tenaciously to freshly green grass. A horse whistled; large and white. He stood beside the road, staring at her with his head over the fence.

She walked over and slid her fingers up under his forelock, smoothed his mane and smelled grass on his breath.

"You remind me of someone I used to know," she said. Poseidon. Back when he was more man than monster, he would turn into a great white stallion and run thundering down the beach. "Earth shaker, they called him. Poseidon, earth shaker."

The horse regarded her with wide black eyes. But he was only a horse. Poseidon was gone.

"If you're planning on running, Henry's Mustang is a better choice than that one."

The horse jumped as Hermes made the scene the way he liked best: out of nowhere in a cloud of dust.

"Hermes."

"Who else? What are you doing out here?"

Athena shrugged. "Killing time. He looks like our uncle, doesn't he?"

Hermes scrutinized the horse. "He's got more dappling on his hocks. Quit fussing over the steed and answer the question."

"Night before battle. I needed to walk."

"Or you needed to get out of the house before Calypso and Odysseus started to make it rock. I heard your little exchange."

"If you were so sure you knew already," she said, "why did you bother to ask?"

"I wanted to know if you would be honest. I should have *known* you wouldn't be." He leaned against the fence and stroked the horse's neck. "You should have let me throw her out of the house when I offered."

"No. She'll still come in handy tomorrow."

Hermes looked into the sky. "Later today, you mean. The sun's almost up." He sighed. "I suppose it is difficult to think about love when there are so many estranged family members to kill," he said, and patted the horse solemnly. He draped his arm across the animal's withers. "Athena?"

"What?"

"Are we really going to kill them? Kill them for real? I mean, they're still . . . our family."

"Hermes, they'd do the same to us."

"Yeah, but," he said, and tried to smile, "I thought we were the good guys."

Kid brother, she reminded herself. It did no good to tell him to stop being childish. To grow up.

"There are no good guys," she said.

"It matters, though, doesn't it? That we feel bad? That it makes us sad that it's all over?"

"Maybe," she lied. But it did make her sad. No matter how twisted they were, and what pain they caused each other, the gods had once had forever. Forever to fight and hate and make up, to switch loyalties and regain trust. They'd been at it so long they didn't really understand what it would mean for it to be finished. They wouldn't, until it was far too late.

She couldn't say any of that to Hermes. Underneath his selfishness and sarcasm he had the biggest heart of all the gods. One more ounce of sympathy, and he'd hesitate in the face of his family. And they would slice him in half for his trouble.

"We're going to kill them tomorrow, little brother. All of them. Just like we killed Poseidon." She pushed the horse's face away, toward the open pasture. "We'll kill them for real, and if there's regret to feel, we'll feel it later."

She slapped the horse on the hindquarters, and he tossed his head and galloped away. Together they watched him go and pretended the snow scattering beneath his hooves was beach sand. Pretended he was Poseidon, running for the surf.

26

IN WAIT

Ares and Aphrodite stood together on one of the many slopes of Olympus. The mountain had infinite surfaces, infinite tunnels and pathways and exits, more plateaus and edges than any mountain should contain. It wasn't a real place. It wasn't a real mountain. Olympus belonged to the gods, subject to only their will, strength, and fancy.

The slope Aphrodite chose that night was black with rocks and overlooked the sea.

"Storms are on my mind tonight," she said. She twined her arms around Ares' shoulders. Below them, waves crashed against the cliff in shades of blue and graphite under overcast skies. "The kind of storm I was born in. I didn't emerge on the half-shell from a gently rising wave, no matter what they say. It was nowhere near that calm. Birth never is.

"I was born from a raging swell, from water breaking on sharp rocks. I was flung onto the sand amidst a kill of sharks and silver fish, tied with seaweed ripped from its bed."

Ares stroked her hair and wondered if it was true. It

made sense: birth in exchange for death, the life of a goddess for the blood of a cove. A hell of a lot more sense than a giant clamshell opening and poof! There she was. But he couldn't know for sure. Aphrodite sounded coherent, but she often did until she started to scream.

"What are you thinking about?" she asked, and lifted her head.

"Nothing, pet."

"Don't lie."

He kissed the top of her head.

"Fine. I was thinking that Athena could arrive any day. With Hermes and her brats. I was thinking how we have to kill them and eat them."

Aphrodite's pert nose wrinkled. "We won't have to eat them, silly."

"Not us. But the Moirae. And through them we'll regain our strength. Athena and Hermes are a meal for us, even if we don't do the actual chewing." He flexed his arm. The cut that had refused to heal was gone. Clotho, Lachesis, and Atropos took care of it when he returned with Panic. A reward? Or perhaps a last infusion of strength so he could better do their work.

Athena's face flashed behind his eyes. So fierce. So bullheaded. So unprepared.

"Ares," Aphrodite said, and tugged on his arm. She gestured to the door, where Panic paced back and forth. "The Moirae call."

The Moirae called. And when they called, the gods went.

Poor Athena. She actually thought she was going to win.

27

ARMING

Athena and Hermes found their way back to the house just after dawn. The sun breached bright and yellow, rising to meet a cloudless blue sky. No orange. No pink. No glorious reds. Just yellow. It was a good omen, maybe. Aidan's eye, peering down, making sure she did as she had promised.

"Nothing will touch Cassandra, brother," she whispered. "I swear."

"What?" Hermes asked. He went into the house and shed his shoes. The kitchen was stocked for a massive breakfast, just for him. The others would eat light.

"Nothing," Athena replied. Somewhere in the backyard, a bird trilled. Down the block, someone started their car. An ordinary day, if not for the faintly audible clang of weapons being packed into bags.

"Can I fix you anything?" Hermes asked. Athena had never been less hungry.

"Save me an egg," she said. "I'm going to check on the packing." She put silent feet to the basement stairs and

stopped when she heard their voices: Odysseus and Calypso.

"It will be all right," Calypso said.

"It might," he said. "It might not. But she thinks she
knows."

Athena bristled hearing them talk about her. She wondered what else they said, when she wasn't there. Had Calypso told him what happened last night? Had they laughed
at her together?

"If you think she's making a mistake," Calypso said, "then
why are you following her?"

Odysseus paused. "Because I always follow her," he said.
Fabric moved, and metal slid against metal. "Because old
habits die hard."

Because you can't let me go without you. Say it.

"I need you to do something for me, Cally."

"Anything."

"I need you to look after Andie and Henry. She'll be pre-
occupied with Cassandra and Achilles. Andie and Henry
are vulnerable."

"But she must know that," Calypso said.

"Of course she does. She's been a general long enough to
know that soldiers die. But she wouldn't tell them that. So,
take care of them, will you?"

"I will. With my life. They've become friends to me."

"Me, too," he said.

Athena backed quietly up the steps. So that's what he
thought of her. That she would let Andie and Henry die.
Sacrifice them, for Olympus, like an offering of blood might
help their chances.

He had no faith, though he'd seen her wage many battles.
Though she was the goddess of war. She had the weapons,
and the Fates were with her. She'd always intended to have

Andie and Henry covered in the back, to face off against wolves or nothing, with Hermes standing guard. The battle would be hard, and there would be pain. But they would win. And it would be a one-sided, glorious victory.

Before the day was over, he would see.

Henry took Andie home to change early. They met her groggy mom, fresh off the night shift at the hospital. Andie hugged her long and hard, so long that her confused mother started to laugh. Andie laughed, too. Henry just stood there with a lump in his throat.

It wasn't long before she'd dressed, in light shoes with good treads, pants with extra pockets, and a jacket. She emptied out her backpack to be filled with knives and other supplies. When she was ready, they got back into Henry's Mustang and sat, his hand idle over the shifter.

"We don't have to go," he said. "They'd track Cassandra if she didn't show, but not us. They wouldn't even come looking."

"That's my line," Andie said. "Andromache's line. 'Don't go, Hector, don't fight.' But we have to, Henry." Her hand trembled over his. "They sent those wolves, and they'll send them again if Athena loses. We can't let them get Lux again. We can't let Cassandra go alone."

She leaned over fast and kissed his cheek. He blinked at her in shock.

"I feel our old lives coming through today," she said. "It feels like I should tie you up. Or stand in front of you. I'm terrified I'll see you die. And then I'll remember what it was like the first time. Pretty dumb, huh?"

Henry reached over and took her hand. It felt like ice, but her fingers twisted through his and squeezed.

They'd have to take two cars, Athena realized. She should've thought of that and rented a van, but it was too late now. Hermes loaded a green canvas pack into the trunk of the Dodge, on top of everything else, right near the front. Another sat at his feet, to go into the trunk of Henry's Mustang.

"Hey." She nodded toward it. "What's that?"

"*That* is a combat medic first aid bag. I may have lifted them from the army base a few days ago."

Good thinking. Inside would be bandages, gauze rolls, suture sets, and antiseptic. Hopefully more than what they'd need.

Cassandra came out, carrying another bag of weaponry. She'd shown up a half hour after Athena and Hermes got back, with Achilles by her side.

"Do you want me to get that?" Athena asked. She stepped toward the car, but Cassandra heaved the bag into the trunk on her own.

"Nope. I want you to keep on standing there with a dopey look on your face." She smiled. "It's fine. I've got it." The smile wasn't exactly warm, but it was something. Better than feathers exploding out of her arm. Athena went into the house. The rest of the packing she'd leave to Andie and Henry. Let the activity calm their nerves. Her hands slid over the smooth, cold surface of her oak dining room table.

Olympus. After all these years, they were going back.

"What are you doing in here?" Odysseus walked up behind her, wiping the blade of a freshly sharpened knife.

"Leaning on a table. What's it look like?"

"Where were you last night?" he asked.

"I'm surprised you noticed I was gone." Her tone was

petty and childish. She pressed her lips together and wished they'd glue that way.

"Of course I noticed. I would've liked to . . . talk to you," he said. He studied the blade under the light and returned it to its sheath. "I know. You don't want any big good-byes. We don't need them. Because we're going to win, right? But I wanted that time. I thought you'd be here."

"Odysseus—"

"Aren't you the slightest bit afraid that I'll die today?"

"You?" She laughed. He wouldn't sandbag inside Olympus, and his hidden speed and strength were more than enough to carry him through. "Not you. Never you. In Troy you charged a thousand swords and no one touched you."

He snorted. "I remember a wicked spear scar that says differently."

"But still, you died in your bed, an old man."

"So I did," he said. He slipped his arms around her waist. "I still worry for you, goddess."

She pushed her fingers into his hair. Henry's Mustang growled into the driveway.

Odysseus sighed and pressed his forehead to hers.

"No more time for this, I suppose."

28

OLYMPUS

Andie's cave wasn't far. Less than an hour's drive. Athena craned her neck over Odysseus' arm to get a look at the speedometer of the Dodge.

"What? Am I not driving fast enough?"

"It's fine," she said.

"If you want me to go faster, just say so. But there's ice on the road."

"There isn't ice on the road. It's almost forty degrees out."

Odysseus gave her sideways eyes. "Not in the shade."

Hermes leaned in between them from the backseat he shared with Achilles.

"Remember the good old days?" he asked. "When mortals just did what they were told?"

Athena pointed at Odysseus. "That one never did what he was told."

Achilles head popped up between them, too, four heads wedged into the front seat, each one wound tight with nervous energy. Today the Dodge was six sizes too small, ten times too slow. Athena glanced into the side mirror, at Henry's black Mustang following close behind. Around her, Hermes, Odysseus, and Achilles continued to chatter, and she tuned them out. When they arrived at Olympus there'd be no time for pondering or nerves. They'd have to be sharp and do as she ordered. So they'd better let it all out now, in the car.

"It wasn't hard to get into the underworld?" Achilles asked.

"Nope, just blood and a boat. Same as always."

"Was Hades there?" he asked.

"If he was, I didn't see him," Athena replied.

"No Hades, and no Apollo, either. Huh." Achilles sat back thoughtfully.

"His name was Aidan," she said. "We call him Aidan now."

"Aidan or Apollo, he wasn't there. And if he wasn't there, where do you think he is?"

Athena glanced at Hermes, who stared back, following the conversation with interest.

"I don't want to talk about this right now," she said. Hermes didn't need to be thinking about their fallen family right before he fought the surviving members. He didn't need to be thinking about what would happen if he died. If he went into battle afraid of the void, he'd get himself killed for sure.

They pulled the cars off the road, into a quiet turnaround just short of the state park. Athena was out first, and she saw the others get out of the Mustang. Andie hugged herself tight, feigning cold to cover her shaking. Henry popped the trunk.

"No," Athena said. "Leave that one packed. In case something happens to the other supplies. The Mustang will make for a better escape pod than this would." She drummed her fist against the hood of the Dodge and accidentally dented it. Odysseus eyed the dent.

"I thought you said we were going to win," he said quietly.

"Pack up," she said, and gestured up the hiking path. She looked at Andie. "How far up the trail?"

Andie shrugged.

"Half a mile? It's just across a stream."

"Okay."

They walked single file, the only way the narrow path would allow. Hermes led, and Athena brought up the rear. The spring melt turned the dirt to mud and loosened the rocks.

"Hermes," she said, "keep it slow. We don't need anyone turning an ankle."

As they crossed the creek, the cave became visible, not much more than a five-by-five black spot in the dirt and stone of the hill.

"Is that it?" Athena asked.

"Yeah," said Andie. "It looks weird, without the leaves and grass. I've never seen it like this before."

"Just wait until we get inside," Hermes said.

"It'll be fine," said Athena. No need to frighten them any more, right from the get-go. "Stop outside the mouth. Let's arm up."

They did it quietly, helping each other secure knives against their sides and legs, sliding blades down into boots. Achilles put his favorite sword across his back. Odysseus opted for a crossbow, but strapped a sword on, too, when Athena threw it at him. Henry and Andie took up the only two spears they'd been able to fit in the cars, and a matching set of shields. Calypso chose long-bladed knives. Athena, Hermes, and Cassandra were unarmed.

"Cassandra," said Athena, "maybe you should take a shield."

Cassandra smirked.

"You are my shield."

Achilles moved to stand beside her. "She's your shield, and I'm your sword."

Odysseus gathered the rest of their supplies and stowed them behind some bare shrubs. It wasn't exactly the best cover, but no one was likely to come along, anyway. The park didn't open to hikers for another month.

"Ready?" Athena looked at Odysseus, and at Hermes. They nodded. "Okay. We switch leads in the cave. Hermes is in the back. I'm out front, with Achilles and Cassandra. Then Odysseus and Calypso. Andie and Henry, keep to the middle, and don't leave Hermes. Understand?"

"Don't leave him?" Henry asked. "What if he leaves us? It's not like we can keep up."

"I won't leave you. I promise." Hermes smiled. "And if I do, I'll be back in a jiffy."

Athena turned her back on them. Now wasn't the time for her to comfort mortals. *She* was mortal. And inside the cave, she would take her godhood back.

She filled her lungs with cold air and felt it rush into her blood. Her heart pumped. Her muscles wound tight.

I am the goddess of battle.

Cassandra squared her shoulders and followed Athena into the cave. As the shadow fell over her head, she knew how it must feel to be a clown loading into a car. Any minute now, she'd run into Athena's back, and then Achilles into hers, and so on and so forth until they were all swearing and squirming in the dark, wedged into a twelve-foot-deep hole with no back exit.

But that didn't happen. They walked and kept walking, and Cassandra couldn't tell when the cave stopped being the cave in the state park and started being part of Olympus, but it did. She breathed deep, expecting to smell salt and wet rock, but the air was cool and scented softly with sweet herbs. She could see, too, and not because her eyes had adjusted. Eyes didn't adjust to the total dark of a cave. But as they went farther she could see more and more.

Walls shifted gradually from jagged stone to smooth, and then from stone to white marble. The ground beneath her feet became an actual floor, and it was fire-warmed and comfortable.

Of course it was. It was the home of the gods.

"Does the old Trojan princess inside you want to fall to her knees and tremble?" Achilles whispered.

"Not one bit," she said back.

"Here. Up this way." Athena turned up a short flight of stone steps. At the top they opened on a small room, the walls covered in relief sculpture depicting gods in flight and in ecstasy, slaying beasts and creating them, storms and victories. Cassandra thought she recognized Hercules and the Hydra. The room was a tapestry of greatest hits.

Athena looked around, and then turned to face them.

"Tell me you know where we are," Cassandra said.

"Of course I do." Athena's voice left no echo, despite standing in a circle of enclosed rock. She sounded sure, but the way she looked around searching the walls seemed confused. Or maybe she was just admiring the sculpture.

Hermes turned in a small circle.

"It's weird, being back," he said.

"It's weird, period," said Andie. The spear shook in her hand. "Where do we go now? Back the way we came?"

"No. Not the way we came. Through the door."

"What door?" Andie asked. There wasn't any door. Not until Athena turned and pointed to the open passageway.

"There are doors everywhere," Athena said. "So be on guard. They'll send things for us, through the walls. Pick us off, one by one."

"How do you know?" Andie asked.

"Because it's what she would do herself," Odysseus replied. "We should get moving. They already know we're here."

"Of course we do."

Aphrodite's bright blue dress fluttered in the open doorway. Her arms braced against either side, and her face emerged from shadow like a cracked porcelain doll, white and painted, framed with hair so golden it seemed artificial.

"Aphrodite," Cassandra growled. Aidan's murderer. Rage seared down to her toes and fingertips. Good. She wanted Aphrodite to be first.

Cassandra ran too fast for Athena to stop her into the hallway as Aphrodite giggled and fled. Her hands were on fire. Her feet pounded so hard it felt like she could crack the marble floor.

Athena shouted, and ordered Hermes and the others to stay behind. But Athena couldn't stop her. Not this time. The heat in her hands would flow over Aphrodite's face. Those wicked blue eyes would fill with blood. The golden hair would melt off her skull.

Cassandra turned a corner. The hall was empty. No scrap of blue dress to follow and no mocking laughter to track. She slowed, listened for footsteps, and heard nothing.

"Don't run off like that." Athena stood beside her and looked for signs of the other goddess. "Follow orders."

"Where the hell is she?" Cassandra shouted. "Where did she go?"

"Where she went isn't the problem," Athena said, and ran her hands over the walls of their small stone chamber. "The problem is, where did *we* go?"

"What?" Cassandra asked. Pissed off as she was, she hadn't noticed at first that the hallway they'd run down was gone. Shut. Disappeared.

"We should go after them. It's been too long."

"Athena said to wait here," Hermes said. He paced at the doorway's dark mouth, but Odysseus was right. It had been too long. Athena should've been able to grab Cassandra by the shirtsleeve and drag her back minutes ago.

"What are we waiting for?" Odysseus growled.

"This is bad," Andie whispered. "This is bad."

"What if Aphrodite got them? What if she got Athena like she did Aidan?" Henry asked, holding his spear at the ready. "We've got to go after my sister!"

Hermes pressed his hands against his skull. His voice grew louder with every progressive word. "*My* sister said that we should wait, and we will give her another goddamn minute!" He closed his eyes. But he above all the others should keep his eyes wide open. He was what they had, if Athena didn't come back. It would be up to him to lead them farther in, or beat a hasty retreat.

But he couldn't retreat. He couldn't leave Athena and Cassandra stuck inside. He looked at Calypso. She could take the mortals out, and he and Achilles could go on alone.

"They're picking us off, one by one," Odysseus said. "Just like she said they would. They'll kill her if we don't hurry. I'll go by myself if I have to."

"You will not." Hermes stared him down and silently

cursed Athena for leaving them. For getting him into this.
The god of thieves was never meant to lead.

"Well?" Cassandra asked as Athena walked the edges of
their chamber.

"Well, what?" Athena snapped. "They've separated us.
Granted, if they had to do it, this is the way I would've
wanted to be broken up. But Hermes and the others . . ."

"They have Achilles," Cassandra said.

"Yes. At least they have that."

"Look, can you get us out of here or not?" Cassandra
flexed her fingers. The heat inside them ebbed with Aphrodite out of sight.

Athena stopped pacing and stared over Cassandra's left
shoulder.

"Don't need to," she said. "The doorway's back."

Cassandra turned. The doorway *was* back, leading to a
familiar marble hall. But somehow she knew that it didn't
lead back to the others.

"Starting to think it was a bad idea to come here?" she
asked.

"No," Athena replied stubbornly. "There was only ever
going to be one way out of here anyway."

Leading Calypso and the mortals through the halls of
Olympus, Hermes had never felt quite so glaringly inadequate. Athena would say a god should never feel inadequate.

"Athena," he whispered. "Where are you?"

He turned a corner, and the hall changed from white marble to black. Sconces lit the way every few yards with small

flames. An ominous hallway. Dark and gold. So ominous that when the growling started behind them, it almost felt appropriate.

"Do you hear that?" Andie asked. She shoved and twisted and tried to see.

"Andie, come up here by me," Hermes said. He held his hand out.

The wolf struck as Andie moved through the line, clogging any route Hermes might have taken to get to the back before it did. And it was so fast. A flash of mangy gray fur, matted together with blood and pus. It rose onto two legs just as it hit Calypso, to sink its teeth into her shoulder. She screamed as it pulled her down.

The close corridor became a cacophony of shouts and shrieks, growls and the sounds of claws on marble, fangs ripping through skin. Hermes pushed Andie to the side, against the wall. Henry jumped for the gray wolf.

It was an impressive jump. He cleared ten feet with barely any momentum and landed straddling Calypso's torso. He jammed the spear down, but the beast dodged, and instead of finding a home in its spine, the spear tip sliced deep along its rib cage. Henry pulled the spear free to try again, but the wolf leaped and fled through a door that hadn't existed a moment before.

"Pain," Calypso hissed through clenched teeth. Henry knelt to help her up, and Odysseus was by their side in an instant.

"I know," Henry said. "Is it bad? Hermes, bring the med bag!"

Calypso waved him off and leaned against Odysseus.

"Don't waste a dressing on me," she said. "I meant that the wolf was Pain. Revenge for my saving you in the woods." She put her hand on Henry's chest. "Thank you."

Odysseus glared at the blood. "This is bollocks. We can't keep on strolling through their funhouse. We came to fight."

"I'm all right."

"You might not be, next time. None of us might." He glanced at the shifting walls. Somewhere not far away, Pain growled again. Odysseus pulled Calypso closer. The damned wolf hadn't given up. It wouldn't give up, not until it got what it wanted, or until it was dead. And it could come from anywhere. From up under the ground, for all they knew.

More snarls sounded from the walls. And then a breathy howl behind Hermes.

"I'd lay odds that was Famine," Hermes said. "And the other growl was Panic. That makes three."

"What about Oblivion?" Henry asked.

"It won't make any noise. But it's here."

"What do we do?" Andie asked.

Hermes clenched his fists. "I know how to kill a couple of elongated dogs!" Of the four wolves, only Oblivion was likely to give him much trouble.

"We know that," Achilles said. "So could I. But these close quarters are a problem. Not even you could move fast enough to stop all of them before they bit through Henry's neck. We could hurt someone ourselves, just shoving them out of the way."

They waited and listened to the beasts.

"What are they doing?" Henry asked.

"They're holding us," said Achilles. "They're only playing."

"No," Odysseus said. "They're keeping us from Athena and Cassandra." He pushed through the line to the front before Hermes could stop him.

Famine materialized out of the wall and dove for Odysseus, long white snout parted to tear his throat out. On two legs it stood taller than any man. Hermes tensed to spring, to intervene, but he'd be too late. The wolf would have Odysseus' jugular stripped before Hermes closed half the distance, before anyone even had time to shut their eyes.

Odysseus twisted out of the way. He brought his knee up into the diving wolf, and the strength in his leg sent it rolling. He leaped after it, and his knife blade flashed as it slid under Famine's thin jaw into its brain. Odysseus lifted the corpse. One jerk of his shoulder flung it neatly to thud against the marble wall.

He looked back at their shocked faces. "One down. Three to go."

29

FATALISTE

"How did you do that?" Henry asked.

Odysseus led the way down the hall, walking fast up stairs and around corners, headed always toward the growls and snarls of Ares' wolves. But none attacked. They must've gotten the message.

"You've never shown that kind of skill before," Hermes said, "that kind of movement." He wondered if Calypso knew, but she seemed as astounded as he was. Achilles, too, watched Odysseus warily, with a dark look on his face.

"That was only practice," Odysseus said. "Why strain yourself training?"

"You didn't show it in the field, either," said Hermes. "When we faced down Ares in the rain forest, you were as much use as a dishrag."

"Hey. I never said I could stand against the god of war."

Achilles narrowed his eyes. "I can't believe you didn't say anything," he said in a low voice. "All this time."

"What? So she could run me to the ground in training

like she does you?" He nodded over his shoulder at Henry and Andie. "Listen. I did it for you, right? If she knew what I could do, she'd figure it out. And you don't want her to figure it out, Henry."

"Figure what out?" Henry and Hermes asked together, and Odysseus smiled.

"Later. After we find your sisters. And after we all make it out of here alive."

Cassandra's legs thrummed with an impatient pulse. The halls of Olympus went nowhere. They walked down twisting halls, through doorways and rooms painted gold, filled with sculpture and ornately carved tables.

"How did you ever live here?" she asked Athena.

"What? You don't like it?"

"I hate it. I feel like a mole trapped underground after some asshole tamped the opening to my burrow shut."

"Yeah, but look at all this museum-quality shit," Athena said, her voice dull. She walked partially crouched, ready for anything and only paying slight attention to Cassandra's words. "Besides, we're not underground. We're in a mountain." Athena threw open a door and stepped out.

They were outside. Under blue sky and yellow sun, with grass thicker and softer than Cassandra had ever felt beneath her shoes. All around them hills rolled and peaks soared, none higher than the one they had climbed.

"Cassandra, are you all right?"

"All right?" she breathed. "I'm in damn Narnia." She gestured outward, to the green splendor, silver mountains capped in mist. "What could be so abysmally, unnaturally wrong?"

"Good. Then let's go."

"Look," Cassandra said, "I'm as impatient for a kill as you are. More, probably. But let me get my head straight."

"All right," Athena said. "But don't take too long."

Up the hillside a simple wooden door led back to the interior of the mountain. Cassandra wondered where Andie and Henry were. But they had Hermes, and Achilles, and Calypso. And she had Athena. She looked at the goddess, waiting impatiently.

The sooner I kill the lot of you, the sooner they'll be safe.

Cassandra started to walk up the hill, and the voices came. Crashing through both ears.

(CAREFUL OF THE EDGE, CASSANDRA. THOUGH THERE ARE SO MANY WONDERS TO SEE ON THE WAY DOWN. MILES AND MILES AND MINUTES AND MINUTES BEFORE YOU BREAK ON WATER AND ROCKS. SO MANY WONDERS YOU WOULD NEVER SEE UNLESS YOU JUMPED. UNLESS YOU DOVE AND HELD YOUR EYES WIDE AGAINST THE WIND)

The voices were so strong she stepped back toward the edge and half expected her heel to land on nothing but air. Her stomach tumbled up into her throat, and the mountain tilted like a horse bucking.

"Athena!"

"What? What's wrong?"

"I don't know." Laughter rang through her head. She could barely hear Athena through the racket.

(AWAY FROM THE EDGE, CASSANDRA, AND WALK QUICKLY. ONE FOOT THEN ANOTHER FOOT THROUGH THE DOOR AND TO OUR CHAMBER. WE WISH TO SEE YOU, OUR CHILD: THE CURVE OF

YOUR CHEEKS, THE FALL OF YOUR HAIR. WE WOULD HAVE A WORD WE WOULD HAVE MANY SO HAPPY YOU ARE HERE)

Cassandra pressed her hands against her ears.

"Who are you? Stop talking!"

Athena tried to take her arm. But through her nausea, Cassandra lumbered past her, lurching like a drunk, trying to get to the wooden door and through to the other side. Hoping that then the voices would stop.

Something was in Cassandra's head. Something Athena couldn't see or hear. She followed close on the girl's heels as she stumbled into walls and dragged herself forward. It was the Furies. It had to be. One more little trick Hera had managed to keep up her sleeve.

"What are they saying to you?" she asked. "Don't listen, Cassandra. They'll try to drive you mad." Cassandra didn't answer. There was nothing Athena could do besides make sure the Furies died first, when they got to where they were going.

Cassandra moaned painfully.

"It'll be a hell of a thing if we have to do this alone," Athena whispered. "Just us, and you half-mad. You'd better hope the others aren't far behind."

Lights lit up in Athena's chest. They were close. The halls grew warmer and smelled sharply of herbs and smoke. Her pulse quickened, and her muscles coiled. Any door might be the last door.

"Cassandra, you should get behind me now," she said, too late. Cassandra turned a knob and pushed through.

Athena burst in behind her and put her arm out across Cassandra's chest. Athena's eyes swiveled to take in everything, and came up short. Hera was there. The braziers burned and skittered orange against her stone cheek, all but healed. She smiled, and she could almost use her whole mouth to do it. But Hera wasn't the most important thing in the room.

"What are you?" Cassandra asked.

"Who are you talking to?" Athena blinked. Something blurred her eyes and made her head swim. The room was lit only by firelight and the setting sun, but it was too bright. The air was too thick to breathe even though the far wall was open air, cut rock and columns, looking out over the sea. Her eyes watered. She barely made out the dark shape of Ares, standing on the opposite side of the room.

(WE SEE YOU, GODDESS OF BATTLE. NOW SEE US)

Athena's grogginess disappeared, wiped clean like a hand swept across a fogged mirror.

There they stood. Or sat. With the tricolor silk laid over them she couldn't tell. Three disfigured women, raised up on a platform of marble. Three crumbling, withered monoliths of women, twisted together. Athena's eyes traveled from their red, black, and silver hair, to their arms, grown into each other's stomachs.

"The Moirae," she whispered.

Atropos, the black-haired one in the center, and the only one still beautiful, took her eyes off Cassandra. Her gaze made Athena want to crawl into a hole.

(KNEEL)

Athena didn't think. She knelt with reverence and haste. Anyone watching would have thought she wanted to. That doing it was her decision.

She couldn't look at Hera. Couldn't stand to see her smug expression of triumph.

[333]

The Moirae were here, and they stood with her enemies. Fate had never been with her at all. It was too late to warn the others.

Too late to tell them that she'd been wrong.

Cassandra stood still in the center, between Athena and the Moirae. They ordered the goddess onto her knees, and Athena's kneecaps struck marble as she obeyed.

They made Athena obey. It almost made Cassandra like them.

"I've heard of you," Cassandra said. "The Moirae. The Fates. They Who Must Not Be Named. Is it true? Are you the gods of the gods?"

She didn't really need to ask. Invisible leashes wound around the necks of every god in the room, from Hera to Ares, tethering them to the sisters. And the dark one in the middle had thrown a rope around Athena easy as roping a lame calf. It could be good. Leashed gods were easy targets.

(COME CLOSER, CHILD)

The words pulled her, but their voices were softer in her head. Whispering instead of ringing like cathedral bells.

(COME, AND BE GRATEFUL FOR THE GIFT WE GAVE YOU)

"What gift?"

(PROPHECY)

"That wasn't your gift. It was Aidan's, and it was a curse."

(COME KNEEL)

"No." The leash wouldn't go around her, she realized. And now that she had her eyes on them, they could bombard her brain all they wanted. It would be no different than if they screamed in her face.

(NO?)

[334]

"That's what I said. I don't take orders from a Franken-stein monster in patchwork silk." She looked back at Athena as the burning in her hands spread up her arms and into her shoulders. Soon, she'd be able to taste the fire in her throat. "I don't take orders from anyone."

(YOU ARE OURS)

"It would seem not," she said, her eyes on Aphrodite's deli-ciously terrified face, hiding behind a pillar. Time would stop while she watched it melt. So many gods, ripe for the picking.

"Athena, stand up," she said, and willed Athena's legs to move. Athena trembled and started to sweat.

(YOU WILL NOT)

"I will," said Cassandra.

A door she hadn't noticed flew open on the other side of the room, to the rear of Ares and Aphrodite. Achilles and the others spilled through.

The weight of the Moirae disappeared from Athena's shoul-ders when the others burst into the room, and she slipped her foot under her and tensed, ready to spring. For the time being, no one moved. Hermes and the rest fanned out into the back, their arms out as if to ward off evil, their weapons raised. Cassandra lifted her arms, too. Even Ares. The two groups looked between each other, held in limbo, a Mexican standoff with no guns. Athena was very aware of the heart in her chest, and how the Moirae would explode it if she tried to move against them. But she would. The distraction might be their only chance.

"Finally found you," Achilles said. "Orders or a plan might be good about now."

"You think I have one for this?" Athena asked through clenched teeth.

(ACHILLES) The Moirae strained toward him. Atropos extended her lovely hand. (IMMORTAL ACHILLES)

"The Moirae," Hermes whispered. His eyes were wide and rimmed with tears. Shame kicked Athena straight in the gut.

Achilles held his sword out, pointed at Atropos.

"Cut them!" Athena shouted. "Kill them!" If Cassandra could disobey, Achilles could, too.

Clotho and Lachesis shivered in their husks. Atropos ignored her. She was too busy admiring her weapon. Achilles. The other weapon of fate.

(YOU ARE OURS. AS CASSANDRA IS OURS. WITH YOU, WE WILL DEVOUR THE GODS)

Across the room, a nervous wave passed through Hera, to Ares and Aphrodite.

"Don't listen to them, Achilles," said Cassandra. "We're not theirs."

But they were. The Moirae were the gods of the gods. Nothing could stand against them. And Achilles only fought for the winning side. He would never charge the cannons believing he would lose. He just wasn't the type.

"Get away from them, mate," Odysseus said, and walked slowly closer. "They don't have anything good in mind for you."

(COME, ACHILLES. COME TO US, AND RISE AS AN IMMORTAL. AS A TRUE GOD)

"A true god?" Achilles asked.

Athena closed her eyes.

(YOU ARE WHAT YOU ALWAYS WERE. KILLER OF MEN. KILLER OF HEROES. SHOW US. SHOW US)

Achilles looked down, dazed, at the sword in his hand. Athena didn't even have time to scream before he turned and threw it.

But Cassandra did. Cassandra, and Andie, and Hermes, they all screamed and moved toward Henry. Only Henry wasn't the target.

Athena's heart beat once. The sword caught Odysseus in the chest, and came out his back.

Calypso screamed. Everyone screamed. Blood soaked into Odysseus' hands and dripped from his lips.

Inside Athena's head, the world slowed to a crawl. Wolves snarled. Calypso fell to her knees and tore at her cheeks. Someone shouted Athena's name.

"No," she said.

Odysseus slid to his knees, and something inside of her snapped. Everything else fell away: Hermes crouching low and fighting off attacking wolves with Andie and Henry stabbing spears beside him, Cassandra turning her murderous eyes back on the gods. None of it meant anything. Only Odysseus' blood, and his fading heartbeat, mattered.

Athena sprang away from Hera, away from Cassandra. She crossed the room in three strides and pulled him into her arms.

"Odysseus."

I love you.

"Athena!" Hermes shouted, and for an instant the world returned: a vulgar clash of metal and claws, screams and hateful laughter. She pressed Odysseus tightly to her chest.

"No," she said.

Athena ran to the open wall of columns and leaped out. She dove and took him with her, straight down the sheer face of Olympus.

———

Athena jumped. She jumped.

It was all Hermes could think. He stared with his mouth hanging open at the empty space where his sister had just been. Then Andie screamed, as Oblivion raked its claws down her back.

"Andie," he whispered. He turned and kicked, and Oblivion crashed into a wall. The Moirae screeched in his head, in all their heads. Ares moved toward Henry, and Hermes flashed forward and punched him in the face. It wasn't much, but it gave him enough time to yank Henry out of the way.

It wouldn't work for long. Hermes had to get them out of the mountain. Out of this horrible trap.

"Cassandra!" he shouted, but she paid no attention. She was murderous, furious over Odysseus, screaming that she'd kill Achilles, too, for what he'd done. But she crept closer and closer to Hera.

"Ares!" Hera screamed. "Atropos, please! Keep her from me!"

Ares turned, but Cassandra was already too close. Atropos, Clotho, and Lachesis did nothing, safe behind their Achilles shield.

"Get away from me!" Hera shouted and clambered backward. "Ares! Aphrodite!"

"Mother!" Aphrodite shrieked, but Ares held her by the arm.

"It's too late," he said.

He was right. It was too late. Hermes felt heat off Cassandra all the way across the room, and Hera started to stiffen and shudder before the girl even touched her. Ares shoved Aphrodite against a wall and started forward, calling to his mother.

Henry stepped bravely and stupidly into his path.

"Hurry, Cassandra!" he yelled. "Do it!"

"No, damn it!" Hermes hissed. "Henry, you idiot!" He moved to tug the boy back, but Panic leaped for Andie, making him grab her and spin her out of the way. The wetness of the blood soaking her shirt made his stomach lurch, but she landed solidly and thrust her spear through Pain as it came for her hamstrings. The weight of its falling body pulled the spear from her hands, but it didn't matter. Pain was down and dying in a stinking heap.

Hermes' eyes twitched from scene to scene: one more dead wolf, Ares seconds away from turning Henry into a splat on the wall, and Calypso on her knees, weeping, oblivious to Aphrodite, who drew closer with an eager expression.

"Too much, too fast, even for me," he muttered. He grabbed a brazier and threw it at Aphrodite. Hot metal and orange coals bashed into her chest. She screamed, and her dress caught fire. Ares forgot all about Henry and ran to her rescue.

"Two birds with one brazier. Finally, some progress."

But not enough. They had to go.

"Cassandra, we have to get out of here! Cassandra!"

"No! Not yet. Not now." She dodged Hera's arm, and Hermes winced. Even a glancing blow would turn Cassandra's head to pudding. But Cassandra ducked low. One of her hands trailed along the underside of Hera's arm, and it hit the floor with a solid thump, granite clear up to the shoulder.

"My god," he breathed. It was so fast. So incredibly lethal.

Hera screamed, and the sound only brought Cassandra on faster. A touch here, a shove there, murdering a goddess in bits, and the whole room paused to watch as Hera trembled and jerked. As she cried for Ares and Aphrodite, telling them to get the head, the head, whatever that meant. As she tried to protect her own head, putting her stiff, stone arms in front of her face.

Her pleas to Ares and the Moirae unheeded, Hera finally looked at Hermes.

"Stop her, please!" she begged.

The fear in her eyes was terrible.

"I can't," he said.

Hera strained under Cassandra's touch, and then, all at once, her screaming stopped. Hera was dead. Past the point of recovery or miracles. A stone statue, her face forever frozen in a twisted howl of pain.

"No," Aphrodite keened, and reached behind a column. What she pulled out was something Hermes never thought he'd see again. Poseidon's head.

It was severed and ragged at the neck, but remarkably well preserved. His uncle's dead jaw hung slack, ringed with swollen, purple lips. The eyes remained intact but had no color. Just white orbs, not so dissimilar to Hera's marble eyes. Aphrodite lifted the bloated, still-wet thing to her mouth and whispered into its ear.

"Shit," he whispered, and called to the others. "Come on, move! She's calling the sea!"

Water rushed up the sides of the mountain like thunder, ready to serve the last of Poseidon, to crush them and drown them. Hermes looked between Andie, Henry, Calypso, and Cassandra. He'd never get them all out in time.

"Cassandra, now!" he shouted.

"No!"

He darted to Calypso. "Come on. Get up!" But she wept and remained slack. He couldn't get them all out. He could only carry two. The first wave crested and broke into the room, cold and frothy and furious. He cursed and made his choice, going for the ones he wouldn't have to drag kicking and screaming. He grabbed Andie and Henry, and fled Olympus.

The water cut a strange, deliberate path through the room. Gallons of it surged and splashed against the confining edges of the door, so hard it reminded Cassandra of Wile E. Coyote hitting a wall when chasing the Road Runner.

But no roadrunner was ever as fast as Hermes. Andie and Henry were gone. Safe. They'd make it out.

The thought was a shy whisper in Cassandra's angry brain. One small, unimportant piece compared to the other part that killed gods. Fire burned inside of her, inside and all around. She glowed with it. Hera was stone beneath her fingers. A few seconds more and she'd be reduced to rubble, then dust.

Water slipped up into her shoes and drenched her feet in cold. Cold enough to snuff part of her rage out like a candle. She glared at Ares and Aphrodite. At the Moirae and Achilles. She couldn't burn him up with a touch, no matter how much she wanted to.

So what? If I kill the others, what does he have left?

"Don't make me slice you up, princess," Achilles warned. But he only guarded the Moirae. Ares and Aphrodite were fair game.

Ares held Aphrodite around the waist. She hugged Poseidon's head, and the water didn't touch them.

"You think an ice bath is going to stop me?" Cassandra asked, and Aphrodite wailed. She stepped forward, treading water to the knees. Ares glared at her, and thrust Poseidon's head in her direction. Salt spray and a strong wave rose up like a wall, crashing into her and knocking her to the ground. She spit and sucked air and tried to get to her feet. But Ares was no fool. Through the water, she saw him run, and take Aphrodite with him. They disappeared through a door, and the door disappeared right after.

"No!"

She coughed, and her limbs sagged in frustration. The fire inside her flickered and grew weak. But she could find a way. A way through the walls to Aphrodite.

Cassandra took a step, and heard Calypso cry. She looked back and saw Calypso on the floor, drenched to the waist. The stupid girl would probably stay there, weeping for Odysseus until she traded tears for the sea. The water rose so fast, already up to Calypso's ribs. Another minute and it would be too deep to run in. Cassandra glared at Achilles and the Moirae, protected from Poseidon's waves. Only the barest inches of water touched Achilles' feet.

"You can't get past me, princess," said Achilles. "Take her and go."

Cassandra looked again at Calypso.

"This isn't over," she growled.

"It is today," Achilles said as Cassandra turned and clutched Calypso around the waist, throwing her arm around her shoulder. It took most of her strength, but she got the nymph to stand and dragged her toward the door they'd come in through.

(YOU CAN'T GO. YOU ARE A WEAPON OF FATE)

"I am," she said. "Just not in the way you intended."

Cassandra pulled the door closed behind them to keep some water in the chamber, and then shook Calypso into a run. "Come on. We've got to move! Move, damn you!"

Damn you. I could've killed them all.

EPILOGUE

Even with Hermes' speed, they almost didn't make it out. The winding rooms and corridors of Olympus thwarted them at every turn, sending them into dead ends and up-side down staircases. The water churned up to their waists. Currents dragged them under and fought them hard, as if the sea knew it was chasing the god who'd killed Poseidon. In a room full of false doors the water finally closed over their heads, tossing them so Hermes had to twist himself between the walls and the mortals. By luck and panic, Andie found the right door, and Hermes scraped and clawed his way toward the surface.

They broke into the dank reality of the shallow cave of the state park, coughing brine, soaked, and freezing. Hermes jogged the last steps out into daylight and fell onto one knee, with Andie and Henry clutched onto his sides like barnacles. He hugged them tight, proud of them for hanging on.

Henry coughed the last of the ocean from his lungs and looked around.

"Cassandra?" he asked.

"She wouldn't come."

Henry blinked. "You have to go back." He rolled away and stared into the black spot of the cave.

"Henry," Andie said, her breath ragged. "He can't go back. It's submerged."

"We can't leave her there!" He looked at Hermes. "You can swim, can't you? You can hold your breath."

Hermes shut his eyes. If he went back, he'd be going for her body. And he might run into Ares or the Moirae on the way down. But he would go, if they wanted him to. He didn't have much more to lose.

Andie's eyes widened, and she pointed. "The cave!"

The ground shuddered beneath them. Hermes put his hands out, ready to grab their shirts and yank them down the trail. But the quake stilled. When he looked back, the cave had disappeared.

"That's not possible," Andie said. "Where did it go?"

Hermes walked to the side of the hill. The cave was gone. Not closed up, or fallen in, but gone, like it had never been there at all.

He stared at it, at brown grass and weeds and roots. At impossibility. Nothing there for him to fight. Nothing to dig out. No way back to the place they'd been moments before. No way back to Cassandra.

Or to Athena.

His whole body went numb, inside and out. He might've stood all day before that spot, if Andie hadn't sneezed.

"Come on," he said. He pressed his hands to her back, to staunch the blood from the wolf's claw marks. But the blood was slow. She'd heal, nothing left but a set of scars on her back to match the Nereid wounds on her stomach. "We have to get you dry and warm, before you catch pneumonia." He walked to the patch of shrubs where they'd hidden their supplies. "I'm not going to lose everyone."

He brought them back to the house, and tried not to think about how empty and quiet it seemed. He sent Henry into a warm bath, and dressed Andie's wounds. He set out warm sweaters and flannel pants and towels. When they were dressed, soup waited on the stove. It wasn't until it was gone, and another half pot besides, that anyone really spoke.

"What are we going to do?" Andie asked.

Henry stared down into his bowl. "What am I supposed to tell my parents?"

I don't know, Hermes wanted to say. *I don't know, but if you need me, you can leave a message at the French Riviera.* But that's not what his big sister would do. It wasn't what she'd want.

"Cassandra and Odysseus," Andie said, and started to cry. "And Athena. Cally. Are they really dead?"

Hermes put his arms around her. "Whether they are or not, we'll find them." He squeezed her, careful not to squeeze too hard. "We'll find them. And until we do, I'll keep you safe." He would try, even though his insides felt like broken glass. He put his hand on Henry's arm. The boy's face was washed out and gray. After a moment, he bent his head over the table and wept.

"It's all right to cry," Hermes said, and started to cry himself. "We're both down a sister today."

(Down, but not lost.)

Hermes blinked as the familiar, air-through-bellows voice whispered inside his head. He almost smelled her: a faint cloud of dust upon the wind.

(You can't think that those girls would succumb to wind

and water. Those girls who defy everything. The instrument of Fate. The goddess born against the gods.)

The faintest hint of a smile curled in the corner of Hermes' mouth.

"Aunt Demeter?"

ACKNOWLEDGMENTS

Boy howdy, writing this one was tough. And a lot of the first draft created by all that writing was a pile of poo, so first off, thank you to Melissa Frain for once again being editor extraordinaire and slicing out the poo with diplomacy, precision, and an uncanny sense of what the story needed. Also thank you for introducing me to City Bakery hot chocolate. I didn't believe her when she said I could only have a shot, not a full cup. But as usual she was right. That is not hot chocolate for rookies.

Adriann Ranta lended her laser focus to this one as well, so thank you, Adriann, for finding those remaining hiccups. Also, she's just a plain great agent, working on stuff when I don't even know it, and then dropping in with amazing, unexpected good news.

A hundred thanks to you both, Mel and Adriann. In addition to being great at your jobs, you're both just plain great, and I'm so glad to be working with you.

I don't know how Alexis Saarela manages to keep everyone's publicity schedules straight but she is always ten steps ahead with everything covered. The best. Publicist. Ever. And a fellow mini donut enthusiast. Thank you, Alexis.

Thank you to Kathleen Doherty, art director Seth Lerner, and the entire team at Tor Teen, who do amazing things for books every single day. How lucky I am that a few of those books are ones I wrote. A shout-out to librarians, teachers, and bloggers, who make the world better by spreading the love of reading. Getting to know so many of you is the best perk of this gig.

Thanks to my parents for thinking everything I write is incredible, even before they read it, and for professing to people that I am the next Hemingway. I'm not. I'm way more macho. But thanks, folks. It's a nice sentiment, and I appreciate it.

Susan Murray, Missy Goldsmith, you know what's up. Ryan VanderVenter, you're a big dumb idiot. Kidding. Just checking to see if you read these acknowledgments.

And always last but never least, to Dylan Zoerb, for luck.